ONE OF US IS GUILTY

By Steve Cavanagh

The Eddie Flynn series

The Defence

The Cross *(novella)*

The Plea

The Liar

Thirteen

Fifty Fifty

The Devil's Advocate

The Accomplice

Witness 8

Two Kinds of Stranger

One of Us Is Guilty

Standalones

Twisted

Kill For Me Kill For You

STEVE CAVANAGH

ONE OF US IS GUILTY

HEADLINE

First published in Great Britain in 2026 by
Headline Publishing Group Limited

1

Cataloguing in Publication Data is available from the British Library

Hardback ISBN 978 1 0354 0830 6
Trade Paperback ISBN 978 1 0354 0831 3

Typeset in 11/14.5pt Adobe Garamond Pro
by Six Red Marbles UK, Thetford, Norfolk

Printed and bound in Great Britain by Clays Ltd, Elcograf S.p.A.

FSC
www.fsc.org
MIX
Paper | Supporting responsible forestry
FSC® C104740

Headline's policy is to use papers that are natural, renewable and recyclable products and made from wood grown in well-managed forests and other controlled sources. The logging and manufacturing processes are expected to conform to the environmental regulations of the country of origin.

Headline Publishing Group Limited
An Hachette UK Company
Carmelite House
50 Victoria Embankment
London EC4Y 0DZ

The authorised representative in the EEA is Hachette Ireland,
8 Castlecourt Centre, Dublin 15, D15 XTP3, Ireland (email: info@hbgi.ie)

www.headline.co.uk
www.hachette.co.uk

This book is for the readers. Hope you enjoy it.

PROLOGUE
Eddie Flynn

The last walk

The best time of your life lasts less than a second.

When you hold your newborn in your arms for the very first time; when you meet the one you know that you will love with your whole heart until the moment you die; when you look around you and realize that everyone you love is happy and well and safe.

It's a fleeting moment of joy.

The worst times of your life seem to last an age.

Right now, I was having one of those moments.

I'd just woken up in the trunk of a moving car.

My head felt like there was a rusty nail rattling around inside my skull. The cut on the back of my scalp was still bleeding, and I could taste the fumes from the exhaust pipe and hear the rumble of tires on the road and the drone of the engine. I couldn't see anything, too dark. The only thing in my vision were occasional white stars that penetrated the black, probably the result of the head injury.

My hands weren't tied. I felt around in my jacket and coat pockets.

No phone. No wallet. No cash. No keys. I put my right hand down, tried to move.

It was too cramped. My feet and legs were tucked up into the corners.

The bed of the trunk felt strange. It wasn't hard plastic. It wasn't that rough fiber that lines most trunk beds.

It was thick plastic.

I felt all round the edges of it.

This plastic had been taped to the inside of the trunk, so that I wouldn't leave any blood, hair, saliva or fibers behind. There would be nothing for forensics to find.

Nothing to prove that this was the car that drove me to my last stop.

Every second in this trunk felt like a hundred years.

This was the moment.

It had been in the mail for a long time.

Some day.

Sometime.

This was always going to happen.

In my life, I've hurt a lot of people. Some of those people I loved. Some I hated. It didn't matter – I always tried to do the right thing, even if it meant killing somebody. I'm a trial lawyer, but I used to be a conman. Some say there's not a lot of difference between the two jobs.

I felt the car slow and lean left.

We were turning.

No idea how long we'd been on the road.

One thing was for certain, we were no longer on the highway. The suspension now had to work hard, and in the trunk every bump sent a fresh shot of pain through my head. We were on a dirt road, somewhere.

The end was close now.

I'd been in tight spots before.

But not like this.

Not with so many unanswered questions. I had a pretty good idea who had grabbed me off the street, though. My ability to get myself into trouble was kind of a gift. Not that my ex-wife, Christine, saw it that way.

I thought of her, and my daughter, Amy. How would they react when they were told I was missing? Judging by the professional approach of the two guys riding in the front of the car, and it was always two guys in a street grab like this, my body would probably never be found.

It was strange, but right then, that was the thing that pissed me off the most.

My family and my friends not being able to grieve properly. Not knowing where I was, but certain in the knowledge that I was dead. I had known loss and pain, and I'd seen the damage it could do to others – their lives torn to pieces. I didn't want that. I definitely didn't want that for my daughter.

Everybody has to go sometime.

And one grave is as cold as the next.

It was the people I would leave behind.

That's what hurt.

I should have seen this coming sooner.

Sometimes, we are so blinded by what's right in front of us, that we don't see the real danger.

The car slowed. The scene that would play out was inevitable.

When the car stopped, the trunk would open. A flashlight would be directed at my face. I would be told to get out and walk. Headed somewhere dark, somewhere quiet. Some deserted patch of old forest, or hillside.

The men would follow me, one of them carrying tools – a shovel and a pick, most likely. The other would have a gun on me. Their flashlights pointed at my back, casting my shadow on the cold ground. And for a while, I would follow my dark shadow.

Then they would tell me to stop. To get on my knees.

To say a prayer.

I will have taken my last walk.

And then I'll be dead.

FIVE MONTHS EARLIER

THE NIGHT OF THE MURDER

Patrick Vanderpool

As Patrick lay naked in the bed, he gazed at the ceiling fan rotating slowly and wondered why he felt so uneasy.

His fingers lightly touched the scar tissue on his right shoulder. A perfect circle of raised, gnarled, red tissue. When Molly had first seen the scar, she'd asked him if it was from a gunshot. He said it was an old wound, and left it at that. Strangely, he had told his wife the truth. Not all of it, but he'd told her it was a burn.

Even though it had happened a long time ago, the memory of it was still hot in his mind. When he was worried, or anxious, he often found himself rubbing the scar to remind himself that he was a survivor.

No matter what.

His heartbeat was just returning to normal. The young woman who rented this apartment, Molly Green, had taken a robe and left the bedroom. He wasn't a man who usually enjoyed looking into his lover's eyes as they caught their breath, or held them close, or kissed them afterwards or whispered sweet things to them in a post coital glow.

But Molly was different. He wanted to feel her next to him. Listen to her heartbeat. Lace his fingers through hers. Smell her hair as she nestled her head against his shoulder. Taste her lips.

And tell her how he felt.

The fan burred as it churned the hot air in the bedroom.

To Patrick, feelings were always complicated, but on those rare occasions when he enjoyed them, he wanted to cherish every moment. When he slept with Molly, Patrick felt like he was making love. That was strange and wonderful.

His father often told him that emotions were weakness. He doubted if his father had ever loved anyone – certainly not any of his wives, and perhaps not even Patrick. When he was a much younger man, he had worried that he would grow up to be just like his father. Ruthless and brilliant, yes, those were qualities that he wanted to emulate. But not the distance and the coldness.

And the cruelty.

Life meant more to him with warmth. Not just from a body beside him, but sharing a connection with a woman that he cared for.

A woman he loved.

But Patrick felt strange. There was no peace. No warmth. Molly wasn't beside him. She never was. After they made love, she usually left the bed. He hadn't fully realized this before, but perhaps as his feelings had grown for her it had become more apparent. Now, it stood out. Emotions create vulnerability. His father was right about that.

Now, he had a strong sense that something was wrong.

It wasn't just his wife Vanessa's general suspicion of Molly. Vanessa was smart and perceptive. He had hidden his feelings about Molly. He had been careful. Of course, he had dismissed Vanessa's concerns in order to hide the affair.

Now, he wasn't so sure.

Perhaps Vanessa had seen something in Molly that he could not.

A clanking sound reverberated throughout the apartment. A noise familiar to all New Yorkers who rented one in an old building with plumbing that sometimes sounded like a marching band playing out of tune. It was the groans of the ancient, cold pipes dealing with a sudden flood of hot water roaring through them.

It wasn't that annoying sound that made him uneasy – he was sure of that.

And it definitely wasn't the fact that Molly was much younger than him. That didn't bother him in the slightest.

Cheating on a spouse had never bothered him before either. He was a rich man, and his father was one of the richest to ever have lived, and with that kind of wealth comes a compromise on morals. His father had cheated on every single wife he'd ever had. When Patrick was a kid, this seemed appalling to him, but now, as an adult, he had inherited much of his old man's ethical flexibility. At thirty-five years old, and already on his second marriage, Patrick was zero for two on the faithful husband meter.

For his father, it was sex and the thrill of the hunt. His father was considering tying the knot for a seventh time. If he did manage to marry again, even in his advanced age, there was little hope that it would be his last. In fact, it would certainly trigger his father's interest in another woman almost instantly. It wasn't love so much as conquest.

Patrick was different. He understood two things.

He was falling in love with Molly.

And he loved his wife.

Perhaps less so now. But he wouldn't have married her if he didn't have that connection. It had only been two years. Not even enough time for a callus to develop on the palm beneath the wedding band he wore. Yet, there was love. It wasn't as hot or as vibrant as he felt toward Molly, but he couldn't discount it. He still loved Vanessa, and now he also loved Molly.

Those two things could be true at once.

Still, he felt something wasn't right. Part of his reptilian brain was calling to him. Trying to warn him. It reminded him of those magic-eye pictures he sometimes saw on Facebook. An ordinary glance shows a perfectly normal landscape scene, but if you look closely, or narrow your eyes, or hold the phone at just the right distance, there's something else in the picture that was previously hidden.

Usually, something sinister.

He sat up, put on his underwear and pants, then his shirt, socks and shoes.

And then it hit him.

Molly. The plumbing.

After they made love, Molly got up right away and went to shower. He racked his brains for an occasion when this hadn't occurred. He couldn't think of one. She always showered afterwards.

Always.

She knew he was married. She had met his wife, Vanessa, many times. Molly even worked from his marital home on occasion, when he was planning media strategy for his electoral campaign. Perhaps it was merely a physical manifestation of guilt – Molly had to go and wash away her sin after she had slept with a married man, but when she returned from the shower she was always just as affectionate. There were no other signs of guilt, such as asking him to leave right away, or not being able to meet his eyes.

Something else was off with Molly.

He stared at the window. The drapes were drawn closed. Below them, Molly's shoes were arranged in a neat row. Two pairs of sneakers, some pumps, some heels of differing heights and a pair of leather Chelsea boots. Something for all weather and most occasions. He opened her wardrobe to reveal her work clothes, mostly blouses and black pants, a few skirts, assorted sweaters and jeans, some sweatpants and leggings.

Her nightstand just had a radio clock on top, and in the single drawer were her contraceptive pills and a bottle of Tylenol. Her phone charger and laptop charger hung from the wall plugs.

There was no personality in this bedroom. No knick-knacks. No photographs. Nothing personal to her life.

He got dressed, listening to the ceiling fan. The constant beat sounded like a clock. A countdown to something.

In the kitchen, he continued to open drawers. Nothing unusual.

Geoff, his campaign manager, probably hired her because she could read and spell, and Geoff wanted to sleep with her. Maybe he should have had her vetted. Patrick wasn't that interested in politics, really. His father had hired Geoff, and funneled money and donors to him, but Patrick knew none of it was really for his benefit. It was all for his father's vision of his son.

In the living space, there was a TV and a couch, and a bookshelf filled with paperbacks, their spines hidden so that only a shelf full of yellow and white paper edges faced into the room. *What a stupid filing system*, thought Patrick. How could you know what books you had, what you wanted to read or even find a book that you knew you already owned? It was for decoration's sake, and nothing else.

He began to pull the books off the shelf, one by one, checking their covers.

He stopped.

The noise from the plumbing was beginning its death spiral. The water had been shut off. He could hear the drip from the shower head leaking into the tub.

He looked at the book in his hand.

It wasn't a novel.

It was a journal.

As he opened the journal, he noticed a gym bag tucked behind the bookcase. It was black with a white Nike swoosh on the side.

He began to read the first entry, his heartbeat rising in time with every line he read.

The pages of the journal creased as he gripped it tighter and tighter.

His chest rose and fell.

His heart rate echoed the speed of the bedroom fan, beating quicker and quicker.

His vision blurred and a teardrop spattered the page.

He had only read the first two pages. He knew then he couldn't read any more.

Too painful.

Patrick moaned softly and wiped his eyes.

Vanessa was right.

The click of the lock on the bathroom door *snicked* open.

Patrick quickly closed and folded the journal, tucked it into the back of his pants, then rolled his shirt down over it.

'What are you doing?' asked Molly.

He didn't answer. Didn't want to risk fumbling for a clumsy lie.

'Is everything alright?' asked Molly.

She stood in front of him, just a few feet away, toweling her soaking wet hair. Her robe cinched tight at her belly, droplets of water running down her shins and over her toes and into the carpet. A pool rapidly developing around her feet.

'Everything is just fine,' said Patrick, his lips drawing into that practiced, winning smile that few women could resist.

He hid the lie behind his eyes, hoping she wouldn't hear the crackle of pain in his voice.

He gazed at her wily, crooked mouth, her bright thick lips, white teeth, the dimple on her chin when she smiled at him, and her brown eyes, flecked with tiny golden sparkles. Her dark, wet hair dripped onto her shoulders, rivulets of water running down her neck, collecting in the well of her throat, and then tumbling over her chest and down to the floor.

She looked so good. So innocent.

But it was only a look. It was only what she wanted Patrick to see.

Now her lips, her eyes, her beauty, her soft words – it was all a lie.

'Are you sure you're okay?' she asked.

Patrick said nothing. He merely nodded.

He was definitely not okay.

His tongue was hard against the back of his clenched teeth. He suddenly realized his whole body was as tense as a compressed spring, his breath trapped in his chest, fists clenched. An electric heat spread over him, from his belly up over his neck and down across his back.

In a curious moment, Patrick was suddenly very aware of how he must look. His control was slipping. He had seen the same look on the face of his father, Julian, many times. Usually right before Patrick was beaten, or that one occasion . . .

When his father had slowly put out his cigar on Patrick's shoulder. The smell, the pain, and the look of satisfaction in his father's eyes had never left him.

The memory of that scar still burned him, even today. The same scar Molly thought had been a gunshot.

Molly's gaze never left his as she took a step back, as if she had suddenly found herself face to face with a growling guard dog. He could see the alarm in her beautiful brown eyes. She moved slowly, carefully. Maybe it was instinct, but her hands reached out in front of her as if to placate him. Her chest began to swell and quickly deflate as her breath quickened.

A metallic taste flooded his mouth. His vision seemed to zoom in on Molly, everything else around him blurred.

Something deep and dark inside Patrick had snapped.

Patrick's life was all about control. That's what money bought, ultimately. The ability to determine his life in any way that he chose.

He took a step toward her.

In that moment, he knew he no longer had control.

No control over Molly.

No control over his life.

No control of his broken heart.
No control of himself.
Emotions are weakness. And they had overwhelmed him.
Now, there was only pain and anger.
The perfect mix for murder.

THE NIGHT OF THE MURDER
Vanessa Vanderpool

She had been parked in the back of this lot for at least a couple of hours now. She couldn't risk the heater. The engine coming to life in her Mercedes would automatically turn on the lights, illuminating her face.

She didn't want anyone to know she was here.

Didn't want anyone to see the cold tears that had streaked her face.

She pulled down the sun visor, opened the vanity mirror. Instantly, a small light flicked on.

Shit.

The fleeting glance she caught of her reflection was enough to know her tears had ruined her make-up. The mascara had run over her cheeks like warpaint. She flipped the mirror closed and slammed the visor back into the roof.

Shit.

She definitely didn't want anyone to see her, but least of all the man who exited through the rear emergency door of the building straight ahead. He was maybe a hundred yards away, but the light above the door just caught enough of him to notice that he wore a dark navy suit and thick wool coat, his tie strung loosely around his neck like a scarf. Vanessa thought he looked well in that coat. She had bought it for him for Christmas. A lousy gift for a husband who had everything. He hurried across the lot and Vanessa slunk down into the driver's seat, fearful that Patrick might catch a glimpse of her in the moonlight, or worse still, maybe he had noticed the light from the vanity mirror.

He glanced in her direction, and she shuffled down further into the driver's seat. She thought, for just a moment, he might have seen her, but he never broke stride and got into his Mercedes, parked fifty feet to her left beside an old Ford and a brand-new Hyundai. Patrick switched on the engine, then drove out of the lot.

Vanessa replayed the scene in her mind – Patrick striding across the dark parking lot, the look in her direction.

Had he seen her?

She thought not.

She waited.

Sat up straight in the driver's seat.

And thought about her husband's tie hanging loose around his neck. When he was getting dressed in a hurry, he would leave their home with his tie loose, slung through his collar, top button open. Just like tonight.

There was no doubting the situation any longer. He was sleeping with Molly.

The affair wasn't in her imagination. It was real. It was happening.

It was still happening.

She had warned Molly.

Vanessa was only thirty years old, but she had been betrayed many times before. Thinking back on it, each time had been unique. The pain was the only constant. It felt hot, like a burning coal in her stomach. The level of anger varied from partner to partner. For the worst of them, the men who she knew she should never have been with in the first place, the anger was less potent, as if their cheating was an inevitability – just part of who they were. For the better men who had passed through her life, the anger was more profound and targeted inwards toward herself. What had she done to make these men cheat?

Tonight, the pain was a ten-foot-high inferno and the anger was just as white hot.

She had warned Molly to stay away. She had trusted her to do the right thing.

And Molly had betrayed her.

She had to end this, one way or another.

Molly had to leave. She had to disappear out of her life. Out of Patrick's life. Forever.

And it had to be tonight.

She reached over to the glovebox. Opened it.

Inside was a small red leather Valentino purse. It was expensive, and secret, and the perfect size to snugly hold its contents. No one knew about this purse. Not Patrick, not Molly, not anyone.

She put the purse in her pocket. Felt the weight. It sank deep into her coat.

Tonight could be dangerous. She had learned to recognize those high points of peril. She might need what was in that purse.

She checked her watch, and after a few minutes she got out of the car and made her away across the jagged stones that filled the lot until she reached the steel door.

She pulled the handle on the door, found it open.

Like last night.

She went through the dark hallway, and then up two flights of stairs.

She stood in front of Molly's apartment door for what felt like a long time, burning in the agony of his lies. Of Molly's lies.

I warned you.

Those three words echoed in her mind, swirling like smoke from the fire of her anger.

I warned you.

She knocked on the door, waited.

Nothing.

She knocked again, harder this time, but to her surprise the increased force on the door opened it an inch. The door had not been fully closed.

She pushed inside, found the apartment in darkness.

Another few steps, in the dark. An arc of light at her back from the hallway. She didn't want to put on lights in the apartment.

She took another step and felt her open-toe shoe sink into the carpet and then something cold and wet swill over her toes.

The carpet was wet. But she couldn't see what was on the floor. Just a dark wet patch.

Maybe water from a leak in the ceiling. Or a spillage.

Or something else.

It was too dark to tell.

She suddenly felt afraid. A creeping dread crawled over her back, making the hairs on her neck stand up.

Even in the faint light, something on the table beside her glinted.

She picked it up, and felt the weight, solid and reassuring. A jewelry box, studded with colored stones.

Vanessa took a breath and went deeper into the dark, the box in her hand.

As she moved, she felt the weight of the red Valentino purse in her coat.

Someone once told her that life can be measured not by what you have gained, but by what you have kept. Most of her life had been loss.

She knew then she couldn't lose Patrick. Not now.

Not now.

She moved further into the apartment.

Her entire body shook with adrenaline.

I warned you and you betrayed me.

Fear and anger coursed through her like a thousand volts of electricity.

The perfect mix for a murder.

THE NIGHT OF THE MURDER
Sergeant John Hardy

Cops in any major city in the United States quickly grow a thick skin.

Death is a daily companion.

Sergeant John Hardy had seen death in nearly all its guises. Elderly men and women, dead for weeks, rotting in their hallways or in their beds. He could usually give a good estimate of how long the person had been deceased judging by how hard he had to push the front door open. The mail stacked up fast, even in these digital times. Old people still preferred paper. When he had to repeatedly shove the door to push through the three-foot-high pile of mail jamming the door, that was usually a bad sign, normally followed by a smell that would stay on his skin for days.

Car wrecks, gun shots, stabbings, beatings, accidental falls, jumpers, strangulations and those who quietly slipped away on the streets, taken by the city under their cardboard sheets as they slept – the cold, and the loneliness, and the city itself taking her daily quotient of souls. Men and women. And children.

He remembered his first corpse.

A pedestrian mowed down by a bus. He remembered every detail of that young man. The awkward, crooked shape of his back and legs. The look on his dead face. He had a vague recollection of the second body – a stabbing. He remembered the utter stillness of the stairwell and the blood that had run down over the steps like a macabre waterfall. He didn't remember many after that.

And there had been many. His resistance to the visceral finality and violence of death had only increased with every passing day and every dead body.

The rookies who had called for his assistance that night hadn't built up their resistance yet. Garcia and Coates were eighteen months on the job. They shouldn't really be working together, but three cops had called in sick for the shift and it was better than sending them both out alone. One less patrol car, but probably safer for both of them.

He parked behind that patrol car, in front of the apartment building, and got out of the vehicle. The city never sleeps. Even now, the first thing he heard was the rumble from a generator across the street, powering lights and machines run by the five-man road-maintenance crew. They had a dumper truck full of hot tarmac, and were filling in potholes. Road crews in Manhattan tended to do emergency work during the day, and maintenance during the night, to minimize traffic disruption. This was no comfort to the locals, who had to listen to diesel generators in the middle of the night.

As he reached the second floor of the apartment building, Sergeant Hardy noticed he was a little out of breath. He needed to get back in the gym. Warming his ass behind a desk wasn't good for his health, but he had gone up a couple of paygrades. His wife was happier, but he sometimes missed the buzz of being a cop in New York City.

Coates and Garcia stood toward the end of the hallway, outside an apartment, hands on their belts. The older of the two, Coates, had his back to the wall facing an open door, his pale face dripping in sweat. Garcia, shorter and smarter, was making notes on the memo app to record key information: a cop's greatest weapon is not their gun, or their pepper spray, it's their notes. They had moved on from physical notebooks to an app, and those notes put away more perps than anything else.

'Sarge,' said Garcia, nodding.

Coates glanced toward the door, covered his mouth with the back of his wrist and then looked away.

'You got all your notes down?' asked Hardy.

'Every detail,' said Garcia. 'We arrived at the property at four forty-one. Spoke to the complainant Alison Karim at four forty-six. That's her apartment up the hall there. She asked what the hell was the point in having a police department if we didn't respond to calls. I told her it was a busy night, and her call had been logged as a noise complaint. We'd woken her up, and she was pretty pissed. She also said it wasn't really a noise complaint – she was worried about her neighbor, a Molly Green. Said she'd heard banging and a commotion. She didn't call on Molly, as she was too afraid. She called us instead.'

'You got no answer when you knocked the door, you called the building supervisor who didn't pick up, you were concerned for the occupant's safety so you forced entry,' said Hardy, looking at the broken frame on the open apartment door in front of him. He said it as a statement, rather than a question, to make sure that if Coates and Garcia hadn't followed the exact protocol, they at least knew now what to record in their reports.

'Correct,' said Garcia.

'Who was first in?' asked Hardy.

Coates held his hand up.

'You alright?'

'Not great, Sarge,' said Coates.

'Go get some fresh air, and don't worry about it. The locker room will bust your balls for a while, but everybody's been there. You'll toughen up.'

Taking a deep breath, Coates thanked his sergeant and made his way down the hall to the stairwell. Hardy stepped into the apartment. Garcia, coming behind him, flicked on his flashlight and shone it inside.

The light fell over a shape on the floor.

Hardy froze.

Sometimes, it doesn't matter what you have seen. There are images that will burn themselves into your mind no matter how toughened it has become.

There's death.

And then there's the violence of murder.

And then there's this.

'My God, turn off the flashlight . . .' said Hardy.

'Sarge?'

'Turn it off!' he said, spinning and barreling into Garcia, fighting to get out of the apartment, into the hallway.

Hardy didn't make it outside. He lost his dinner on the stairs.

Leaning against the rail, he caught his breath, heard footsteps coming up the stairs toward him.

'You okay, Sarge?' asked Coates.

'No, I'm not. Are you?'

'I don't think I'm going to be okay for a while,' said Coates.

'Call homicide. Tell them this is a bad one.'

I

Eddie

Everything changes.

Seasons, global politics, TV shows, sneakers and ice-cream flavors.

Nothing is set.

My father was a con artist who passed the profession on to me. Laws existed, but they only mattered if you got caught. These days, that doesn't matter so much any more. I moved from hustling insurance companies from the back streets to suing them in the courts. A lawyer is a natural progression from the con game. Those two careers share a lot of common elements – same skill set, similar hours and, at least in my case, either profession was likely to get me killed. Maybe that last part says more about me than anything else.

Laws are supposed to apply to everyone, equally.

But no one believes that any more. I never bought it in the first place.

I'm a New York trial attorney and that gives me a bird's-eye view of the sewer. Mostly I practice criminal law, but occasionally I step over to the dark side of civil law, where the real hustlers work.

I sat in court, waiting for the judge to begin a three-day civil case for harassment and false arrest against the NYPD. My client, Errol Jackson, sat beside me in a new suit. It was charcoal gray, and it still had the brand label sewn onto the outside of the right cuff. I didn't know if this was supposed to be a not-so-subtle hint to the jury that Errol had bought a new suit to make a good impression, or, more likely, Errol would take the suit back to the store for a refund after his case was over. His dreadlocks were neat and perfumed, he was freshly shaven and he'd even polished his ten-dollar fake-leather wingtip shoes from Marshalls.

I'd represented him twice before, both times for low-level crime. A year ago, Errol got caught shoplifting a box of baby formula from a CVS, and six months later he was arrested for an alleged assault on his boss – a restaurant manager who had decided to take all of Errol's waiting tips because he was four minutes late to start his shift. Errol denied hitting the guy, who was uninjured, but he admitted to a heated confrontation. Considering this was an all-night restaurant that served hamburgers, waffles and pancakes to drunk people, a heated confrontation was not the worst thing in the world. Before Errol finished his shift, he routinely had to wash the blood off the restaurant floor.

He was a young man with a family, just trying to make enough to keep a roof over their head and food on the table. His older brother, Maurice, was a different story. He'd fallen in with a gang and got busted regularly. He was currently serving a dime for armed robbery. As well as bringing shame on his family, Maurice also brought a lot of police attention down on them too. When Maurice was put away, that attention shifted to his brother, Errol. Patrolman Fabio Gennaro developed a particular interest. Maurice had assaulted him during one arrest, and Gennaro had taken it personally. Now, the whole Jackson family were on Gennaro's shit list.

If NYPD got a report of somebody dropping a piece of litter in that neighborhood, Gennaro would use it as an excuse to kick down Errol's front door. This culminated in an arrest a few months ago when a warehouse was raided ten blocks from Errol's home. Seventy-five flatscreen TVs and ten washer-dryers were taken in that raid, and the nightwatchman, who had been tied up during the heist, got a pretty good look at one of the perps who had trashed the security footage before they left. The nightwatchman gave a description of one of the perps to officer Gennaro, and sure enough Errol's home got searched and he was arrested. They found nothing linking him to the raid, and I got the charges dropped when I tracked down the nightwatchman and found out the description he'd given to Gennaro didn't match Errol.

That was the starting point for today's court proceedings – a harassment suit and a false-arrest claim against NYPD.

In truth, this is rarely a good idea. Pissing off the police doesn't normally work out well. It just so happens that as a criminal defense attorney it was part of my job to piss off the cops. This explains some of the trouble I'd had in my life. There was good sense in backing away from a fight with the NYPD, even if you already had a target on your back, because if anything that target was just going to get bigger, unless you win.

And win big.

In order to win a case against the NYPD, or any other law-enforcement agency, you have to prove that the police lied. This is a high bar to clear. How do you convince anybody that your client, the guy with the rap sheet, is the person telling the truth and the decorated public servant is lying?

Most of the time you don't clear that bar.

Better to settle.

My opponent in this case, representing the city, was Paul Shilton, a career lawyer in a dull suit who took pleasure in denying claims. In Errol Jackson's civil case, Shilton had one piece of evidence that was crucial to his defense – Patrolman Gennaro's police notebook.

The most important tool for every serving police officer in the US is their notebook. They are trained to use it at every call-out. They make notes in real time about interactions with suspects, witnesses, time of arrival at call-outs, scene descriptions – everything.

It's much more than an aide-memoir or a diary. Used properly, the notebook becomes a living record, almost like a separate eyewitness providing corroborating evidence. Realizing the persuasive power of this tool, cops regularly abuse it, sometimes leaving blank spaces in the pages so they can fill in a more favorable version of events later. This is a disciplinary offense that could cost them their jobs, but who's going to find out? Recognizing the potential for abuse of the memo book, a few years ago NYPD developed an app that replaced the leatherbound notebooks so that there was a real time digital record that could not be altered.

But guess what? For the shadier police officers, sometimes the app wasn't working, or they couldn't get a signal, so they reverted to their paper notebooks as a back-up. That way, they could tailor the evidence to suit the person they wanted to arrest and fill in the details later.

In Errol's case, the nightwatchman told me he described a forty-year-old African American with short hair and a facial tattoo to Officer Gennaro. That description didn't fit the mid-twenties Errol, who didn't have tattoos and had very real dreads.

This was what I wanted to discuss with the city's defense lawyer, Shilton. So far, he'd refused all invitations to settlement discussions. I wanted to make one last effort. Before the judge came in.

As I got up, I patted the tall pile of law books I'd arranged on the left side of the defense table and approached Shilton. He was a young guy with a long career screwing people over ahead of him. He stood, with a sour look on his plain face. Tall, slim and pale, I formed the impression he spent his evenings laughing at TikTok videos of law enforcement officers beating up members of the public.

'You don't want to try this case – trust me. We can settle now on favorable terms for everyone. Twenty-five grand in damages for Errol, no admission of liability and we seal the agreement so there's no bad publicity for the city. Oh, and one more thing: Gennaro has to lay off Errol. I want the cops to leave him and his family alone.'

Shilton's voice was high and shrill, as if he'd skipped puberty. 'You're out of your mind, Flynn. I know you've got the nightwatchman waiting outside to testify, but you're forgetting he was held at gunpoint for four hours, he was coming off a fourteen-hour shift and he was too damn tired and traumatized to remember what he told the cops. Gennaro has his notebook entry that corroborates his recollection of the nightwatchman's description of the perp, and of course that description matched your client. Did the nightwatchman write down the description he gave to officer Gennaro? No. *If he didn't write it down that night, it didn't happen.*'

'Gennaro altered the description in his notebook to match Errol after he arrested him. We all know what happened after that. He went back to the nightwatchman, said he'd found the robber, a real nasty guy who had to be taken off the streets, and showed the nightwatchman Errol's picture. But what Gennaro didn't envisage was the nightwatchman being a stand-up guy and resisting the pressure Gennaro put on him to identify Errol. Look, twenty-five grand won't break the city's bank just . . .'

'Did the nightwatchman write down, at the time, the description he gave to Gennaro? No. I already told you, *if he didn't write it down it didn't happen*. There's no way to beat that argument in court.'

'I won't have to,' I said.

'What do you mean?'

'I mean I won't have to make any arguments. I don't need to give an opening statement to the jury, I don't even have to ask a single question. I'm going to win this case without saying a goddamn word. I've got the law on my side,' I said, and pointed at the tall stack of law books.

'Good luck with that,' said Shilton.

I went back to the defense table, sat beside Errol. He had turned around in his seat to talk to his family. His wife, Shavawn, and his grandma, who had simply been introduced to me as 'Grandma', like she was everyone's grandma, sat behind the defense table in the gallery.

Errol looked worried. Grandma gave his hand a reassuring squeeze.

At that moment the judge came into court, we all stood to greet her and then she ushered in the jury as we settled back in our seats.

I opened a page of discovery in the case. A photocopy of Gennaro's notebook. Of course, the app hadn't been working, so he reverted to hard copy. The handwriting was neat and unhurried.

The page number of the notebook on the bottom left-hand corner said 59 in bold letters. I'd issued a subpoena for the real notebook to be brought to court. I didn't have the right to examine it, just for it to be produced in court. Shilton had sent me a copy of the entry relevant to Errol's case – page 59. I wasn't entitled to look at anything else in that notebook because it would contain notes on other police calls.

This was a dilemma that the law couldn't get around. I had a good idea how Gennaro made the false entry recording Errol's description instead of the real description given by the nightwatchman, but I couldn't prove it without the notebook.

But I wasn't entitled to see it, by law.

Shilton rose and made his opening statement to the jury, telling them that if they believed Officer Gennaro, and his contemporaneous note of the description given by the nightwatchman, then this amounted to lawful probable cause for the arrest. He called Patrolman Gennaro to the stand.

The rear doors of the courtroom opened, and a policeman in uniform entered. Gennaro was smaller than Shilton, and much rounder. He was one of those guys who looked like a human bulldog. A ball of muscle and fat, with no neck and a red complexion.

His notebook was clutched tightly in his meaty left hand.

To get to the witness stand, Gennaro had to walk down the central aisle that divided the public seating, go through the pinewood gate that separated the lawyers from the public and then pass between the defense and prosecution tables.

As Gennaro passed by, I leaned back in my chair, stretched out my legs.

My left ankle caught Gennaro's right foot, and he reached out his hands to save himself as he went down, face first.

'Oh my God, I'm so sorry,' I said as I leapt to my feet, maybe too fast, and as I dashed to help Gennaro, I knocked over the fifteen or so law books I had piled on my table.

The heavy books clattered to the floor around Gennaro. I grabbed his left arm, helped him to his feet.

He had turned a brighter red, with embarrassment.

'Are you okay? God, I'm so sorry,' I said.

'Fine,' he said, shrugging off my helping hand. He bent down and picked up the notebook from the floor, and then took the stand and the witness oath while I retrieved my books and put them on the defense table.

Shilton took a second to let Gennaro get settled in the witness stand, then began.

'The jury are well aware of the issues in this trial. It is our case that you recorded a description from the nightwatchman, and that description matched the defendant. Let's get straight to the heart of this matter. Do you have your *original* contemporaneous note of the description provided to you at the scene of the burglary by the nightwatchman?'

'I do. It's in my memo book,' said Gennaro, holding the leather-bound book aloft.

'Just for the record, you didn't record this in the digital app?' asked Shilton.

'There was no signal at my location. I keep a standard-issue police notebook in my patrol vehicle in case that happens, and I used that.'

'And there was no bodycam footage of this conversation?'

'Not usually, not when I am talking to witnesses. I turned on the bodycam when I arrested the plaintiff, Errol Jackson.'

'With the court's permission, please, take your time, and find the relevant entry in your notebook, then read it aloud.'

'Of course, just a second, and I'll find it.'

Gennaro opened his notebook.

The surprise and confusion registered on his face.

I knew what he was looking at. The first page. Something written there that he didn't expect to find. In black marker. Capitals.

DON'T REACT.
I CAN GET YOU OUT OF THIS.
KEEP TURNING THE PAGES.

Gennaro flipped the page.

LOOK UP.

As his head came up, I gave him my best smile.

Then winked and nodded toward the book in front of him.

Gennaro flipped the page.

I'VE GOT YOUR ORIGINAL NOTEBOOK.

When he looked up at me again, he was just in time to see me holding my cell phone over his original notebook, right in front of me on the defense table. After I'd tripped Gennaro, then spilled a pile of books on the floor, I'd switched his notebook for the one he was now reading. I had his notebook open to the page of notes he'd later made. I noticed the tiny scraps of torn paper edges, at the center fold of the notebook. The pages of the book went from 57 to 59. The original description given by the nightwatchman was no doubt on that missing page. I snapped a photo with my cell phone.

Officer Gennaro's rosy pallor suddenly began to fade into a fearful white as he flipped to the next page.

JURIES DON'T LIKE COINCIDENCES.
THE NYPD LIVE LOG APP WASN'T WORKING . . .
YOUR BODYCAM WASN'T ON . . .

Next page . . .

A PAGE HAS BEEN RIPPED OUT OF YOUR NOTEBOOK?

Gennaro flipped to the next page.

TELL SHILTON YOU'VE BROUGHT THE WRONG MEMO BOOK.

On the next page.

SETTLE AND LEAVE HIM AND HIS FAMILY ALONE. YOU'LL GET THE BOOK BACK AFTER.

He closed the notebook, glared at me, his eyes bugging out of his big round head. It took a few moments for Gennaro to gather himself enough to start thinking. But it didn't take him long.

'Your Honor,' said Gennaro, addressing the judge, 'I'm so sorry, but I think I've brought the wrong notebook. Could I have some time to go find the correct one?'

The judge rolled her eyes, said, 'Let's adjourn for fifteen minutes. Mr. Shilton, by then I want an update on how long it's going to take for Officer Gennaro to get his original notebook and bring it to this court. Shouldn't take more than an hour, but I want a firm timeline when we come back.'

With that, the judge stood, and Gennaro almost ran out of the witness stand and grabbed Shilton, taking him to a corner of the courtroom for a hushed and anxious conversation.

'What's happening, Eddie?' asked Errol.

I could only see Shilton's back, but the way he hung his head, and then slumped his shoulders told me all I needed to know.

'Looks like justice is happening, Errol.'

Gennaro shook his head, his blood pressure now getting the best of his fear as he turned lobster red and then stormed out of court, Shilton calling after him.

Shilton gestured that we should talk. I took Gennaro's notebook and put it in my jacket pocket, and joined Shilton.

'Problem with your star witness?' I asked.

'Look, we've been thinking. We're going to take your offer, Flynn. Settled at twenty-five grand, no admission of liability. Settlement agreement to be sealed.'

'I told you I would win this case without saying a word in court, didn't I? Look, I can see you've got a problem with Gennaro. I'll agree no admission, and to sealing the agreement. But my offer of settlement was fifty thousand dollars, Shilton, not twenty-five.'

'What? You told me, not ten minutes ago, you would take twenty-five.'

'You need to get your hearing checked. I said fifty.'

'No, you didn't.'

'Did you write down my offer settlement in your notes?'

Now it was Shilton's turn to change his complexion. His neck flushed red.

'No,' he said.

'What did you tell me? *If it wasn't written down at the time it didn't happen?* Fifty. Take it or leave it. And make sure Gennaro leaves Errol and his family alone.'

Shilton stared at the ground. He was out of moves.

'I'll take it. Jesus, you're not a lawyer. You're a goddamn con artist, Flynn.'

'Believe it or not, I take that as a compliment.'

Errol's grandma damn near crushed my ribcage as she took me in a bearhug. I didn't mind. I was too busy watching Errol and his wife as the dollar signs rolled around in their eyeballs.

Sometimes I really like this job.

My cell phone buzzed, a reminder for an appointment at a white-shoe law firm on Wall Street.

Right then, I got a feeling that my day was about to go downhill rapidly.

2

Eddie

The offices of Buchanan and Duff, attorneys at law, occupied three floors of a skyscraper on Wall Street and even the kid in the back room working the photocopier wore a better suit than me.

I was in a conference room, alone, my hands on a walnut table and a hot cup of coffee in a stainless-steel mug in front of me. It had been poured from a steel coffee pot by an assistant wearing a gold Rolex, before he left me on my own to go fetch the principals I was about to meet. This wasn't my first experience with the behemoth law firms that occupy this town. I wasn't impressed and I wasn't intimidated, despite their best efforts. I knew how to win a trial, and I was damn good at what I did, but I wasn't in their league. In many ways, I wasn't even in the same sport. The floor below them was occupied by an oil company. The business that sat below my office in Tribeca was a tattoo parlor. I was pretty sure that was a Picasso on the wall of the conference room. I didn't have artwork in the office; I was lucky the walls were painted. The only thing that passed for art in my firm was a framed print of four bulldogs playing pool that hung in Harry Ford's office. He was a former judge, my best friend and a consultant with my firm. He knew his way around the law better than anyone in this building. The difference was Harry billed out to clients at a hundred dollars an hour. In this firm, the janitor probably made more than that.

I wasn't in Kansas any more.

The door opened and two men entered the room.

One was tall and broad, wearing a blue double-breasted pinstripe suit, and a pink shirt and pink tie. He had a head of thick, curly red hair, swept back over his scalp with either gel, wax or motor oil. Whatever it was, it glistened as he passed underneath the recessed ceiling lights. He walked in with his meaty hand extended in a greeting. I took it, and we shook hands.

'Glad to meet you, Eddie. I've heard a lot about you.'

'Don't believe everything you hear,' I said.

He threw his big red head back on his shoulders and his belly shook with laughter. It was at this point I noticed his companion: a small man who appeared to be wearing the same suit. Blue pinstripe, but with a white shirt and pink, tile-patterned necktie. In contrast to his big friend, this man was pale and thin. There was a mousy aspect to his features – pointed nose, pinhead eyeballs recessed so far into his skull that they looked like they were afraid of everything they saw, and pale lips drawn back over sharp little teeth. I checked his shoes, and saw the lifts in his heels.

'I'm Rex Buchanan,' said the big man. 'This is Ronald Duff.'

Duff stepped forward and nodded. No handshake. No greeting.

I nodded back.

'Take a seat,' said Buchanan, and sat down opposite me. Duff pulled out a seat at the head of the table, to my left. As he did so, I noticed there was an extra five inches of padding on the seat of that chair, to make sure Duff got close to eye level with the larger men he sat with at this table. It was a small detail, but it told me a lot. This seat was especially made for him. He didn't want the indignity of sitting on a cushion, yet the impression of power he wanted to portray was too important to him to be compromised by his diminutive stature.

'Thanks for coming in, Eddie. I explained on the phone we have a client that we care about very much, but we can't be on the record for them right now. We want you to come on board and work with us on this. It shouldn't be anything more than handholding and advice.'

Lawyers hold on to their most important clients like they're made of gold. It takes a lot to even think about bringing in another lawyer to represent them. It was only done when professional ethics demanded it.

'I appreciate the call. Who is the client?'

'Vanessa Vanderpool,' said Buchanan with some flair, like that name should mean something to me.

I nodded, tried to remember who the hell she was. I'd heard or read the name before, but right then I couldn't place it.

'Sorry, you'll need to remind me . . .'

'She's married to Patrick Vanderpool, Julian's son,' said Buchanan.

Julian Vanderpool was a name that most people knew. He was a newspaper man who got rich in the seventies trading stocks, and used that windfall to buy up more newspapers, then started his own television network in the eighties. Subsequent ventures included publishing companies and maybe thirty radio stations. In the last twenty years, most of his money has come through his news entertainment channel. It wasn't really a news channel, because it favored whatever politicians or political parties happened to favor Julian Vanderpool. The fact that Buchanan called him by his first name indicated a long-standing relationship. Julian Vanderpool had been sued more times than any human being alive, largely because of the way his newspapers and TV networks went about covering celebrities and politicians. Journalistic integrity wasn't high on the agenda. Despite the lawsuits, the divorces, the mergers, the scandals and the pressure traditional media was under from social media and new technology, Julian Vanderpool remained one of the richest people in the world. That meant he had power. Presidents listened to him.

Tech moguls still feared him. And his son, Patrick, would one day inherit his empire.

'So what's the problem with Vanessa? Why do you need me?' I asked.

'It's a long story. Tragic, really. As you may know, Patrick is running for governor, and last week one of his campaign staff was murdered in her home. A young woman named Molly Green. The police have questioned everyone on the campaign, including Vanessa and Patrick, and some allegations unrelated to the murder have emerged.'

'What kind of allegations?'

The little guy, Duff, removed a folded document from his suit jacket along with a pen, and placed them in front of me. It was the first time he'd moved for a minute or two. I'd almost forgotten he was there.

I unfolded the document and checked it over. It was a non-disclosure agreement. Everything that I heard in this room was under client confidentiality. Standard practice.

I signed it. Passed it back. Duff took it without a word, leaned forward, his face just inches from the page, to make sure I'd signed and dated correctly. He turned toward Buchanan and something passed between them, silently. Buchanan continued.

'Thank you for this. Yes, unrelated allegations. It seems there is a spurious lie going around that Patrick was having an affair with Molly. It's nonsense, and he denies it, but the NYPD are on this like flies. It's the only lead they have and they're sniffing around the couple, trying to dig up whatever dirt they can to make a case.'

'Are they trying to say she was murdered by Patrick Vanderpool?'

'We don't know yet, maybe. Obviously, it's total bullshit. Vanessa is standing by her husband one hundred per cent. The problem we face is more delicate. We don't want to be in a position of a potential conflict of interest in relation to his wife, Vanessa.'

'And you can't tell me what that potential conflict might be, because then I would know and I wouldn't be able to represent Vanessa either?'

'We counseled Vanessa and sat with her while she was questioned by the homicide detectives, but we're in a potentially uncomfortable position.'

'So Patrick was having an affair?' I asked.

'Just take it from us, we don't want to compromise Vanessa or Patrick. We've debated this point a few times, and we've decided it would be cleaner, and in Vanessa's best interests, if she were separately represented. In case the police have more questions . . .'

'You mean in case the police ask Vanessa if she knew her husband was having an affair with the victim?'

'Patrick has denied the affair to the police. That brings us to you, Eddie.'

Not exactly an answer to my question. Buchanan was choosing his words carefully.

I leaned forward, said, 'Rex, there's about fifty law firms in this city with the necessary criminal experience, some with hundreds of lawyers and almost infinite resources. I'm not one of those firms, to put it mildly. Why'd you come to me?'

'Don't sell yourself short, Eddie. We've been watching your cases. We know how good you are. As you can imagine, we want nothing but the best for Vanessa. We want to make sure she has the finest representation, and of course we'll make sure you have all the resources you need.'

Bullshit.

At least most of it. I'd made a reputation for winning tough, high-profile cases, sure. I know my way around a courtroom. But I'm small time. They wanted me because they thought they could control me and more importantly, control the narrative coming from Vanessa.

'Did she or Patrick have anything to do with this murder?'

'Asked and answered, Eddie. They're both clean. We don't know who the hell murdered Molly Green in that apartment. Could have been an ex-boyfriend, a freak she met on the street or Hannibal Lecter. We have no clue. But the one thing we do know is Patrick and Vanessa had nothing to do with it. Now, compensation—'

'How do you know she didn't do it?'

He paused, looked at me. Then said, 'We know, okay?'

'Have you asked her?'

'What are you, a criminal lawyer or a priest?' said Buchanan, laughing.

'I'm not much of either,' I said, 'but I can usually spot a liar from fifty feet away. It will be a condition on whether I take on her case, that I'm satisfied she's innocent. Otherwise, no deal.'

Buchanan glanced to his right, to the silent, stone-faced little man in the pinstripe suit sitting on his booster chair.

He nodded.

'That's fine with us,' said Buchanan. 'Now, as I was saying, compensation. A thousand dollars an hour, plus expenses sound fair to you?'

'Let's say fifteen hundred an hour, and I don't need any of your people or resources, no offense.'

'Fifteen hundred is fine, but . . . we would really like Vanessa to have a familiar face with you on this one, a consultant, not directly employed by the firm. Someone to help steady the ship, plus half a dozen assistants. They'll all be officially working with you on secondment from the firm.'

'One lawyer only. I don't have a lot of office space.'

'Deal. I'll set up a meeting with Vanessa for later today.'

'What can you tell me about Molly Green's murder?'

'I'll give you a copy of our case file. We don't have much, got the coroner's report—'

'How'd you get a hold of that?'

'Can't say. We have contacts, Eddie. It just happened to come to us.'

'What was the cause of the death?' I asked.

Buchanan and Duff exchanged looks again.

'Inconclusive. There was only a probable COD, subject to further investigation,' said Buchanan.

'Come on. I'll read the damn report. Just spit it out,' I said.

'Probable cause of Molly Green's death was decapitation,' said Buchanan.

'Jesus, why is that only a *probable* cause?'

'Because a full examination was not possible?' said Buchanan.

'I don't understand,' I said.

When Duff spoke, he startled me. He had been quiet this whole time. And his voice was dry and cracked, as if it had come through the trunk of a dead tree instead of a throat.

'A full examination of the body wasn't possible because her head is still missing,' he said.

3
Eddie

The Second Avenue Deli, now located on Third Avenue for reasons that I still don't understand, had about the best pastrami sandwich I'd ever tasted. Some people preferred Katz's Deli, and I wouldn't argue, but in this part of town there was nothing better.

Harry Ford wrapped his hands around the famous sandwich, took a bite. I started with the French fries, because they're the best. Harry, when he was still a judge, had been my mentor and we'd grown into best friends. He didn't just use law books for show, like I had that morning – he'd read them. He also drank a little more than was good for him, which these days meant his legal knowledge wasn't as sharp as it used to be. Harry blamed that on his age, not the booze.

Under the table, Harry's dog, Clarence, whined softly. Harry took some smoked ham from his side plate, fed it to Clarence.

'I let you bring the dog in here, but I didn't say you could feed him,' said a passing waiter.

'He's an assistance animal. And he ordered his own plate,' said Harry.

'What does he *assist* you with?' asked the waiter, with a derisory sneer.

'He bites rude waiters,' said Harry.

The waiter raised an eyebrow, moved on.

'I don't like the sound of this case,' said Harry.

'If it was up to you, we'd never take any cases,' I said.

'If it was up to me, we wouldn't take the kind of cases that get us into trouble. We'd be poorer, but we wouldn't have as many scars. And we might have more personnel.'

Recently, my partner Kate Brooks had left the firm.

Justice in America doesn't come cheap. And I'm not talking about legal fees. Delivering justice takes a little piece of your soul. Kate had done the right thing, paid the price for it and now she wanted some time to herself, to adjust. She was a good person. Honest, true, loyal and one of the finest lawyers of her generation. That either made her totally suited to life in criminal defense or completely unsuited, depending on how you looked at it. She could do the job better than me, but she never wanted to cross over the line.

The scales of justice in this city aren't balanced. The prosecution has all the weight and leverage. Sometimes you had to bend the law a little to even up those scales.

Kate Brooks wasn't someone who bent the rules. So, for now, she wasn't a lawyer.

'If somebody is innocent and they need my help, I've got no choice, Harry. I have a responsibility.'

'There's always a choice,' he said. 'You made a mistake a long time ago. When you took on that case, you didn't know your client was guilty. You've been carrying that around like an anvil on your shoulders. Time to put it down, kid. You can't save everybody.'

'I can try.'

'And, eventually, you'll fail. And that's okay too.'

'Not today I won't. Will you come with me to meet this client?'

Harry put down his sandwich, took a sip of water.

Clarence nudged his leg. He put the whole plate of ham on the floor and stroked Clarence's back as he ate. I remember when Harry took Clarence in. I can't say that Harry found him on the street, because it was just as true to say that Clarence found Harry on the street.

'She's a Vanderpool, Eddie. Nobody in that family is innocent,' he said.

'She married into them. She's not a real Vanderpool.'

'That's even worse. Imagine joining that family voluntarily.'

'You don't need to agree with her politics, or her husband's, to help her. I don't think she did this. It's just a feeling I have, but I want to meet her and make sure. Then I'll fight for her. What I don't know for sure is why the firm is farming her out to us?' I asked.

'Sounds like they know Patrick was having an affair with the victim. But, right now, Patrick is denying there was an affair to the police. That's risky if it ever comes out that he lied. There's your conflict. You have a married couple at war. No lawyer could represent them both.'

'If rumors of an affair between Patrick and Molly are true, and can be proven, then Patrick is in a lot of trouble.'

'If the affair is real, it makes Vanessa a suspect, too,' said Harry. 'Hell, even if the affair didn't happen, and it was only rumor, it wouldn't be the first time a jealous spouse took out their anger on a love rival by mistake. It's equally plausible that Patrick killed the victim to hide the affair. He's gearing up his campaign to run for governor. This couple sit on top of a tall mountain of wealth, privilege and power. They've both got a long way to fall. In my experience, those who have the most to lose are willing to go the furthest to save themselves.'

'This is messy. But it might all be smoke and mirrors. If Vanessa is innocent, I want to help her, regardless. Are you in?'

'Kid, if you want this case, then I'm with you. Always.'

'What kind of a mutt is that?'

Rex Buchanan was a corporate lawyer with north of a hundred million dollars in his bank account, he owned prime real estate in several countries, commanded an army of vicious litigators and was in every conceivable way an extremely powerful man.

But he'd just insulted Clarence. And Harry. And right then, standing in Rex's office, I felt sorry for him.

'This is Clarence,' said Harry. 'Where I go, he goes.'

'He's not exactly a pedigree,' said Buchanan.

Harry bent down toward Clarence, who gazed up lovingly at his owner.

'Clarence,' said Harry, 'meet Rex. He's not a dog, despite his name. But if he keeps insulting you, he'll be dragging his sore ass all over this nice carpet.'

'No offense intended,' said Buchanan. 'I just never saw a dog like that before. What breed is he?'

'He's a Heinz 57. All kinds, like the ketchup. Clarence has about fifty-seven varieties.'

'We don't normally let dogs into our offices.'

'You don't normally let people like *us* into your offices,' I said.

'Take a seat, gentlemen. I'll bring in Vanessa. I left the file over there on the coffee table.'

He left, and Harry and I took a seat on his couch. Buchanan's personal office was about the size of our entire firm. I lifted the file from the glass coffee table. Opened it.

It was a thin file – some bio information about the client at the beginning.

Vanessa Vanderpool was thirty years old, two years married to the older Patrick Vanderpool who was now in his mid-thirties. She currently resided on the Upper East Side, although a number of other properties were listed, including a Hamptons residence, a house in Malibu and apartments in Paris, London and Zurich.

The bio described the marriage as *committed*. A strange word to use. It didn't say loving, or devoted, more like two people who had made a decision some years ago and had decided they had to stick to it.

Molly Green started working for Patrick's political campaign as a PA three months ago.

There was nothing in the file about Patrick or Vanessa's relationship with Molly.

I turned to the medical examiner's report.

Short and ugly.

Cause of death could not be determined as the victim's head was still missing. There was some bruising on the arms, consistent with some form of assault; a cut about an inch wide on the bottom of her left foot; and her head had been severed between C3 and C4 of the spinal cord. It was not a clean cut. Due to the rough, uneven nature of the lacerated skin of the throat, the medical examiner had determined that a saw blade of some kind had been used to remove the head.

In addition, there was bruising around the throat. It didn't say in the report, but I guessed that could have been caused by the decapitation.

Harry and I read together.

When we'd finished, I threw the file down on the table and sat back.

'A man did this,' said Harry.

I nodded.

The door opened and a tall woman in a black coat walked in. She wore black pants, a cream silk blouse and a white cashmere scarf. Her long hair had once been a shock of blond, but she had allowed a little of her natural gray to come through it. It made her look older than she might first appear. Her skin showed no signs of wrinkles, nor of any surgical treatments.

'Eddie Flynn?' she asked.

We stood and shook hands, and she flashed a smile with rows of perfect white teeth. Same for Harry when I introduced him.

She knelt beside Clarence, gently stroked his head as he gazed up at her. She took longer with the dog than us. Then she smiled and sat opposite, crossing her legs. She wore Chanel perfume, although I couldn't tell exactly which kind. I just remembered the scent, the same as my ex-wife used to wear.

'He has a gorgeous face,' she said, watching Clarence.

Vanessa Vanderpool waited for us to take the lead. She had the confidence and ease of the wealthy. When I didn't say anything, I saw her eyes narrow toward us and her lips purse. She rested her chin on delicate fingers.

'How are you?' I asked.

'It's a difficult time, but we're all working through it. How are you, Mr. Flynn?'

'Please, it's just Eddie and Harry. Do you know why we're here?' I asked.

'Rex explained it's better for me if the firm doesn't represent both of us. He recommended you. I don't have a problem either way, but Rex mentioned before you would take me on as a client you wanted to know if I did it?'

The way she said it, confident and earnest with a serious tone, she wasn't making light of our request, no matter how unusual it might seem.

'Rex is right. We don't represent people who want to use us to evade justice.'

'Not a very good business model for a criminal defense attorney.'

'Maybe not, but we all sleep better in our moderately priced apartments. I can see you're not one for idle talk. So let's get to it – did you kill Molly Green?'

Her eyes flashed at me.

She looked at me straight.

'I'm actually really glad that you asked this, and please, I didn't mean to come across as flippant before. It's so horrible what happened to that young woman. I'm not worried about the police, because I didn't do anything wrong. But I know Rex wants me to be protected and he's probably right. Trust is very important to me. I want someone to represent me who truly believes in me. Someone who I can trust. So let me say it out loud for you – I didn't kill Molly Green.'

I said nothing. I could feel Harry's eyes on me.

'Thank you, Mrs. Vanderpool,' said Harry. 'We understand the police are still carrying out investigations. What can you tell us about the victim?'

'I hardly knew her. It's so sad.'

'When did you first meet Molly Green?' Harry asked.

'I think I met her briefly after she was hired. You should understand, initially Patrick ran his campaign from his office in mid-town. I only called in occasionally. When he ramped up the campaign and started working from home in the last six weeks, I saw her more often. We exchanged some pleasantries if we both happened to be in the kitchen at the same time, getting coffee or whatever. I sat in on some meetings where she took notes, but she was Patrick's PA. I didn't really know her. I'd be surprised if we ever spoke more than twenty words to each other in the whole time she was there.'

'What was she like? What was your impression of her?' I asked.

'A hard worker. She was quiet. Did what was asked of her. Very organized, I recall. She always had an iPad in her hand, sorting out Patrick's schedule. Jesus, she was so young. So smart and beautiful. It's so tragic. I just can't wrap my head around it.'

'What would you talk about with her?'

'Just to say hi, or I might ask her how the campaign was going or how her day was, that kind of thing. Just out of politeness, you understand. She worked for Patrick – we weren't friends or anything.'

'Was your husband close to her?' I asked.

She leaned back in her chair, said, 'She was an employee, nothing more. Patrick can't even remember the name of his father's current fiancé. He's not big on personal details. She was a hard-working PA, and that's all.'

'Where were you on the night she was killed?' I asked.

'I was at home.'

Another straight shot. Only this line seemed like it was practiced. It was short, clipped. No details. The kind of shut-down answer that might have been suggested to her by Buchanan. There was a lot more digging left in this hole: What did you do at home that night? Did you watch TV? Did you cook? Did you order food? What did you eat? Was Patrick with you? If so, was he there the whole night? What time did you go to bed? Were you on your phone that night? Did you make any calls?

These and a million more questions came to mind.

'Did you ever visit Molly Green's apartment?' asked Harry.

She leaned forward, opened her mouth to speak, but then hesitated. Her eyes fell on Clarence briefly; when she looked up again she seemed to have found her answer somewhere on the floor.

'No, I've never been to her apartment.'

I could've probed further, Harry too, but a first meeting with a potential client was not the place to push back.

'We will have some more questions for you once we know more about the case. In the meantime, if you have any contact from NYPD, you must call us immediately,' said Harry.

'I will. Patrick has worked so hard to get where he is now. I don't want anything to upset that. But more importantly, someone murdered that young girl. I want that person found. I want justice for Molly. Thank you for your time. It was a pleasure to meet you both,' she said, then stood and left.

When the door closed, Harry said, 'Well?'

I've been a conman all my life. I can spot a lie a mile away. Nobody bats a thousand, but I got pretty close.

'What do *you* think?' I asked.

'I think we should take her on as a client. There's no guarantee she'll even be charged. We don't know enough about the case, and for now there doesn't even look to be any evidence against her or her husband apart from rumor. Let's do it,' said Harry.

I nodded, said, 'Okay.'

'That's it?'

'That's it.'

'Wait, do *you* believe her?' asked Harry.

I shook my head, said, 'I don't know. Everything about the case tells me she's not the person responsible. Particularly the injuries to the victim. I just— I don't know. I can't seem to read her. I don't know if that's a good thing or a bad thing. It's clear Buchanan and his associates have already drilled her on how to answer questions. She's had practice. Maybe that's what's sticking in my throat. For right now, let's see where this goes. I need some air. Tell Buchanan we're in.'

EXTRACT FROM PROSECUTION FILE – VICTIM – MOLLY GREEN DOD – FEBRUARY 17TH (estimated).

Notes on Security Camera 2 – victim's building (rear service entrance), compiled by Detective Lorraine Carey.

All time logs correspond to timestamp on security footage.

20:43 – Female, mid-20s, curly black hair, long mauve coat, black calf-length boots, approaches the service door. Female is positive match for VICTIM (MG). She opens the security door with a key fob. Door opens outwards. She hesitates. Turns around.

20:44 – Male, mid-thirties, dark suit, dark overcoat, light hair swept back, joins the female at the door. Male is probable ID as Patrick Vanderpool (PV). He looks around. Puts his hand on her lower back. They enter the building. Door closes.

22:18 – Male, probable ID as PV, exits the building through the service door.

22:31 – Female, blonde hair, tied back, long brown overcoat, white blouse and white pants, approaches the service entrance. She stands by the entrance door.

22:32 – Female looks up at security camera. Positive ID on female as Vanessa Vanderpool (VV).

22:32 – Security door opens. VV enters the building.

23:58 – VV exits the building through the service entrance. She carries a large black Nike gym bag with a white swoosh in her left hand.

4

Vanessa Vanderpool

January 3rd
Six weeks prior to the murder of Molly Green

Vanessa let the warm water run over her hands, rinsing the soap from her fingers – watching as the suds washed over her gold wedding band, and the diamond engagement ring.

She told herself she was clean now.

She had a thing about cleanliness. Some nights, her hands would sting from her moisturizer. Her skin raw, sometimes her knuckles cracked and bleeding. It was a combination of the excessive, maybe compulsive handwashing and the cold this time of year.

Every time she washed her hands it felt like a reset. That she was clean.

She turned off the faucet, braced her hands either side of her sink and leaned over it, head down, breathing in and out, willing her mind and body to slow down.

Everything was going to be alright.

A sharp pain at her temple. Advil or Tylenol would take the edge off.

She had a lot to do today. Final preparations for her anniversary party.

She moved away from her sink, to her husband's. Opened his medicine cabinet.

He had old bottles of shower gel, unused bottles of cologne and several toothbrushes in jars, and of course his meds. Vanessa took a bottle of Tylenol from her pants pocket, opened it and took out one capsule, which she carefully placed on the curved rim of the sink basin.

She returned her attention to her husband's medicine cabinet, found the bottle of Vicodin. That would do nicely. As she reached for it, she saw something hiding behind a bottle of mouthwash on the middle shelf.

She moved the mouthwash aside and saw a small, silver gift bag. She lifted it clear, opened it and gazed inside, then removed the slim jewelry box.

The name of the maker was engraved on the slim box.

Seinfeld, NY, Est 1948

She had seen this name before, on the box that had contained her engagement ring. She couldn't help but glance at that ring now, still as breathtaking as the day when she'd first laid eyes on it. Seven carats, oval diamond cut by Seinfeld's to enhance its brilliance. She knew that Patrick would propose to her when he took her to Seinfeld's on a shopping trip. It was in the diamond district of Manhattan, as you might expect, but it didn't have a store front. This was a place that only took customers by appointment, up a flight of stairs to a nondescript steel door, security cameras everywhere, and into a room displaying some of the world's finest jewelry. Presidents and Saudi princes alike bought their diamonds from Seinfeld's, each piece bespoke and handcrafted, with the maker's mark engraved upon the exclusive white gold, which was their trademark. Her left and right ring fingers had been measured that day, and she knew why, even as she tried on some of their plain white-gold pieces, and pretended that she hadn't figured out his plans.

She knew now, standing in her bathroom, before she even opened this rectangular box, that something special was inside.

Opening it, she stared.

A delicate white-gold bracelet.

Studded in diamonds.

Easily a six-figure piece of jewelry.

At least he'd remembered it was their anniversary next week. No, she was being unfair. This was a gorgeous gift. She had known him for two and a half years. In the early days, a beautiful gift like this would have stunned her. Now, despite the glorious nature of the jewelry, she was no longer stunned. It brought a strange sense of comfort. Or calm, perhaps. A reassurance that he still loved her.

She quickly closed the box, put it back in the gift bag, and placed the mouthwash in front of it. Then she took his bottle of Vicodin, opened it and poured a couple of the capsules into her hand.

Only one, she thought.

She swallowed the white capsule, then examined the Tylenol she'd left by the sink. Same shape, same color. Only if you closely examined it would you notice the difference.

She popped it into the bottle of Vicodin, then closed it and returned it to the cabinet. She didn't want Patrick to know.

'I might have to cancel that Hamptons thing,' said Patrick, from the bedroom.

Her breath caught in her chest. The callous way he had thrown out that statement. No regard. No thought for anyone but himself.

She looked again at the gift bag, just visible behind the mouthwash.

'By thing, you mean our anniversary party?' she said, eventually. 'I'm going to the house this morning to check out the new décor. Let me know,' she said.

*

'Mel, I might have to cancel the party at the house,' said Vanessa.

She was kneeling on the tiled floor of the upstairs main bathroom in the Hamptons house. The phone was on the floor, on speaker beside cleaning products, cloths and two other items.

'Is there something wrong? Are you okay?' asked Mel.

Melissa managed the house in East Hampton. Vanessa had spent a lot of time and money getting the house ready. New furniture, new lighting, new appliances. A refresh. The house would have a new, nautical theme. Mel had helped oversee the work and organize the anniversary party, including all the invitations.

'I'm fine, Mel. I'll let you know. I saw the kitchen is nearly finished.'

'If we do cancel and the caterers ask why we're postponing, is there—'

'Just tell them it's Patrick's campaign. Something came up. Thanks, Mel.'

She hung up the call.

Vanessa had already cleaned the sink and toilet, taking time to clean around the back of the toilet cistern. Now she looked at the other items on the bathroom floor. A six-inch flathead screwdriver and a roll of duct tape. Vanessa tore off a strip of tape about five inches long, put the screwdriver handle in the center and then crawled over to the toilet bowl. Reaching around, she placed the screwdriver on the back of the toilet cistern, then pressed the tape down.

Peeling off another section of tape, she placed this over the first section, to make a cross, ensuring that there was no way the tape would peel away. It had to be secure.

She picked up the tape, got to her feet and gave the bathroom one final look. This would work.

Stepping out of the bathroom into the wide second-floor landing, she put the duct tape back into the bag of supplies she'd picked up from town. As part of the nautical theme, Mel had ordered decorative ship's lamps – ornate glass domes with metal handles that traditionally burned kerosene. They looked like hurricane lamps, with their glass chimneys. Vanessa filled the four lamps on the landing with the oils she'd bought, then put the bottle back into the bag beside a two-hundred-milliliter bottle of her favorite perfume and a can of engine starting fluid.

Not that there was anything wrong with the engine in her Mercedes.

Before she left the bathroom, she checked the lock. It was an old-style mortice lock, with a keyhole on either side, and the key kept in the lock on the bathroom side of the door. She tested the lock from both sides of the door. Made sure it was working. Sometimes the old handles or latches on the doors became stiff.

She was ready for the party. At last.

She grabbed the bag, went downstairs, picked up her coat and locked up the house. Pressing the car fob, the trunk of her Mercedes opened.

Vanessa placed the brown paper bag inside, next to her gym bag.

It was a Nike bag.

Black.

With a white swoosh.

She got into her Mercedes and switched on the engine.

A text came through as the car connected to Apple CarPlay.

The text was from Molly Green.

Patrick says cancel the Hamptons party.

Vanessa had been planning this party for months. In meticulous detail. The decorations, the catering, the band and the guests, including Patrick's father, Julian. Nailing that man down to a date that suited him had been hell. The date had to accommodate him, or he wouldn't show.

She would reschedule.

She had time.

Her plan would work out just fine.

The bracelet was a lifeline she could cling to.

She had suspected Patrick wasn't happy, but that could have been the stress from his father, who was pushing him into another run for governor. She wondered if that was all that was wrong. Even though he'd made her cancel their anniversary celebration, it didn't mean he wasn't happy. He wasn't planning to leave her. After all, he had bought her something truly beautiful.

Everything would be fine. She just had to hold the marriage together a little longer.

She breathed in and out. Exhaled the anger from her body, letting it steam the window. She sent a text to Melissa to cancel the party.

She swore. And drove home to Manhattan, and Patrick.

Vanessa parked the Mercedes on the street, climbed the steps and entered the house. She stopped and looked into the dining room, now re-christened the war room.

Geoff Gilbert stood in the corner, his arms folded, watching a TV mounted high on the wall, showing a local news channel. There was a piece about a shooting in Brooklyn that had taken place in broad daylight – an attempted mugging gone horribly wrong. Gilbert's thinning hair was badly managed by him discharging some kind of spray onto the top of his scalp every morning. In terms of disguising his baldness, it worked, from a distance perhaps, in the winter. In the summer, when it got really hot, Vanessa occasionally noticed a trickle of what looked like black molasses dribbling down the side of his face.

'We've got to pin this on Coleridge,' said Gilbert. 'Heidi, I want Patrick prepped on this and on the six o'clock news to call out Coleridge's soft approach to crime. Take a hard line when you're pitching this – we're not blaming Coleridge for the death, but in reality, it's a result of his policies. You got it?'

Heidi, a twenty-something blonde in a blue Chanel suit, furiously made notes and said she would get right on it. She was one of the staffers in public relations and her striking appearance was all that mattered to Geoff when he hired her. Her beauty was only marred by a constant vacant expression on her face, as if she had lost something important but couldn't remember what it was or where she had put it. Geoff only hired pretty young women. He was more interested in their dress size than their résumé.

At the table sat Patrick, and beside him Molly Green.

Close beside him.

It was a long table. With plenty of space. Patrick had his suit jacket off, draped over the back of his chair. His tanned hands rested on his chin as he watched the news. He wore a blue tailor-made shirt, a yellow tie and a vintage gold Rolex Submariner on his wrist, with gold and ruby cufflinks that Vanessa thought were way too gaudy. They made him look as though he owned a private island. Which, of course, he didn't. Not yet.

His father had two.

Molly was in a green silk blouse. Her short, dark hair curled over her delicate features, a contrast to her pale skin. Her head was down staring at the iPad on the table. It wasn't overly warm in the house, the temperature set at a steady seventy-five degrees throughout. And yet Molly had more buttons open on that fine green blouse than one might expect.

'How's things in the war room?' said Vanessa.

Molly's head shot up from the iPad, startled. She glanced at Patrick, then shuffled her chair an inch away from him.

'Darling,' said Patrick, 'you're back. How's everything at the house?'

'It looks great. Don't let me keep you from your plotting. Molly, do you think we could have a quick word?'

Like all of Geoff's hires, Molly was another beauty. She had once heard Geoff at a party, parroting a line from another politician, making the claim that he didn't have the smartest campaign team, but he definitely had the hottest. And Molly was hot. Perhaps too hot. But of course Vanessa wasn't thinking of the woman's body temperature and those open buttons on her blouse. Molly was sitting far too close to her husband.

It made Vanessa uneasy.

She had learned to trust her instincts.

Molly smiled, got up and followed Vanessa past the row of shopping bags in the hallway, and into the kitchen. It was a great space, with an imposing marble-topped kitchen island and a vast twelve-ring stove. Vanessa had only ever lit one ring, for morning eggs. She was largely uninterested in food. Coffee was another matter. There was always a pot brewing. She poured herself a cup, then opened the refrigerator, found the almond milk and poured a little into the coffee. She turned to the counter, pulled out a drawer and her fingers hesitated over the neat pile of silver teaspoons.

Memory can be cruel.

Images flashed through her mind.

A pair of pliers gripping the spoon handle.

The flame of the blow torch bowing as it hit the bevel of the spoon, fire spilling from its edges as if it was liquid.

The head of the spoon blackening, and then glowing.

The hissing, the smoke and the smell of her own burning flesh.

And all this accompanied by the fear she had felt in that moment, alive again within her chest.

It played out in microseconds in her head, the moving images clear and crisp, accompanied by a sound. The sound she had heard as her flesh seared—

She grabbed a spoon, slammed the drawer shut and stirred her coffee.

She turned to face Molly and leaned her back against the counter.

'We'll reschedule the Hamptons party,' said Vanessa.

'Thank you. That frees up Patrick for the podcast recording. I'll confirm with the bookers?'

'Of course. It's what Patrick wanted,' said Vanessa.

'His father seemed pretty insistent. It's a huge podcast with millions of streams. He cares a lot about Patrick's campaign.'

She noticed that in the time Molly had walked behind her, from the dining room to the kitchen, she had taken the opportunity to do up two buttons on her blouse.

'I think he wanted to tell you himself, for sure. Sorry about the text,' said Molly. As she said this, her left arm swept up to stroke a loose hair behind her ear and the sleeve of her blouse rolled down to her elbow, and Vanessa saw . . .

The bracelet.

Fine white gold.

There was no mistaking it.

The bracelet that Patrick had been hiding in his bathroom cabinet.

The bracelet that Vanessa assumed would be her anniversary gift.

Vanessa opened her mouth to speak, but realized that she had said nothing. Her mouth was open, dumbly, her breath trapped in her chest.

Vanessa angled her gaze, making sure no one else was about to wander into the kitchen.

'How long has it been now?' asked Vanessa.

Molly's eyebrows knitted together, just for a moment, trying to find the right context for the question.

'Oh, I've been with the campaign for three months now.'

'I didn't mean that. I meant how long have you been sleeping with my husband?'

Molly's lips curled tightly together, her eyes flaring at the bald accusation.

Vanessa heard footsteps in the hall, held her finger over her lips. When she spoke again, it was at normal volume. 'How are you fitting in with the rest of the team? Heidi still giving you a hard time?'

'Oh, ahm, no, not at all. We work great together, actually,' said Molly, mirroring Vanessa's voice level. She must've heard Patrick's approach, and wanted to play along. 'I feel like I've finally got a grip on the way things work in the campaign office.'

Vanessa blinked slowly, signaling that she understood the subtext. And that Molly understood that Patrick was way off limits.

'I'm so glad,' said Vanessa. 'It can be difficult. You know, fitting in? Most PAs don't last this long in the job.'

With a tiny cock of her head to one side, Molly appeared to register the implied threat in Vanessa's statement.

'Patrick has been great. I'm all up to speed with—'

'Did I hear my name being used in vain?' said Patrick as he wandered into the kitchen. He moved straight for Vanessa, putting a proprietary arm around her waist.

'Not everything is about you,' said Vanessa. 'I'm just asking Molly if she's finally found her feet. It's not easy, running after you and making sure you're organized and on time, and in the right place.'

'Molly has been a breath of fresh air. She's doing great,' he said, and stood beside Vanessa so he could face Molly.

'Thank you both,' said Molly. 'I'm really grateful for the opportunity. I enjoy the job. I really do. You've both been so kind and, well, really generous.'

As she spoke those last two words, she emphasized the point by placing her finger on her chin, flashing the same wrist on which hung the bracelet.

Vanessa's jaw clenched.

'I'd better get back to Geoff in the war room. He wanted to go over your schedule for the week. There's a lot of meetings still to finalize and I have calls to make,' said Molly.

She spun around and headed for the door.

Before she reached it, Patrick called after her. 'You're doing great, Molls.'

So, he had a pet name for her now, too.

'Is she really doing great?' asked Vanessa.

'She's wonderful, yeah,' he said. And then, after a moment, 'Why do you ask?'

'I don't trust her. Something about her feels off, like she's hiding something,' she said.

'That's all in your head. She's fine. Look, I'm really sorry about the party. My father said the campaign comes first.'

'It's okay,' she said, then broke from her husband's grasp, turning to face the kitchen window. In the reflection, she saw him walk away.

With every step, his gaze fixed on the figure up ahead.

The figure of Molly.

Vanessa knew right then that Molly could destroy everything. She also knew Molly had courage. She had stood there, in Vanessa's kitchen, and flaunted that bracelet. That was brave, or stupid. Or both. There was a lot more to this young woman than Vanessa had first thought.

Vanessa could no longer ignore this situation.

Molly Green was a lot smarter than the ditzy wannabee models that Geoff usually hired. What was worse, Molly seemed to be hiding that intelligence.

There was no other way around this. Molly had to be dealt with.

One way, or another.

5
Patrick Vanderpool

January 3rd
Six weeks prior to the murder of Molly Green

'I might have to cancel that Hamptons thing,' said Patrick, from the bedroom.

As he let those words into the air, he froze in front of the bedroom mirror, his tie pinched between his fingers, collar up, ready to make his attempt at a half-Windsor knot, head cocked to the side, listening for a response from their adjoining bathroom.

Nothing.

Volcanoes don't suddenly erupt. There are warning signs – harmonic tremors, deformations in the surrounding earth, rising magma, temperature changes and a strong odor of sulfur. He thought for a moment she hadn't heard him, but he couldn't hear the faucet running, or the high drone from a hairdryer, so he guessed that she heard him just fine.

'By thing, you mean our anniversary party?' she said, from the bathroom.

Shit.

'I'm going to the house this morning to check out the new décor. Let me know,' she said.

He heard her heels first, on the inch-thick polished mahogany flooring that she'd had done last year. Amazing – how he could tell his wife's mood by the sound of her heels on the floor.

She swished into the bedroom, dressed in dark pants, a cream off-the-shoulder cashmere sweater with a huge collar, and a thick black leather belt with an oversized gold buckle cinched around her waist.

He was expecting some comeback.

'My father moved heaven and earth to help Geoff set up the podcast interview. You get more ears and eyeballs on YouTube and Spotify than primetime TV these days. I can't let my father down. You know what he's like . . .'

She nodded, and said nothing, but she smiled at him as she left.

He thought about that smile while he finished dressing. It wasn't a loving look. It was something else. Her eyes had been pinched, her lips tight.

That smile had been full of pity. She knew what Julian Vanderpool was like. Patrick had told her some of the stories. She knew he didn't want to be governor, or mayor, or congressman, and he sure as shit didn't want to work for his father, but there was no escaping him. Julian had high ambitions for his son, and Patrick could not let him down. He always did what Daddy told him.

Always.

He felt angry at her now. He didn't want her pity. He wasn't some schmuck. He was a Vanderpool.

As his father continuously reminded him.

Before going downstairs, he went into the bathroom, opened the cabinet above his personal sink, moved the mouthwash to one side and grabbed the gift he had hidden there.

An electric thrill quivered across his back as he put it in his pocket.

As Patrick sat in his war room, previously his dining room, he stared at the top of Molly Green's head. Like always, she had her eyes down, pointed at her iPad screen. She flicked through the days on a calendar app, making notes on her phone of the important meetings, which were color-coded red.

'I've got something for you,' said Patrick.

She looked up, and he handed her the gift bag he'd been hiding in his bathroom cabinet.

She opened it, and her mouth gaped as wide as the lid on the box.

'Oh my God, it's beautiful,' said Molly.

'Here, let me,' he said, and took it from the box, then laid it over her wrist and fastened the clasp. Her gorgeous eyes danced with the glare from the diamonds.

'It's from Seinfeld's,' he said.

'Are you kidding me? It must have cost a fortune.'

'It's not that. I . . . I just wish it was something else.'

'What?'

'A diamond ring,' he said softly, almost a whisper.

She checked the door, listened for a moment, then leaned over and kissed him.

'I need you to sign off on these campaign ads,' said Heidi before she strode into the room.

They broke apart, both of them grinning like teens in love.

Molly looked up, watching Heidi stride confidently over to Patrick. Heidi was tall, blonde, good-looking. She put the mock-up ads in front of Patrick, leaned over him and turned her head toward Molly.

'These look fine to me,' he said.

Heidi smiled at both of them. It was a knowing smile.

Geoff came in and turned on the flatscreen TV mounted on the wall.

'You've got to see this news report. Heidi, wait here. I need to put a hold on those ads. We might want to change the copy, emphasize Coleridge is weak on crime. Wait till you see this.'

He found a local news channel, turned up the volume.

The front door opened.

Heels on the floor.

Vanessa was back.

Patrick ignored whatever Geoff was mouthing off about on the news, lightly touched Molly's arm. She smiled at him, and he flicked a finger at the bracelet. Molly glanced at it, then rolled her sleeve down over it and put her arms on the desk.

'How's things in the war room?' said Vanessa.

Molly's head shot up, startled. She shuffled her chair a couple of inches away from Patrick.

'Darling,' said Patrick, 'you're back. How's everything at the house?'

'It looks great. Don't let me keep you from your plotting. Molly, do you think we could have a quick word?'

Molly got up and followed Vanessa into the kitchen.

Patrick needed something to drink. With Geoff on the warpath, it was going to be a long day. As he entered the hallway, he heard whispering from the kitchen. Slowing his pace, he made sure to make his footsteps quiet as he approached.

Molly had her back to him.

Vanessa was glaring at her, then she flicked her gaze toward him and then straight back to Molly.

Her eyes softened, she leaned back, her shoulders relaxing.

When Vanessa spoke again, it was back to a normal conversational volume, 'How are you fitting in with the rest of the team? Heidi still giving you a hard time?'

He needed to be more careful. Molly needed to be careful too. Vanessa was not to be underestimated. She had impressed his father when they'd first met.

Be careful, he told himself.

Or this would all end badly.

6
Eddie

The justice game is strange.

I'd gotten used to almost every aspect of it in my time, but one thing I never adjusted to were the variations in pace. You could spend months with very little happening on a case, and then it suddenly explodes and you're running around trying to put out fires, the pressure insane and everything on the line.

This is the game.

The fact that it is played with people's lives doesn't seem to matter to most.

It matters to me.

It had been two weeks since I'd agreed to take on Vanessa Vanderpool as a client. She'd signed a retainer agreement and deposited fifty grand on account. A much larger retainer than I normally accept. Hell, I was still representing guys who paid me in boxes of tomatoes, laptops, TVs and whatever else fell off the back of a truck on the Jersey turnpike.

My cell phone vibrated. The display said – Princess.

I picked up. 'Hi, Amy.'

My daughter was turning sixteen soon, as my ex-wife Christine liked to remind me. When I say soon, I mean in around four months, but with the level and extent of my ex-wife's planning that meant very soon. A party had been scheduled in a downtown hotel restaurant for family and friends, a limo booked for a ride around Manhattan for Amy and her friends and an after-party in a private room below the restaurant also confirmed. No alcohol, of course. I got daily updates on who had accepted invites on a group chat entitled *Amy's Sweet 16.*

I was bad at planning, of course, and nobody knew that like my ex-wife. My involvement in the preparation was to hassle people into returning their RSVPs and paying for everything. In the grand scheme of things, I got off lightly.

'Dad, Keisha is having her sixteenth in the city in a couple of weeks, and Mom says it's okay if I stay at your place afterwards as long as you drop me at the party and pick me up.'

'Sure, glad to have you. When and where?'

'I'll text you the details. Keisha's parents will be there so I don't need a chaperone, I won't drink any champagne and I'll be ready to be picked up at midnight.'

'Okay, well, maybe we could grab some dinner before I drop you off . . .'

'I won't have time, Dad. Plus, there will be food at the party. I'll text you. Love you.'

She hung up before I could say anything back.

It would be good to see her, even if I was just a glorified Uber driver for the night. I could still take her for breakfast – the pancake place we both like.

I got up to fetch some coffee. Denise, the office secretary, was peeling the cellophane off the box of a brand-new laptop.

'You want some coffee?' I asked.

'Sure. Slab O'Neill paid his bill, by the way,' she said.

'I take it he didn't give you a receipt for that?' I asked, nodding at the laptop while pouring two coffees from the bun flask.

'Nope, but I needed a new computer. I told you last week, Q key stopped working on mine. I've been re-writing Harry's legal briefs to avoid words with the letter Q in them.'

'You got a nail file?' I asked.

'Yep, I know. Get rid of the serial number on the battery.'

The phone rang on her desk. She picked up.

'Eddie, it's Detective Lorraine Carey for you. She's calling about Vanessa Vanderpool.'

'I'll take it here,' I said, and handed Denise one of the coffees.

'Detective Carey, Eddie Flynn. How are you?' I said.

'We'd like your client, Vanessa Vanderpool, to come down to the precinct and answer some questions. I'm calling to make those arrangements,' said Carey.

I hadn't come across Carey before, and she sounded authoritative. No hint of nerves. She was used to dealing with defense attorneys, yet she sounded quite young on the phone.

'No small talk? No pleasantries? Just straight to business – is that how this works now?' I asked.

'I thought you were a busy man, Flynn. Didn't think you'd have time. Don't you bill by the hour?'

'I was just trying to be friendly. Do you have new information you want to share in the Molly Green case?'

'I'm not discussing the case on the phone. We want your client to come downtown and answer some questions.'

'I know most of the detectives in your precinct, but I don't believe we've met.'

'I made detective a year ago.'

'If you don't mind me asking, you're how old?'

'Twenty-six.'

'Then you're one of the youngest detectives in the NYPD. Congratulations, that's a real achievement. How do your colleagues feel about—'

'We need your client to come in and answer some questions,' she said, cutting me off.

'Is she under arrest?'

Silence. Then . . .

'No, not at this time.'

'Are you sure you don't want to talk about the weather? Because if you keep me on this call for another ten minutes, I can charge my client for a full half-hour.'

A sigh on the other end of the line.

'So she's not coming in?' she asked.

'Now I understand how you made detective so young.'

There was a loud *CLICK*, which you only hear these days from people in offices slamming a phone handset into its cradle.

Damn, I missed that sound.

'Is she mad at you?' asked Denise.

'I have that effect on certain people,' I said, looking around the office. Only Harry and Clarence were in.

'Where's Bloch?'

'She's in Chinatown on a private assignment.'

'What's she doing there?'

'She's trying to get robbed.'

'You said that like it's something that should make sense to me.'

'What can I say – that's our Bloch.'

7
Bloch

New York, like most cities, goes through changes with administrative policy, migration, the economy, social and cultural dynamics, and political earthquakes. The result is usually mixed, but the current climate felt worse than perhaps other challenging eras.

Crime, which had plagued New York in the seventies and eighties, rendering parts of the city no-go areas even for cops, was going through a statistical spike. So much so that the NYPD, the mayor's office and the district attorney's office couldn't do what they normally did and massage the figures to make them look a lot better than they were in reality.

It was all over the news. Every day.

Robberies, homicides, burglaries, sex crimes and hate crimes were rising. Had been for a while. But nobody realizes they're being cooked until they see the water in the pot bubbling.

Manhattan was on the brink of boiling over.

Cops were stretched thin on the ground. It was Christmastime for anyone with no prospects, no self-control and a dubious moral relationship with the law. And that was just the government.

Bloch wore a Yankees baseball hat and shades, blue jeans, Doc Marten boots and her usual blue blazer over a white tee. A laptop bag was slung over one shoulder, and she had her cell phone in her hand with the Maps app open as she made her way along Mott Street. Chinatown has the largest population of Chinese people, per square mile, anywhere in the West. It's one of the city's tourist highlights, and a constant delight for New Yorkers who like good food, friendly people and colorful streets.

This time of the day, it was Tourist City.

And Bloch looked like any other tourist.

On purpose.

She stopped. Looked up at the buildings, then back at the phone, as if she was trying to get her bearings. Really, beneath the sunglasses, she was checking out the four white guys huddled outside Mann's Chinese restaurant, smoking cigarettes, and deciding which one would come up behind her and snatch her laptop bag, and which one would take her phone.

They appeared to have decided that the big guy in the Knicks shirt was going for the bag, and the smallest of the crew would take the phone. The small guy could grab the phone and run, whereas the laptop bag required more brute strength.

Bloch turned her back to them, pretending to be guided by the phone. She faced the window of a Chinese grocery store, kept an eye on the reflections in the glass of the two men crossing the street toward her. The little guy had a shaven head, black sweatpants and a black shirt. He broke left as he crossed, so he could come up on Bloch from her left, running fast, right past her, snatching the phone out of her hand. Then the big guy would hit her from behind, grab the bag.

That was the plan.

The little guy disappeared from her view, but Bloch heard his sneakers flapping on the sidewalk, as he started his run toward her.

Bloch tensed.

She wasn't nervous.

She was getting ready.

Phone in her left hand, outstretched. Transferred her weight onto her right foot.

The little guy was moving fast, maybe ten feet from her now. Coming in from her left.

She threw her weight onto her left foot as he stepped forward, then using the momentum, she swung out her right boot, heel first, leg raised, and stamped down.

It had to be timed perfectly, stepping into the path of the runner moving at speed.

Her boot smacked onto the top of the little guy's shoe, and if he had been standing still, he would have felt some pain. But he wasn't standing still. He was running. The problem for the little guy was that while his body was still moving at speed, his foot wasn't. It was trapped flat on the sidewalk.

The sound of his Achilles tendon snapping was much louder than the small bones in his foot breaking, or indeed his ankle dislocating. When major tendons break, it's like a gunshot. The little guy collapsed, face planting into the sidewalk where he slid along with a horrible scraping sound until he came to a stop, five feet away, a trail of blood from his ruined face behind him.

Bloch slipped the messenger bag off her right shoulder, and continued her turn in one fluid motion, letting the strap fall to her hand, then flinging out her arm, spinning on her heel, as if she was tossing the hammer at the Olympics, and watched as the messenger bag swung into the surprised face of the big guy in the Knicks shirt.

There was a dull thump as the bag hit him on the left cheek and mouth, the arc continuing into his nose, his feet leaving the ground, such was the force of the swing.

Bloch wasn't worried about her laptop. It was still in Eddie's office, at her desk. And she was pretty sure the five-pound red clay brick in her laptop bag wouldn't be damaged either.

The bag had excellent padding.

The guy's face didn't. His nose broke left and a great gout of blood erupted into the air.

Their two pals stood frozen to the spot outside the restaurant. Their cigarettes stuck to their lips as their mouths opened in shock.

'You want to help your boy pick up his teeth?' she asked.

One of them slapped the other on the arm, said, 'Let's go,' and they both sprinted away.

A stocky, elderly Chinese man in a brilliant white shirt and black pants came out of Mann's restaurant and approached Bloch.

'You didn't get all of them,' he said. 'What if they come back? They've been hanging around here for weeks, robbing tourists. The police do nothing. You said you would stop them all.'

'They're not coming back, Mr. Mann,' said Bloch.

She leaned over the big guy, who was lying on his back, his hands over his mouth, blood bubbling up through his fingers.

'Hey, you! Knicks fan,' said Bloch as she unsheathed Maggie from the shoulder holster. She held the Magnum 500 in front of the guy's face, his eyeballs bulging with terror as he looked at the massive handgun.

'You come back here I won't go so easy. Do you understand?'

The man scrambled backwards on his elbows, his face leaking blood all over his shirt.

He tried to speak, but between the blood and the missing teeth, Bloch couldn't make out what he said. Whatever it was, it sounded perfectly agreeable.

At that moment, a car came down Mott Street, stopped in front of the Knicks fan still trying to crawl away. The engine backfired, a cloud of flame and black smoke rising from the exhaust pipe. Then the engine stalled.

To say it was a car was perhaps too loose a description. It looked as if it had been designed by someone who had never seen a car before, but who'd once had a car described to them over the phone. It was brown, dirty, dented and those were the good points.

Gabriel Lake got out of his Pontiac Aztek with a squeak and a whine from the driver's door. His black suit jacket and pants looked to be in about as good a shape as the car. His white shirt was creased, and although his curly black hair had been washed during his morning shower, it hadn't been combed since a democrat was in the White House.

'What's going on?' he asked.

'Community relations program,' said Bloch.

'Eddie's looking for you,' he said. 'We've got a case.'

8
Eddie

In a trial, knowledge is half the battle.

You cannot go into a trial knowing less than the other side. That way you walk into walls, get ambushed and are made to look a damn fool. The other half of the battle is knowing what to do with the knowledge you have. Like most things in life, the parallel to poker is clear. It's like seeing two aces on the flop when you've got the other two in your hand. Don't mean a damn thing if you don't bet the right way. Go too hard and you scare off the other players. Bet too low, you're not going to get the maximum return for your winning hand.

Trial law is the same.

First, you read the players.

Gabriel Lake walked into my office, Bloch behind him. Two of the best investigators I'd ever worked with. Lake was ex-FBI. One of their finest behavioral analysts. He kicked down doors belonging to serial killers. He was a weird guy, slightly at odds with the world. Although, he didn't see it that way. According to Lake, the world was slightly at odds with him. His mind was like a wind turbine in a hurricane, and that meant he didn't have room in his brain for everyday matters like dressing well, music, movies – frivolous things that others enjoyed. The only thing he was meticulous about, apart from investigative work, was food. He ate well, which meant he didn't really eat what most humans would call food. He was, however, fiercely loyal, and a deadly enemy. Bloch, in particular, was fond of him, in her own way. Or at least in as much as Bloch could be fond of anyone.

'I had to send Lake out looking for you. Did you get robbed?'

Bloch nodded.

'How many people did you send to the hospital?'

She thought about it, held up two fingers.

'Anybody I gotta worry about?'

She shook her head. Bloch didn't say much.

'There's movement in Vanessa Vanderpool's case. Cops want to talk to her.'

'What about?' asked Lake.

'They didn't say.'

'So are you going to go along and find out?' he asked.

'Absolutely not,' I said. 'She's not under arrest, and no good comes from talking to the NYPD. Whatever it is they've found out, they don't have enough to arrest her. Not yet. We need to know what their next move is and get ahead of it.'

'What's Vanderpool's deal?' asked Lake.

'She's intriguing. Clarence liked her, and she liked him. I'm not sure we're getting the whole picture from her, but I don't think she killed that girl. The cops might have something they can use to falsely pin the murder on her, or something that changes my mind about representing her. Either way, I want to know now.'

'Why'd you take this case if you don't trust the client?' asked Bloch.

As usual, Bloch cut to the chase. It was right then I noticed Harry leaning against his office door, listening in. For most lawyers, it's not a problem. Client's lie to their lawyers all the time. I don't work that way. I can't put a dangerous person back on the street. I'd been down that road, and no amount of money in my pocket makes me feel any better about it.

'I took the case because I don't trust her husband or her former lawyers.'

'What do you mean?' asked Harry.

'Buchanan and Duff lied to me and Vanessa. There are plenty of friendly firms they could've approached to offload Vanessa. Instead, they came to us. We've got a reputation for results that they can use to sell us to Vanessa as to why it's a good move for her, and we're smalltime enough for Buchanan and Duff to think they can either control us or crush us. Their real client is the Vanderpool family. I think they could be setting up Vanessa to take the fall for Patrick. Right now, that suspicion is reason enough to represent her.'

'What do you want us to do?' asked Lake.

'The cop who called me is Detective Lorraine Carey. She's way too young to be the lead on this case, so find out who her partner is on the investigation. This is a high-profile murder, so they'll keep their shit tight at the precinct. They don't want a cop leaking anything to the press. Find out what you can about Carey and her partner. You won't get near the crime scene, so don't bother trying. I want to know where Carey and her partner have been, particularly any meetings with potential expert witnesses.'

'What are you gonna do?'

'I'm going to speak to the governor. He's going to be Vanderpool's opposition in the election. If there's dirt on Patrick or Vanessa Vanderpool, you can bet their political opponent has it.'

9
Eddie

I'd often heard being the governor of a major US state is one of the hardest jobs in the country.

They should try working as a defense attorney in Manhattan.

Or waiting tables for twelve hours in one of the busiest cities in the world.

I didn't buy the rhetoric.

Neither did Harry.

We sat on a red leather bench at the end of a long marble hallway in the governor's mansion. The thick double doors to our right led to the reception area, and then the grand offices of Governor Fairfax Coleridge III. To name even one kid Fairfax seemed unfortunate to me. To do it twice looked like bad luck, but three times begins to look like carelessness, as a famous Irishman once said. Coleridge's administration was running out of excuses too. A state with this much wealth and deprivation wasn't easy to manage. Nothing like a double shift waiting a large section of tables in a busy restaurant, but no walk in the park.

The fact that we were here at all was entirely down to Harry Ford. Retired judges were not the class of people that could be ignored by city or state officials. Not even when they came out of retirement to join disreputable criminal defense firms.

'How do you want to play this?' asked Harry, keeping his voice low.

'He's a career politician and a dedicated public servant. There's really only one way to play it.'

Harry nodded, said, 'Alright, dirty it is.'

The double doors opened beside us and a millennial in a suit two sizes too small for him said the governor would see us now.

We went through the ornate reception area and another set of oak double doors to a large office. Crimson carpet, oak-paneled walls, two large windows, a desk that looked like it was for somebody more important than Fairfax Coleridge III – who sat behind it in pinstriped pants and red braces hanging off the shoulder of his white silk shirt.

Binders, documents, pens and a laptop spread out over the desk.

Fairfax didn't get up, or even raise his eyes from the page in front of him as we walked in.

Harry and I stood behind two leather chairs that faced the governor's desk.

I grabbed one, began to pull it out so I could sit down, but Harry touched my arm. I looked at him and he shook his head. I hated this bullshit. Power had its own etiquette in this city. You had to know how to play nice and kiss the ring.

After ten seconds of silence, Fairfax put aside the document, raised his head and leaned back in his chair.

'Please,' he said, gesturing that we should take a seat.

Harry and I sat down in front of him as he smiled and laced his fingers together over his stomach.

'How's retirement treating you, Harry?'

'I'm busier than ever. That's why I'm here. I take it you know my colleague, Eddie Flynn?'

His gaze fell on me, the fake smile remained frozen on his face.

'Only by reputation. Nice to meet you, Eddie. So what can I do for you gentlemen?'

Now this was the tricky part. The murder of Molly Green was headline news. But it was scant on the details and no suspects had been formally identified. The media were waiting, patiently, for any hint that NYPD were treating the Vanderpools as suspects. When I say media, I mean only certain newspapers, websites and TV channels. Most of the big news outlets were controlled by Julian Vanderpool, and I guessed he would be damned if his son was ever going to get any negative headlines from one of his puppets.

I couldn't tell Fairfax we were representing Vanessa, nor could I say we were representing someone in the family. I had to keep it a little vague. All the same, I had no doubt Fairfax knew exactly what was happening in the investigation. We just had to dance around each other for a few rounds before someone threw a hard right hook.

'Patrick Vanderpool is gearing up to challenge you,' I said. 'I'm sure you've done your homework. We're representing certain interests at the moment, and we don't want Patrick's political ambitions to put a target on his wife's back.'

'I see. You think I can just call up the police commissioner and get Vanessa, or even Patrick, arrested for murder? Is that right? You think I'd use my office for political gain?'

'Drop the bullshit,' said Harry. 'You'd sell your grandmother if you thought it would help you stay in office.'

The fake smile widened into something more genuine as he said, 'How do you think I got elected in the first place? Don't worry. I'm all out of grandmas, Harry.'

'If you come after the Vanderpools, it will look like a political prosecution,' said Harry. 'What's that fake word they use? Lawfare?'

'I've asked the mayor and the commissioner to keep me informed on the progress of the investigation, but I can assure you, I have no input into the case.'

'Because you've got a whole other pile of dirt you can throw – is that right?' I asked.

'Listen,' said Fairfax, leaning forward and putting his elbows on the table, 'with the money Pat Vanderpool can call upon for political donations, I gotta be willing to protect myself. In this day and age, being convicted of a crime is no guarantee of political jail. Not in this country. And I'm not interested in Vanderpool painting himself as the victim of a political witch hunt. That will only boost his poll numbers with his base. Plus, his father's media company . . . I'm not worried so much about newspapers any more – it's the troll farms.'

'Troll farms?' asked Harry.

'He posts an article online. Within seconds it's on TikTok, Instagram, X, Facebook, posted by thousands of trolls, some real influencers but mostly amplified by bots. It's a tsunami of shit. Like all nuclear threats, the best way of stopping it is to have your own warhead and point it at the most vulnerable person. I don't have one yet, but I may be close.'

'If you got this missile, where would you aim it?' I asked.

'Patrick, of course. Look, I'm not stupid. I know Buchanan and Duff look after the Vanderpools, and with the greatest of respect, you're no Rex Buchanan, Eddie. So I'm guessing they've farmed Vanessa out to you. Be careful. What's in your client's best interests and what's in Patrick's best interests may be very different.'

'Which is why we're here,' I said. 'If there's anything you know about her husband that could help protect her, or anything about her that might damage her defense, then I need to know.'

He leaned back in his chair, his fingers tapping the desk as he looked at each of us in turn and then nodded his head, gently. It looked like we had an understanding.

'I've got some of the best PI firms in the city working for me. They looked into Patrick, but got very little, apart from one thing. I have to be very careful about how I say this, because not all of this information came to me through entirely legal means. The private investigators hit a brick wall with this, but they all suspected there was more to discover. You've got Bloch working for you. If I sent you in the right direction, and you found something explosive that I could put in a warhead and aim it at Patrick, would you be willing to share that information in the spirit of mutual co-operation?'

'As long as you stay away from my grandma, I might be willing,' I said.

He laughed, said, ''Teresa Chase. That's all I can give you. There's something there, but I can't say any more. Not that you need any more. The name will lead Bloch down the right path, but she'll need to work fast. There's something else you should know, and it didn't come from me.'

He checked his watch, then said, 'In about thirty minutes, homicide detectives are going to arrest Vanessa Vanderpool for the murder of Molly Green.'

10

Bloch

'Why can't you buy a real car?' said Bloch.

She sat in the passenger seat of Lake's Aztek as they followed the beige Crown Victoria through the streets of lower Manhattan.

'This is a real car. It's inconspicuous,' said Lake.

'It's hideous. It sticks out like a sore thumb.'

'Yeah, but it's not threatening. Nobody is going to expect anyone with motivation, a mission, or any kind of agenda to be driving a car like this. This is a vehicle for people with a low profile, and low expectations. If this car makes it to the end of the block, it's an achievement.'

Bloch shook her head, keeping her eyes on the road as the Crown Victoria pulled up outside a bagel shop. Lake was two cars behind. He steered into a space on the opposite side of the street, twenty feet behind the Crown Vic.

A young woman with auburn hair got out of the driver's seat of the Crown Vic. She wore black jeans and a black winter coat. The bulge on her right hip let Bloch know she was carrying. Detective Carey was one of the youngest homicide cops Bloch had seen. She looked like she just graduated from the academy. No way should she be in a major homicide investigation unless her partner was a seasoned veteran, and she was being groomed for a fast-track promotion.

A vast head came out of the bagel shop, looked around and then the rest of the body followed. The head alone must've weighed seventy-five pounds. It was almost square, pale, and surrounded by a curtain of brown hair, which only accentuated the bald dome on top which was wide enough to use as a couch table.

The man had small eyes, a mouth that could swallow a bagel whole, and no neck. A white shirt the size of a sail on a small boat stretched over the torso of the man and was secured into his pants with a thick leather belt. A dark necktie didn't reach as far as his navel, and in a strange way almost acted as an arrow pointing to the man's bloated stomach. He had a brown paper bag in his left hand, and what Bloch presumed was his suit jacket in the other.

She took out her phone, snapped a picture. She didn't recognize him, but was pretty sure Eddie would know him.

The big man waved to Detective Carey.

Then turned.

Another man came out of the coffee shop. He was taller, probably just as wide, but in contrast carried about as much body fat as the other man's neck. He was younger, with a square jaw, dressed in black and wore a thin beard.

The two men spoke.

It was only then that Bloch saw the package in the bald man's hand. A bulky manuscript-sized envelope, sealed with Scotch tape.

Bloch took another picture of the two men in conversation. The man in black pointed at the package, gave it to the big bald man, then slapped him on the shoulder and departed, checking up and down the street as he did so. Carey didn't approach or talk to the man in black.

'That looks suspicious,' said Lake.

Bloch nodded.

The bald man then folded himself into the front passenger seat of the Crown Vic, severely testing the suspension of the vehicle. When Carey got into the driver's seat, she turned to the man, then put on her siren and blazed out of the parking space into traffic.

Lake pulled out behind her.

'Is that a cop she just picked up?' asked Lake.

'Must be. The other guy in black didn't look like police.'

They followed the police car through the streets, but lost them as they turned North and headed toward the upper east side of Manhattan.

'We're never going to catch up. Not in this shit-heap. Pull over here. I'll take the subway,' said Bloch.

'We don't know where they're going. How are you . . . ?'

Lake paused. Bloch waited for the other shoe to drop.

Lake said, 'Detective Carey called this morning, they want to interview Vanessa. Got stone-walled. She's got the sirens on and her lead detective in the car – they're going to arrest her right now.'

Bloch said, 'Call Eddie,' then got out of the car and ran into the subway.

By the time Bloch exited the subway on East 77th Street, climbing the steps to emerge in the milieu of the city once again, she was bathed in sweat and breathing hard. It was still winter, and while the subway was warmer than the streets above, the sweat was nothing to do with the temperature nor the exertion.

Bloch hated confined spaces, but more especially had a phobia about being underground. Still, it hadn't stopped her. She just suffered through it. That was what made her strong. She worked out every day, hit the gun range twice a month and ran three times a week. She didn't want to do any of these things, but knew that she *should* do them – that the long-term benefits outweighed the short-term effort and pain.

The pain and difficulty was the point. It meant when she experienced adversity in any part of her life, she had the mental clarity and physical memory of being able to go through it and get to the other side.

She sprinted to Third Avenue, turned left and ran to 81st.

By the time she turned the corner she saw Vanessa being led from her home in handcuffs and placed into the rear of Carey's Crown Vic.

Shit.

She was too late.

II

Eddie

The precinct interview room stank of stale sweat, vomit and something else I didn't even want to think about.

Sitting beside me on a cold steel chair, Vanessa was dealing with this better than I had expected. Once the cuffs came off, and she'd been processed, I had gotten to see her briefly. We were waiting for Detectives Ben Larkin and Lorraine Carey to come in and begin their questioning.

'What if they . . . ?' began Vanessa, and I put my finger to my lips.

'Everything you say in here is recorded. Know that before you speak. My advice, like I told you, is to say nothing. Let's see what they have. Remember, they want *you* to talk. They think they can get you to slip up. Here's the thing, even if you tell the truth in here, that can go against you in court. Words, phrases, nods of the head, even your intonation, it can all be twisted around if this is ever played in court for a jury. Say nothing. And watch your demeanor. You're on camera too. This is not a safe place for us to discuss strategy. We've been through this. Now, considering everything I've just said, do you still want to ask me something or can it wait until I get you out of here?'

'It can wait,' she said.

The door to the interview room opened and the young detective came in. Lorraine Carey was just under five feet tall, slim and pale with long, fine brown hair that stretched way down her back. The file in her arms looked as if it weighed more than her. She set it down on the steel table.

The next figure through the door was the same one Bloch had sent me a pic of not thirty minutes ago. A huge bald guy in a suit. She asked if I knew him. I didn't know him, not exactly. We'd had a few run-ins, but I certainly knew his reputation. Detective Ben Larkin had been a football player in college. Linebacker, naturally. Considering his sheer mass, he could take up most of that back line comfortably. Some who saw him felt sorry for him because of his size, but little did they know he was mostly muscle. Sure, he'd grown a gut, but I imagined he could comfortably pick me up and put me through this steel table with one hand.

The truth was, most cops didn't feel sorry for Ben Larkin, and it was all because of his reputation. Ten years ago, he didn't have the gut, his star was on the rise in the department and he closed cases with efficiency and diligence. Then everything changed. Larkin fucked up an arrest, mislabeled and lost evidence, and lied about it all in court. The perp was a Wall Street broker accused of attempted murder of his girlfriend. Thanks to Larkin, the guy walked. And Larkin never recovered. He spent the next ten years riding a desk, mostly filing other people's overtime reports. Instead of putting away bad guys, he started putting away donuts.

It was a sad story. And Larkin became a poster boy for what happens to cops who mess up.

The other man in the second picture Bloch had sent, the guy dressed in black who had given Larkin a package, I didn't know him at all. Never seen him before. But he didn't look like a cop.

The steel chair legs groaned as they took Larkin's weight. They were an odd pairing.

Something wasn't right with this picture, and it wasn't the fact that Carey looked like Larkin's lunch.

Carey began the interview by reminding Vanessa of her rights, and then opened the binder in front of her.

'We've been talking to individuals involved in your husband's political team,' began Carey. 'His campaign manager, Geoff Gilbert, and the rest of the staff, including Heidi Swanson. When you were interviewed two weeks ago, you told NYPD officers that you didn't really know the victim, Molly Green. And that you hardly spoke to her. You also said you didn't know of anyone who might want to harm Molly. Is there any part of your answer you want to change?'

I watched Vanessa closely. She took in the question without her expression changing. No surprise, no shock or alarm. She sat upright in the chair, legs crossed, back straight, hands relaxed in her lap. A blank look on her face. As if she was waiting for something.

Her lips parted, and I leaned forward and put one elbow on the desk, just to remind her that I was here, which in turn hopefully reminded her to keep her mouth shut.

Vanessa said nothing. She just stared at Carey.

'Not talking, huh? Smart. Too late, though. You should've had Mr. Flynn in your corner two weeks ago. Turns out, your husband's team have a different recollection to yours. They say you were close to Molly. That you two regularly talked together. Alone. Tell me, what had Molly done to make you so angry?'

Again, Vanessa said nothing. This is more difficult than it sounds. Sitting there, listening to police accuse you of something terrible, it's natural to want to fight back, to stand up for yourself, to tell them that they've got this all wrong. Vanessa was playing the game well. Showing real restraint.

'You also told us you had never been to Molly Green's apartment. We've got you on security camera visiting the apartment the night of the murder. Do you want to change that statement?'

Clients lie. To their lawyers. To the police. To their priest. The world turns and the sun rises. What else is new? Vanessa had not been the first client to lie to me. She would not be the last. People lie for all kinds of reasons. It doesn't automatically mean they're guilty.

The ground shifts beneath your feet in a murder case. Happens all the time. But you don't expect your client to be the one who moves the earth. I was too long at this game to feel a sense of betrayal, but now I had questions for Vanessa. Not here. Not now. But soon.

'We found your DNA in Molly Green's apartment. How did it get there?'

Vanessa blinked, slowly. Perhaps a subtle recognition of what was to come.

In that moment, it looked like she'd taken a knockout punch, and she was trying to shake it off.

She said nothing. No reply.

'Was it the fact that Molly Green was sleeping with your husband? Is that why you killed her?'

Now we had motive.

'Still not talking? Okay, let's cut to the chase. Vanessa Vanderpool, we're charging you with first-degree murder.'

I took time studying Vanessa's face.

Cold. Frozen. No reaction to her life collapsing right in front of her.

Still, there was perhaps something in her eyes that spoke to me.

Her expression told me a lot.

It was the kind of resignation that comes to those who know they have already sealed their fate by their own actions. That karma, or even that loose concept of justice, had just arrived to even the score. I'd seen it before.

It's the kind of expression you see on the faces of the guilty.

12

The Journal

Dear Reader,

I don't know who you are. Maybe you're someone special to me. You're not family. I know that much. They've all gone now. Maybe you are someone who knows me, but it's unlikely. Chances are, if you're reading this, you're a stranger.

I think it's better that we don't know each other. I have a tale to tell. And by the end of this you will understand everything.

But not yet.

Not all at once.

I need you to understand what I've done. This record is not for me, not really. It's for you. A written record of everything I did, and why I did it.

So far, no one knows about this diary. I'm keeping it hidden from everyone. Especially Patrick.

I think it helps, putting it all in writing. It helps keep my head straight. It reminds me that I am not who they think I am. It keeps me sharp. Focused. When you tell lies all day, it's easy to get lost in them. Sometimes, but just sometimes, I feel like I'm disappearing into the role I'm playing. I think it must be the same for actors sometimes. Method actors who just stay in character even after the director yells cut. They become the person they are playing for months, right up until the last day of shooting.

I sort of know how they must feel. Just occasionally, I get lost too.

This diary is my map back to me. And your map to the truth.

It may be complete, or not. I don't know how long I can do this without them finding out. I hope it's for long enough to find the truth. If not, you will have to use what's here to piece together the rest of it. If I haven't finished this, I'm sorry. But there's probably a good reason for that.

Because there's a good chance that if you're reading this diary I have failed.

And I'm dead.

Not just passed on after a long and happy life, but murdered.

You might grieve for me. You might not. I'm no innocent. Not any more. I have lied and cheated to get close to him.

Close enough to destroy him.

I understand that revenge is a dangerous path. I think of it sometimes like I'm trying to catch a wild animal, like a tiger that has become a man-killer. You have to get close enough so that it falls into your trap. But how close? Close enough that its claws might tear your flesh.

Close enough that it might just kill you.

I have accepted the risk. You should know that.

If I am murdered, I need you to understand that I am not the first person Patrick has killed.

And I probably won't be the last.

13
Eddie

'Everything will be fine,' she said.

Normally, I'm the one who says those words. Or something to that effect.

This was the first time I'd heard that phrase from a client.

But that's what Vanessa said as she was booked for murder.

Nonchalant. Like this was just an administrative error that would be quickly corrected. A minor inconvenience. And it wasn't just the privilege talking. It was either the kind of supreme confidence that comes with wealth and power, or it was something else. It could have been the knowledge that she was innocent.

Innocent people always believe they will be freed.

In the beginning, anyway.

Then they meet the American Justice System.

Beliefs can change pretty fast in a courtroom.

I told her I would work on her bail. She would be out in a couple of hours. Even as I spoke, her words were still echoing around in my head. Sending goosebumps over my flesh.

Everything will be fine.

I hoped, for her sake, that she was right.

I told the booking sergeant to make sure she had a cell to herself. He looked her up and down. Nodded. The criminal justice system treats people differently according to their status. It shouldn't be that way, there was nothing in the constitution or the statute books to even hint at it. Quite the opposite. The line was that everyone was equal under the law.

The only problem was that justice is a business, like everything else in America.

Health. Birth. Imprisonment. Even death. Somewhere, somebody was making money from every part of life in the good old US of A.

Walking out of the precinct, I had a million thoughts running through my head and I needed some fresh air and perspective. With the sidewalk beneath my feet, and my back to the precinct building, I looked up at the ash-gray sky, took a lungful of gasoline fumes from the traffic rolling by and tried to get my head straight.

As a con artist, I had survived by listening closely to my instincts.

Right now, every part of me was itching to get away from this one. I had a bad feeling. Something wasn't right here. The circumstances of this case didn't add up. The only thing I was certain about was that I didn't trust my client. Did that make her guilty?

It might.

And then again it might not.

She was hard to read. One minute, I believed she was innocent. The next, my gut was telling me to run far and fast from this case. Staring straight ahead, my mind elsewhere, I didn't fully register the large black SUV that pulled up at the curb. I paid no attention to the two men who got out of the front of the car.

Not until they stood right in front of me.

One had short black hair, and a puffy face. Huge shoulders that looked like melons stuffed under his shirt collar. Zits on his neck and cheeks. He looked to me like he was in his mid-twenties, so I guessed his adolescent acne was probably behind him. Then I saw the veins bulging in his neck, his skin tone a vivid, dark pink.

All signs of heavy anabolic steroid use.

He wore a black woolen overcoat over a black suit. Lace-up boots, not shoes.

The man next to him was shorter but wider and about the same age. He had cropped, bleach-blond hair with a scar running across the top of his head. Same woolen overcoat. Same black pants. Same boots.

Both men held their arms way out from their body, the result of overdeveloped lats. They each stood with their feet shoulder-width apart, knees slightly bent. They were probably used to handling other human beings who didn't want to be handled.

'Mr. Flynn, you're to come with us right now,' said the blond one.

'I'm a little busy right now. You'll need to make an appointment with my office,' I said, and widened my own stance. Took my hands out of my pockets, but it had been a while since I'd buried a glove in a heavy bag.

They looked like they were trained fighters. They were about fifteen years younger, forty pounds heavier than me, with tons of gas in their tanks and lots of hours on the mat.

But what I lacked in youthful vigor I could make up for with experience, pure cunning and fighting dirty.

'This can't wait. We gotta take you now,' said the blond guy.

'I think the two of you together could get me into that car, but you'll both be sore for weeks after. Think carefully.'

The rear door of the SUV opened and a small woman in a gray suit dropped her heels to the curb. The car wasn't that tall, but it was too big for this lady. She was in her early thirties, red hair and a patch of freckles over her pale skin. A leather shoulder bag and sunglasses. She walked right up to the two men, who turned and acknowledged her presence, then swung their attention back to me. Even though she was small, there was a quiet authority in her manner.

'I was hoping we could do this in the back seat, instead of on a street corner,' she said.

'I bet you say that to all the guys.'

She stared at me. I'm not normally rude to strangers. But two guys who looked like they were about to throw me into a car and take me God knows where didn't exactly make me feel polite. Nor did the woman who appeared to be their superior.

'Sorry, just a joke,' I said. 'My mother told me never to get into a car with strangers.'

'My name is Samantha Voss. I'm a consultant attorney instructed by Buchanan and Duff. I'm your liaison in the Vanessa Vanderpool case.'

I remembered Buchanan offering me a whole team of lawyers to work on Vanessa's case. I had objected and agreed to only one. I figured that whoever he sent me would relay every detail back to Buchanan, and I guessed it was easier to keep an eye on one person instead of a team. All the same, I had no idea what a consultant attorney might be. Perhaps some formal legal separation from the firm, to ensure there were no technical conflicts of interest.

'Pleased to meet you, but there's no need for you to be here. I've got it covered.'

'The reverse is true, Mr. Flynn. You have a meeting that you must attend. I will ensure Mrs. Vanderpool is bailed within the hour.'

'Very kind of you, but I don't have a meeting in my schedule and I'm not letting you anywhere near my client.'

'*Our* client, if you care to check the terms of your retainer. I have a copy here if you'd like to see it. In addition, Mrs. Vanderpool will struggle to use joint marital assets as capital for a bail bond and joint cash reserves cannot be utilized either. The man you're about to meet will pay Mrs. Vanderpool's bail bond, in full, as long as you meet him. So get in the goddamn car, or I'll go explain to *our* client why she has to spend a night in a jail cell because her other attorney fucked up her bail.'

The blond guy smiled. I got the impression that this wasn't the first time he'd seen Voss get the better of somebody.

'I don't play well with others. Why don't you go represent

Mrs. Vanderpool, and I'll go home. I've had about enough of this situation.'

'The man who is waiting to meet you won't tolerate that, I'm afraid,' she said.

The blond guy stepped closer.

I got the message.

There were two of them, and they were both bigger and stronger than me. I could probably take one of them, maybe, but not two. This was only going to go one way. Either we all got into the car, bloodied and bruised, or we got into the car without the theatrics, and I bided my time.

'Who is this asshole who wants to meet me?'

'You'll see,' said the blond guy.

14
Eddie

Not many people own houses in Manhattan.

Fewer own two.

Fewer still own a whole block.

Only one person lived in two townhouses, knocked together, on his very own block.

Flanked by the men in overcoats, I stood in a vast marble hallway that reminded me of City Hall. A collection of Fabergé eggs sat on a hall table, casually, no security glass surrounding them. Above them, I was pretty sure sat a Jackson Pollock painting that stretched high above onto what would have been the second floor, if they hadn't taken this ceiling away to create an entrance to drop the jaw of any billionaire. Right there, just on that one wall, with those eggs and that painting, was more money than I'd ever seen in my life.

An archway below the winding marble staircase led into a secluded garden. A door opened upstairs, and a man stepped onto the landing and started walking down the staircase. He made the guys standing beside me look small. A huge man, with a jaw like a wash basin, legs that were the size of my torso and pale arms impossibly swollen with muscle and decorated with what looked like military tattoos. He wore black pants and a black tee. Tight hair in a buzzcut. Graying at the temples. His skin was waxy, and white. Like a marble statue.

A handgun was visible on a quick-release holster on his hip.

Only when he was halfway down the stairs did I notice the little guy behind him. The small man wore the same outfit, but on him it looked like he was modelling babywear. The skin on his shaven head was mottled with age, and the hairs on his arms were thick and white, making him look like he'd reached both hands deep into a cotton candy machine. He held a thick cigar in his hand, smoke swirling around his face, and his lips were worm-like and slightly purple. He wore sunglasses in thick black frames, his skin was tanned and I got the impression this was a permanent effect, which he topped up via weekends in the Caribbean.

The big guy said, 'Did you search him?' in an accent that I couldn't immediately place.

The two guys in overcoats looked at each other, shrugged. The blond said, 'The guy's a lawyer. He ain't gonna be carrying.'

The big guy tutted, looked at me and said, 'Hands up.'

That's when I recognized the South African accent. I raised my arms, stood still as he searched me. Sweeping my legs, arms, torso. He took my phone out of my pocket, switched it off, said, 'You'll get this back later.'

The small man said, 'Julian Vanderpool,' in a heavy Brooklyn accent, 'let's talk.'

No handshake. No smile. All business.

He set off through the archway beneath the stairs to the garden. I followed, the big guy stalking behind me. It was then I realized this wasn't an outdoor garden. It had a glass ceiling, and a temperature control to keep the exotic plants and tropical trees in good health. I could feel the wave of heat as soon as I saw the glass above me.

Julian folded himself into a rattan chair, crossed his legs and gestured that I should take the chair opposite. I sat down, watched him take off his sunglasses and place them on a table.

His eyes were hard to look at. The irises were strangely blue. The color of a Scandinavian lake in summer. What made them strange was that the irises were not surrounded by the usual white fibrous tissue. Instead, it was red. As if every capillary had burst. Staring into his eyes was like looking at two sapphires resting in bowls of blood. When he placed the cigar between his lips and smoked, it almost looked like he had three burning eyes.

'You've got promise, Flynn. I've followed your cases. You're good on your feet. You know how to work-over a witness and talk to a jury. I like that. The only thing holding you back is that conscience of yours. That's weakness. If you were serious about your career, you'd have some heavyweight clients. I can make that happen – oil companies, pharmaceuticals, politicians – I can open the right doors for you, Flynn.'

'No, thanks,' I said.

His lips drew back over a row of small, rounded teeth, in what I guessed was a smile.

'Moral pride is this country's great sickness,' he said.

'My conscience is my greatest weapon. It stops me from representing oil companies, big pharma and politicians.'

'Then consider this as your wake-up call. Your real client in this case is *me*.'

'Like I said, I don't represent the guilty.'

He threw his head back and laughed.

'You don't have a choice, I'm afraid. I'm going to put up Vanessa's bail through a shell company. She'll be out on the street today and I'll make sure her trial happens in record time. You just be ready.'

'I didn't know you controlled the courts as well as the media.'

'You'd be a fool if you underestimated my sphere of influence. Let's be clear: my son is running for office. He is my priority. In an ideal world, I'd like his wife cleared, clean and fast. I want this shit gone in three months, tops.'

'You got a magic wand I could borrow?'

Julian leaned forward, said, 'I've got the media, two hundred and thirty billion dollars and a contacts list you wouldn't believe. For now, you will proceed as instructed. If things change, your instructions will change.'

'I only take instructions from clients.'

'You're not getting this, are you? Don't worry. You will. For now, you will defend Vanessa and you'll do a good job. If she gets convicted, so be it. I couldn't give a fuck. What I do care about is my son. The DA will go after her, but you, my friend, you're going to keep my son's name out of this courtroom and out of your mouth. If you do what I tell you, I will make you a rich man. If you accuse my son in order to get Vanessa acquitted, you're walking into hell. I have more money than God, but you know what I spend most of it on?'

I said nothing, just stared at him.

'Insurance. Bad things happen all the time. *You*, you're my insurance policy. I look after my family, Flynn. Do you care about your family? Your daughter wants to go to college some day, right?'

My jaw clenched. My throat tightened.

He leaned forward, said, 'I could get her into Harvard with one phone call, full scholarship. Or I could get her blacklisted from every decent college in the country. I can have the FBI, the IRS and the justice department investigate your friends, your ex-wife, your fuckin' landlord, even the guy who delivers your mail – they can all be eating oatmeal in a federal penitentiary for a very long time. You? I could have you on a plane to a fleapit max-security prison in Lagos in the morning. Don't you get it? Don't you know who is in charge now? All bets are off with this administration. There are no laws, and there are no rules. Not any more. Not for guys like me. In my time, I've brought down presidents, movie stars, princesses, prime ministers and governments. You? You're breakfast, Flynn. Now, get the fuck out of here and do your job.'

I wanted to say something.

I'm good at comebacks. I don't take threats well. I could be out of my seat with my fist in Julian Vanderpool's scrawny throat before his gorilla could stop me.

But right then I didn't. I let my fingertips curl into the palms of my hands, tightening into fists.

I turned and looked up at the big guy.

'What's your name?' I asked him.

He didn't answer, instead unfolded his thick, tattooed arms and slid his thumbs behind the waist of his pants. Right hand inches from the pistol on his hip.

'Are you still here?' said Julian, the tan on his cheeks seeming to deepen, a vein growing in the side of his neck.

I sat there, didn't move.

I relaxed my hands, spoke calmly, trying to keep the emotion out of my voice.

'If Vanessa is innocent, I'll help her. But not for you. If you know me, you'll know I don't respond well to threats. Especially threats to my friends and family. Let me do my work, keep the hell away from me and the people around me. Then we won't have any problems.'

'You really don't get it. I'm your boss, your father, your savior and your executioner. I'm all things to you, Flynn. Now go.'

I didn't move an inch.

Julian's anger turned to surprise. He was a man who was used to people snapping to attention, and doing everything he said, immediately.

I leaned back in the seat.

Julian tutted, said, 'Dekker, get him the fuck out of here.'

The gorilla stepped toward me, a mean look on his face.

He grabbed the collar of my shirt, pulled me up off my seat and turned, then shoved me toward the hallway.

I didn't resist.

The blond guy and his pal waited in the lobby, sweating in their overcoats.

Just before we reached them, I felt the gorilla tensing his arm. He pulled me back, then pushed me forward, almost punching the back of my neck, such was the power and speed of the movement. I lost my footing, put my hands out as I fell and even though I got them beneath me, I still hit my head on the marble floor.

The overcoats grabbed me by the arms, and lifted me off the floor with ease, just as the first drops of blood from the cut on my right eyebrow fell over my shirt. I heard my phone clattering on the floor. They let me pick it up. Then they wheeled me around and toward the street, blood dripping into my eyes.

It was okay. The cut was worth it.

I'd gotten what I wanted. I'd pissed off Julian Vanderpool enough for him to call his bodyguard to get me removed.

The gorilla's name was Dekker.

He was the second man in the photo Bloch had sent me. The big guy who had met Detective Larkin at the bagel shop and given him something in an oversized envelope.

I didn't know who he was, or what his connection was with Larkin, but now I had his name.

There are layers of mystery in every murder. This one was thicker than most. There were a lot of things about this case that didn't make sense. One thing I was sure of: nobody was telling me the truth.

It was time to start finding out what had really happened to Molly Green.

15
Eddie

'Did you ask Julian Vanderpool about Teresa Chase?' asked Harry.

'No, not until we know more about who she is and what the hell she has to do with the Vanderpools. Pat Vanderpool's political opponent seems to think it's something that could jeopardize Pat's political career. It's a weapon. You don't pull a weapon like that out of the bag unless you know how to use it and— Ow!' I said.

'Sorry,' said Denise as she dabbed some cotton wool on the cut over my eye. I could smell the disinfectant from the swab. Denise had soaked the thing in iodine.

I sat on the desk in the conference room, blood on my shirt. Collar open, neck tie in the trash.

Harry leaned against the doorframe while Denise cleaned the wound. Lake sat beside Harry and Bloch, who was listening but also on her laptop.

'Did the little demon lawyer get Vanessa out on bail?' I asked.

'She did,' said Denise. 'She called and left a message for you. Vanessa wants to meet with Ms. Voss and you.'

'I'll look forward to it . . . Yikes, that stings. You're going to blind me with that thing. I'd rather die from an infection.'

'Don't be such a baby,' said Denise, then pressed the wool swab down harder. Held it there. I gritted my teeth. After a few seconds, she let go and said, 'There, the bleeding's stopped.'

'Thanks,' I said, then rubbed the back of my neck. I had a monster headache coming on.

'So what do you make of all this?' asked Lake.

'I was hoping my investigators and my mentor might have some ideas,' I said.

'Dekker, Lee Harold, emigrated to the US from South Africa when he was fifteen. Former Navy Seal, originally based out of Little Creek Naval Base in Virginia Beach,' said Bloch, reading from her laptop screen. 'He transferred at the rank of Master Chief Special Warfare Operator to the CIA's Special Operations Group and retired two years later. Worked as a merc for a while, which is why we have a profile online. And some headlines. He was part of a team that was investigated following the war in Afghanistan. Allegations of alcohol and drug abuse, and sexual assault within the unit. He denied all the allegations and because he was already out of the service nothing happened.'

'He sounds delightful,' said Harry.

'We need to know what was in that package. What did Dekker give to Detective Larkin, and why?' said Lake.

'Could he have given him some piece of evidence so he could frame Vanessa?' asked Harry.

'That doesn't make a whole lot of sense,' I said. 'Julian doesn't want any mud on his son, Patrick. He can't run his campaign on bringing down crime stats if he's married to a murderer.'

'Could it have been a bribe? To make sure the cops focus on Vanessa instead of Patrick?' asked Lake.

'I don't think that makes sense either. Vanessa and Patrick are tied together, at least politically. And the cops on this case are their own mystery. Ben Larkin is a has-been, and his partner is greener than Vermont. If even one of them was on this case it would be out of the ordinary, but both of them?'

'This isn't an ordinary homicide. All the power players in this town are watching,' said Harry.

'When the suspects include the ultra-rich and powerful, you can bet this investigation will be closely handled, every move debated and signed off by the top brass,' said Lake.

'Okay, find out the shift pattern for detectives on the date and time the body was found. It could be that Larkin and Carey lucked out and were just the only homicide detectives available and someone let them ride the case out this far. If they weren't on that shift, then we need to find out who was and how this case got handed to the dream team.'

Bloch nodded and got up to get to work.

'Wait, I need something else. Fairfax, the governor, mentioned a woman's name – Teresa Chase. I looked online, couldn't find a single thing about her. We need to find out who she is and talk to her.'

'If it's not connected to our case, then why do you need to know about her?' asked Lake.

'Julian Vanderpool threatened me. Threatened everyone here, too. If Teresa Chase has dirt on Julian, or his son, then I want to know. We're going to need some leverage.'

'What are we gonna do?' asked Harry.

'We're going to talk to Vanessa. It's time we had a heart to heart. Then I want to talk to her husband.'

'You sure that's a door you want to open?' asked Harry.

'That's a door we have to kick down. Somebody cut off a young woman's head in her own apartment, and I don't think it was our client.'

'You didn't sound so sure when you said that, kid,' said Harry.

'She lied to us, but there has to be a reason. Maybe she's

protecting her husband. We have to make it clear to her that the best defense in this case is giving the jury an alternative suspect and that's Patrick Vanderpool. I don't care what Julian says, we have to do the best for our client, whether she wants that or not. And that means we have to go after her husband with everything we've got.'

16

Vanessa

Some silences are so heavy they are practically deafening.

The small woman who sat beside Vanessa in the back of the town car had not said a single word since she'd got in. Ms. Voss was an independent counsel, hired by Buchanan and Duff as a consultant to assist with Vanessa's case.

Vanessa didn't believe any of it. There was only one person who was being protected in this arrangement, and that was Patrick. Voss could explain all the technicalities she liked in order to appear independent and unbiased, but there was only one name on the check that paid her fees – Julian Vanderpool.

The silence gave Vanessa time to think.

Time to take in the developments of that day. The arrest, the questioning.

Time to absorb it all, calmly.

Time to plan.

The town car pulled up outside Vanessa's home, and Voss opened her door and got out. Vanessa followed, stepping onto the curb beside the lawyer. As Vanessa stood, she towered over Voss, but in truth she felt much smaller than her diminutive attorney. Here was someone not to be underestimated. Voss had a hard, angular face, overdeveloped calves and muscular body to match the taut features.

She looked like a masonry nail in a red wig.

And Vanessa knew who was swinging the hammer.

Voss spoke softly, but her diamond-cut words were hard.

'When you meet Flynn tomorrow, you tell him nothing about what we have discussed. He's an idiot. He has his beliefs about the justice system and a set of morals he sticks to. This is his weakness. We are going to exploit that to get the best out of him. Patrick will ask you what happened in the police station. You'll tell him exactly what I told you. You were arrested, the police have evidence, but we don't know the precise nature of that evidence yet. We'll know more in a couple of days. The trial will be heard quickly. This will all be over in a few months. Tell him everything will be alright. You're going to get acquitted, and then you two can put all of this behind you. Got it?'

Vanessa hesitated, her throat dry and mind reeling. She was shaking, but not from the cold. Voss wasn't shaking. She stood very still, like a goddamn statue, gazing up at Vanessa.

Then Vanessa nodded, said, 'I've got it.'

After a moment, Voss's head cocked to the side. It was a strange movement. She never broke eye-contact with Vanessa, and no other part of her body moved. The gesture could have been made by an animatronic puppet. Alien and cold.

'We discussed this. I'm sure this isn't the first time you've lied to your husband. It won't be the last. Just go and tell him you don't know what case they have against you, but everything will be alright,' said Voss, then without another word she got back into the town car and slammed the door shut. The car rolled away.

Vanessa watched it go, unable to see Voss through the tinted windows, but she knew the woman was watching her.

For a few moments, Vanessa stood on the sidewalk, her back to the brownstone home she cherished. Patrick was inside, waiting for her.

She could feel him.

Not like a wife feels her husband. Not like a lover feels their partner. That sense of warmth, of love and security.

She could feel him like a presence in the dark.

As she walked up the steps to the front door, keys in hand, she thought about turning and running. She could leave now. And never have to enter this house again. Never have to see his face again.

The front door opened.

Patrick stood there in a blue shirt, the skin below his eyes swollen, hair tousled, as if he'd just woken from a nap.

'I heard the car. Are you alright?'

Vanessa stared at him for a moment, unable to say anything.

But then she remembered her role. She remembered what she had to do. Voss's sharp words ringing in her ears.

'I'm alright. Everything is going to be alright,' she said.

He didn't embrace her. That wasn't his way. He had not been raised in a home that comforted loved ones, nor a home that understood love at all.

He simply stood aside, beckoning her to come in.

She took a deep breath and stepped into the hallway. The door, with its heavy steel plate on the back for security, slammed behind her, making her jump. But to Vanessa, right now, that door wasn't there to keep people out. It was there to keep her in.

'What did the lawyers say?' he asked.

'She— They said the trial will be fast. It will all be over in a few months and then we can put it all behind us.'

He stepped in close behind her, so that when he spoke his breath was hot on the back of her neck.

'That's wonderful news.'

She moved on, through the hallway toward the kitchen. Grabbing a bottle of water from the fridge, she drank deeply. Patrick stood behind her. She'd heard his footsteps on the floor, and sensed his presence coming ever closer. He was gauging her responses.

Trying to get a handle on her demeanor, so he could properly assess where he stood and how this case could affect him.

'Do you want something to eat?' he asked.

She put the water bottle on the counter, keeping her back to him. Then she shook her head.

There was something else on his mind. Something he wanted to know. He just hadn't asked it yet.

'I need to rest. I need to sleep,' she said.

'Of course. Just one thing . . .' he said.

This is it.

'Did they mention Molly's bracelet?'

She spun round, gazed at him. He leaned against the kitchen island, his arms by his side, legs crossed – a casual display, but the keenness in his eyes betrayed his portrayal of casual indifference.

'What?' asked Vanessa. 'What bracelet?'

'The diamond bracelet she wore. Did they mention it?'

Picking up the water bottle, Vanessa made for the hallway and the stairs.

As she passed him, he grabbed her upper arm, fast, causing her to jolt and spill a little of the water on her blouse.

'The bracelet. Did they talk about the bracelet?' he asked again, this time with an edge in his voice.

'No,' she said, and then shrugged away, and pulled, but he held on to her arm, his fingers digging into her flesh. He stared into her eyes, trying to gauge if she was telling the truth.

Fear is a funny thing. She thought she should be used to it by now. She had lived with it long enough. Not every day, but somehow it was always there. It could come from the look in the corner of Patrick's eye, the way he gripped a coffee cup, the sliver of ice in a single word from his crooked mouth or even from the way he breathed.

He was a severely damaged man. His father had seen to that.

Badly damaged people hurt others.

This is the way of things. This is what Vanessa understood above everything else.

Because she was damaged too.

Vanessa knew fear like she knew her own face. And yet, when it arrived, like right now, it always felt fresh and new – pulsing through her veins, crawling over her skin, licking with a cold tongue on the back of her neck.

Fear, however familiar, was always a stranger.

He let her go.

She turned away quickly, her chest rising and falling faster and faster, as the fear took her in a gentle, icy embrace. She clambered up the stairs.

'Vanessa,' he called out. She was moving away from him, fast as she could, and she didn't want to turn back. Not for anything.

'Stop!' he yelled. 'You and I need to talk.'

'I don't want to talk to you. My lawyers said I shouldn't.'

'We have to talk. I have things I have to say. Whether you believe it or not, I don't know. I loved her, Vanessa. And part of me still loves you. There's something I have to tell you . . .'

17
Patrick

He heard the town car pull up.

Patrick was out of his seat in an instant, at the bedroom window, peeking through the blinds. There on the street, Vanessa was talking to a short woman with red hair, in a business suit. The consultant Buchanan had arranged – Voss. He recalled seeing her once before, consulting with his father. She was cold, detached. A real killer was how his father had described her.

His stomach tightened.

Voss and Vanessa were talking on the sidewalk.

He took the stairs quickly, and ran to the hallway, opening the front door just in time to see Vanessa standing there, keys in hand.

'I heard the car. Are you alright?' he asked.

'I'm alright. Everything is going to be alright,' she said.

He stood aside, letting her come in. He didn't want to chance an embrace. It would only make her uncomfortable and he needed her to talk. He slammed the door shut behind her.

'What did the lawyers say?' he asked, following her through the hallway.

She slowed, said, 'She— They said the trial will be fast. It will all be over in a few months and then we can put it all behind us.'

He stepped in close behind her, thought about grabbing both her shoulders, spinning her round and screaming at her. Telling her she had better come clean about everything the police knew, about everything she had told them.

His hand snaked out, but he dropped it. He couldn't risk it. He had to get her talking on her own steam.

'That's wonderful news.'

He followed her into the kitchen as she took some water from the fridge, then closed it and stood facing the counter with her back to him. She opened the water and drank.

A single thought pulsed in his mind as he stared at the back of her head, the water bottle at her lips.

She can't look at me . . .

She's told them about me and Molly.

'Do you want something to eat?' he asked.

Keeping her back to him, she put the water bottle on the counter. Her head followed it down, focusing on the counter, exposing the back of her neck, and the honey and vanilla skin stretched taut over the ridge over her spine.

She shook her head. 'I need to rest. I need to sleep,' she said.

'Of course. Just one thing . . .' he said. 'Did they mention Molly's bracelet?'

She spun round and stared at him. Patrick didn't want to spook her. He tried to appear as nonchalant as possible.

'What?' asked Vanessa. 'What bracelet?'

'The diamond bracelet she wore. Did they mention it?'

Without answering, she took her water bottle and was about to storm off.

Without thinking, he grabbed her upper arm, stopping her, spilling some of the water from her bottle.

'The bracelet. Did they talk about the bracelet?'

'No,' she said, and tried to wrestle free. Was she lying? He tried to detect anything other than fear in her eyes.

He let her go.

What the hell was she doing? Vanessa was a survivor – he knew that at least. When they'd met, and then dated and she agreed to be married, Patrick was under no illusions. He loved her then, but part of him always questioned her love for him. That wasn't unusual. He was rich beyond what most people could imagine. Every relationship in his life was affected by his wealth. It became a screen through which he saw the world and the world saw him. How much did anyone really love him for the man he was, and not the man his bank account made him?

Patrick was taught very little by his father. They had never played catch in the garden, never went fishing, never had a beer together, never went to a ball game together and never really talked. Not a real conversation. Julian expected him to learn by watching him. As a young man, he would shadow him as he toured the floor of the smoky newsroom, sat behind his huge desk and barked orders, and on one memorable occasion Patrick had been brought into his father's office to witness something that would mark him for life.

He had spent the morning on the black leather couch reading his comic books while his father made calls from behind his huge desk – older and bigger than the president's Resolute desk, or so his father had told him. Those kinds of things were important to his father.

Bigger. Stronger. Faster. More expensive.

These were the words and phrases that brought something close to happiness to his father. It wasn't true to say he had friends, but if another billionaire bought a new yacht, or a new Bentley, then his father had to have a bigger one, a faster one, and preferably one that nobody else could have.

The desk was specially built. This was the helm of the ship that steered his father's business.

Patrick looked up from his Superman comic to see a gray-haired man in a shiny silvery suit walk into his father's office and take a seat in front of that slab of wood. The chair that faced his father's desk was small and uncomfortable, forcing the occupant to sit upright. This was Mr. Cherry. Boris Cherry. The name always made Patrick smile. It was unusual and he didn't know people could be named after fruit. He'd seen the man often at his father's apartment and at social gatherings when Patrick had been forced to wear a necktie and pants that were way too stiff. At these events, Boris was often introduced to people as *Julian's number two*, which also made Patrick giggle at first, because he didn't know it meant Boris was almost as important as his father – he just thought it sounded like he was his father's turd.

'Come over here, Patrick,' said his father.

He put down his comic and joined Julian on his side of the desk.

'How are you, my boy?' asked Boris with a nervous smile.

Patrick had nodded and smiled back. He didn't talk much in those days. His father said he blabbered too much, so he had been purposely quieter in his presence.

'How long have we known each other? Twenty years?' asked his father.

'Maybe longer. What's up, Julian? Is there something I can do?'

Patrick stood by his father's chair, his hand resting on the desk, his fingers feeling the grain of the polished wood. When his father didn't say anything for a few seconds, Patrick got nervous. He saw Boris shifting in his seat, trying not to look scared. His father could shout a lot. And that was always scary.

'You know I don't have time for bullshit, Boris. You're out. Get your fucking coat and get out of my sight,' said his father.

The man sat still for a long time. His pale, glassy eyes were suddenly wet. The man took a handkerchief from the breast pocket of his suit, and covered his mouth as he sobbed.

'But . . . I've done nothing wrong . . . I . . . I've always . . . My wife, my kids, how am I going to look after them?' said the man, slobbering through his words.

Julian stared at the man. His cold, red eyes burning into the man's flesh.

'Look at that, Patrick. Have you ever seen anything more pathetic,' said his father, and then pressed an orange button on the big panel of buttons on his desk phone.

Two security guards came into his father's office, slid their arms underneath Boris's and lifted him out of the chair, sobbing, and carried him from the office.

'Why did you do that?' asked Patrick.

'He was getting too comfortable,' said Julian. 'I'm godfather to his kid. I was best man at his second wedding. He was my number two in this business for a long time. But you know what? I don't trust him. There's no one you can trust in this world other than your family. Do you hear? *Nobody*.'

'Did he betray you?'

'I never gave him the chance. You can let people in, but only so far and for so long. Sometimes, you've got to let them know who you are. He's shit on my heel, son, and I just scraped it clean.'

Right then, Patrick felt very sorry for Boris. He swayed on his heels, and his tummy began to do that weird thing. He had never seen an adult cry before, and it made him feel frightened.

'Don't you feel sorry for him, son. Not even one little bit. Empathy is the enemy. Empathy is weakness. You watch and learn from your old man. Some day you could be president. I could make you a great man.'

If that was what it took to be a great man, Patrick knew then, as he knew now, he didn't want to be one. It was his father who had betrayed Boris. And he had enjoyed it.

His father had always been there for him, not with love and support, but with money and power. All Patrick's problems had been solved that way, his drinking, his drug habit, hundreds of thousands on rehab, but not one kind word.

Just pain. Pain and betrayal. That was who his father really was.

Patrick didn't want to be this great man any more.

His hand reached for his right shoulder, and began tracing the scar there through his shirt. It felt hot and itchy.

He followed Vanessa and stood at the bottom of the stairs as she raced up them.

'Vanessa,' he called.

She ignored him, and continued upstairs.

'Stop!' he yelled. 'You and I need to talk.'

'I don't want to talk to you. My lawyers said I shouldn't.'

'We have to talk. I have things I have to say. Whether you believe it or not, I don't know. I loved her, Vanessa. And part of me still loves you. There's something I have to tell you . . .'

18

Bloch

The truth doesn't come easy.

Detective work is a laborious, detail-driven process of elimination. For a private detective, it's slightly different. You come into a situation where an investigation has already been conducted. The stones have been overturned, or at least most of them. The job then becomes examining what was beneath those stones afresh, without bias, without a suspect in mind, without prejudice. And then you look at the little rocks. The ones the police didn't bother to kick over. What story lies under there.

In the end, and in the beginning, it all comes down to hard work and good eyes.

Bloch ended the call on her cell phone, stared across the table of the diner at Gabriel Lake. There was a hint of gray in his stubble, and at his temples. He was still in his late thirties. The bags under his eyes, the gray hair and the wrinkles on his face weren't from age. They had worked together for long enough now. Her partner didn't sleep much, didn't really eat a lot, didn't work out and hadn't unpacked the boxes in his apartment since he'd moved in a year ago.

His fingers tapped lightly on the table as he stared at the remnants of the poached eggs on his plate. This was a guy whose motor revved high all the time, the needle constantly hovering over the red line. His mind never rested, not fully. Judging by the time of night she had received texts from him, she knew he didn't sleep much either. He had spent his life hunting monsters. Real monsters. Serial killers, mostly.

You can't run on red for long. Sooner or later, something was going to blow.

And Lake did blow, from time to time. Usually when he found his prey. For a former FBI agent, he had a casual disregard for the system. It was his pushback against this system that almost got him killed. Someone in the bureau had set him up, making sure he walked into a kill house full of armed men – drug dealers protecting their product.

Lake had been carried out by the paramedics on a stretcher. The dealers came out in body bags.

This had scarred him, both on the outside and the inside. In his soul.

Now, when Lake found a monster, he didn't hesitate.

Bloch wondered if Lake being a killer somehow helped him find others who shared his dark nature.

'What did you find out?' he asked.

Bloch drained the last of her coffee, folded up the wrapper of her blueberry muffin and tossed it on her empty plate.

'Carey and Larkin weren't on shift when the body was found. They weren't even partners,' said Bloch. 'Carey got her detective promotion the day the body was found. This is her first homicide. The whole precinct is talking about it. The captain is pissed too.'

'So he got orders from higher up the chain of command. Somebody with power put a rookie and a world-class fuck-up on a high-profile murder. Doesn't make sense,' said Lake.

'It makes sense if that person wants to control the investigation.'

'Any hits on Teresa Chase?' he asked.

'Not yet. My contact checked most of the databases, nothing

showing in New York. She's doing a wider search, and she's still waiting for VICAP results.'

The violent criminal apprehension program was a database of unsolved violent crimes statewide. While it had its drawbacks, it sometimes helped identify violent offenders through victim profiles and common patterns.

'Do you still have your forensic kit in that . . . *car*?' asked Bloch, checking her watch.

'Yeah, why?'

'Larkin and Carey are not flavor of the month in the precinct. The rest of the detectives see the Molly Green case as a promotion ticket. They're pissed. There's a patrolman named Terry Johnson due to perform a check on the crime scene at seven. He's a friend. And his brother is homicide, one of the people Carey stepped over to land this case. Terry will have a fresh crime-scene seal with him when he performs his check.'

Lake glanced at his watch, tapped it. It was an old digital Casio. The face was scratched and the LCD display was fading out with the rapidly diminishing battery. He pressed the side button, adjusted his view to block out the light, but still couldn't read the display.

'What time is it?' he asked.

'Time you got a new watch. It's five thirty. The building is a half hour from here.'

'We can take my car.'

Bloch said, 'We want to get there today. Get the kit. We'll take my Jeep.'

West Harlem, 135th Street, a line of gray-brick apartment buildings sitting opposite the Bus Stop Diner on the corner of Broadway. The buildings were four stories high, with a solid steel-fronted security door leading to the lobby and a bank of apartment buzzers on the wall. Bloch made a call, the door buzzed and Lake pushed it.

A single elevator served the residents, with a staircase to the left. The walls were either painted yellow or had aged into that color.

No cameras anywhere.

They took the elevator to the second floor.

A cop in uniform waited in the hallway. There were four apartments on each floor. They passed two apartments to get to the cop who stood outside a door with a yellow seal, about the same size as a dinner tray, stuck over the frame and the door.

The cop held a fresh seal in a packet in his hand. As Bloch and Lake approached, they put on black disposable gloves so as not to contaminate the scene.

'You've got ten minutes. You haven't seen me. I haven't seen you,' said the cop.

He turned, took a key from his pocket and used it to split the seal, then unlocked the door and stood back.

The apartment was in darkness, curtains drawn. Bloch found a light switch, flicked it up. The door opened into the living space of the apartment.

'Watch your step,' said the cop.

Bloch looked down, saw a large dark stain on the gray carpet. It was about three feet wide and crusty, a pool of blood that had soaked into the fibers. The stain was in the middle of the floor. This area had a couch facing a TV and a bookshelf with dusty paperbacks, their yellowed pages facing outwards instead of the spine, perhaps arranged this way for aesthetic purposes.

A single door on the right stood open and Bloch could see a tiled wall and a small sink through the gap. The bathroom.

Beyond the living area, divided by a breakfast bar, was a small, neat kitchen. White cupboards, steel sink, a microwave, an oven below and an electric stove on top. Nothing on display in the kitchen, not even a dirty coffee mug.

To the left of the kitchen was a small bedroom. The double bed had been stripped to the bare mattress, and there was a wardrobe, a chest of drawers and some shoes arranged on the floor in a line below the window. Bloch took her time examining the mattress. No traces of blood.

Generic art hung on the walls of the bedroom, black-and-white photographs of the Manhattan skyline. Same in the living area and the short hallway leading into the apartment.

Apart from the bloodstain on the carpet, there were no signs of a struggle, no signs of violence. Nothing out of place.

Bloch sniffed.

'You smell that too?' asked Lake.

'What is it?' asked Bloch.

The odor was strangely familiar, a chemical of some kind.

'Smells like a solvent of some kind,' said Lake. 'It's like the solvent forensics use to lift fingerprint DNA. Although this is way more concentrated.'

The odor was strongest close to the front door, around the staining on the rug.

'Maybe something used to treat the bloodstain?' asked Bloch, then knelt down and sniffed at the floor.

She recoiled, holding her wrist over her nose.

'No, they haven't used anything on the carpet. I can still smell the blood.'

Lake went into the bathroom. Bloch returned to the bedroom and began going through the drawers. Underwear, socks, sweaters, jeans. Dresses and coats in the wardrobe. She went into the kitchen and began pulling open cupboards and drawers. Just ordinary kitchen items. She abandoned the kitchen, moved to the living area.

A coffee table between the couch and the TV had a glass top. A dozen pens sat in a coffee mug. The mug was old and had a faded picture of a windmill on one side. There had been some writing on the back, but it had faded away. It had been through too many cycles in a hot dishwasher. Two large heavy books were arranged beside it. One on coffee and one on industrial design in architecture. A thin coating of dust lay on the top of the first book. Bloch opened the books, leafed through the pages.

She stood, examined the bookcase, took a few books at random and flicked through the pages – nothing.

Lake came around the corner, said, 'Check out the bathroom.'

She followed him.

The bathroom was tiny: toilet, baby sink, low bathtub with a shower and a yellow curtain. White tile on the walls, a single extractor fan on the wall and nothing else.

There was the same chemical smell in the bathroom, especially around the small sink.

'I already checked the whole room with a black light. No trace of blood, saliva – nothing,' said Lake.

'Look for prints,' said Bloch.

She reached into Lake's bag, took one of his bottles of fingerprint powder and a large brush and went into the kitchen. She coated the brush in the powder and began to quickly cover the counter, the drawer handles, the sink. Then went back to the bedroom, dusting the door handles, wardrobe and drawers, even the shoes on the floor.

'I got nothing. What did you find?' asked Lake.

Bloch stood, shook her head.

'You ever seen anything like this?' asked Lake.

'No, you?'

'Never. Let's get out of here.'

They packed up, and were walking toward the front door when Bloch stopped. A framed print hung on the wall. On the other side of this wall was the bathroom. It was painted white, just like the other walls, but this print caught her attention.

It was Monet's waterlilies. Colorful, vibrant.

Wrong.

Bloch turned and approached the next picture she could find, this one above the TV. Another black-and-white Manhattan skyline. She ran her index finger along the top of the frame. It came back with dirt. She went back to the Monet print. This time, the other finger.

Clean.

Bloch looked at Lake, said, 'Somebody cleaned this. The whole place has been wiped down.'

She gazed at the stain on the floor. Something terrible happened here. A life taken. A body mutilated. Whoever had taken this woman's life had been careful to clean up after themself. This was a killing that had a cold edge. Something clinical and precise.

And planned.

In the car, on the way back to the office, she called Eddie.

'We got a look at the crime scene,' she said. 'There's a wide bloodstain from blood pooling on the carpet in the living area. Probably where the decapitation occurred. Everything else has been cleaned.'

'Cleaned? By the NYPD? By the landlord?'

'Not the landlord,' said Lake. 'First thing they would do is tear up the carpet. Bloch means the whole apartment has been cleaned. There's not a single fingerprint in the place. And that's not all. There are no photographs of Molly Green. No mail. No ID. No laptops, no phones, no iPad, not even a goddamn charger plugged into the socket. The tech is probably in the inventory of exhibits taken by police, but there's more. There was no bedding. Just a bare mattress. There are no bath products, no toothbrush, no toothpaste, not even a towel. There is not a single trace of Molly Green in the whole apartment apart from her clothes and shoes.'

'What does that mean?' asked Eddie.

'It means she's been erased,' said Bloch.

'Why?' asked Eddie.

Bloch said, 'Don't know yet, but if we find out why then we've found the killer.'

19
Eddie

'I just want to go on the record,' said Harry, 'to say I think this is a bad idea.'

For a moment I said nothing, and dug my hands deeper into my overcoat. We stood together in silence gazing up at the brownstone home of Vanessa and Patrick Vanderpool. It was dark, but not late. And this wasn't a social call. We hadn't yet climbed the porch steps to knock on the door. No one had noticed our presence. It would be the easiest thing in the world to just walk away.

But I couldn't. I had one of the richest and most powerful men in the world standing on my neck, and willing to put his boots on the throats of the people I loved if I didn't do what he wanted.

There was no way out. Not yet.

I had questions.

Especially after Bloch and Lake's investigations.

Why were Carey and Larkin on this case? Who had put them there? And who had cleaned the crime scene where a young woman had been murdered and her body mutilated? And what the hell did all of this have to do with Vanessa Vanderpool?

'Knowledge is power,' I said.

'If you think you're going to get the truth here, then we've come to the wrong place.'

'I didn't say I'd get the truth. Clients lie. Most of them. We just need to figure out why.'

I put one foot in front of the other until I was facing her front door and rang the bell.

An intercom and camera were fixed to the wall beside me.

'Who is it?' said a male voice.

'Eddie Flynn and Harry Ford for Vanessa,' I said.

Silence.

I heard footsteps on a hard floor. The door opened.

Patrick Vanderpool wore a pale blue shirt, with a stiff white collar. Red silk braces held his gray pants high above his hips. He had a wide mouth and angular lips, a sharp nose and keen blue eyes. His hair was graying, and naturally curly; he kept it short and swept back. He wore a gold pinky ring with a black square and some kind of symbol on it that I didn't recognize. It was on the same hand as his wedding ring. No other jewelry, no tie. His cologne was powerful enough to make a camel sneeze.

'Mr. Vanderpool, we're your wife's lawyers. We need to see her,' said Harry.

He stood there for a moment, his hand on the door, as his gaze shifted between me and Harry. He seemed to linger on Harry.

'Did she call you and invite you over?' asked Patrick.

'No, we need to see her right away,' I said.

'She's in bed,' said Patrick.

His eyes widened, and lips parted as Harry stepped inside the house and said, 'You'd better wake her up, then.'

He looked like he was trying to find the right words to get rid of us. I followed Harry inside before he could find them.

'It's important, Mr. Vanderpool. Let her know we're here,' I said.

The door slammed closed behind us, and Patrick marched past, arms swinging.

'Wait in the living room,' he said.

The living room had two couches facing each other, with a coffee table in between. A gold-trimmed mirror hung above a grand marble fireplace, and a bay window overlooked the street.

I sat next to Harry. We listened to Patrick's leather shoes on the stairs, and when he was far enough out of earshot, I said, 'Charming, isn't he?'

'Buchanan and Duff have told him there's a potential for this murder to come back and bite him on the ass. We're the outside help. That means we are the ones who might be doing the biting. He's right to be a little wary of us,' said Harry.

'You always see the good in people.'

'Why do you think I took on a conman as my clerk when he was fresh out of law school?' asked Harry.

'Ouch.'

'Be careful what you say in here. Let's take her out of the house. Go back to the office. This is not the place for a hard conversation,' he said.

Footsteps on the stairs. Two sets. One heavier, one much lighter.

Patrick led Vanessa into the living room. He had his left hand in hers, down by his side. She had changed into navy linen pants, a white T-shirt and sandals. I saw Vanessa tug her wrist, as if to get Patrick to let go.

But he held on, tightly. They sat together on the couch opposite us.

'Mr. Flynn, Mr. Ford. Is everything alright? Is there a problem with bail? I wasn't expecting you,' she said.

'We need to talk, Vanessa. Say, Mr. Vanderpool, would you mind?' asked Harry, in as polite a way as possible, to subtly suggest that he take himself elsewhere.

'Would I mind what?' asked Patrick, narrowing his eyes. There was a little fastball in that question.

'We need to talk to our client in private,' I said. 'If that's okay? It shouldn't take long. Maybe you could make some coffee.'

'I don't make coffee,' he said. 'And whatever you've got to say to Vanessa you can say to me.'

His eyes locked on to me. I realized that I hadn't yet seen the man blink. I understood how some people would find him intimidating. I didn't speak. Neither did Harry. We just sat on the couch. There was no other way we could put it other than to tell him to get the hell out. I saw Vanessa noticing his demeanor. Saw the realization in her eyes. She knew her husband better than almost anyone, and she had that keen ability to read her spouse's moods. She spoke slowly and softly.

'Darling, they need to talk to me privately,' said Vanessa.

'It shouldn't take too long,' said Harry. 'Brewing a pot of joe would take your mind off things, and help warm up this old man.'

'Patrick doesn't know how to make coffee, I'm afraid,' said Vanessa.

We didn't say anything. I guess growing up rich means you don't have to make your own coffee. I wanted to ask if he knew how to wipe his own ass, but I decided now was not the time.

He got up, suddenly, the fingers of his left hand still interlaced with Vanessa's right. He pulled her up with him and strode to the door, practically dragging her out of the room. I leaned back on the couch so I could get a better view. In the hallway, Vanessa yanked her hand away, breaking his grip, but instantly he took hold of her other wrist.

Harry, who was also leaning back, took hold of my arm as I tried to stand. He pulled me back down. I looked at him and he shook his head. Harry knew me well enough to spot my triggers. I kept my anger in check. Just.

Patrick's grip tightened.

I stood up. Took a breath. Tried to de-escalate.

'Vanessa, maybe we could go somewhere private to talk. Also, for your husband's sake, I think it might be better if you stayed somewhere else for a few days. The press haven't found out about your arrest yet, but it's coming. I'm sure Patrick doesn't want paparazzi camped outside the house. There's a lot of media outlets that would love to run this story. That wouldn't help his election hopes.'

They whispered, and I couldn't make out what they were saying, but Patrick let her go.

'You're right, Eddie,' she said. 'I'll just go pack a bag,' and she darted around him and ran upstairs.

Patrick stared at me. Once Vanessa was out of earshot, he spoke. 'Since when are you so concerned about my political career?'

Harry came out of the living room, said, 'We want what's best for Vanessa, and her family.'

'She's your client. Not me. Don't get involved in my affairs,' he said.

'I met your father today. He was concerned about the Molly Green case affecting the family. You're right, Vanessa is my priority, and you are her family. So I guess I should be following your father's advice and try to protect all of you.'

'I don't need your protection.'

'Of course not, Patrick,' I said.

'It's *Mr.* Vanderpool. You know who my father is. You know how powerful my family is,' he said, spittle flying from his mouth. His blood was up, his shoulders tensed, eyes locked on me. 'Show me some goddamn respect,' said Patrick.

My fingers curled into fists.

'Sorry, *Mr.* Vanderpool,' I said. 'I don't care who your daddy is. If I ever see you hurting your wife again, I'll knock you the fuck out, with all due *respect*.'

He froze.

Uncertain what to do.

'Let's go,' said Vanessa as she appeared in the hallway, carrying an overnight bag and a coat in her arms.

She didn't look at her husband as we left.

Not one word was spoken.

Which said a lot.

I sat in the back of Harry's car with Vanessa.

'Thank you,' she said. 'I know you mean well. But you shouldn't have done that.'

'Is he always like that?' I asked.

'Sometimes.'

'Has he hit you before?'

She looked out the window at the city.

I said nothing. She said nothing.

We drove on in silence for a time. I realized that tonight was not the time to ask her hard questions. I needed to know more about the prosecution's case. Then we could all lay our cards on the table.

Harry asked her what hotel she wanted to stay in, and that it should be somewhere out of the way. Somewhere she had never been to before. We settled on a Hilton Garden, and Harry made a left and headed downtown.

'You need to lie low until this case is over. Don't call anyone else apart from me.'

'What about the other lawyer, the woman, Voss.'

'I need you to fire her, but not yet. For now let's ghost her. I need time to think.'

'So what happens now?' she asked.

'Now we wait for the prosecution evidence. Your father-in-law has all kinds of powerful friends. This trial will come on fast. Voss will help move that along. Once we know exactly what kind of case the DA has, we can fire Voss, start investigating and get ready for the fight. I don't want to ask you a lot of questions right now. Let's do it later, when we know more. But there is one thing. Have you ever heard the name Teresa Chase?'

'No, should I have?'

'One of your husband's political opponents mentioned the name. Said they knew about her. My investigators have come up a blank, so I thought you might know.'

'Sorry, I never heard the name before,' she said.

'What was Patrick whispering to you before we left?' I asked.

She turned to look at me, and I saw again the fear in her eyes.

'I can't say it.'

'What do you mean?'

'I can't tell you.'

'You're safe with me, you know? It may take some time for you to properly feel it, but I actually do want to help you, Vanessa. I'm not doing this for money, or my reputation, or for some kind of bullshit publicity. I only take cases on when I want to help someone. I think you need help. I think you're holding a lot back. I can't help you if you won't tell me the truth.'

She glanced away, through the raindrop-speckled windows, lit with the lights from the hotel.

When she turned back, the fear had dissipated. She had made a decision.

'It's been a difficult day. Give me some time. Let me get my head clear. And then I'll tell you everything.'

20

Eddie

A week passed with Vanessa hiding out in the Hilton Garden downtown.

I'd gotten the call from Voss the morning after Vanessa checked in, asking where our client might be. I told Voss I didn't know. She said I was lying to her, and I told her she was correct. I said Vanessa needed some processing time. And that I would be in touch when we got discovery in the case.

The prosecution discovery arrived in my office on a wet Thursday morning. Denise signed for the package from the police officer, and brought it straight to me and Harry.

Hard-copy pages, a booklet of photographs and everything duplicated on a pen-drive. Harry inserted the pen-drive into his computer. I sat at the edge of his desk with the paper and photograph book.

It's always my way to look at the pictures first. I want to see what story the crime scene tells on its own, without having first read the other evidence. It's a way of keeping the mind open. If I knew the prosecution narrative already, it might taint my view of the photos.

The DA doesn't send the defense all of the evidence. The rule is they disclose the evidence they want to rely on in court, plus any evidence they uncover that might be helpful to the defense.

There were only five photographs.

So few that they should have come with their own alarm bell.

The forensic photographer would have taken dozens of pictures.

Of the five, two were wide shots of the apartment, the headless corpse of a young woman in the foreground. She was lying on the floor, chest down, arms by her sides, legs straight. She was naked and pale.

I remembered the autopsy report mentioned a cut on the sole of her left foot. There was no close-up of that cut, but the second picture was from the reverse angle, so I could just about see the small dark line on the sole. Her feet were dirty, perhaps from walking around the apartment barefoot.

There was no glass on the floor. Nothing was broken. No furniture disturbed.

A final picture was a close-up of what looked like a jewelry box sitting on a steel desk. This photo wasn't taken in the apartment. The box was studded with either crystals or semi-precious stones. An exhibit sign beside the box gave me an approximation of its size and scale. About eight inches long, five inches wide and six inches deep, styled to make it look as though it was a treasure chest in miniature. It looked heavy. Three stones were missing in the right corner of the box, just where some dark staining was present.

I flipped through the photobook again, then checked the binder of documents and the envelope, just to make sure I hadn't missed anything.

This wasn't a case of what the pictures told me. It was more about what they were trying to conceal.

'Do you have five photographs on that pen-drive?' I asked.

'Just looked through them,' said Harry. 'Only five. That's got to be a first for a murder trial. You can bet they took about a hundred pictures. Where are the rest of them?'

'They're in the DA's file. They're focusing on the body, maybe minimizing the cleanliness of the rest of the apartment. I can see the sense in that. Bloch said the scene was way too sanitized.'

'You read the witness statements yet?'

'Just about to do that.'

'Fair warning: they don't help us.'

'Give me the highlights.'

'Patrick's campaign manager, Geoffrey Gilbert, says that Vanessa kept a close eye on Molly. That she was jealous of her, and suspected that Molly was trying to seduce her husband.'

'That's not good.'

'Wait till you get to forensics. We don't have the full report yet, but it looks like Molly's blood was found on that ornate jewelry box. There's also another set of DNA on the box, probably from skin contact. It's Vanessa's.'

'Our client's DNA and Molly's blood on that box is the DA's case.'

The DA had nearly all that they needed to get a conviction, right here. During a heated argument, Vanessa hits Molly over the head with the jewelry box, killing her. I couldn't see exactly how they were going to make the case that Vanessa cut off Molly's head, nor why she would do such a terrible thing. That was a big problem here for the prosecutor. I could see a competent DA convince a jury that Vanessa killed Molly in a fit of jealously because she believed her husband was having an affair with her, but I couldn't see anyone proving that Vanessa then decapitated her victim.

Harry said, 'Then there's this,' and clicked on a file.

It opened a video. Security camera footage from an emergency exit at the rear of the building, out by a small parking lot. The footage was time stamped. It showed a man who looked like Patrick Vanderpool going into the building, coming out a while later. Then a woman, who was clearly Vanessa Vanderpool. When she left, she was carrying a gym bag.

'Shit,' I said, 'you know what they're going to argue, don't you?'

'Yep,' said Harry. 'The DA will say Molly's head is in that gym bag. That it was a desperate attempt to hide the evidence of her crime. We have to go talk to her. See if there's an explanation for this.'

'What if there is an easy explanation?' I asked.

Harry leaned back in his chair, crossed his legs. He tossed aside the laptop, laced his fingers over his stomach and let his thumbs roll over each other. This was Harry's way of thinking, and relaxing. It somehow helped his mind wander onto paths that led us out of a myriad problems, but this time it was different. Harry wasn't thinking about our case. He was thinking about me. I could tell from that deep, penetrating look he gave me. Not that he busted this expression out often, but when I saw it I knew he was trying to dig his way into my head. Harry already knew what I was going to say. But he didn't speak. He just sat there, quietly, waiting for me to give it breath and let it float into the air around us, so that we could get a good look at it, taste it, see it for what it really was and try to figure out how we felt about it.

I let the thought breathe as I said, 'Maybe the easy explanation is our client is guilty.'

Harry said nothing. He nodded, acknowledged it was out there. Let the thought permeate.

Then said, 'Are you asking me if I think she killed Molly?'

'I'm asking,' I said.

'No,' said Harry, flatly and without hesitation.

'Why not?'

His gaze drifted off. Then he said, 'You're much better at reading people than me, but I just don't think she cares about Patrick enough to kill Molly Green.'

'That's dark,' I said.

'He's rich, but I'd guess that Vanessa would do well out of a divorce. I think he's controlling her, Eddie. There could be some violence in that relationship too. You've been thinking the same thing. It's just a matter of time before she tells us. Spousal abuse coupled with her husband's infidelity would give her strong grounds for a favorable divorce. The best thing to happen to Vanessa is her husband's affair with Molly.'

'Then why is she lying to us? Why is she not telling us the whole story? And now the DA can prove that she lied to police. She told them she'd never been to Molly's apartment. Now they've got her DNA on a possible murder weapon, and thanks to a security camera they can prove she was there on the night of the murder and lied about it to everybody. There's a lot of heavy lifting to do before we could persuade a jury of reasonable doubt.'

'And yet the murder doesn't make sense to me,' he said.

'Then what are we going to do?' I asked.

My phone rang – Bloch.

'I finally got a lead on Teresa Chase,' she said, no greeting or small talk. All business.

'Who is she?'

'Lake and I are on our way to East Hampton to find out. We were looking for victims, crimes, deceased, but this morning I tried a different kind of search. Got a hit. Teresa Chase is a missing person.'

'Missing? For how long?'

'Six years.'

'Do we have any kind of link with the Vanderpools yet?'

'Just one,' said Bloch. 'According to the reports, the last person to see her alive was Patrick Vanderpool.'

She said she would check in later when she knew more and hung up.

Harry and I spent the afternoon going through the discovery, over and over again, re-reading everything. Denise made an appointment for us to call at Vanessa's hotel that evening. I wasn't looking forward to this, but it had to be done.

I heard footsteps coming up the stairs to our office. Fast, excited. A light step.

I knew exactly who it was. I got up and opened my office door, stepped into reception and was standing there when Amy walked in. She was carrying an overnight bag, wearing her jeans and a hoody. A dress was in a travel bag.

'Dad, you haven't forgotten,' she said.

'Of course not. Harry and I can take you to dinner, then we've got to see a client while you're at the party and when you're done I'll pick you up.'

I heard heavier footsteps on the stairs, and Christine followed Amy inside.

'He's forgotten,' said Christine.

'I haven't forgotten. I've been looking forward to tonight. I swear.'

'Are you excited for the party?' asked Denise.

'Stressed. I don't have time for dinner. I've got to do my make-up and get ready. Dad, can we go back to your place?'

'Sure, let me grab my coat. Christine, how are you?'

'Fine, just don't forget to pick her up.'

'I won't. Jesus. What makes you think I forgot about today?'

'Because we were supposed to meet at your apartment. We just came from there.'

Denise got up from her desk and muttered something about getting Harry to sign a discovery motion.

'I'm sorry. I knew it was today, I just lost track of time,' I said, and then tried to change the subject. 'How's Kevin?' I asked, politely.

'He still has a functioning memory,' she said.

'Come on, Dad. Let's go,' said Amy.

She was smiling, trying to head off the argument that was brewing between me and her mother.

'I'll be right there,' I said, and turned to get my coat.

'Eddie,' said Christine, and I turned. She had followed me to get out of earshot of Amy.

'I'm sorry. I know you've got a lot on your mind. I can tell when you're on a big case. A lot of everyday stuff gets pushed out of that big brain of yours, especially when you're dealing with life and death trials. I'm sorry. I shouldn't have said anything.'

'It's fine. Don't worry about it. And don't worry about her – she'll have a great time.'

'That's what I'm worried about. Remind her she promised no champagne, no alcohol of any kind.'

'I will.'

She turned away, and kissed Amy goodbye before she left.

Harry came out of his office with Clarence, who bounded toward Amy. She knelt down and nuzzled him, and giggled when he rolled onto his back so she could stroke his stomach.

'I'll meet you at Vanessa's hotel later. I gotta drop Amy at her friend's party.'

'We can blow this off till tomorrow, you know?' offered Harry.

'I can't. I need to know where the hell we're going with this case, and why our client lied to everyone, including us.'

21
Bloch

The time it takes to get from Manhattan to East Hampton varies according to the time of day, and the time of year.

It was the tail end of winter, spring was promised and the traffic on the freeway was light. Two and half hours, for the one-hundred-and-ten-mile trip. In the summer, the same journey can take anywhere between four and seven hours. East Hampton is a rich getaway town for the Manhattan elite. With its beaches and old-town feel, it's a haven for millionaires looking to summer on Long Island. You won't get a house with a pool for under eight million, and the mom-and-pop stores on Main Street have all but been replaced by Prada, Gucci and Ralph Lauren. The Clintons summered here, Robert Downey Jr. lives in a converted windmill and the most in-demand addition for properties in the area isn't a tennis court, or a heated pool, it's a helipad, so the super-rich don't have to spend seven hours fighting through the traffic on a Friday night.

Bloch pulled her Jeep off Montauk Highway, so named after one of the indigenous peoples who were forced, bribed or hoodwinked out of their land. Another sharp left brought them into the parking lot of East Hampton Police Headquarters, just behind the local airport.

Bloch found a space, and killed the engine. No police vehicle in the lot was more than two years old, all fitted with the latest tech. A police helicopter sat behind the station. For a small-town police force, they were better equipped than most city cops.

'It's more like a country club than a police station,' said Lake.

Bloch nodded.

They got out of the car and entered the building. It was a few years old now, but to Bloch, any place that smelled of fresh paint was new. The desk sergeant looked as though he'd just had the same kind of cosmetic surgery as the building. It was a hell of thing, policing the rich. Of course, the police force wasn't there to keep order among the millionaires and billionaires – mostly they were there to stop homes being robbed by outsiders and to keep in check the staff who lived west and south of the village, in considerably smaller homes, who cut lawns, brewed coffee, drove Ubers and did the laundry.

The Christmas tip jar for this station would've funded a precinct in the Bronx for a month.

'Bloch for Captain Landry,' she said.

The desk sergeant looked up from the mirror on his desk – he had just been admiring his tan – and picked up the phone.

'Say, what kind of moisturizer do you use?' asked Lake.

Bloch rolled her eyes.

'Depends if it's my morning or night routine,' said the sergeant. 'Mostly, I use L'Oreal for daily moisturizing. In the evening, I prefer something aloe based.'

Lake nodded. 'Thank you.'

As they took a seat to wait for the captain, Bloch said, 'Aloe?'

'It's good for you,' said Lake. 'You should try it.'

'Sometimes I don't understand you.'

'What's wrong with moisturizing?'

'What's wrong with buying food and putting it in your refrigerator? What's wrong with ironing a shirt? Or shaving more than once a week?'

'I've got my priorities straight,' he said.

'Miss Bloch?' said a voice.

Standing in front of them was a middle-aged man in uniform – black pants, white shirt with insignia, black and gold epaulettes that came with the rank. He sported a thick, graying moustache that might have come with the rank too. A row of three silver pens sat in his shirt pocket, neatly held in place by their clips. The shirt was clean and diligently pressed.

'Captain Landry,' she said, and stood to shake hands. 'It's just Bloch.'

'Pleased to meet you, Just Bloch. And this gentleman?'

'He's not important,' said Bloch.

'Do you have your identification?' Landry asked.

Bloch handed over her private-investigator's license. Landry glanced at it, threw it on the desk of the sergeant and asked him to take a photocopy.

'Just for our records, you understand,' he said. 'What about Mr. Unimportant?'

'He's with me,' said Bloch.

'Does he have a license?'

'Why don't we talk in your office?' asked Bloch.

Landry pressed his thick fingers onto his hips. He said nothing. And didn't move again for a time. He was putting up a roadblock of sorts. There was no getting around this.

'I don't usually like giving my name,' said Lake. 'I don't have a PI license. I'm not insured or regulated as an investigator. I pay my taxes, I'm polite and I obey the law, most of the time. You don't have to worry about me. I'm just assisting Bloch.'

'You want to talk about Teresa Chase, I'm going to need your name and identification.'

'I might have an old Blockbuster Video membership card, if that helps?' asked Lake.

'Your name will suffice.'

'Gabriel Lake.'

'You're *him*.'

Lake stared at him. Landry stared back.

'I thought you'd be bigger,' said Landry.

'I get that a lot,' said Lake.

'So you're not a licensed investigator in the state?'

'I'm consulting.'

Landry stared at him, and rolled his tongue along the inside of his cheek, mirroring the thoughts rolling around in his head.

Finally, he said, 'Well, the two of you can come on back to my office. Professional co-operation is the cornerstone of good policing. Just out of interest, who is your client?'

'We can't release that information,' said Bloch.

'I understand. Come on. You want coffee?'

Bloch nodded. Lake shook his head.

'Bring us a couple of fresh cups, along with the ID,' said Landry to the desk sergeant.

The captain's office had more screens and tech than Bloch was used to. Two monitors sat on his desk, another wide screen hung on the wall and a TV with the local news played in the corner, with the volume down low.

Landry clocked Bloch taking in the room.

'It pays to be up to date. I can monitor every officer on shift at any time from here. Take a seat,' and he waved to two leather chairs facing his desk.

A thin file with a blue cover sat there. It was old and the cover was curled up at the edges. Landry sat down and opened it. Bloch leaned forward.

There were perhaps ten or twelve pages in the file. No more.

A paltry body of work for a missing woman.

The desk sergeant came in, handed out the coffees, took the ID from his back pocket and handed it back to Bloch. She took a sip from her coffee. It was hot, but not fresh. It tasted of old coffee machines that brewed twelve hours a day and gave every pot the same stewed flavor.

'The coastguard handled this for the most part,' said Landry. He'd eyed Bloch sizing up the file. 'Teresa Chase had been swimming off the east shore. She was there one minute, gone the next. Riptides, you see. We were called out, as is routine, took some particulars and then handed it over to the coastguard. Tragic accident. Not much more I can tell you.'

'She drowned?' asked Lake.

'It would appear so. Body was never recovered.'

'Tell us about her,' said Bloch.

'She was twenty-eight years old. No immediate family. She'd lost both her parents a few years before in a car wreck. Had a half-sister, somewhere, but we couldn't find her and she never came forward. Teresa was an English grad, worked a little in the local paper, writing up movie reviews, restaurant reviews, that kind of thing. Nice girl, by all accounts. Such a shame.'

'Who reported her missing?'

Landry leaned on the desk, covering most of the open file with his forearm.

'A local, who was on the beach.'

'Did you get a name?' asked Bloch.

'Sure, doesn't matter much. They did the right thing – called it in straight away. Coastguard was in the water fast. They did everything they could to find her. It's just one of those—'

'Do you mind if I take a look at the report?' asked Bloch.

'Like I said, not much to it.'

'This local, was his name Patrick Vanderpool?' asked Bloch.

Landry swallowed a mouthful of bitter coffee, then said, 'Why, yes it was.'

'Were they friends? In a relationship?' asked Bloch.

'Whether they were or not, doesn't matter much when you're searching for a body ripped out to sea. The riptide doesn't care about that, now does it?'

Bloch thought for a moment, said, 'I take it you have a report from the coastguard about the search?'

'Sure do.'

'Can I look at that report?'

Landry hesitated.

Lake spoke for the first time. 'If we saw that, it might go some way to confirm that everything possible was done to save Teresa. That kind of thing can be of comfort to some people who have lost those who were dear to them.'

'Sure,' said Landry, tearing the report out of the file.

It was a single page, recounting the report from the coastguard and their searches, including geographic coverage, an examination of the tides and theories of possible locations based on that. The first thing Bloch did was look for the name of the reporting officer – Winchester, Paul. Detective. And she scanned the rest of the document, but took her time. She had all she needed.

Handing the report back to Landry, she asked, 'Is there anything else you think might be important?'

Landry held up the thin file, and said, 'We don't have much. It's really a coastguard matter.'

'Do you think it would be worthwhile talking to the lead officer on the case?' she asked.

Landry coughed, leaned forward and placed his elbows on the desk.

'He's not with us. Not any more. He had some personal issues. Mental health, that kind of stuff. He took early medical retirement. He won't be able to tell you anything more than I've told you. And, well, I feel sorry for the guy. This job takes a toll – you know that. I wouldn't want him disturbed. Plus, the kind of meds he's on – probably doesn't remember his own name half the time, never mind anything else.'

Bloch took another drink of coffee, set the mug down and said, 'Thank you for your help.'

Together, Lake and Bloch got up and he escorted them out of the building.

'Sorry you had to come all this way for that. Good to meet you both,' he said.

They all shook hands. Lake and Bloch walked silently to her car.

Once inside, the car doors closed, they watched as Landry stood in the lot, his hands in his pockets.

Neither of them said anything. They didn't need to. Bloch fired the engine, and waved at Landry as they left. In the rearview, she watched him turn and head back inside.

Lake had his phone in his hand. Staring at the screen.

'I've got a Paul Winchester in Sag Harbor.'

'Give me the address,' said Bloch, pointing to the navigation screen. Lake punched in the address. It was an hour away.

'What did you think?' he asked.

'I think at least half that file is missing. Sometimes it can be difficult to distinguish between incompetence and a cover-up.'

'Landry isn't incompetent. Did you see those pens in his shirt pocket?' asked Lake.

Bloch had noticed them, but had given them no further thought. That's not how her mind worked. She had a hard time reading people. She had a basic understanding that Landry had been cautious about what information he had given out, and didn't want anyone poking around in their old case. But the same could be said for any number of cops. Nobody likes having their work judged in hindsight.

'I saw the pens. So what?' said Bloch.

'His shirt was fresh on today, right out of the dry-cleaning wrap. He keeps those pens in his pocket to make notes, corrections, additions, all in different colors. His desk, his dress, his entire office was neat and orderly. He is a meticulous man. He's not worried about anyone judging police work from his precinct. Plus, he stood in the lot, and he made sure we left. At least we know one thing about him.'

'What's that?'

'We can't trust a word he said. The police, at the very highest level, are covering something up for Patrick Vanderpool.'

22

Eddie

Traffic in Manhattan is never as bad as you think it might be. That's not to say that it's good. It's often quicker to walk if you're foolish enough to go out in rush hour. This was a Thursday, coming up on six, but I was still able to make good progress. A lot of people who worked in the city were still taking two days to work from home. Thursdays and Fridays were much better now than they used to be.

'You look amazing. Have a great time and be safe,' I said.

She was touching up her lipstick in the side mirror. I don't know how it happened, but it seemed to me that very suddenly my kid was becoming a young woman. She wore a navy dress, navy shoes, a pink denim jacket and had her hair tied up.

'Don't drink any alcohol, and no drugs,' said Harry, from the back seat.

'I'll bear that in mind, Harry,' she said.

'I'll text you later and make sure you're okay,' I said.

'Dad, I have my cell. Don't text me. I'll be fine. If I need you, I'll call. I promise. See you at midnight,' she said.

I pulled in outside the hotel. She got out and ran to a group of young girls who had just gotten out of a Humvee and were standing on the sidewalk. I buzzed my window down to give a final warning of no alcohol, and I heard the excited high-pitched screaming that passed for a greeting. They were headed for one of their first big parties. That's the thing about your daughter turning sixteen. Most of her friends were also turning that age too, and there seemed to be a full roster of parties planned. Only a few in the city, though.

I watched her get lost in the crowd. Harry got out of the back of the Mustang, pulled the seat back and sat in the front.

'She'll be fine,' he said. 'Let's go get this over with.'

I sighed, pulled out into the traffic and headed over ten blocks to see our client in a different hotel.

The suite that Vanessa occupied had a living area, a double bedroom and a separate dining area. I didn't get a look at the bathroom, but I guessed it was probably half the size of my whole apartment. It would cost more for one night in this hotel than I paid for my first car.

We set up in the dining area, the prosecution discovery spread out on the table. First, we let her read, then gauged her reaction. There was some surprise, sure, especially at the statement from Geoff Gilbert.

'He's lying, you know?' she said.

'Okay, so you were never jealous of Molly?' asked Harry.

'No, and we never fought. We never had any harsh words . . . For God's sake, I barely even spoke to her. She was just someone who worked for Patrick – to me, anyway. He's worried about his job. If Patrick's campaign gets blown up by this case, he's out of work. They're all protecting him.'

I'd decided we had gotten so far down this road wearing our kid gloves. Time to put on thirty-three ounces and start fighting.

'You're still lying to us, and that has to stop,' I said.

She was about to speak, but whatever words were about to be spoken froze on her lips when Harry opened his laptop, swiveled it round so the screen pointed at Vanessa and hit play on the security footage.

She watched in silence. Dispassionate. Cool.

The footage ended.

She leaned back in her chair, stared at us.

Didn't say a goddamn word.

I laid it out for her.

'The DA is going to show this video to the jury. He's going to remind them that you told the police that you'd never been to Molly's apartment. You lied about this. He's going to make the case that you either knew, or suspected, that Patrick was sleeping with Molly. That you waited until he left her apartment, then you went inside. And when you left an hour or so later, you had her head in that gym bag.'

Her reply came fast.

'When I left, she was alive.'

Harry and I looked at each other.

'What was in the gym bag?' I asked.

'Patrick's change of clothes, spare toothbrush, change of underwear, socks and spare shoes. I told Molly she had to stop seeing him. She agreed.'

'You lied to us. You lied to the police. You told them there was no affair. You told them you had barely spoken to Molly. You told them you'd never been to the apartment. If you didn't kill her, then why all of these lies?' I asked.

Her head fell forward and she stared at her shoes. Her back, which had been straight before, hunched in a perfect arch. It was like watching somebody take off a disguise.

She looked at each of us in turn, but didn't speak.

'Don't tell us you were trying to protect your husband's political career,' said Harry. 'We've seen how he is with you. Other than a very misguided sense of loyalty, there's no reason to protect him.'

'I wasn't trying to protect him,' she said, finally. 'I was trying to protect her.'

'Molly?' asked Harry.

She nodded.

'Why should we believe any of this?' I asked.

Vanessa rolled up her sleeves and displayed her arms.

'Jesus,' said Harry.

'At first, he used his hands,' said Vanessa. She spoke softly, but there was power and sorrow in every word. 'It didn't take long for things to get worse. We were married a year when . . . It was our first anniversary . . . He thought I wasn't appreciative enough of the jewelry, and the dinner, and the ballet. That's when he started to burn me. The first time it was a cigar, but it got worse. He would heat spoons on the stove or with a kitchen blowtorch. He laughed when the hot metal touched my skin. I remember that. I don't think I will ever forget it. He said burns were a reminder – to avoid weakness.'

She fell silent. The sunlight from the window sparked in a tear that ran over her cheek as she rolled down her sleeves.

She said, 'He's careful. He won't hurt me where someone could easily see. It didn't start this way. It took time.'

It doesn't matter if you live paycheck to paycheck, or if you're staying in a hotel room that costs two grand a night, the feeling of powerlessness, of vulnerability, that sensation of being trapped in a nightmare, feels just the same for everyone.

I wanted to help her.

She sat down again, her face flushed hot with embarrassment.

It takes a lot to confess that you are a victim.

'The night she was murdered, tell us what happened,' said Harry.

'I confronted her about Patrick. She denied it at first, but I told her I knew. I guess she felt guilty. I saw his gym bag in the corner of the living room. I said I was taking his stuff. That she had to stop seeing him. That she had to call the office in the morning and tell Geoff that she'd quit and she wouldn't be back. And that was it. I took his bag, and I left.'

'How did your DNA and Molly's blood get onto that jewelry box?' I asked.

There it was. The DA's case, laid out for Vanessa's response. If we couldn't find a reasonable and rational explanation for this, the jury would again revert to the simplest explanation – that the blood was on the jewelry box because they fought with it, and only one of them is still alive. That's a three-minute deliberation and a guilty verdict at the end of it.

'I have no idea how my DNA got onto that jewelry box. I've never seen it before in my life.'

That wasn't a reasonable explanation, but right then, that didn't trouble me much. It was the way Vanessa gave her response. She'd clenched her hands, leaned forward, stared me straight in the eyes and spoke clearly and cleanly – like she was trying to persuade me.

Clients who tell the truth don't have to persuade their lawyers of anything. They give their responses honestly and without affectation. I hadn't spotted Vanessa's tells yet, not all of them at least. But this . . . this was concerning.

I was pretty sure she was lying about the jewelry box.

Did that make her a killer?

For me, maybe not. For a jury?

No doubt.

And I wasn't doing her any favors by holding back.

'Vanessa, if the DA presents this evidence in court, and you say that you've never seen that jewelry box before, you will be convicted.'

'I can't help that. I'm telling you the truth.'

'I don't believe you,' I said.

'Maybe, in time, you will.'

'The security footage of you leaving Molly's home shows you carrying a gym bag. Where is that bag now?'

'I left it at home. It had Patrick's things in it. I checked for it the other day, searched the house, he must've thrown it out.'

'He must've seen you'd brought the gym bag home from Molly's apartment. Did he mention it to you?' I asked.

'He didn't need to. He must've known I was there at the apartment. What's he going to say? Thanks for bringing my things home from my mistress's apartment?'

Harry and I looked at each other.

'Why are you still with Patrick?' asked Harry. 'You could've left him. I know it's not easy, but lots of women find the courage to walk away.'

'I stayed because there's nowhere else on this planet I could go to be free of him. He has power like you wouldn't believe. My life would be hell wherever I went. I know I can never be free of him. Not unless he decides to divorce me. Maybe then he might let me go. Or maybe my head just ends up missing.'

'You think Patrick had Molly killed?' I asked.

'I don't think so – I know.'

'How do you know?' asked Harry.

'Because the night you came to my house, the night I left, before you got there, I was about to go upstairs to get away from him and he stopped me, told me he had something to tell me. He said we shouldn't have secrets. He told me he loved Molly. And he loved me, but there had been an accident. He hit her, and killed her. He didn't mean to do it. He said he came back later and tried to hide the evidence by . . . you know . . . Jesus, I need your help. I didn't do this. You have to believe me.'

23
Vanessa

For Vanessa, hiding her emotions and true feelings was as easy as riding a bicycle.

She'd been doing it all her life.

But sometimes, very rarely, people fall off their bikes. They hit a rock they didn't see coming on the trail, the front wheel buckles and twists, the bike lurches and the rider is thrown into the dirt.

Flynn gazed back at Vanessa as the door to her hotel suite closed. He didn't hide his heart. This guy wore it around his neck. Sure, she had read about him. Knew he was cunning and incredibly smart. That he could manipulate judges, juries and witnesses, and outsmart prosecutors, but those things were performative. She could look into Flynn's eyes at any time and see exactly what he was feeling. He was a good man.

She wondered if he could see into her heart. She had to be careful with this one.

A tear formed and she felt its warmth as it snaked over her cheek.

The door closed.

Vanessa walked to the peep hole, and peered out.

The hallway was clear. Flynn and Ford were gone.

She put the security bolt across the door.

Wiping her face, she took a moment to breathe. Closing her eyes, she relaxed her shoulders, rolled her neck. Exhaled. Her heartbeat was still high. But she was gaining control.

Hiding her emotions.

Like riding a bike.

'They've gone,' she said.

The luxury hotel had not held back on décor, furnishings, fittings and trim. She heard the handle on the bedroom door turning like a rifle pin sliding another round into the chamber. There was only the faintest whisper from the door opening. And then the soft brush of leather shoes on the thick carpet.

Vanessa returned to the living area of the suite and folded herself into the couch.

'You did well,' said Samantha Voss.

The lawyer stood over Vanessa. It was rare that Voss looked down on anyone, given her size, but when she did Vanessa got the impression that Voss enjoyed it.

There was a lot of trouble in that small woman.

'You did exactly what you were supposed to do. Just keep talking to me, and listening, and we'll keep Flynn on your side. Just remember, I'm in charge.'

'If you're in charge, why don't you just represent me?' asked Vanessa.

'Because I have all the knowledge, tactics and experience, but I'm not Flynn. Think of it like horse racing. You can train a horse all you want, but some are just faster than others – it's genetics. There's no fighting it. Flynn is a thoroughbred. Trust me – there's very few people in the country who can do what he does. He's going to build a defense for you, but he can't use what you've told him against Patrick. Remember that. Remember, that when the time comes, Patrick is to be protected at all costs.'

Vanessa didn't want to be in this position. Voss, Patrick and Julian in one corner, Flynn in the other, and nowhere for her to go in between.

She let Voss out of the room, promised to let her know when she'd heard from Flynn.

Leaning against the hotel room door, she let the cold wood cool her face. Then put on the security chain, went to the bathroom and washed her hands.

Over and over.

Until her skin was raw.

Vanessa closed her eyes again, and let her head fall to her chest.

It was hard to keep so many lies alive. Like spider webs. Threads spreading out and overlapping. And when the wind or a twig or something else broke one single strand, she had to get over there and repair it, lest the whole structure collapse.

The trial threatened everything. She just had to get through it. To do that, she needed to trust in the right people and hope that in the meantime, her web held together.

She needed to keep it strong for a while longer.

She just needed time to catch the right person in that fragile web.

Then, she could devour them.

24
Patrick

There was nothing in this world that made Patrick feel weaker, or smaller, than sitting outside his father's office waiting to see him.

The townhouse had been finished when Patrick was fourteen, but his father didn't move in until Patrick was close to sixteen. It had taken some time to furnish it and complete the snagging works. Considering it was really two townhouses converted into a vast mansion, Patrick hadn't been surprised it had taken five years. On the third floor, the walls were covered in dark oak paneling lined with paintings of hunting scenes with men in red jackets on horseback, surrounded by hounds in woodland. Each picture was illuminated by a lamp above it with a green glass shade. This floor of the house looked like an old English golf club lounge. Patrick sat on a green leather studded couch. His right foot tapped on the oak herringbone floor, giving a beat to his anxiety that echoed down the hallway to the sturdy oak door at the end.

He rubbed his hands together, trying to expel more nervous energy.

The door at the end of the hall opened and Dekker took long strides toward him.

'Go on in,' he said.

Patrick got up without a word, met Dekker's gaze for a moment.

The South African was hard to read most days. He had that dead look in his eyes, as if he had seen the worst of humanity and was resigned to being a part of it. Standing half a foot taller than him, and considerably wider in the shoulders, Patrick felt even more like a naughty child summoned to see his father.

He made his way to the open door, stopped, turned back and saw Dekker had been watching him. There was something calculating in that look, the way that butchers look at a side of beef – deciding where the prime cuts would lie.

Patrick entered his father's office and shut the door behind him.

The old man, dressed in a white shirt and red tie, sat behind his favorite desk, one of his five-hundred-dollar cigars between his fingers, the same kind he always smoked. Similarly, the desk was the one that used to be in his office in Manhattan. Now, it was in a much smaller, darker room. Bookshelves behind his father were lined with novels he had never read and pictures of him with various world leaders. Among the photographs: his father having dinner with Colonel Gadaffi, playing bridge with Saddam Hussein and posing on the steps of his private plane with Henry Kissinger. He wondered if these infamous men knew at the time they were posing with an equal.

His father was a different kind of monster, but no less dangerous.

And considerably wealthier.

As he sat down, he stared at the wood grain on the desk, and the deep layers of varnish. Anything to stop him from having to look at his father's blood-red eyes.

'We're not going to let any of this harm your chances in the election,' said his father, smoke curling from his caterpillar lips.

'I don't see how. This kind of scandal, the shit just sticks,' he said.

'No doubt about it. But there is something we can change. We can change who the shit sticks to. We have to make sure that it's not you. But I need to know if you're up for this, Patrick.'

For the first time that day, Patrick raised his head and stared into his father's blood-soaked eyes and said, 'Of course, Dad. I mean, I know how important this is to you. You've done so much for me.'

'Good. At last you're thinking with your head and not your dick. You got yourself involved with two fuckin' dangerous women. We need to make sure the right person goes down for this. You're going to testify against Vanessa at the trial.'

'That will be difficult. It'll all come out, about me and Molly. What if they ask questions about Teresa?'

'Are you really that fuckin' stupid? Wait, don't answer that. You're running for public office, so clearly you're not the brightest spoon in the drawer. This is now damage limitation. I never wiped your ass when you were a baby, but Jesus H. Christ I've been cleaning up plenty of your shit since then. Wait, you're not using again, are you?'

'No, I'm still clean. No drugs.'

'Drinking?'

'In moderation. You know it was never the booze that was the problem. Not really.'

'You're my fuckin' problem. Do you know that? I've had to carry you your whole life. It's time to stand up now, son. You're going to testify against her. You're going to say there was no affair and that she was crazed with jealousy.'

'But if I accuse her of the murder, won't her lawyer just accuse me?'

'Voss is keeping an eye on things for us. And don't worry about Eddie Flynn. He's under control.'

Control had multiple meanings when it came from his father's lips. Patrick was under his father's control, and so were a great many men. But none of them were loyal. Not to a man who ruled through fear.

'This has to look right, Patrick, for the election. So you're going to see Rex Buchanan, and you're going to file for divorce.'

Patrick looked back at the desk as he said, 'Won't that piss off Vanessa? You said it yourself – she's dangerous. If I accuse her, she'll accuse me.'

'You're a joke. Do you know that?'

'Dad—'

'Shut up. Do you remember Boris Cherry?'

An image flashed in his mind of Boris sitting where he sat right now, across the same desk from his father. Boris and his father had been close for twenty years, his right-hand man. And he had made Patrick watch as he fired him. Made him watch Boris plead for his job. Made him watch Boris cry like a child.

'I remember you made me watch you fire him,' said Patrick.

'Right, and do you know what happened to Boris afterwards?'

Shaking his head, Patrick said, 'I remember he died, but I don't remember how.'

'I had him blacklisted in the industry, Patrick. The only job in media Boris was going to get was sweeping the floors on the night-shift at CNN. He killed himself six months after I fired him. And do you know what, son? When I heard about it, I was so glad I'd fired him. I knew, right then, I'd made the smart decision. You remember how he cried? He was weak. I always knew it. And when Boris stepped off the roof of his building that just confirmed it for me. Look, I'm not an animal. I sent a wreath to his widow. Something small and cheap. Just so she could be sure of how little I thought of her late husband. Only the strong survive, son. And you're going to get past this whole thing. You're going to get elected in New York, and in five years' time, it's the White House.'

After a few seconds, Patrick realized his mouth was lying open and he was staring dumbfounded at his father. They had never spoken about Boris since that day Patrick saw him fired. He had heard about Boris's death, but he had no idea of how his father truly felt. Not until this exact moment. It was not a surprise, but it was difficult to hear nonetheless.

'You have to be strong, for once in your life,' said Julian, and took another drag on his cigar. Patrick watched the ash glow red, and shivered.

Julian saw his son's reaction, and followed his gaze to the stogie in his hand. He took the cigar from his lips and blew on the hot, smoking tip, and smiled.

'Nothing is more important than getting you into office. You're going to divorce that bitch wife of yours, but we're not going to finalize the divorce until after the trial and she's convicted. That way you won't have to pay her any alimony. Then we get back on the campaign trail. Okay?'

Patrick nodded.

'Say it,' said Julian.

Patrick's mouth moved but no words came.

'Say you're going to testify against her.'

'I'm going to testify against her.'

'Say you're going to divorce her.'

'I'm going to divorce her.'

'Again.'

He was a frightened boy again, sitting in his father's office. Filled with hate and fear.

'I'm gonna divorce her.'

'Louder . . .'

'I'm gonna divorce her!'

'What is weakness?'

'Empathy is weakness,' answered Patrick.

'Are you weak?'

'No, Pops, I'm not.'

'Because if you can't do this, there's an alternative . . .'

Bile instantly filled Patrick's mouth. He swallowed it back down, and balled his fists to stop his hands from shaking.

'I'll do it,' said Patrick.

'You'd better. If you can't, then Vanessa is going to do something very stupid. The pressure of the trial and the weight of her guilt might just be too much. People in that kind of situation think there's only one way out. So man up, son. Or I'll have to make sure Vanessa throws herself off the roof of her hotel.'

25
Eddie

I sat down on the barstool and ordered two large glasses of bourbon.

The bar was quiet, dark and smelled of stale beer and old wood. Just the way I liked it. Two drunks sat in the corner surrounded by empty beer bottles and shot glasses. Their conversation was low and slurred. There was no music. Two holes in the wall behind me, a dangling electrical wire in the center and old, yellowed paint from a previous decoration job told me that a customer had ripped a jukebox off that wall at some point in time. Either the act of yanking the jukebox off the wall had been a performative act of musical criticism, or more likely the closest thing at hand to hit someone over the head with. Didn't matter. I was grateful for the quiet. There's only so many times you can listen to 'Free Bird'.

My young bartender had all the dedication to the profession of a college kid working three jobs to make his rent. He lazily poured the Jim Beam into two glasses, straight. Set them on the bar. Didn't place any napkins under the glasses. Didn't ask if I wanted ice. It wasn't an ice and napkins kind of place.

Harry took his seat beside me and dropped his leather satchel at his feet.

He reached for his glass, his fingers freezing in mid-air as he noticed the drink in front of me.

He didn't say anything. Didn't need to. He watched me stare at my glass, a decision in front of me. I'd been sober for years. The odd drink aside. Not falling off the wagon exactly, just running alongside it for a spell. Harry picked up his drink and took a long sip.

Smacked his lips and set his glass down.

The bartender stepped away, took out his phone and leaned on the bar, flicking his finger across the screen, watching TikTok videos.

Harry picked up his glass again, swallowed the contents and set it back down on the bar ceremoniously and with enough force to prick up the bartender's ears. He continued to gaze at his phone.

'You can't get the staff these days,' said Harry.

'I could ask Denise to collect Amy. I'm thinking about having a drink,' I said.

He picked up my glass, took a sip and placed it back down in front of him.

'You don't want to drink. You want some peace,' said Harry. 'You don't know what the hell happened in Molly Green's apartment. You want to believe Vanessa, but something doesn't feel right. I know how your mind works. You want to quiet the storm. It's not going to happen. It will be waiting for you in the morning along with a hangover that would level a building.'

'I know it's not worth it, but I hate this. In the best-case scenario, we're going to have Vanessa telling a court her husband confessed to her that he killed Molly Green. The one thing I was warned not to let happen. Julian Vanderpool will come after all of us. I know his type. And it's not going to get us anywhere, because Patrick is going to deny he ever said that to Vanessa, and he's going to make the DA's case for them. The jury will buy the woman scorned argument and Vanessa goes to jail for murder. Maybe that's right? Maybe that's wrong, I just can't tell for sure.'

'If only it were that simple,' said Harry. 'You might be the best lawyer I ever laid eyes on, but you don't know the law.'

'I know enough, but for the obscure legal stuff I've got this consultant in my firm who used to be a judge. He's old, he's drinks too much and he's wildly eccentric. Walks around with an old Colt 1911 strapped under his arm and brings his dog everywhere. I don't know if you've heard of him?'

Harry smiled, but only for the briefest of moments. Whatever was on his mind wiped that smile away fast.

'*The People* vs. *Dudley*, 1969,' he said.

'That's supposed to mean something to me?'

'Spousal privilege,' said Harry. 'Confidential communications between spouses induced by the marital relationship are privileged. The protection is owned by the spouse who made the communication.'

'You want to tell me that again, in English?'

'Vanessa can't testify that Patrick confessed to murder.'

'Say what?'

'It's an old legal maxim that was passed down from English common law, and it's now protected in statute and a long line of case law. It comes from the time when women were legally seen as chattels of their husbands. Property, in other words. But in more recent years, the privilege protects both spouses. If she tried to testify that her husband told her he was the Zodiac killer, that he had Jimmy Hoffa buried under his back porch and he stole the Lindbergh baby it wouldn't be inadmissible testimony. It's just as sacrosanct as attorney–client privilege.'

'Holy shit.'

'Exactly. So it doesn't matter what he told her. It's confidential, privileged information. She can't testify that he confessed.'

'Not even in her own defense?'

'Nope. The law seems to think that protecting the sanctity of marriage is more important than the truth.'

'What if she blurted it out in front of the jury?' I asked.

'The judge would declare a mistrial, and Vanessa would go to jail for contempt of court.'

'And people think that being a con artist is a dishonest profession.'

The bartender was still engrossed in his phone. Harry finished my drink, slammed the glass on the bar. The young man turned around. Harry pointed at the glass.

'You want two more?' he asked, as he approached.

'I want a Pepsi for my friend, and another two for me. In fact, just leave the bottle. I don't want to distract you from your phone.'

'Are you sure? I'd have to charge you for the whole bottle, even if you don't finish it.'

Harry counted out his bills, put them on the bar, said, 'I'm sure I'll manage.'

The bartender poured me a Pepsi, then went back to the corner of the bar and his phone.

'So we've got what looks like a murder weapon, with both the victim's blood and our client's DNA on it. Vanessa lied to the police saying she'd never been to the victim's apartment, but she's on security footage entering and leaving the victim's apartment on the night of the murder with what looks like the victim's head in a gym bag. Her husband was having an affair with the victim so there's plenty of motive. Our defense is our client was being abused by her husband, she was afraid and that's why she lied, and that same abusive husband has confessed to our client that he killed Molly, but we can't use that in court or tell anybody else? And even if we do try to pin this murder on the husband, his father, who is one of the most powerful men in America, is going to come after us with everything he's got. Have I missed anything out?' I asked.

'That's about the sum of it. Plus, our client didn't just lie to the police, she lied to us. Who is to know if she's telling the truth now? Maybe she's lying about the confession, so we stop looking at her and start focusing on the husband.'

'I need something a lot stronger than Pepsi.'

'Have you heard from Lake or Bloch?' he asked.

'No, let's hope they find something useful.'

My cell phone vibrated.

Princess.

I checked my watch. I wasn't due to pick up my daughter for several hours.

I answered the phone. 'Amy, how's the party? Is everything okay, sweetheart?'

The voice on the phone was one I didn't recognize.

'Mr. Flynn, this is Keisha. You need to get here right now. Something's wrong with Amy.'

26
Bloch

Sag Harbor has some of the most expensive real estate in the world. Not a place where you'd expect to find retired police, especially those living off their pension. The churches were plenty and ornate, built to honor those lost at the sea. Windmills had been preserved here, as in East Hampton. This was an old town, built on the proceeds of whaling, a community that had grown rich on the profits from flesh.

Like a lot of the United States where there is prosperity, you don't have to look hard to find old bloodstains in the dirt.

Bloch and Lake drove around a neighborhood that you'd expect to see in 1950s family movies. Vast white timber-frame homes, side by side on lush green lawns, separated by white picket fences. An array of electric cars and Italian sports cars in the driveways. At the end of one street, they pulled up outside a home that was set apart some distance from the rest. It was much older, as if the development of newer, larger homes had sprung up around it and this one had stayed put, defiantly. It was smaller than the others, and in need of some attention. The paint had flaked from the boards, the lawn was patchy and thick with weeds in certain places.

They climbed the stoop and stood on the porch. Bloch rang the doorbell.

A heavy-set man in an over-sized plaid shirt and faded, baggy blue jeans opened the door. He had a receding hairline, a faint beard and slight twitch in his left eye. Either the clothes belonged to someone else or he had lost a lot of weight recently.

'Can I help you?' he asked.

Bloch noticed he stood side-on to the door. The right side of his body beyond view. His right hand hanging at his hip. She knew there was a piece in that hand. A quiver in the man's voice let her know he was nervous.

'Mr. Winchester? I'm Bloch. This is my partner, Gabriel Lake. We're private detectives. Could we come inside and talk?'

'What about?' said the man.

'We're investigating a disappearance. An old case of yours.'

'Can't help you,' he said, and began to close the door.

'We just spoke to Captain Landry. We got the impression that maybe we didn't get the whole story. Thought we would talk to you,' said Lake.

Winchester hesitated. Stared at them.

'You got ID?' he asked.

Bloch showed him her PI license.

Winchester looked at Lake.

Lake smiled, warmly.

'You're the fed they talk about?' he asked.

'Used to be.'

He took Bloch's license, studied it. Looked at her again.

'You're *that* Bloch. I didn't know you two were working together.'

'It's safer for everyone if someone keeps an eye on him,' said Bloch.

'Come in,' said Winchester, swinging open the door. As he turned to walk back down the hallway, Bloch saw him snick the safety catch on his Colt and drop it into a holster on his right hip.

He led them into a pleasant kitchen, old but well cared for. Country-style pine cupboards, a polished stove and a drip coffee machine, which judging by the smell had just finished brewing. They sat at a round kitchen table at his invitation, and both said they would certainly take coffee. Bloch knew Lake wouldn't drink it, but he knew well enough to accept hospitality when it was offered, to help build rapport.

Winchester brought the coffees, sat down beside Bloch.

'Landry said you took medical retirement. How are you doing?' asked Lake.

'Like shit, mostly. I took the pension, but it was that or be fired.'

'What happened?' asked Bloch.

Winchester took a sip of his coffee, eyed them both for a second then put his mug down, seemingly after he had made a decision about what to say next.

'I heard of you both. I know you by reputation only. Enough that people seem to think you're both straight-up so I'll cut to the chase. I was forced out of my job not because I was bad at it, but because I was thorough and competent. And I didn't take a hint that I should stop asking awkward questions. If you're here to see me, then it's about Teresa Chase. I knew it soon as I laid eyes on you.'

'We saw the file in Landry's office. Didn't seem like much to go on for a disappearance at sea? What kind of questions were you asking?' asked Lake.

'The right kind. You see, you saw the Teresa Chase file. That says she disappeared, suspected drowned in an accident. But that's not what happened. At least I don't believe it. I don't believe Teresa Chase drowned.'

'You think she was murdered?' asked Bloch.

'I do, but I can't prove it.'

'Of course not – hard to prove anything when you don't have a body,' said Lake.

Winchester's eyes locked on Lake.

'Oh, I got a body.'

'You found a body in the sea?'

'Nope. Found a woman's corpse buried in the woods. 'Bout the same age as Teresa. Been dead about the same time as she had been missing. I think the report of her being lost at sea was a distraction. No one was going to look for her body in the woods if she had been suspected of drowning at sea. Yep, far as I could tell, that body was Teresa Chase.'

'Wasn't there a formal identification of the body?' asked Bloch.

He stared out of the window for a moment, and tensed, as if he thought he had heard someone in his backyard. Bloch and Lake sat still and quiet. After a few moments, Winchester looked back to his coffee mug. He stared into the black liquid as he spoke.

'We couldn't formally ID the body. It's not so easy if the body don't have a head.'

27
Eddie

The tires on the Mustang screamed as I slid to a stop outside the hotel where I'd dropped off Amy.

I leapt out of the car, Harry behind me.

There, outside the hotel, sitting down on the sidewalk with her back against the building.

Amy.

Surrounded by the same group of girls who had been squealing with delight not hours before.

Her head was on her chest, and the girl who I guessed was Keisha knelt beside her, with her arm round Amy's shoulders.

'She's been sick,' said Keisha, 'but she still doesn't look good.'

I knelt down, cupped her face in my hands and lifted Amy's chin. Her eyes were half closed and her skin was hot to touch. The other girls outside were shivering in the cold. Vomit had flecked Amy's dress.

'What the hell happened?' I asked.

A cacophony of high-pitched, panicked voices rang out all at once.

'One at a time, ladies. It's okay,' said Harry.

'We don't know,' said Keisha. 'She was fine then she stumbled on the dance floor, and we sat down together and had some water.

Then she got really drowsy, said she was feeling sick. I said I would call you and then we went outside. She vomited and now she's barely conscious. But I swear she didn't have any alcohol. On my life, I swear to God, she—'

'Okay, okay,' I said, and bent down to my daughter.

'Amy, can you hear me?' I asked.

She groaned, leaned over and a little more sick came up.

That's when I saw the flash.

I looked up.

A guy in a black coat was taking pictures with an expensive-looking camera.

'Get the hell out of here,' said Harry.

The guy let the camera drop from his face, smiled and then turned and ran.

'What the hell was he doing taking pictures? Does he think we'll sue or something?' said Keisha.

'What are you talking about? Do you know that guy?' asked Harry.

'He was working behind the bar earlier,' said Keisha.

Harry and I exchanged a look.

'Thank you, Keisha, we can take it from here. Harry, get the door. We're going to the hospital.'

'Dad, these clothes stink,' said Amy.

She was lying in a hospital bed. I'd brought my gym bag from the trunk of the car. She was wearing gray sweatpants and a Black Key's T-shirt. She had a butterfly needle on the back of her hand that was attacked to a saline drip that hung above the bed.

I patted her head with a damp towel, said, 'They may stink, but they don't have vomit on them.'

'Sorry, Dad.'

'Don't worry about it. I can get the car cleaned. I can't get a new daughter.'

The young doctor who had seen Amy earlier threw open the

green curtain that surrounded the bed. He didn't look that much older than Amy.

'How're you feeling?' he asked.

'I'm pretty mad and I think I might have had a mild heart attack,' I said.

He looked at me.

Amy smiled, and laughed for the first time that night. I felt better as soon as I heard that laughter. It was one of the best sounds in the world.

'Actually, I was asking your daughter,' said the doc.

'He knew that. He was just trying to make me laugh,' said Amy. 'I feel a lot better, thank you.'

'Good, well, your vital signs are all improving. Heart rate is way down, your temperature returning to normal. How's the stomach?' he asked, and took a pen flashlight from his pocket. He checked Amy's eyes.

'Feels weird, and sore, but not like I want to be sick.'

'Good,' said the doc.

'Was it the food?' asked Amy.

The doc looked at me. I nodded.

'Amy, do you know what a roofie is?' asked the doc.

'What? Rohypnol?'

'Not exactly in this case. But something similar. Thankfully, your body rejected the drugs quickly. If you hadn't vomited so quickly after drinking it, things might have been a lot worse. You'll have a headache soon, but we're flushing your system and giving you everything that you need to make a full recovery. By tomorrow morning you'll be feeling a lot—'

'What the fuck is going on?' shouted Christine as she burst through the curtain. I stepped aside and she grabbed Amy in a hug. She had been crying on the way here, I could tell.

The doc said, 'Your daughter had her drink spiked. She's well on her way to recovery. Your husband did everything right and she—'

'He's not my husband,' said Christine.

Right on cue, Kevin came by the bed, out of breath and flushed from running.

'She's going to be fine,' I said, and patted his shoulder.

'Thank you, Eddie,' said Kevin, and joined Christine and Amy in a hug.

I looked up at the ceiling, blew out a breath. I had been panicking too. I had tried not to show it, for Amy's sake, but now that the emergency had passed I felt my heart rate beginning to drop.

My phone buzzed.

Text from Denise.

What's going on? Is Amy okay?

I hadn't had time to talk to Denise. Neither, I thought, had Harry.

Another text. This time she had sent me a link.

I clicked on it.

The link took me to X.

A photo of Amy, lying on the sidewalk outside the hotel, vomiting. And me kneeling beside her. But this wasn't just a photo.

It was the picture from an article. I read the headline.

Famous Manhattan Lawyer's Daughter Caught in Drug and Alcohol Disaster

I clicked on it.

The article was from a gossip Substack and it referenced numerous posts on X, Facebook and Instagram from what looked like a mixture of bot accounts and social-media trolls.

There were hundreds of posts, all with that same picture.

And something else.

A link to another gossip column.

LIKE FATHER, LIKE DAUGHTER. BOOZY NY ELITE LAWYER EDDIE FLYNN COMES TO THE AID OF HIS DRUNKEN DAUGHTER IN ILLEGAL NIGHT OF DEBAUCHED DRINKING!

This was from the *Daily Post*.

An online news site.

Owned by Julian Vanderpool.

'I'm just going to text Keisha—' said Amy.

I snatched the phone out of her hand.

'Dad?'

'Eddie? What the hell?' cried Christine.

'Don't let her see your phone,' I said as I ran out of the ward. Harry was standing in the hallway outside. His face contorted in disgust as he stared at his phone. His head shot up when he heard me running toward him.

Denise must have sent him the same message.

'Thanks, Harry. I'm sorry. Ask Denise to pick you up,' I said as I ran past him.

'Eddie! Eddie! Don't do it! Stop!'

He kept calling out, even as I ran past the bank of elevators and took the stairs, fast as I could, down two flights and then out the side doors to my car.

By the time I pulled up on the corner, the brakes were burning and beginning to fail on the Mustang. And there was a terrible smell from the clutch. I think I might have burned it out snatching fourth gear from first after that last set of lights.

I got out, popped the trunk, took a straight tire iron from the hidden well beneath the trunk floor and slid it up inside the sleeve of my jacket. I held the steel head in my palm, closed the trunk and turned the corner.

The two guys who I'd first seen accompanying Voss stood either side of the front door. They were wearing the same black overcoats. The same black luxury SUV was parked in front of them at the curb.

The blond guy with the scar running through his hair was closest to me. I was coming up on his left side, and kept close to the building to block the view of his pal. The blond guy heard my footsteps, turned toward me.

For a moment, he was confused.

I wasn't supposed to be here. He hadn't been asked to come get me. This was a picture that really didn't make any sense.

His stance widened and he spun toward me as I sprinted the last ten feet and dropped my right shoulder so it hit him square in the chest, full speed. A hundred and eight-five pounds of pissed-off father knocked the wind straight out of him.

He went down hard, and it was lucky for me he was so solid because I just bounced off and didn't go down with him. His buddy, the stocky body builder with a bad steroid rash got his hands up, ready to fight.

I opened my left land.

Let gravity fill it with the handle of my tire iron.

His eyes widened as I swung it up, over my head, and he raised his arms to block it as I stepped forward.

I swung down hard, and at a sharp angle.

I didn't want to kill him.

But when the tire iron hit his right knee he probably wished he was dead.

He went down screaming.

His buddy rolled around on the ground, clutching his chest where I'd put my shoulder into his sternum. He was panting, trying to get air. I rolled him into the recovery position, stood and threw the tire iron straight through the driver's window of the SUV. The hazard lights and alarm flared.

Then I pushed the front door open and stepped inside.

Another set of double doors stood four feet in front of me. This was an inner hallway and on my left was a security panel with a digital keypad and a large green button marked ALARM beside it.

I smacked the alarm button and pushed open the double doors.

As the alarm rang out through the house, I found myself in the marble hallway I'd been in some weeks ago. Corridor to my left.

Another to my right. A hallway dead ahead that led to the conservatory and a staircase sweeping up beside. Fabergé eggs and art that cost more than most Manhattan apartments.

Cupping my hands in front of me, I stared straight ahead and stood very still.

Footsteps to my left. Coming up fast. I turned casually and saw another security guy, dressed all in black. Younger than the others. He saw me standing in the hall, casually, and slowed as he approached. He stood in front of me in a wide stance, hands ready in case he needed to tackle me. There are various types of intruders. A man in a nice suit and tie standing still in a hallway doesn't fit the bill.

Before he could speak, I said, 'Something's burning.'

'Burning?'

'Yeah.'

He dropped his hands, said, 'What's burning?'

'Your balls.'

I took one step forward and planted my left foot, swung my right leg into a kick that would score a forty-yard field goal.

He was regretting that wide stance as he clutched his groin and dropped to the floor, mouth wide open, sucking in air, unable to scream.

I got down on one knee, as I heard someone else approaching on my right. I rolled the guy on the floor onto his side. To anyone who hadn't seen me give him an almighty kick in the balls moments ago, it would look like I was trying to help the guy out.

'What the hell happened?' said a voice behind me. He stepped in close, trying to look over my shoulder. Whoever he was, he had a deep voice and I saw the toe of his military boot step in close to the body of his pal on the floor. I got up fast, driving myself into a standing position, using all the power in my legs, and I turned and caught the new guy right under the chin with an uppercut.

He staggered back and I grabbed his tie with my left. Hit him three hard shots with my right as his legs folded underneath him. I didn't need the third punch. He was out cold in two, but it was already on its way to his jaw. I still had hold of his tie as he went down. Didn't want him to crack his skull on the marble floor.

Soon as he was safely on the ground, I let go of his tie and spun round.

Dekker was almost down the stairs. Behind him, tying off a silk dressing gown, was Julian Vanderpool.

'What the fuck?' said Dekker when he saw the two guys either side of me, one rolling around on the floor with his hands between his thighs, the other letting out a loud snore.

I ignored Dekker, looked right past him at Julian.

'My daughter? You drugged my daughter?' I asked, my right fist still clenched.

'I didn't drug anyone. I asked my guy for some pictures and a story, and that's what I got. Good coverage, don't you think?'

'She's only fifteen, you son of a—'

'I just wanted to make sure you remembered who is in charge,' said Julian. 'The news cycle moves fast. Tomorrow the tabloids will be full of the story of Vanessa's upcoming trial and a statement from Patrick confirming he's filed for divorce. We're cutting Vanessa loose. If she tries to blame my son for the murder, I will crucify the both of you. Consider this a *warning*, Flynn.'

'After what you did tonight, you've made up my mind. You're a tough old sick son of a bitch. I can't hurt you. Not directly. But I can hurt him. He's the only thing you care about, and I'm going to make sure he suffers, and that *isn't* a *warning*. It's a goddamn guaranteed golden ticket and I'm Willy fuckin' Wonka.'

'You busted into the wrong house,' said Dekker.

'I don't walk into any place without knowing how to walk out again,' I said.

'You're an intruder. We can shoot intruders,' said Dekker.

'Dekker, don't kill him. Put one in his knee, for being a prick,' said Julian.

The alarm belted off the walls.

I stood very still. Watched Dekker reach for his side arm.

Heard that click from the quick-release holster.

The gun was in his hand in a flash. He adjusted his aim, and I watched the barrel angle down.

He smiled, relishing the moment. He would enjoy the squeeze of the trigger, the kick from the gun, the crack of fire and the delicious moment of pain and ruin as the bullet found its target.

His smile broke as his gaze flicked over my shoulder.

'NYPD! Drop the gun! Drop the gun!'

He instantly raised his hands, let the Glock fall to clatter on the steps.

'Down! Get down!' came the cry.

I turned slowly, my hands in the air.

Two uniformed cops with their guns drawn. One on me, one on Dekker.

I don't walk into any place I don't know how to walk out of.

In this case, I might have to be carried out in cuffs, but I knew the NYPD response times in this area, especially a personal alarm in the largest private home in Manhattan.

There's nothing like a police escort when you need it.

I got onto my knees and stared at Julian.

Rage filled his bloodshot eyes.

I lay down, put my hands behind my back and quickly felt a knee in my spine, and heard the jangle of handcuffs.

'Glad to see you, officers,' I said. 'I just heard the alarm, thought it was a fire and ran in to help. You know, it's a real piece of luck you're here. I was about to call you. Somebody stole a tire iron out of my car.

'What the hell is going on?' said one of the cops.

'I got a permit for that piece,' said Dekker.

Nobody explained the situation. Julian said nothing. He just glared at me.

'This isn't finished,' he said.

The cop hauled me to my feet. I stared at Julian and said, 'You got that right. I'm just getting started.'

28
The Journal

The first time I met Patrick Vanderpool I wanted to throw up.

You have no idea what it's like.

Some people are comfortable telling lies. It comes as naturally to them as breathing. I struggled with it, even as a kid. My mom always knew it was me who had accidentally dropped a plate on the kitchen floor, or left a window open by mistake, or stained the couch – even when I denied it as sweetly as I could.

She could just tell.

Could Patrick tell?

It was late, and I was in his office, copying. I heard his voice before I saw him.

He was talking to Geoff, that lech. I turned round, caught a glimpse of them both in the hallway. They were laughing and slapping each other on the back. The laughter had a cruel quality to it. As if the only enjoyment these men could have was at the expense of someone else.

I turned my back, focused on the copier.

It was after seven, and almost everyone else in the campaign office had gone home, with just a few staffers in the mailroom licking envelopes and folding posters for the next day's drop.

'So you're the new girl,' said a voice.

It wasn't Geoff's Brooklyn drawl. This voice had an education and money behind it.

I turned to see Patrick leaning against the desk, looking me up and down. He had a smile on his face, but there was no warmth to it. He looked at me like I was rare steak. The thing about men with power is that they can't help but remind people of it, even in their smallest gestures. It hangs off them like a bad smell.

'How long have you been here?'

He put an emphasis on the 'you', as if I was some gold-plated Ferrari he'd just discovered in his garage.

'About a month, now.'

'A month? How come I haven't . . . You know what? Never mind. Thank you for all of your hard work on the campaign. Together we can really rebuild this state: restore it to what it used to be, you know?'

I smiled and said of course, and added that I was rooting for him to win.

He cocked his head, looked me up and down and said, 'As much as I really appreciate all your efforts, it's getting a little late to be working. You want to get out of here and go somewhere?'

I played the innocent.

'Go where?'

'Anywhere . . . ah . . . Why don't we go get a drink and you can tell me what you think of the strategy? I assume you've seen the latest poll numbers?'

'Sure, that would be fun. And yeah, I saw the numbers. The needle is starting to move in our direction.'

'Spectacular,' he said, throwing his arms wide. He smiled and his gaze lingered on my legs.

I'm no fool. I knew what he wanted, and it wasn't my take on campaign strategy or poll numbers. Don't think I'm an innocent in all this. I know exactly what I'm doing.

I do.

I promise.

I'm not under any illusions.

This is where I knew it could go.

Maybe where I hoped it would go.

And it's not because I'm attracted to Patrick. I just need to get close to him. Real close.

I need this man to trust me.

If that means he gets into my bed, then so be it. I told myself I could do it.

Then I felt his fingers brush against the small of my back, and the wave of revulsion and anger that followed it.

I swallowed it down.

Could he tell?

'Why don't you grab your coat and I'll call for the car.'

The bar was one of those well-hidden places on the fourteenth floor of a skyscraper. There was no sign for the place in the lobby, and nothing outside the building to indicate that it was even there. But this was the sort of place that not only didn't need to advertise, it didn't want to. The lighting was low, with ornate crystal lamps on each table, a black floor, black leather furniture and a long black marble bar. More lighting behind the bar sat in the gold filigree recess that housed the shelving for spirits. Almost every table was occupied, and apart from the low, unnerving jazz track, it was quiet enough that no one had to raise their voice to be heard.

'You like this place?' he asked.

'Yeah, it's very cool. Too cool for me.'

'You belong in places like this,' he said.

I looked around at the other women in the bar. Sleek, dark cocktail dresses and heels. I was in black jeans and a charcoal low-cut tee. Boots though, which I was now grateful I'd chosen that morning instead of my beat-up Nike Cortez.

'I'm not dressed for somewhere like this,' I said. 'I'm not even *sure I have anything to wear that would make it look like I fit in here.'*

'Don't be silly. You're the most attractive woman in the room.'

I smiled, and tried to hide the embarrassment by staring into my drink and stirring it with my cocktail straw. He'd ordered for me, of course.

'You think I suit a place like this?' he asked.

'Sure, you're, well . . . you know who you are. I mean, you can go anywhere.'

'I wasn't talking about money, or power. I mean look around. Half of the guys in here are models. Or they look that way. I know I'm a little older, but I'm not out of place here, am I?'

That was my cue. He'd let me know he was into me, now he wanted to know if the feeling was mutual. If you didn't know him, and you didn't know who his father was, I guess on a pure aesthetic level he was physically attractive. Good body, a big smile, cheekbones, blue eyes and that slightly roguish hair, which was kinda preppy, but in a good way. He dressed smart and smelled of money – there was that too.

I gave him a smile, said nothing for a few seconds, then bit my bottom lip, and flashed him a coquettish look. Like he was handsome, but I didn't want to admit it.

'Your looks make you fit in just fine,' I said eventually.

He liked that, took the compliment with a sip from the same muddy cocktail we were both drinking.

'I get the impression there's something you're not saying. You think I'm too old for this place?' he asked.

'No, I don't think that at all,' I said, and stirred my drink.

'What then?'

'Well, people come to places like this to meet their lovers. But you're not a single man, Patrick,' I said.

It was the first time I'd used his name. And he liked the way it sounded on my tongue.

'Does that bother you? I only ask, because you're very beautiful. I like you. I like you a lot.'

I almost said I didn't mind at all. That would have been the easy thing. To give him what he wants. To fall willingly into his bed.

To make him trust me.

But that would be a mistake. Not yet.

I reminded myself this man had everything he'd ever wanted in life. To deny him gave me power, and only made him want me more. He liked the chase. If I gave in to his desires too soon the whole thing would fall apart way too quickly.

'Thank you,' I said. 'It's not just your situation – it's mine. I work for you. We only just met, really.'

'Of course, no problem. So what do you like to do in your spare time?'

'What spare time? Your office is pretty busy, but you know, at the weekends I like to read and go for a long run. Sometimes I just chill in bed the whole day and watch old movies.'

He nodded, and said that sounded fun. I knew what I wanted to say next, but wondered if it was too soon. Was I playing this at the right pace? I took the chance.

'What I really love is the ocean,' I said, and he leaned forward, put his elbows on the table and gazed into my eyes.

'My parents moved around a lot – my father was in the military. But I remember we had five good years in Monterey, at the Presidio. In the summertime, me and my friends would cycle to Del Monte beach and just spend the whole day there. It's so beautiful. Those summers used to feel like they lasted for a whole year. If I wasn't swimming, I would just sit and stare at the water. It was so peaceful, especially early in the morning. Before we moved to Monterey, I'd never seen the ocean, but it got into my bones. I love it so much. That's the one drawback to living in the city. Yeah, there's beaches, like, hours away, but it's not the same. It's too crowded. There's too much noise.'

'You know I have a house in the Hamptons? A beach house?'

'No way,' I lied.

'It's amazing. I get up in the morning and stare out at the ocean, then I get coffee and walk right out my back door onto the beach. And there's no one else around. Just the sound of the waves hitting the shore.'

'That sounds like heaven,' I said.

'Would you like to come out there with me sometime? Maybe for a weekend?'

I couldn't believe my luck. Yes, I said. I would like that very much.

I knew he had a house in East Hampton. I'd stared at it for hours on Google Maps. I'd found the floor plans in the District Planning office and studied them. I'd walked past it on that same beach dozens of times. And a dozen times more I'd run past the driveway on the country road leading to it. I knew who his nearest neighbors were, and even got a tour of their property, posing as a potential buyer, to see if I could get a better look at Patrick's house. I knew everything it was possible to know about it.

But I'd never been inside.

If I played this right, then that was about to change.

I could feel my pulse quickening, and I let the excitement bleed into my voice.

I said, 'I'd love to spend a weekend with you in the Hamptons.'

'Then that's a date,' said Patrick.

Pain. Loss. Grief.

These were my companions. These were my guiding stars.

They had led me here.

They would lead me to the truth. The truth was in that house in East Hampton. I knew it in my heart.

Pain, loss and grief don't take things away from you, not always. If you use them right, they can give you something back.

They would give me revenge.

29
Bloch

The sun was disappearing behind the black trees when Winchester had finished telling all he knew of the Teresa Chase case to Bloch and Lake. The window behind him framed the sunset perfectly. A row of fields stretched to the horizon and the distant tree line. So involved in telling his story, Winchester hadn't seemed to notice the dying light. The small kitchen was now dark, and only when he had finished, and picked up his empty coffee cup, did he flick on the light switch as he made his way to the machine for a refill.

Bloch was glad of the light. The tale was dark enough, and so perhaps it had been fitting for Winchester to tell it while the light faded into dusk.

He was convinced the body that had been found in the woods by a father and son hunting had been the body of Teresa Chase. Absent her head, of course. The discovery had been made some months after Teresa had reportedly been swept out to sea. Ordinarily, when a partial body is recovered, there are procedures and investigations that in most cases lead to a positive identification.

The fingerprints taken from the body were not in the system.

Dental records were no help here.

There were no distinguishing marks of any kind. No tattoos. No scars.

The DNA profile of the body was not in the missing person's database. Teresa's apartment had been cleared out by her landlord, and the place deep cleaned, as was his usual method. So there wasn't even an identifiable hair fiber on a hairbrush that they could tie to Teresa to be used as a base sample of DNA for comparison to the body.

Following an MRI scan, there were no signs of any old fractures or evidence of surgical procedures that can sometimes be used to identify people – particularly any metal plates, which usually have a serial number that can be linked back to an individual, the surgeon and the hospital where the surgery was undertaken.

Nothing.

Well, there was one thing that could have been done, and this is what caused Winchester serious problems.

Teresa Chase had no living relatives that could be traced. She had a half-sister, on her father's side, named Willow Chase, but apparently she was a drug addict who had fallen so far off the radar that no one knew how to trace her. Cousins were not good enough, and Teresa's parents had both been deceased more than five years.

Winchester had asked permission from Captain Landry to obtain a court order for exhumation of her parents, Steven and Deanna Chase, so that their DNA could be compared to the unidentified body.

Landry had refused, point blank. Said there was no evidential basis for obtaining an exhumation order. He didn't care that the partial body was roughly the same age as Teresa, and had been dead around the same amount of time Teresa had been missing.

There was nothing more Winchester could have done.

Now, Bloch replayed his story as she sat in his dark kitchen.

Bloch felt Lake nudge her knee with his. He flicked his eyes to Winchester. Bloch came out of her reverie and followed Lake's gaze. Winchester leaned over the kitchen counter. His eyes shut tightly. His shoulders jerking.

Tears fell on the oak countertop.

'We're sorry to have upset you, Paul,' said Lake.

He took in a huge breath, wiped his face with meaty hands.

'It's alright, it's just me being stupid . . . It's . . . It's ah . . . I failed her. I failed that girl. I know it's Teresa.'

'You did everything you could,' said Bloch. 'You can hold your head up. Can't say the same for Landry.'

'He's scared,' said Winchester. 'That's why he canned me when I went behind his back to the judge for the order. Goddamn judge refused me straight out, and told me he'd already spoken to Landry about how there was no evidence to exhume Teresa's parents. They don't want the truth coming out. I think that son-of-a-bitch Patrick Vanderpool killed her, either in a rage or by accident. I just know it. And they're protecting him because of who his father is. You know how much the Vanderpool's donate to the local police fund?'

Bloch shook her head.

'Neither do I, but I know it's more than the five hundred and seventy-five thousand dollars Vanderpool paid for a fleet of new police cruisers.'

Winchester suddenly spun round, sprang to the window and stared out. Bloch began to say something and Winchester raised his finger to his lips. He was listening.

Bloch and Lake exchanged looks.

Some of what Winchester had told them sounded outlandish. Bloch was not a great judge of liars, but she was aware that for some people it is much easier to believe there is a conspiracy and a cover-up when perhaps the actual problem is merely incompetence. This can be a particular problem for those who have lost something. In Winchester's case, going behind Landry's back to the judge had been the final straw. He had been told to take medical retirement and forget about Teresa Chase, or be fired. He took the retirement package, but he had not forgotten about Teresa. The tears, just moments ago, were testament to that, but perhaps more. Bloch got the impression that Winchester had been one of those rarer breeds of police officer who not only cares about victims, but feels a moral compulsion, something akin to a personal mission, to see that they have justice.

Yet, he was hearing things. Bloch and Lake shared a highly developed sense of danger. She could admit that Lake's was more finely tuned than hers. And neither of them had heard or sensed anyone outside Winchester's property.

He had been a good cop. And he may have had a point about Teresa Chase. Or he may have been mistaken.

Bloch had failed to mention that they were currently working on the defense team for Patrick Vanderpool's wife, who stood accused of murdering and beheading another young woman named Molly Green.

One thing was fairly certain in Bloch's mind.

'Thank you for everything you've told us,' said Lake, getting up.

Winchester didn't take his eyes from the window, not until they were almost at the front door.

'I probably should've closed the door in your faces, for all the good it'll do me,' he said.

'Thank you anyway,' said Bloch as they left. The heavy door slammed shut behind them and Bloch listened to two separate bolts slotting across the door, and then the rattle of a security chain.

Once safely inside Bloch's Jeep, Lake asked, 'What do you think?'

'I think he may be on to something.'

'You sure?'

'Nobody cans a detective with his rep, experience and clearance rate unless you want to cover something up. It's what happened to him because of the Teresa Chase case that makes me think he's right. I do know one thing for certain – he's paranoid.'

As they drove out of the street, they passed a Land Rover Defender with blacked-out windows parked at the curb. It was parked sufficiently far away from Winchester's house to be barely visible due to the bend in the road, but it was still in a position to notice everyone coming and going from the property. The Land Rover had not been there when they'd arrived. Bloch would have noticed. She saw Lake checking out the side mirror, keeping the Land Rover in view as they headed out toward the highway.

'I think you're right about the cover-up,' said Lake, 'but I'm not sure you're right about Paul. Just because you're paranoid, doesn't mean they're not out to get you.'

30
Paul Winchester

It was always the same dream.

Since he was eight years old.

He was sitting cross-legged on the rug that lay in the center of the floor in his old living room. Barefoot, wearing his Captain Caveman pajamas and watching *Sesame Street*. It was the summer, but there was nowhere to go. Both his parents were at work, and they didn't want him wandering. Mom would be back anytime. He just had to wait.

He was feeling hungry. She should have been home by now.

When she got home, she would fix him a PBJ and serve it on a little flowery china plate with a cold glass of milk. He was worried now. She was really late.

He thought about going into the kitchen and making his own PBJ, but he'd tried that a few weeks ago and it didn't work out. He had torn the slice of Wonderbread to shreds trying to spread the hard peanut butter, just out of the fridge. The strawberry jelly wasn't a problem, but putting it all together was impossible for him. He thought about just getting a spoon and eating from the jars, but he liked the combination of sweet red jam and salty peanut butter on sugary thick white bread.

He missed his mom.

The credits started to play on *Sesame Street* as Big Bird and the kids on the street waved goodbye.

That's when he saw the flashing red and blue lights on top of the police car as it pulled up outside his house.

He saw the big cop, the tallest man he'd ever seen, get out. He had a white uniform and black aviator sunglasses with gold rims. And a hat. A hat kinda like those that cowboys wear except it had a golden-colored cord wrapped around the base of the crown like a band. That hat came off as the cop knocked on Paul's front door. He could smell the chewing tobacco on the big cop's breath as he knelt down and told him both his parents had been killed.

And they were never coming home.

That was the point, usually, when Paul would awaken, startled and upset and disturbed, and strangely with the same odor of that chewing tobacco in his nose.

But not lately.

Not for a while.

In the last few years, there had been another part of the dream.

The part he was seeing now.

The part where he lay down on the living room floor and rolled around, crying hysterically. And as he rolled, he suddenly felt something cold against his eight-year-old cheek. When he opened his eyes, he saw the headless, naked corpse of a woman beside him.

She was crying too. Even though she didn't have a mouth, or eyes, or a head. He could still hear her wailing.

That's the new part. That's the part where Paul wakes up.

Like he did tonight.

He was sweating and panting. Sitting upright in bed.

This time, it was different.

He could still hear the headless woman wailing.

A terrible fear filled his chest, and chilled every inch of his flesh until he felt as if it was being pulled off his bones.

Then he realized it wasn't the headless Teresa Chase haunting his dreams. The security alarm on his phone was shrieking.

He grabbed the handset.

The alert told him someone had breached the motion detectors in his backyard, and out front.

He'd heard this siren before. Raccoons, mostly. Especially out back.

But never had they triggered alarms at the front *and* back of his home.

Raccoons don't attack in a pincer movement, covering all exits.

Only people do that.

Paul drew the Colt from the quick-release holster bolted on the side of his nightstand. He stood in his vest and boxers, barefoot, still panting, but a different kind of panic now washing his system.

This was real. This was actually happening.

He shouldn't have spoken to those private investigators. He knew it then, and he knew it now.

But he did the right thing. He had told them everything that he had known, everything that he had believed, and everything that he couldn't prove. They were professionals, Bloch and Lake. Both had fearsome reputations. They wouldn't stop until the truth finally came out, and then, maybe then, he would stop hearing Teresa Chase's corpse crying in his dreams.

He opened his bedroom door quietly, held the pistol out in front as he padded to the top of the stairs. The floor below sat in a heavy, pregnant darkness. He held his breath, listened to his heart thumping, the blood coursing through his veins and resounding in his ears, the sound almost deafening.

What were his options?

He could wait until they tried to get upstairs.

Bad choice.

He would be cornered up here. No way out.

He had to go down.

Cautiously, the pistol shaking in his hands, he stepped lightly and slowly down the stairs, his bare feet feeling the ribbed pattern of the carpet, his eyes wide, his every sense on high alert.

He froze.

The second to last step. The board was loose. It would groan as soon as he put weight on it.

In this dense quiet, it would be as good as sending up a flare to mark his exact position.

Fear took hold of Paul. He had known terrible fear before, when that tall policeman came to his front door all those years ago. He knew it was because something awful had happened to his parents. And still now, years later, that fear visited him often. It was a paralyzing cold, as if he had fallen into a freezing black lake.

That's what downstairs looked like to him. Pitch black. Cold.

And filled with fear.

His teeth began to rattle, and he clamped his jaw shut. He took the pistol in his right hand, reached out and took the rail with his left. He would need to step over that loose board. Stretching out his right foot, he put it carefully onto the last step and was able to see a little way into the hall. As he picked up his left foot to bring it down, he overbalanced and pulled on the rail to stop himself falling.

The rail *creaked.*

His right hand shook so violently that he almost dropped the gun. And he couldn't suppress a whimper escaping his lips. It wasn't the fifty-five-year-old Paul on those stairs – he was now that frightened boy again.

That's when he saw the flashlight. At first, it pointed straight at the floor. He could just make out the man who had stepped into view. Dressed in black, with a black ski mask covering his face. The flashlight was attached beneath the barrel of a pistol and part of it shone on the silencer that elongated the barrel.

Everything happened in slow motion. The light swept up toward him.

Paul couldn't move.

Couldn't extend his arm. Couldn't even point his weapon at the light.

He wasn't that kind of cop. He had never even had to draw his gun before, not in all his years of service, and now it showed.

'No,' he said quietly.

Just as the flashlight beam swept up and over his body, he collapsed on the stairs, dropping his gun.

And a huge sonic *BOOM* rent the air.

Paul closed his eyes. But even before then he was conscious that the light from the flashlight had disappeared.

He didn't feel any pain. And he wondered if he was dead. If this is what death feels like.

Then he opened his eyes and saw the flashlight on the floor, pointed toward the window.

He blinked as another figure appeared from the darkness, and grabbed his hand.

'You're alright,' said Bloch.

His vision cleared as he stood, and felt Bloch's grip on his wrist. She helped him down the last steps.

He glanced down and saw that the man in black lay still, some distance away from the stairs. His balaclava was now oddly shaped, as if half his head had collapsed. The stain on the wall behind the man and the glint of Bloch's magnum in her other hand told him everything he needed to know.

'You saved me,' he said.

'We came in through the fields at the back. But don't thank us yet. This isn't over,' said another voice.

He squinted, saw Gabriel Lake, who was on his knees, peering out of the front window of the living room.

His senses began to return, the shock lessening.

It was then he heard the engine, and followed Lake's gaze through the window to see a large black SUV, with no headlights, pull up outside his house.

Three men, all in black, got out of the vehicle. They wore black ski hoods, and they held stocky assault rifles in their hands.

'Everybody down,' cried Lake.

31
Bloch

Winchester let out a cry of pain as Bloch pushed his face into his hardwood floor and kept it there.

At first, he had resisted.

Then, within a second, the shooting started.

They lay pressed to floor.

The weapons were silenced, but the sound of firing was still audible. Not as loud as the sound of bullets ripping through windowpanes, wood-paneled walls, and then tearing up the TV in the living room and the crockery in the kitchen beyond. It was a shotgun house, so-called because you could stand on the front porch, with the front and back door open and fire a shotgun through the house without hitting anything but air.

These rounds were not going out the back door. One bullet must have gone clear through some of the old plumbing as a jet of water burst through a hole in the back wall and sprayed the kitchen floor.

The tinny sound of recoil from the assault rifles was as fast as a beat on a brass cymbal. After fifteen, maybe twenty seconds, the firing stopped.

Bloch heard boots on gravel, working hard and getting fainter.

One of the men, at least, was headed round the house for the back door.

She turned to Lake, but he was already getting to his feet and heading toward the kitchen. Ducking underneath the spray from the burst pipe, he whipped round, one-eighty, swung to his knees and put his back to the kitchen island. The back door was behind it. Bloch was still lying flat on the floor at the bottom of the stairs, but she pushed herself forward, left ear to the ground, straining to see into the kitchen.

She could just make out the back door. Bloch and Lake had left it open when they'd come in. The first intruder must've come round the front and used a side window in the parlor.

She could see Lake, but she was far enough away, with just her head low to the ground and her eyes jutting past the living room doorway, that anyone coming through the back door likely wouldn't see her. Not through the spray from the ruptured pipe.

Lake looked at her. Nodded.

She nodded back.

They'd worked together long enough to have an unspoken language. Bloch said so little that it had developed faster than usual.

Silently, the back door opened a little farther. A masked man carrying an assault rifle came into the kitchen, sweeping the weapon left and right, checking the corners for targets.

Military trained, thought Bloch.

She nodded to Lake, and kept her eyes on the man at the back door.

Lake scooted onto his belly, wrapped his arm around the kitchen island, until the Glock was pointed in the right direction, and fired three times in tight angles. He couldn't be sure, but at this distance, one of those quick shots was bound to hit the man standing in that doorway.

One of them did. The round tearing through the side of his boot.

The man dropped and the back of his head hit the floor. He just had time to look up to see Lake, standing over him now, the Glock pointed at his face.

Lake pulled the trigger.

The back of the man's head hit the floor again.

This time, it would stay there.

Bloch rolled over, looked toward the front of the house.

Listened.

It was so quiet. So dark.

And then the clouds shifted.

Moonlight drifted through the bullet holes in the front of the house. From the living room to the hallway, shafts of light angled through the holes to cast pools of silver on the floor.

And then one of the shafts of light went dark, way over to her left in the living room. Then it lit up again, and another shaft was extinguished, like a candle being blown out. Someone was outside, moving across the front of the house toward the door. Slowly, silently, unaware that the moon was showing their exact position.

The magnum in Bloch's hand followed the path of the man outside.

Then, to her right, the shafts of moonlight in the hallway were broken.

Two figures converging on the front door.

Bloch felt around on the floor with her left hand.

Picked up Winchester's Colt.

She held both guns at arm's length, pointed at the dark spots where the intruders blocked the moonlight. Holding her breath, her arms got closer together, as she kept a bead on each target.

Closer and closer, her aim converging on the front door.

Bloch pulled both triggers. The magnum kicked, punching through the wall, and then sending a much thicker column of light into the house. She tossed the Colt, brought both hands on the magnum and focused on the second target, firing three times.

She got up, dropped the empty magnum and picked up the Colt, kicked open the front door and saw the two bodies on the front lawn. Both dead. One had his arm severed at the elbow – a stray shot from the magnum.

'Clear,' said Bloch.

'Clear,' said Lake.

'Get out of here,' said Winchester weakly.

She whipped round. Winchester lay on his back. Two bullet holes on his left side from the first barrage of fire through the house. Blood bubbled from one of the wounds. The round had penetrated at least one lung.

'Call 911,' said Bloch.

Lake came into the hallway, dropped to his knees and took out his phone.

Bloch put both hands on the wounds, leaned down, applying pressure. Blood spewed from Paul's mouth and a coughing fit took him.

Lake began dialing.

'S-stop!' said Winchester. 'Too late.'

'Help me,' said Bloch.

He was bleeding too fast. She couldn't stop it. A large pool of blood was already getting bigger beneath him.

'Don't call anybody. I won't make it,' said Winchester. 'And I don't want either of you here when Landry arrives. Give me my gun and get the hell out of here. If you don't, Landry will make sure you both go to jail for this. I know it.'

Bloch and Lake exchanged a look.

'Take . . .' He tried to speak again, but another bloody coughing fit cut him off. His breath gurgled, but with great effort he managed a whisper.

'Take my phone. It has all the files on the Jane Doe and the . . . the security feed from tonight. Get him. Get Vanderpool. Take it, take it and get the . . .'

His eyeballs turned upwards, and his head lolled to one side as the last breath left his body.

Lake looked around, then ran upstairs and came down again quickly with Winchester's cell phone in his hand.

'We've got to go,' he said.

Bloch rocked back onto her heels and stood.

'Are you hit?' she asked.

'No, I'm good. You?'

'I'm not hit. But I'm not good,' she said, and looked at the blood on her hands. It was almost black in the moonlight.

'He's right. Let's go. If they want to cover this up, they won't want to advertise that two possible perps escaped. Right now, it looks like Winchester took out his attackers.'

'My slugs don't match his gun.'

'Landry will know we were here. If he comes after us, we'll deal with him. But right now let's not get caught at a multiple homicide scene in his jurisdiction.'

'Check the bodies,' said Bloch.

Lake went into the kitchen, Bloch turned over the man in the hallway: no wallet, no ID. No cash. She pulled down his black sweater from the neck, checked his shoulders.

A tattoo of an inverted dagger surrounded by a laurel wreath. She snapped a picture on her phone. No point taking a photo of this guy's face. He no longer had one.

'Check their arms for tattoos,' she said.

She checked the two bodies on the front porch. No IDs, and one of them had a tattoo on his right forearm of what looked like multiple stars from a compass laid on top of each other. She took a pic of this and their faces. These guys had MP5s, small military submachine guns. Bloch made her way to the Land Rovers, checked the glovebox. There was a single file in there, and in the trunk an extra bag of magazines for the MP5s, and nothing else.

She took the file, and together they left the same way they had come, through the field at the rear of Winchester's property to Bloch's Jeep. She used what was left of her water bottle to wash her hands, and within ten minutes they'd found the highway and were pointed in the direction of Manhattan.

'Did the guy in the kitchen have any tattoos?' asked Bloch.

'None. How come you asked me to look?'

'The way they moved. They were ex-military. Take a look,' she said, and handed him her phone.

Lake examined the tattoos, took out his phone and began searching.

'The inverted combat knife in the laurel wreath is a pretty generic special forces tattoo, but this one, the compass rose, this is more specific. Wait, here we go – it's South African Special Forces.'

'Dekker is South African. He was US military, but I'd bet in his merc days he made plenty of connections with his home military special forces,' said Bloch.

Lake said, 'Mind if I look in the file?'

Bloch nodded and he took it from the back seat.

There were only a few pages.

The first was an old photo of Paul Winchester, ten years and twenty pounds ago. It listed his current age and address and had a list of his weapon permits. The other two pages, Lake didn't need to read too carefully.

'It's us,' he said.

'We're targets too?'

'Maybe,' said Lake, 'or maybe we're just persons of interest. One thing is clear. Paul Winchester died because we went to see him and Captain Landry was responsible. He tipped off Dekker, or his boss, but Dekker is the one who arranged the hit team. He probably served with at least one of those men back there. At some point I should probably kill Dekker. Just to be on the safe side.'

'I don't think you should do that,' said Bloch.

'How come?'

She glanced at her hands on the steering wheel, dark ridges of dried blood still visible in the fine creases of her skin.

'Because *I* want to kill him,' said Bloch.

32

Eddie

'Flynn!'

My eyes opened and a wave of pain shot up my spine and into my neck. My suit jacket was a poor pillow and the wooden bench in the holding cell wasn't doing my back any favors.

I dropped my legs to the floor and sat up, rubbing my neck. I hadn't slept much. Maybe an hour or two. They'd brought in a tweaker at some point during the night and he bounced off the walls for another hour, screaming and crying and telling everyone else in the cell that there was a giant cockroach in his apartment who was eating all his breakfast cereal and hadn't been paying rent. The other four guys in the cell were regulars. Even the gangster, who could have put the one-hundred-and-ten-pound tweaker in his shoe, knew there was no way to threaten the guy to get him to shut up. And beating the crap out of him would only make things worse. Only thing to do was sit quietly and wait for the meth in his system to dissipate.

'Flynn! You want to stay here or what?'

The cop standing at the door to the holding cell had one hand on his equipment belt, his palm resting on his can of pepper spray, just in case anyone wanted to make a run for it when he opened the cage for me.

I stood and stretched my back. Grabbed my jacket and turned to my cell mates.

'Darius, hope that thing works out with your sister,' I said. 'Andy, if your lawyer can't figure out a way to plead your case down to one charge, call me. All the best to you guys. Stay lucky.'

'Bye, Eddie,' said Darius and Andy, and the rest of them waved or wished me well, apart from the tweaker, who was now sleeping softly underneath the bench in the corner.

I approached the door. The cop unlocked it and let me out.

'Thanks for your hospitality,' I said.

'You're welcome. Sounds like you had fun in there, Flynn.'

I stepped out, heard the door slam closed behind me.

'I had good company, but the bed was terrible and the room service sucks. Don't expect a five-star rating on Tripadvisor.'

I followed him down the hallway, through detention clearing to the desk sergeant. There, on what looked like a much more comfortable bench, sat Harry. He stood when he saw me coming, but there was no greeting.

'Released with no charges. Sign here, Eddie,' said the desk sergeant, who handed me a plastic bag with my tie, shoelaces, money roll, phone, watch and my father's Saint Christopher medal on a silver neck chain. I thanked him, signed for my property and tossed him the pen.

'I don't want to hear it, Harry,' I said.

He held up his hands and said, 'We can do it in the car.'

I walked with him outside and across the street to his old, green convertible sports car. I hated it. I liked some British cars, but not even the Brits liked this thing. Even though it was cold, the sun was out and way too bright for my liking. Harry had the top down.

'Can we put the top up?' I asked.

'Mechanics in four different garages can't figure out how to fix the roof of this car. At least it's not raining. Besides, you look like shit and don't smell much better. The air will do us both good.'

'I don't need a lecture right now,' I said, lowering myself into the passenger seat, and wincing at the shooting pain in my back. I was going to pay for sleeping on a bench all night for at least a week or two.

'Too bad – you're getting a lecture,' said Harry as he got in, and tried and failed to start the engine. He pumped the gas, pulled the choke, then tried again and this time it eventually coughed to life. He reversed out of the parking space. After a couple of tries and a good deal of swearing, he managed to wrestle it into first gear and hit the gas.

'You'd get better results lecturing the clutch in this thing. Neither of us are listening.'

'You're lucky you're not on your way to central booking for aggravated assault, property damage and God knows what else. I think Julian Vanderpool and his head of security didn't want to file a complaint because then they would have to admit on record that a lawyer in a cheap suit blew through a whole security team with nothing more than a tire iron and charm. You're a lucky son of a bitch. You could have been going to jail. You could have lost your law license.'

'I'm beginning to think losing my law license might be in the best interests of my long-term health.'

'Joke all you want, but there are people who care about you.'

'How's Amy?' I asked.

'She's okay. She still hasn't seen a phone. Christine saw the articles, and Kevin and her are trying to get a court injunction to have the pictures taken down.'

'That's not going to work, but let them try. It'll keep them busy. If she's busy, she won't blame me for this.'

Harry took his eyes off the road long enough to give me a withering look.

'Is she that pissed?' I asked.

'She's livid. She knows this is fallout from one of your cases. She asked me if this had something to do with one of your clients and I pleaded the fifth, but Christine isn't stupid. She was talking to Kevin about going to court and getting an order restricting your access to Amy.'

'She what?'

'She won't do it. I persuaded her to think about it. Focus on Amy for a couple of days. When Christine calms down, she'll see things differently. I hope. But look, beating up a handful of Julian Vanderpool's security men just to threaten him isn't going to help Christine see sense. You've got to calm down. When are you going to realize you're a lawyer? You've got to leave that other life behind.'

'Doesn't matter if I'm a lawyer or a bricklayer. This is me.'

'This is why Kate . . . This is why she left,' he said.

I could tell by the hesitation that he didn't want to say it. But the bitterness in those words swam around the car for a while. My law partner had bailed because she was a good person, a straight shooter, who used the law to help our clients. But the law doesn't work. And I can't live with that. I'd been down that road and people got hurt.

When the law fails, I have no choice but to do things my way.

'Any word from Bloch and Lake?'

'Yep, they're waiting for us in the office. They had an eventful trip to East Hampton.'

'How eventful?'

'Possibly a major break in our case and five men are dead.'

I listened to Lake lay out what had happened yesterday in East Hampton, and all they'd learned from Captain Landry, and more importantly the late Detective Paul Winchester. The South African ex-special forces ops stank of Julian Vanderpool's right-hand goon, Dekker.

We sat in silence for a time.

'Can't we use this to help Vanessa? It's a hell of a coincidence – two decapitated victims both with relationships to Patrick

Vanderpool immediately before their deaths? That's a defense, right?' asked Lake.

'We can't use Patrick's confession to Vanessa,' said Harry. 'But if we can somehow prove Teresa Chase is the unidentified decapitated body that Winchester found then that is a defense. But we're risking one hell of a firestorm from Julian Vanderpool.'

'Looks like the fire has already started,' I said, gazing at my phone.

I passed it to Harry, then Bloch and Lake crowded round him to take a look.

Patrick Vanderpool had issued a statement. He was immediately filing for divorce from his wife due to her alleged involvement in the murder of one of his close political aides.

'We should talk to Vanessa,' said Harry.

I rubbed my forehead, then raised my arms above my head and stretched my aching back, forcing my spine to curve until I heard a satisfying click.

'I need some coffee,' I said.

Denise appeared with a mug in her hand. I took a drink. It was almost cold, but I didn't care. I needed the fuel.

'This case has two suspects. Our client and her now estranged husband. The police haven't looked at Patrick for a reason. And it's not just the security camera footage showing Vanessa as the last person to be in that apartment. The same thing that happened in East Hampton is happening right here. The cops are helping steer the investigation away from Patrick Vanderpool. Two women who were having a relationship with him end up dead and decapitated. That's beginning to look like a pattern. If we can prove it,' I said.

Bloch and Lake exchanged a look.

'Why were the bodies decapitated?' I asked.

Lake sat on a desk, said, 'There are various psychological factors involved in a deranged murder. Mutilation takes many forms. Decapitation, without other evidence of bodily mutilation, is uncommon.

Usually, we only see it in certain extreme religious or cultural murders from certain fundamentalist groups. But I don't think we're in that territory. I know that certain serial killers would carry out full dismemberment, so they could scatter the victims remains over a wide area. That's a dispassionate tactic, designed to help the killer elude detection. The Route 66 Taskforce is dealing with that right now. They might find an arm in one state, and a torso in another. It makes investigation incredibly difficult.'

'But it's just the head that's missing,' said Harry. 'That doesn't . . . Wait . . .'

'It does make sense,' I said.

Bloch, who had been sitting in an armchair, listening intently, stood up, a bright look in her eyes.

'It makes establishing cause of death near impossible,' said Bloch.

'What do you mean?' asked Lake.

Bloch, Harry and I were tugging at a theory, but Lake wasn't quite there yet.

'In a criminal case,' I said, 'the prosecutor has to prove all of the factual elements of a crime. Think about it. They need to prove how someone died. If these women died from head injuries, then removing the head completely robs the prosecutor of being able to prove the cause of death. They don't have the skull and the brain to examine. They don't know if the victim was strangled, pummeled with a hammer or a rock, or a knife, or even shot. All they know is the victim's head was removed postmortem. It means that even if the cops did find a murder weapon they wouldn't be able to prove it was used to kill the victim.'

'That's really smart, and ice cold,' said Lake. 'It also gives us a major problem. Even if we can conjure a miracle to prove that Jane Doe is Teresa Chase, we can't prove she was killed the same way, or by the same person as Molly Green.'

I said, 'Not right now, but the decapitation is enough to link Patrick if we can prove the body is Teresa Chase. We've a short window before Vanessa's trial. Julian is still going to pull every big lever he's got to get this trial on quickly. He wants it over and done with to put time between the verdict and the election. He wants his son in power and nothing is going to stop him.'

'How are we going to prove any of this?' asked Bloch.

'Didn't you say Teresa Chase had a half-sister?' I said.

'Willow Chase, but that's a dead end. Winchester looked for her for years,' said Bloch. 'She was a junkie who moved away and dropped out of the world long before Teresa was murdered. Chances are she's dead too.'

I said, 'If she was a serious junkie, there's every chance she was arrested. That means there might be a DNA profile for her somewhere. If she is dead, then we need to find her anyway. Maybe she had a husband, or a partner, someone who might consent to allow a DNA test.'

'That's a real moonshot,' said Lake.

'Then get your rocket fueled,' I said. 'Harry, can you go talk to Vanessa?'

'Sure. Where are you going?'

'Those pictures of Amy are still online. I have to make a call,' I said, putting on my coat.

'Who are you going to call?' he asked as I headed for the door.

I stood at the doorway, everyone's eyes on me, waiting for an answer.

I shook my head, opened the door and made my way down the steps to the street.

Once outside, inhaling the cold Manhattan air, I huddled into my coat and started walking. I didn't have a burner phone, and I preferred my call to this number wasn't located in a cell tower near my office. Protection for the team, not for me.

There was no going back now. I was in this with both feet. All I could hope for was that I was the only one who got burned.

It was five blocks before I found a payphone. I used quarters for the call.

The phone rang three times before it was picked up. I said hi.

'Eddie Fly, how you doin, Flyman?'

I had known the man who answered my call for over thirty years. At one time, we were like brothers. In many ways, we still were. We helped each other when we could. He was someone I could always rely on to do the wrong thing at the right time.

His name was Jimmy the Hat.

'Not so good, Jimmy. I need some help.'

'Money or muscle?'

'Something a lot worse.'

I'd guessed it would take a day. Maybe a day and a half.

But in less than eight hours I found myself driving to a nice suburban neighborhood in Queens. Jimmy used to say that he was in the problem-solving business. It's a much more polite moniker than saying you run the major Italian crime family in New York, but in a way problem-solving wasn't a bad description, even if some of the problems he solved were very much of his own making.

When family was involved, problems tended to get solved quicker.

Still, eight hours was pretty fast.

It was dark when I pulled into the driveway. I hadn't been out here in a few years, and in some ways I was glad to see the place. The lawn was neat and well kept, as always. The house must have had a fresh coat of paint not too long ago. A Cadillac with purple and silver-flecked paint took up the entire driveway. Compared to my Mustang, the Caddy looked like an aircraft carrier. The homeowner's Dodge Ram was on the street, outside the house. I guessed his van was in the garage.

I pressed the door buzzer, and as I waited I thought about the events that would've taken place in the last eight hours.

I guessed that the identity of the photographer wouldn't have taken long to establish. The hotel where Amy had attended the party wasn't part of a major chain and only a few years old. There's a lot of carefully curated and managed bureaucracy to navigate before you can open a hotel in Manhattan. There are dozens of permits required, fire safety regulation standards to be met, hospitality and food safety certificates to obtain, then there's the unions whose staff will provide the beating heart of the hotel.

That's a lot of red tape to get tangled in. Happily, or unhappily, depending on your point of view, for a fee and a modest ongoing monthly percentage, all of these potential pitfalls with unions and city departments can be navigated swiftly and smoothly. It's not cheap because there are a lot of union leaders and city officials who have to be given a lot of brown envelopes, but it can mean the difference between opening and running a hotel and not opening or running a hotel.

If you wanted things done in Manhattan, you paid Jimmy the Hat.

I imagined the purple Caddy and the black van in the garage had paid a visit to the hotel, and the occupants of the vehicles entered the security suite and viewed security camera footage where they identified a certain newly employed bartender, who was really a paparazzi working an angle. That bartender's name, address, social security and phone number would have been swiftly provided to the gentleman in the purple Caddy and his tall, quiet companion in the black panel van.

Then it would only have been the small matter of identifying the real-time location of this bartender, and inviting him into the quiet gentleman's van for a ride here, to his home.

Tony Two Fucks opened the front door. It was difficult to tell, at first. A solid reinforced barrier of a door had been opened to reveal an equally impenetrable barrier of flesh.

'Eddie Fly, ya fuck! How the fuck you doin'?' said Tony.

Some people ask why Tony is called Tony Two Fucks – that is, until they hear him speak.

'I'm okay, Tony. Denise said she's keeping a lasagna warm in the oven for you.'

'Fucking A, I love Denise's lasagna. I think she's half Italian, you know? She denies it, but I'm pretty sure. Come on through, we're out back.'

My secretary and Tony were dating, and as a result even a reminder of Denise tended to help Tony moderate his cussing. Denise didn't mind it, but she worried about what her mother thought of Tony's language and had been training him to broaden his vocabulary. As a result, he was rapidly becoming Tony One Fuck, which was about the best that could be hoped for. Tony No Fucks wasn't on anybody's bingo card.

The custom license plate on his Caddy read TNY 2FCKS.

He might need to get that changed.

He led me through the house and out the back door to a spacious yard with a separate one-story purpose-built building about the size of three shipping containers laid side by side. It had its own central-heating system to include state-of-the-art temperature controls. Soon as I walked in, I felt the high humidity and the heat. It was really hot in here. It had to be.

For the pets.

The interior was divided into two spaces by a thick wall of triple-glazed glass. It was dark on the other side of the glass, but I could make out a bed of straw on the floor over there. The space I stood in was clean and set up like a workshop. Tools hung on the walls, along with an assortment of handguns, shotguns and assault weapons. A large worktable sat in the middle of the room with a vice at each end. But this wasn't a conventional worktable. First, it was solid steel, and it had a series of purpose-built holes drilled through the center, for drainage.

The paparazzi photographer who had drugged Amy lay naked on the table, held down by thick leather straps on his wrists, thighs, waist and ankles.

On the other side of the table, wearing a leather apron over his bare chest, was the Lizard. His moniker hadn't been given to him. He had insisted on that name and it wasn't solely because of the large reptile tattoos he had on his arms and legs.

'Eddie, the Lizard is glad to see you,' said the Lizard.

He often referred to himself in the third person, which creeped me out, along with most other people he knew, but strangely nobody thought to mention it to him. Certainly not in moments like this, when he held up the twelve-inch filleting knife to the LED lamp hung over the table, and inspected the edge of the blade.

The paparazzi didn't say anything, which was understandable considering there was a ball gag strapped over his mouth, but I heard a high-pitched whine escape from behind the gag when he saw the Lizard holding that knife.

'What's his name?' I asked.

'He's called Cory Hill,' said Tony. 'Freelance. I had a look at some of the pictures in his home studio. Likes to take photos of female celebrities in short dresses when they're getting out of cars. Fuckin' perv.'

Tony handed me Cory's phone.

I approached him and he was able to angle his head just enough to see my face. His eyes bulged in fear, his chest rising and falling rapidly, fighting for breath, sweat soaking his body, panic making his frame shake so hard he was practically vibrating with fear. I reached behind his head, unlatched the restraint and took off the gag.

'Please, I'm sorry. Let me go . . . I swear to God, I'm sorry . . . Help! Help!'

I stared at him, and said, 'You can scream all you want, but this room is soundproof. What happens next is up to you, Cory. Is this your phone?'

He nodded.

I held the phone up to his face and it unlocked. I opened the tab for emails and started scrolling.

'You sent photos of me and my daughter to an editor at the *Manhattan Star* and the *Daily Post*. The trolls have picked up this article and run with it. How much did you get paid? Oh, twenty-five thousand? Not bad. Here's what's going to happen now. I'm going to email this guy from your phone and tell him that the twenty-five grand will be refunded. You're coming clean, Cory. You're going to say those photos are not real and were made with AI. The editor will take them down straight away. Does that sound okay to you?'

'But . . . but . . . the pictures were real,' he said. 'I'll . . . I'll be blacklisted. I won't be able to sell a picture anywhere after that. Please, I'll split the money with you—'

'I don't think you understand the full picture here,' I said. 'No pun intended.'

I gestured to the security glass. The Lizard stepped forward and knocked it.

Cory's gaze flitted from the glassed enclosure, to me, then Tony, then the Lizard.

'What? What's going on? Wha— Jesus fuckin' Christ, fuck! What the fuck are those things?'

'You shouldn't fuckin' swear so much,' said Tony Two Fucks.

Out of the gloom, just visible in the low-level LED lighting, two huge reptiles moved toward the glass. The largest one came right up to the Lizard, looked at him and a long black forked tongue licked the glass.

'Good boy, Ernie,' said the Lizard.

'This is Ernie,' I said. 'The smaller one is Bert. They're Komodo dragons. And they're hungry. My friend here works in disposal. In a digital world, it's increasingly difficult to make a body disappear. Bert and Ernie solve that problem. They can rip through two hundred pounds of flesh and bone in no time.'

'They don't like the teeth, though,' said the Lizard. 'Teeth don't digest. They show up as little pearls in their turds. It's easier on them if we take your teeth out when we chop up your body.'

'W-what?' said Cory.

'I think your career as a photographer is over, one way or another,' I said as I typed out the email to the editor on Cory's phone. It didn't take long. I let him stew in his panic. He watched as the Lizard laid out his tools on a leather cloth – a pair of pliers, his filleting knife and a bone saw.

'So what will it be?' I asked. 'I can send this email, and you send back your fee for the photographs and play along nicely. Or I send the email, and you just disappear.'

'Wait! Let's talk! I can get them to take the pictures down, but I can't say I doctored the images. There's got to be another way.'

'He's not getting it,' said the Lizard. 'Maybe he'll understand better when I've cut his foot off.'

He picked up the filleting knife.

'No!' screamed Cory.

'You drugged his daughter,' said Tony. 'If it was up to me, I'd cut off your fuckin' hands and feet.'

'I'll do it! I'll do it!'

I hit send on the email, used his face to log into his banking app and found the payment for the pictures. Wired it back to the sender. Christine had already sent an email threatening to get an injunction to have the articles removed. Now, with written confirmation from the photographer that the picture was fake, it would come down fast.

'We know where to find you, so make sure you don't change your mind,' I said.

'Anything you want. Just let me go.'

'Let him loose,' I said.

Tony and the Lizard removed the straps and Cory, still trembling, sat up on the table.

'Thank you, I swear I'll play along. Just let me go and I swe—'

He didn't see the Lizard throwing a right cross – it was too fast – but I saw the flash of his fist and Cory's head rocking and then it hit the back of the table.

'If it was the Lizard's kid I wouldn't chop him up,' said the Lizard. 'Just give him a small cut and throw him in there with Bert and Ernie, then grab some popcorn.'

'I thought about it too,' I said.

'It's a mistake, letting this prick live,' said Tony.

'We've got nothing to worry about,' I said. 'He doesn't know where he is, and I guess you're going to leave him unconscious on a street corner somewhere, so he can't lead the cops here. He knows our names, but he won't go to the authorities. He's got no proof of anything other than a couple of bruises and a couple of loose front teeth. Besides, he doesn't want the cops asking the hotel questions about one of their guests being roofied. He's not connected to any criminal enterprise, and he's scared shitless. We'll be okay. Thank you both for what you've done. I'll thank Jimmy personally next time I see him.'

'You okay, Eddie?' asked the Lizard.

'Not really, but what's new.'

'If you need anything, call the Lizard,' said the Lizard.

'I'll bear that in mind. Give Bert and Ernie an extra pork chop tonight.'

'You want to come back to the apartment for lasagna?' asked Tony.

'No, thanks,' I said, looking at the dragons. They eyed Cory hungrily as he lay unconscious on the table. 'I lost my appetite.'

I didn't tell Tony that Denise had brought me one of her lasagnas for lunch just after she started at the firm. While it was a nice thought, Denise wasn't much of a cook. The lasagna didn't really work as food, but I remember thinking at the time that it would make great loft insulation.

Denise loved Tony, and so she loved cooking lasagna for him.

Tony loved Denise, and he loved eating her lasagna.

And that made me happy.

I left the Lizard's house, fired up the Mustang and dialed Christine's number on speaker as I headed back into Manhattan.

The call went to voicemail. She wasn't talking to me.

'Christine, the picture and the article will be taken down within the hour. The rest of the videos linking to it will all be deleted within a day or two. I took care of it . . .'

Hesitating, I tried to decide what else I should say. What kind of apology could I make that I hadn't made before, a thousand times over.

'I'm sorry,' I said. 'I love her so much. I love you too. You know that. I just . . . I don't ever want anything bad to happen to anyone because of me. You were right to move on. You were right to get me out of your lives. If you want, I'll stay away. For as long as you think it's right. You don't need to go to court. I won't fight you. I just want you both to be safe. I hope Amy is okay. I hope you're okay. Give my best to Kevin. He's a good guy. And he'll be a better father to Amy than I ever could.'

I hung up, stared at the road ahead.

As I went over the Queensboro Bridge, the lights from the city blurred and swam.

I blinked the tears out of my eyes, wiped my face.

Sometimes driving is strange. I didn't have a particular place I needed to be, and no destination in mind, but somehow my hands turned the wheel and I found myself headed downtown, and then toward Chelsea.

By the time I pulled up at the curb outside a Korean noodle shop, the rain was beating the hood of the Mustang. I got out of the car and hustled into the noodle bar. It only took a matter of seconds, but I still had to stand on the entrance mat and brush rivers of rainwater off my coat. I ordered a bowl of the chicken ramen and a diet soda, then took a stool at the counter facing the window. The food didn't take long. I leaned over the bowl, letting the heat from the broth warm my face, but I still felt my wet shirt clinging to my back. I would dry up soon. I wasn't bothered by it. The cold reminded me I was alive.

As I ate, I glanced up at the apartment building facing the noodle shop.

Third floor. Seventh window from the right.

A lamp in that apartment cast a warm glow on the ceiling. The rubber plant that sat on the window ledge of that apartment had grown since I'd last been here. People who aren't doing so well tend to forget the little things. I took the relative health and prosperity of the rubber plant as a reflection of the wellbeing of its owner.

I ate my noodles, used the big wooden soup spoon for the broth and then popped the tab on my diet Pepsi. The broth was salty, but I liked it that way. I always ordered the same thing here.

Sat in the same place.

Stared at the same window.

Then something happened that I didn't expect.

A young woman in a long brown overcoat left the building. The rain had eased a little, but she waited by the entrance for a few seconds until a tall young man in a black overcoat came out and opened a wide umbrella. She linked arms with him and smiled. He smiled back.

The last time I'd seen the young woman she was standing outside her little run-down rental home in the Bronx, some years ago. She was staring at a large leather bag I'd left on the front step, with a white envelope on top of it.

The envelope had her name on it.

Hanna Tublowski.

I'd watched her read it, then stare at the leather bag, then look around for who might have left it. That's when I'd hit the gas on my old Mustang and drove away before she could see me.

I had once represented a man accused of attempting to kidnap her. I'd gotten him off, even though I'd realized at the end of the trial that this man was guilty. The jury acquitted him, and the first thing he did was go after Hanna again. I stopped him before he killed her, found her bound and badly wounded in his house. Before the cops showed up, I had broken my hands on the guy's skull, but it didn't stop me from beating on him, driving my busted hands and elbows into his ruined face until I almost passed out. He survived, and my legal career very nearly didn't. Harry had saved me. At that time of my life, I didn't want saving. I'd let that young woman down. I hadn't listened to my instincts, but more importantly I hadn't listened to someone who really was a victim. And they had been hurt, badly, because of me.

I carry a lot of scars. Bullet and knife wounds mostly.

None have cut so deep as finding Hanna Tublowski in that house, knowing I had helped that monster to escape the justice he deserved. I'd called the cops and paramedics as soon as I'd found her, and this time he couldn't escape the law. He went to prison for a long time. He's still there, and he still has to eat all his meals through a straw. But that is no comfort to me.

The bag I'd left Hanna all those years ago had three quarters of a million dollars inside: money I'd swindled from the Russian mob. I wasn't seeking forgiveness. There was none. I wanted her to have something to use to build a new life.

From time to time, I checked in on her, here, at her new apartment. I sat in this noodle shop across the street, ate hot ramen and kept an eye on her. She had gone to college, and now had a good job in an architectural design firm. I remember, a couple of years ago, smiling when I first saw that rubber plant in her window.

Now, she had a partner.

Together, they stopped at the side of the curb and checked the traffic, then crossed the street, right in front of the noodle shop. I lowered my head, stared at my broth. When I looked up again, they were walking past the window. Hanna was laughing.

I never approached her. Never spoke to her. I just needed to know she was doing okay, that I hadn't completely ruined her life.

And to remind myself that I had made a mistake. And that I would never make that mistake again. I would only take cases where I believed my client was innocent, and I would fight for them with everything I had. No matter what. No matter how dangerous it was for me, personally.

That's why I no longer had a wife, or a daughter in my life.

I was still paying my debt to the young woman who had almost died because of me.

That was a debt I would take to my grave.

I pushed the bowl away, finished my soda.

I was making the same kind of mistake with Vanessa. I thought of the scars on her arms from old burns. The violence I witnessed toward her, from Patrick. It didn't matter that Vanessa had lied to me. I had to trust my gut. My instinct. I had ignored it before, and that had almost killed Hanna.

I wouldn't ignore it again.

I had to trust my heart.

Pulling out my cell phone, I dialed Bloch's number.

'Our number one priority is to prove the Jane Doe in Winchester is Teresa Chase. I have no idea how we do it, but there's got to be a way. That's Vanessa's only shot. And watch out for Dekker. He's the connection between Julian, Patrick and the murders. They know you two spoke to Winchester. They know I'm coming after Patrick. They're going to make a move and we need to be ready.'

'Lake should stay with you and Harry,' she said.

'I need both of you on this investigation.'

'Who is going to watch your back? The Vanderpools already sent a hit team to kill Winchester and this thing is only escalating. You might be next.'

'Harry's got his old service weapon for protection.'

'And what have you got for protection?' asked Bloch.

'All I need is an envelope, a box of donuts, a remote mic, a phone and a cigarette lighter.'

She said nothing for a moment, no doubt wondering what the hell I planned to do with this disparate collection of items.

'Never underestimate the power of self-preservation,' I said. 'I think you and Lake should take another look at Molly's apartment. That scene doesn't make any goddamn sense. It's been bothering you. I can sense it.'

'It's not just that it's clean,' said Bloch. 'It's been sanitized. And yet they supposedly left behind a jewelry box with both the victim's and Vanessa's blood on it?'

'That's part of our defense, but we need more,' I said. 'How well can you clean up a murder scene without leaving something behind?'

'We could go back, but we would need more time,' said Bloch.

'I'll get a court order if I have to. Just be ready. Bring your forensics guy, Raymond.'

'What are we going to find that we didn't already see?' asked Bloch.

'The picture, the water lilies print. You said it was out of place. Start there.'

'It's just a picture that doesn't match the rest of the décor. So what if it has been cleaned?'

'It bothers you.'

'Yeah, it does.'

'Then go find out why.'

TRIAL

33
Eddie

A murder trial is not about truth.

It's about who tells the best story. Is it the defense? Or the prosecution? Who has presented the most likely and probable version of events to the jury? Even if the prosecution has told a good story, have they proven their case beyond all reasonable doubt?

Where is the truth in any of this?

I used to say the truth has no place in a courtroom. I'm not sure about that any more. In this world, right now, the truth has become more ethereal. More pliable. America is divided. The world is divided. Each side has their own truth. Their own facts.

What happens to the world when nobody pays attention to the truth?

The answer is simple.

It's war.

That's what a trial really is. A battle.

And we all had exactly the same method of warfare – questions.

Normally, a question seeks truth. But not in a murder trial. Here, a question is a weapon, a trap, a shield and a sword. Questions can alter perception, confuse, change facts, manipulate memory and even alter time. I had a lot of questions to ask in this trial. For the past two months I had been sharpening them in my mind like finely edged blades.

Glancing over at the prosecution table, I saw the assistant district attorney in charge of this trial, Kurt Riley, scribbling notes on a legal pad. No doubt he had a few daggers to throw my way.

Despite his youth, he was a talent. Not only did he have a natural gift, but he worked at it too. He was the first person in the office and the last to leave. He didn't drink, didn't smoke and didn't socialize with anyone in the workplace. His focus was on his cases, and his healthy lifestyle regime. His suit was too tight, after the fashion of young men in their late twenties who spent too much time in the gym listening to podcasts on creatine dosing. He was an angular man, from his jaw and cheekbones to his triceps and quads, all of it accentuated by the ill-fitting suit, the jacket button straining to stay closed over his wide chest. I'd done my research on my opponent. He was a rising star in the DA's office, a graduate of Brown University, but despite his excellent grades he had no real connections in the legal world. He needed to make a name for himself, and the DA's office often provided a platform for talented trial lawyers to make the jump into private practice.

As much as Riley wanted to win this trial for his ego, and his boss, the DA, there was no getting away from the fact that the trial presented him with an opportunity. He would use the high-profile murder of Molly Green as an audition.

He rose from behind the prosecution table, walked solemnly to the center of the courtroom and stood in front of the jury. His voice was deep and authoritative.

'Members of the jury, you have a decision to make at the end of this trial. It's not going to be a difficult one. The defendant, Vanessa Vanderpool, murdered Molly Green. We will prove this to you. For now, just take a moment to look at the defendant . . .'

The five men and seven women on the jury turned to look at my client. I'd already told her what to do in case she saw the jury looking at her. She should stare right back. Standard instructions to defendants. Only the guilty hide their eyes from those who would judge them.

Vanessa had dressed in a navy business suit and white blouse, her blonde hair tied back, with little make-up, tasteful jewelry. But there was no hiding it. Even a casual glance told you this was a woman of wealth and privilege.

'Right now, Vanessa Vanderpool has everything. Not only is she rich, but she has power. And it's that power which corrupted her. People with power don't give it up too easily. That power flowed from her husband, the respected politician, Patrick Vanderpool. The defendant was jealous of her husband's beautiful new personal assistant, Molly Green. This jealousy festered into paranoia. The defendant convinced herself that Molly was trying to seduce her husband. If that happened, she could lose everything. She became convinced she had to protect herself. Her wealth. Her marriage. On the night of February seventeenth, she went to Molly's apartment, and confronted her . . .'

Riley pointed to a large screen facing the jury.

An image appeared. His assistants had put it up there from the laptop linked to the screen. A woman in her mid-twenties, with curly dark hair, a warm vanilla skin tone and a beautiful smile stared at the jury members.

'This is Molly Green. Her youth and beauty were destroyed that night. The defendant fought with Molly in her apartment. But this wasn't an argument that got out of control. Vanessa Vanderpool visited the victim's apartment that night with one intention – murder. The defendant's DNA was left behind on a jewelry box in that apartment. That same jewelry box also had the victim's blood on it. We will call a DNA expert and a forensic crime scene expert to prove that it was the defendant who took the victim's life in this savage attack, using this box as a weapon. And then, in her rage and jealousy, she mutilated the victim's body. It is our case that the defendant struck the victim with that jewelry box, crushing her skull. To hide her crime, the defendant decapitated the victim. This is shocking, I know, for all of us. Yet it shows the premeditation and planning of this murder. You might look at the defendant, and think she is not capable of such a terrible act. Don't be fooled. Follow the evidence. We will not only prove that this happened, but we will show you security camera footage of the defendant leaving the victim's apartment building with a gym bag in her hands. And we all know what is in that bag, ladies and gentlemen. The footage will show you Vanessa Vanderpool trying to hide her terrible crime by disposing of the victim's head. Don't let her get away with this murder. Listen carefully to all of the evidence. We will prove to you beyond a reasonable doubt that Vanessa Vanderpool is a cold-blooded killer. And you, ladies and gentlemen, will give justice to Molly Green by finding the defendant guilty.'

He paused, turned to the screen, looked at the picture of the victim.

The jury followed his gaze.

Without another word, Riley strode back to the prosecution table and sat down, leaving the jury to drink in that image of young Molly Green. A picture of youth, vitality and all the possibilities of life. No one could look at that woman and not feel the sadness and tragedy of a life cut short.

I saw that sadness on the jurors' faces. Some of them let their compassionate looks wander from the image of Molly, down to Vanessa, and their expression hardened as they gazed on the defendant.

Young prosecutors play this trick often. It's compensation for inexperience. You see, there's lots of things they can't teach you in law school, and you don't learn it running trials, not right away. It takes time. In the early years of an attorney's life, they focus on the evidence, the testimony, cold, hard facts.

What they don't know how to do is win the jury's hearts.

A verdict in a murder trial is supposed to be a neutral, unbiased assessment of the evidence and nothing else.

That's how the law works.

But that's not how people work.

Ordinary people have great analytical minds. But most of us make decisions with our emotions, not our brains. That's what young DAs haven't learned yet.

We do it every day, in every single decision. The COO of Ford, Kumar Galhotra, once said that building a car involves making a hundred thousand rational decisions, with the sole purpose of persuading a buyer to make a single emotional one.

Riley's rational approach was on point. I couldn't fault it.

His blades were razor sharp.

He'd drawn first blood.

Judge Elizabeth Tanner, a relatively new judge in her late fifties, slid her eyeglasses to the end of her nose as she stared at me. Like all judges, she was appointed by politicians. There were rumors floating around that Judge Tanner had granted a lot of favors in order to get this appointment. That didn't bode well. I had resolved to keep a close eye on her.

It was my turn now.

Defense opening statement.

I knew what I had to do. I'd done this a thousand times.

I stood up, left the defense table and made my way to the center of the courtroom and stood before the jury. I took up the same position Riley had. It was a psychological trick. If I stood exactly where he'd stood, and then gave another side to the story, this would have more impact. The jurors' minds would register it more deeply as a true alternative version of events. It was like holding up a mirror and reversing an image.

I felt the pressure building in my head.

Turning, I scanned the faces watching me from the gallery. Harry sat beside Vanessa at the defense table, his eyes locked on me.

Behind him, on the end of the second row of the public seating, Voss sat with a pen in her hand and a legal pad on her knee. Vanessa had fired her, as I'd asked, so there was no reason for her to be here. Buchanan and Duff were acting for Patrick in the divorce. It was still early days in that process, and we were leveraging the divorce case to help with the defense. Bloch had a mission today, doing some work for the divorce case, which wouldn't help the divorce at all, but might help us in this courtroom.

I didn't do divorce cases, as a rule. It was much dirtier than crime and more complicated – two people who had at one time wished to spend the rest of their lives together, and now they hated each other and wanted to rip their former partner's guts out. And those were the uncomplicated cases.

In this divorce, there was money. Shit tons of it. And Buchanan and Duff had taken all the kinds of precautions that come with protecting the Vanderpools, including a prenuptial agreement with an iron-clad sunset clause. Sunset clauses are legal markers that reflect the evolving rights of spouses as the marriage continues, and protections for Patrick. In this case, the prenup stated that Vanessa had basically no martial rights until the marriage was two years old.

She had cleared that bar, but there was still an almighty battle ahead.

Her divorce case didn't matter right now. If she was convicted, she would get nothing. This trial was way more important.

The courthouse was packed with journalists and politicos. This case was going to cause ripples for Patrick's election hopes, no matter what. The only question was, would it be a small undulation on the surface, or a tidal wave that would bury his political ambitions in the stain of sex and murder?

I had my hopes.

I let my eyelids fall closed.

Took a breath.

I thought of Hanna Tublowski sitting on the window ledge of her apartment, happily watering her rubber plant.

I opened my eyes.

Opened my mouth.

Gave the jury my full attention.

And spoke . . .

'Members of the jury, have no doubt, this case is unlike any other to have come before this court. The decision you give at the end of this trial will be the most important of your life, because my client's life hangs in the balance. It doesn't matter that she has nice clothes, money in the bank or that she has what some of us call privilege. She's entitled to be treated just like any other citizen. But – let's be clear – she is not any other citizen. My client in this case has suffered a great injustice. The police have targeted her for this murder. They have not looked at other viable suspects, and instead of investigating what really happened to Molly Green on the night of February seventeenth, they have sought only to make sure my client is convicted of Molly Green's murder. Take a look at the victim again . . .'

I had not changed the screen, deliberately. I'd left Molly's smiling, vibrant, youthful face on full display for the jury, so I could hold up a mirror to Riley's case.

Reframe the story.

Take the DA's strongest case and throw it back in his face.

'That young woman deserves justice. This is what our city and our justice system demands. Mr. Riley doesn't want you to see the truth. He wants Vanessa Vanderpool convicted. He wants to protect the powerful people that surround this young woman's life, and her death. This is your oath as a juror – you will faithfully try the defendant and render a true and honest verdict according to the evidence. I would ask you to be mindful of that oath. Our society is built upon it. It is a light that will guide you through the trial. You carry that lit torch with you today, and every day for the duration of this trial. Follow that light, and above all follow your hearts. By the end of this case you will know, in your very soul, who really murdered Molly Green. And it's not the young woman at the defense table.'

I took a moment and looked over the jury. The seven women and five men stared at Molly Green's image once again. This time, I saw something different in their eyes. There was sadness for Molly. Some of them sat up straight, or blinked, and then looked at Molly's face again.

This time, none of them looked at the defendant with anything approaching anger or disdain.

My strategy was to hold up a mirror to the prosecutor's case, and let the jury see that the reflection in there was not what Riley wanted them to see. The mirror really showed someone else. The real killer.

So far, I'd built a little frame for that mirror. The surface was dusty and distorted. Throughout the case, I had to sharpen the image. Bring it into focus.

And away from Vanessa.

I sat down next to her, and put a hand on her wrist, patted it. She whispered to me . . .

'Thank you for that . . .'

I kept my voice low, said, 'Don't thank me yet. We've got a long way to go. And things will get worse before they get better.'

'Your Honor,' said Riley, 'the People call their first witness, Alison Karim.'

Here we go.

34
Eddie

As Alison Karim took her oath to tell the truth, the whole truth, and nothing but the truth, I sat quietly wondering if she would lie.

She finished the oath, and sat down. Judge Tanner, her silver hair expertly blow-dried in a salon most mornings, gave the witness a welcoming smile.

I'd never appeared before Judge Tanner before. I didn't know her mind. I did know that she'd been a lawyer for some of the most corrupt companies on the planet, and protected them from the law for decades.

I wondered if she had left that mindset behind.

Judges don't normally smile at witnesses, but in this case Judge Tanner had read the case file and knew Alison Karim was what lawyers call an independent witness. She was just an ordinary member of the public whose everyday life had brought them into contact with a crime. While she clearly knew the victim, they were no more than acquaintances who occasionally passed each other in the hallway. More importantly, she had no connection with the defendant, so whatever testimony she gave would come with a lot of weight.

In other words, nobody was going to be gunning for Alison Karim.

Judge Tanner could welcome her with all the benevolence of her office. This was a witness who would tell the truth.

If things played out the way I'd anticipated, it wouldn't be the first time I'd seen a judge have their preconceptions blown out of the water.

'Miss Karim, what is your age, occupation and address?' asked Riley.

'I'm fifty-nine, I live in the Duraplex building, apartment twenty-seven, and I work from home as a customer-service assistant.'

'How long have you lived at that address?'

'Eleven years, now.'

'Did you know the occupant of apartment twenty-six?'

'Yes, my neighbor – well, she was a neighbor for a while, Molly. Molly Green.'

'How long did she live there?'

'Oh, not long. Maybe four or five months at the most.'

'How well did you know her?'

'Not well, not really. I remember her moving in and I think I helped her with a few boxes of books in the hallway. I'd heard noise, I opened my door and saw her struggling with all her bags and boxes. She was real nice, asked if I wanted water or anything. Yeah, very polite.'

Assistant district attorney Riley knew his way around a witness. His first questions were short, with short answers coming back. He asked them quickly, building up a rhythm, allowing the witness to get used to hearing their voice in court. The equivalent of a warm-up at the gym. Getting the blood flowing.

'Did you know what her job was?' he asked.

Now he was going to start lifting some weight.

'She worked in politics, I believe.'

'How do you know that?'

'I met her in the elevator one morning. She was going to work and she was buttoning a pin, like a political pin, onto her jacket. I can't remember what it said, something about voting. Some slogan. We got talking and she said she was working for Patrick Vanderpool who was going to be running for governor next election.'

'Was that the extent of the conversation?'

I leaned forward. Riley had expected Alison Karim to give a fuller answer. She was leaving some important detail out of that answer and Riley was giving her another shot, even a mild prompt to get her to reveal it.

'No,' said Alison, 'I said I wasn't into politics. I'd always thought it was too complicated for me and asked if she liked her job. She said she loved it, but that like any workplace there are problems. She said she was getting a hard time from her boss's wife.'

Riley's head lowered to the binder on the prosecution table in front of him. He licked his thumb and turned a page. Pure theatre. He had a lot more confidence than I'd anticipated. He wasn't scanning the trial bundle for anything in particular. He was just wasting time. Letting the jury fill the silence in the room with that last answer from the witness. Allowing it time to cement in their consciousness.

The victim was getting a hard time from her boss's wife – the defendant. The jury would remember this.

'Miss Karim, let me turn now to the night of February seventeenth. Do you recall anything out of the ordinary that evening?' asked Riley.

'Why yes, I remember hearing raised voices. The walls in my apartment have pretty good sound insulation so I don't normally hear anyone else. Just lucky, I guess. But that night I heard an argument. It was pretty heated. At first, I wasn't sure where it was coming from. I thought maybe from the apartment upstairs, but then it seemed louder when I was close to the bathroom which is right near my front door. So I opened my front door, stepped out into the hallway. It was pretty clear it was coming from Molly's apartment.'

'Did you knock on the door and ask if everything was alright?'

'Not right then, not at first. People argue, you know. And it wasn't really bothering me. I thought I would just give her some privacy. It would be embarrassing for everyone, you know, if I'd knocked right then.'

'Do you recall what time this occurred?'

'It was pretty late. I'm not exactly sure. I had the TV on and the late news was on. That's all I remember.'

'You said you didn't knock at first. Was there then a time when you did knock on the door?'

'Yes, like I said, I ignored it at first, then I went to bed. I couldn't really hear much in my bedroom. I was trying to get to sleep when I heard a scream. It was very clear to me. This was someone screaming for their life. And then I heard nothing. I jumped out of bed, put on my robe and slippers, went out into the hall and I knocked on Molly's door a few times. I hollered asking if she was alright. I didn't hear anything after that, so I was real worried. I went inside and paced around a little, not really knowing what to do. I made a hot milk, and thought about it and eventually I decided to call the police. I don't know what time I called them.'

'The time of the 911 call is logged. Just one more thing. The scream you heard, you said it was female. What about the raised voices you'd heard earlier?'

'Both were female. I'm one hundred per cent sure about that.'

'Thank you, Miss Karim. Please wait there. Mr. Flynn may have some questions.'

As Riley sat down, he didn't throw any smiles, nods or winks to his assistants on the prosecution team. He had put a lot of points on the prosecution scoreboard with this witness, and he wasn't about to brag about it. There was no ego in this performance. He was going straight for the win.

As I stood, Harry handed me some documents.

I didn't ask him for them.

There was no need. Harry had seen the same line of attack that was building in my mind.

Before I could ask a question, I noticed Judge Tanner peering over her eyeglasses at me. The look wasn't exactly curiosity. There was a warning in that expression, and some trepidation at what I was about to do. Her gaze left me for a second, her attention drifting behind me, to someone in the crowd.

I turned quickly, saw Voss sitting upright, beaming a smile as she casually folded her arms. When I turned back to the judge, it was clear to me she had been eyeballing Voss.

Occasionally, when my cash flow drops, I spend a weekend in Reno, or Atlantic City. I can't go back to Vegas. I've too much heat on me in that city, and not just from the desert. There's a lot of ways to cheat at poker. The easiest way to clean up at the Texas Hold'em table is not to double up with a ringer at the table, contrary to some opinions. The smartest way to wipe out even world champion poker players is to have a secret agreement with the dealer, who can make sure your opponent has a good hand, and that you are dealt a better one.

I'd done it myself, and seen it done to me a couple of times at least.

Just now, looking at Voss and Tanner, I knew the judge had loaded the deck against Vanessa.

Well, I didn't know for sure, but I had a strong suspicion.

I needed to ask the witness one question.

And see if the judge answered it.

35
Eddie

'Miss Karim,' I said, 'are you lying to this jury because someone paid you, or are you lying because the district attorney's office forced you?'

'Mr. Flynn!'

The judge answered my question.

Riley had sprung out of his chair to object, but he wasn't as fast as Judge Tanner. He stood there now, mute, as if he was surprised by the judge's outburst.

'Before you accuse this independent witness of lying under oath, I presume you have strong evidence to put before this court to back up such a serious allegation,' said the judge, sending tiny cannonballs of spit from her mouth that sailed over the bench and then were lost from sight before they hit the polished wooden floor.

I looked at Harry.

His expression changed, his eyebrows crowded in a frown and as he lowered his head he shook it from side to side, almost in disbelief.

The judge had either been leaned on or was bought and paid for by Julian Vanderpool. Didn't matter which, we were now in serious trouble. It's hard to build a defense for your client when the judge refuses to let you pick up a single brick.

With Judge Tanner staring at me, and getting angrier by the second while she waited for an answer, I thought about how I should play this. Having to make massive tactical adjustments in seconds in a murder trial during cross-examination is sometimes called thinking on your feet. But it's much more than that. It's like trying to adjust an invasion plan in the middle of a battle.

The judge's eyebrows sat almost at the top of her head while she waited for an answer.

She was expecting me to say no, not yet. Not at this time. Some delaying tactic.

'Of course I have evidence, Your Honor,' I said.

Her eyebrows stayed put in a look of incredulity.

'Have you shared this so-called evidence with Mr. Riley?' she asked.

'He shared it with me,' I said. Then, before she could say anything else, I shot the next question at the witness.

'Miss Karim, let's start again. You made a call to 911 on the night of the murder, correct?' I asked.

'Yes,' she said.

I held up the document Harry had given me, so the jury could see it in my hand.

'The dispatcher recorded that conversation,' I said, and slapped the page down on my desk. Harry was already handing me the second document. Again, I held it above my head.

'When the police responded to your call, you spoke to Officer Garcia, and he recorded what you told him about hearing raised voices. Do you remember talking to him that night?'

'Yes, I do,' she said.

I slapped that down, took the next document, brandished it for the jury.

'And during the initial investigation, you spoke to Detective Ben Larkin and he recorded your statement. Do you remember talking to him?'

'Of course,' she said.

I gathered all three documents, asked that they be handed to the witness.

'Is that your signature at the bottom of that statement?' I asked.

She gazed at the document, said, 'Yes, that's my signature.'

'In total, Miss Karim, you spoke to three different people in law enforcement, the dispatcher, Officer Garcia and Detective Larkin, and they recorded everything you said. In none of those statements did you mention that the raised voices you'd heard were both female. Correct?'

She stared blankly at the pages in front of her.

'I'm not sure. I think I did,' she said.

'You *think* you did. So, Miss Karim, are you telling this jury that all three of those officers can't do their jobs properly, that they are all three so incompetent that they forgot to include that crucial piece of information?'

'No, but I think I might have mentioned it.'

'You think you might. A minute ago, you thought you had. Now you're only speculating?'

'I can't recall exactly what I said.'

'Well, you signed that witness statement as being an accurate and true account of what you told Detective Larkin. Were you lying when you made that declaration?'

'No way. I wasn't lying. Everything I told the police is the truth,' she said.

'I think that's right. All three statements record the truth. But right now you're lying to this jury. You're embellishing your testimony to suit the prosecution's case. Isn't that right?'

'I'm just telling the truth.'

I took a breath. Let the witness sit with her denials for a moment. A natural pause, to indicate I was moving on to another point.

Really, I was formulating the next question in my mind, making sure it was perfect.

Of course, there's no such thing as the perfect question.

There's only the perfect answer.

This question was bait. I knew the answer already. Miss Karim was smart, and she would give the smartest answer she could.

'Hearing raised female voices from the victim's apartment wasn't the only thing you lied about. You didn't tell the dispatch officer, or Officer Garcia, or even Detective Larkin that the defendant was having a hard time with her boss's wife, did you?'

Even before I could finish the question, I saw the wheels turning in the witness's mind. It was written all over her face. At first, some apprehension, then the answer came to her and she just waited to deliver it.

Harry leaned forward. Out of the corner of my eye, I saw Riley gripping his pen in his fist.

'I wasn't lying about that. When I spoke to those officers, I didn't think Molly having a hard time with her boss's wife was relevant,' she said with some satisfaction.

Having delivered her answer, she nodded and smiled.

Riley relaxed his grip on the pen.

It was a plausible and accurate explanation. The smart explanation.

Or so they thought.

'I see, so it wasn't relevant because the police didn't have a suspect at that time, right?'

'Right,' said Miss Karim.

'So you accept that your testimony today is materially different to the statements you gave the police on previous occasions?'

'Well, yes, but I explained that.'

'Of course you did. You explained that you changed your testimony once the police arrested Vanessa Vanderpool, right?'

'Well, I . . . I don't think of it that way, I mean . . .'

'Miss Karim, all three statements you gave to the police were made before my client was arrested, correct?'

'Yes.'

'So you altered your testimony today to suit the prosecution's case against my client?'

'Objection, Your Honor,' said Riley, leaning over the desk, his pen in his hand like a dagger he wanted to stick in my back. The judge was giving him her full attention. She was going to sustain his objection, no matter what I said. She didn't want the rails coming off this prosecution so soon. 'This is not the way this happened, Your Honor. Mr. Flynn is misrepresenting the facts to the—'

I cut off Riley before he could get the objection sustained.

'Your Honor, if Mr. Riley wants to testify, he can get on the witness stand any time he likes, but there's no need. He already has this witness lying for him in order to make his case.'

The jury heard that. I could tell by the squeak of the old mahogany jury chairs. They make that sound when a juror moves, usually leaning forward or swaying back. Any activity like that from the jury is good.

It means they're listening.

'Objection sustained. The jury will disregard Mr. Flynn's last statements and his last question. We'll take a short adjournment. I want counsel in my chambers, right now. That means *you*, Mr. Flynn.'

It's difficult to gauge how well a trial is going. There are so many little indicators, but often they don't add up to much.

When I saw Harry smiling, and a thick vein pulsing in Riley's red throat, I took it as a good sign. If the prosecutor's blood pressure was higher than mine, then either the DA needed to change their diet and exercise or things were going well for the defense.

Even though Judge Tanner had told the jury to ignore the last exchange with the witness and the DA, they wouldn't forget it. People are always more swayed by something they see or hear that just so happens to be something they weren't supposed to see or hear.

A small victory with the first witness.

I had a bad feeling there wouldn't be many more victories in this case. Even this tiniest of wins would come with a heavy price.

And the judge was about to collect.

36
Eddie

'I was warned about you,' said Judge Tanner.

She had slumped into her chair behind the desk in her chamber. Riley and I stood side by side, facing her. Rubbing at her temples, she looked from the prosecutor back to me. Cupping his hands in front of him, back straight, chest out, Riley looked like he was in a principal's office at military school. Did they have principals at military school? Or did they have a rank? I didn't know and had no inclination to find out. I was letting my mind wander because I didn't want to get angry.

I was already pissed at having to fight back against a judge who had been bought and paid for by Julian Vanderpool, even though I couldn't prove it. I couldn't even say it. Not here. There was no point. It would only make my situation worse, if that was possible.

As a criminal defense attorney, you're always battling against the juggernaut that is the system. No matter how you can manipulate it, or slide past some of those more dangerous pieces of legal machinery, the system won most of the time. Added to that were prosecutors and judges with their own agendas. An innocent person has a better chance of cleaning out the casino at a roulette table than getting a fair trial.

Fighting that fight every damn day takes a toll.

I was tired and disappointed and pissed as all hell.

'*You've got to watch Flynn*. That's what I was told,' said Judge Tanner. 'I just didn't think for one second you'd try to sabotage this trial so early.'

I said, 'No need to apologize, Your Honor. Clearly you underestimated me.'

She stared back at me, open-mouthed.

Riley took one step to the side, putting more distance between me and him. He blew out his cheeks in a false demonstration of incredulity.

'I can't believe you said that,' she said, shaking her head.

'I get that a lot.'

'The *audacity*,' she whispered.

'Tell me about it. I don't blame you for being pissed at me. Here I am, having the *audacity* to put up a defense for my client who has been framed for a murder she didn't commit. I mean, it's outrageous. If I were you, I would report that kind of behavior to the New York Bar Association.'

Her back straightened, her neck arched and the anger fed some iron into her words.

'Oh, don't you worry, Mr. Flynn. I will be making a complaint to the Bar Association about your behavior. In the meantime, I'm fining you a thousand dollars for contempt of court.'

At the mention of a fine, her eyes narrowed.

Riley looked serious, and nodded in agreement.

'I will instruct the jury, again, to disregard that last exchange between you and Miss Karim. I'm tempted to have your entire cross-examination excluded. If you test me again, I will have no hesitation in doing so.'

'You know, there's a seat free beside Mr. Riley if you'd prefer just to sit at the prosecution table. It might make things clearer for the jury.'

'Are you seriously alleging that I am biased?' she shrieked.

'Are you seriously alleging that you're not?' I asked.

'If you wish to file a motion for my recusal then do so. But this disrespect stops right now. And to make sure you don't forget, let's make that fine *two* thousand dollars.'

I heard Riley whisper, '*Wow. Two grand.*'

He was trying to make me blow up.

I glanced at him, shook my head. Then forced all of my rage down, down, down, into my shoes and through the floor. I needed a clear head if I was going to defend Vanessa.

Reaching into my pants pocket, I took out my thick billfold, removed my silver money clip and counted out hundred-dollar bills.

'What on earth are you doing?' asked Judge Tanner.

I threw a stack of hundreds on her desk.

'This trial is going to last at least a week. Here's *five* grand. It'll be easier if I just opened a tab.'

37
Eddie

'How did that go?' asked Harry.

'Not one of my finer moments,' I said.

We stood in the hallway, outside the courtroom. Vanessa was in the consultation room, having some privacy and peace away from the courtroom. Even though neither the press nor anyone else was allowed to take pictures inside the court building, she didn't want to be around the crowds of media gathered to watch the trial, who all stood around now, keeping one eye on us or typing into laptops balanced on their knees or furiously using their thumbs to make notes into their phones.

'It seems when Patrick Vanderpool isn't on trial this case suddenly has a lot of media interest from all areas,' said Harry.

'Yeah, and did you see who else has come out to watch? Voss is here,' I said.

'Didn't Vanessa fire her?'

'Yeah, but she's still here. And I'd say it's not idle curiosity. If Voss is here, then she's on somebody's dime. Probably Julian's.'

'I'll keep one eye on her. And the other on you. I still don't know what happened in Tanner's chambers.'

'She fined me for contempt. She's instructing the jury to disregard some of the witness's testimony. I don't think it matters so much. The jury heard it. And they were really listening. If nothing else, we've shaken them up. Maybe if the judge allows us to put forward some kind of defense the jury might even get to consider it?'

'Don't bet on it,' said Harry.

'How's Vanessa doing?'

'She's holding up. She's tough, Eddie. Maybe tougher than we know,' said Harry.

'What makes you think that?'

'I don't know. Sometimes it's the way I see her staring off into the distance. She doesn't scare easily. She's been through a lot with Patrick. I think the divorce is on her mind too. That's a whole other dirty game.'

'I need to find her a real divorce lawyer when this is over. It's not our field.'

Harry leaned against the yellowed, stained marble wall, shook his head.

'Does she even know what you've been up to with Patrick's divorce lawyers?'

I shook my head, said, 'She signed the retainer agreement, which gives us a broad discretion to act in her best interests.'

'We have to tell her,' said Harry.

'No, not yet.'

Harry shuffled his feet, scratched his head and said, 'I don't like keeping things from clients. Especially not something like this.'

'It's worse when clients keep things from us.'

He gave me an admonishing look.

'Come on. It's not the same. I'm not comfortable with it.'

'Me either, but look at it this way – yeah, she's tough, but she's been through a lot, and I can't get her hopes up and then crush them if we're wrong.'

'Why haven't you told her?' asked Harry.

There was no point in lying to Harry. Some people just see through all your bullshit.

'I don't completely trust her,' I said.

'We have to tell her. If this blows up in our face and a judge finds out what we did without our client's permission, neither of us will practice law again. We've got no choice.'

'Do you always have to be right?' I asked.

Without another word, I followed Harry to the private consultation room where we'd hidden Vanessa from the reporters.

Vanessa sat at the desk quietly as Harry and I took seats opposite her.

'There's something we just need to let you know,' I said. 'Bloch and a colleague are on their way to Patrick's house in the Hamptons. They're looking for something which might help us in this case.'

'What has the Hamptons house got to do with anything?' she asked.

'Maybe nothing, maybe everything,' said Harry. 'We just have a duty to tell you we're carrying out investigations. Just in case you have any objection.'

'No, not at all. I'm just amazed Patrick let you into the house.'

I fell silent. Harry nudged me under the desk.

'Well, he knows we're there, but I may not have explained the real intent behind the visit to his lawyers, Buchanan and Duff.'

'I thought so. Look, you do whatever you think is best. I really appreciate everything you're doing for me.'

Harry smiled, and told her we were due back in court in a few minutes.

'I just need to use the bathroom,' she said, and we left the consultation room. Vanessa walked down the hallway and into the ladies' room.

'Have you heard from Lake or Bloch?' I asked.

'Lake checked in. Patrick is hunkered down in his father's house. Dekker and a full protection team too. They haven't moved for two weeks,' said Harry.

'Still keeping a low profile, as we expected,' I said. 'And what about Bloch?'

Harry checked his watch, said, 'She's managed to wrestle our forensic expert into a new suit, so she should be starting work any minute.'

'She needs to hurry. We're running out of time.'

38
Vanessa

Vanessa's hands rested on her lap beneath the table in the cramped, dirty client consultation room in Center Street courthouse.

'There's something we just need to let you know,' said Eddie. 'Bloch and a colleague are on their way to Patrick's house in the Hamptons. They're looking for something which might help us in this case.'

Underneath the table, Vanessa's fingernails bit into her thighs. She squeezed and felt the sharp points of her manicured nails in her flesh.

What she had learned about lying was that sometimes, to keep the reaction from your eyes, from your face, you have to let that expression come out somewhere else. Lies build pressure. The façade that she wore could crack if someone hammered on it hard enough. That pressure had to be released.

'What has the Hamptons house got to do with anything?' Vanessa asked.

'Maybe nothing, maybe everything,' said Harry. 'We just have a duty to tell you we're carrying out investigations. Just in case you have any objection.'

She tensed her core, used her diaphragm to help keep the tremors from her voice. 'No, not at all. I'm just amazed Patrick let you into the house,' she said.

Flynn said nothing. But in that silence he told her everything. He had lied about this to someone, but he wasn't prepared to lie to Vanessa.

'Well, he knows we're there, but I may not have explained the real intent behind the visit to his lawyers.'

'I thought so. Look, you do whatever you think is best. I really appreciate everything you're doing for me.'

Harry smiled and said, 'No need to thank us. Better get ready to go back inside in a few minutes.'

'I just need to use the bathroom,' said Vanessa, and it had taken every part of her will not to wince at the urgency of how she had delivered that line.

But from their reaction, they had probably thought it was just the anxiety at having to go back into that courtroom.

Relaxing her hands, she smoothed down her pants, stood and then followed the two men into the hallway, turned and headed toward the ladies' room, went inside and checked the four stalls.

Empty.

She stood at the sink on the right, furthest from the door, and stared into the smeared, cracked mirror. The woman in the mirror stared back. Somehow, she was different. Her eyes looked harder. Her skin paler. She believed in the soul, and wondered how much of hers was left.

Death changes people. She wondered if she was the woman in the mirror now, or if there was a way back. Only time would tell.

Her hands trembled as she took her phone from her purse and opened the secure messaging app. She typed with her thumbs. The message would be sent securely and would disappear within the hour. But it would be read.

And it would be understood.

Flynn's people are searching the Hamptons house.

She hit send, dropped the phone back into her purse and looked at her hands. They were clean.

In the mirror, those same hands looked dirty.

She hit the hot water faucet, held her hands beneath the running water then pumped soap into her palms and worked it in between her fingers. Using her nails, she scrubbed her knuckles, her cuticles, every inch, and then rinsed.

The water was too hot, and her skin burned red.

And she held her hands beneath it, biting her lip against the pain.

She had to be clean. She had to wash off the dirt.

Somewhere either in Vanessa, or in the woman in the mirror, she knew her hands would never be clean.

Because she understood one thing now above all else.

You can't get away with murder on your own.

39
Bloch

'Why do I have to wear a suit?' asked Raymond.

Bloch gave him a stare from the driver's seat of her Jeep.

He swallowed, stared out the front window, said, 'You didn't have to get dressed up.'

'I'm not the one playing a part,' said Bloch. 'I'm just being . . . me.'

He pulled at the collar of his shirt with a finger, then yanked his tie down and began wrestling with his top button. They had been parked in a laneway for half an hour, waiting. And with every passing minute Raymond had grown more uncomfortable. He wasn't used to wearing a suit and tie, and at first he had balked at the idea and refused flat out. It had taken Harry to persuade him. A visit to Harry's tailor on the west side with the promise of an indulgent lunch at Patsy's Italian restaurant had sealed the deal. Harry complained that the following week he had to take his tailor out to lunch at Patsy's to apologize. His tailor was seventy-nine years old and he'd never cut a suit for a man who'd shown up to his business in a pair of camo shorts and a Napalm Death T-shirt.

Even Bloch had to admit it was a nice suit. Well cut to Raymond's generous figure. He had even had a haircut, but had drawn the line at shaving off his goatee. Harry had managed to slip the barber a twenty to accidentally trim it.

A silver BMW pulled up outside the electronic security gates. A single occupant. A young man in a dark suit and blue shirt. He got out of the BMW and waved at Bloch. She fired up the engine of the Jeep, flashed the lights. The BMW driver opened the gates with a key fob, then drove through, Bloch following.

'Do up that tie, Raymond.'

'It's strangling me,' said Raymond.

'I'll strangle you.'

Raymond buttoned his shirt and straightened his tie.

The driveway was a narrow single lane that snaked through a crop of old trees. The BMW crawled along, and Bloch followed close behind. After close to a minute, the trees thinned to reveal the large shingled house. Bloch had never seen this kind of architecture outside of the Hamptons. The house was covered in wood shingles, from its base up and over the roof. The small individual wood shingles had darkened with age and weather, and were darker still on the canopy that covered the entrance porch.

Parking beside the BMW, Bloch got out and met the young man in the sharp suit. Raymond had picked up a hefty black bag from the trunk of the Jeep and joined them.

The house was a vast pile, and obscured the ocean behind it, but not the smell. Bloch inhaled deeply. She loved the smell of the sea.

'Mr. Corbett?' asked Bloch.

He nodded and handed Bloch his business card. In his other hand he held a set of keys.

B. Corbett, associate at Family Law and Matrimonial Department, Buchanan and Duff, attorneys at law.

'This shouldn't take too long,' said Corbett.

'It will take as long as it takes,' said Bloch.

'How long does it take to appraise a property?' asked Corbett.

'To do it properly, it will take some time,' said Raymond.

'Can I see your business card?' asked Corbett, to Raymond.

Raymond said nothing. Bloch said, 'He's not in the realtor

business any more. He just does private appraisals and valuations for the market.'

'I'll need his name for the file,' said Corbett.

Bloch said, 'My name is—'

'I know who you are. You're Flynn's enforcer. Sorry, I meant *investigator*. Who is he?'

'He's the realtor. He's with me,' said Bloch. 'You'll see his name on the valuation report when *Mr.* Flynn serves it on your firm.'

'Fine, you want to make it that way. No problem. You know, this is a total waste of everyone's time. The house is a pre-marital asset. There's no way a judge is going to let this fall into marriage property. Your client is never going to see a dime from this house in the divorce.'

'I'm not a lawyer. I'm just here to make sure he gets to value the property. Let's get this done,' said Bloch.

Without another word, they followed Corbett to the front door. He unlocked it, and as the door opened the security panel in the entrance hall began to beep intermittently. Bloch was on his heels, watching as he punched in a four-digit code into the keypad to shut off the alarm system. As he pressed the hash key, a louder and more satisfying beep echoed through the hallway to signal the deactivation of the intruder warning.

An ornate armchair sat in the corner of the hallway, and Corbett took out his cell phone and folded himself into the chair.

Bloch looked around the vast hallway with its central staircase leading up to the first floor. The house had a nautical theme, with a ship's wheel above the door, varnished oars nailed to the opposite wall, telescopes and barometers, and natural wood.

A typical grand Hamptons summer house.

'Don't take too long,' said Corbett.

From his heavy black bag, Raymond brought out a light bar and switched it on. Instead of white LEDs, the bar emitted a strange purple glow. He began running it over the floors and walls.

'What the hell are you doing?' asked Corbett.

'Checking for mold and dry rot,' said Raymond. 'This is an old house. I don't want any arguments about the property valuation based on remedial works from the husband's realtor if they're not necessary. I know how the game is played.'

Bloch couldn't resist a smile. Raymond was playing the part. Even if, despite the suit and haircut, he still didn't quite look the part.

'This isn't going to be fast, is it?' asked Corbett.

Bloch picked up Raymond's bag, followed him into the kitchen as he swept the light over every surface and said, 'Get comfortable, Mr. Corbett.'

This was the second time in as many months Bloch had followed Raymond with that strange light. The last time, they were in a much smaller property.

Molly Green's apartment. A court-sanctioned forensic examination for the defense.

Raymond was Bloch's forensics guy. Had been for years. He worked from a private lab in the city, and always had time for Bloch. She was one of those people who was good to know. While becoming friends with her wasn't easy, it paid off, and once they had discovered that they both had a fondness for Hong Kong cinema the friendship became easy.

If Bloch was in a particular hurry to get quick results on a forensic test, she would bring in the test sample with a Blu-ray for Raymond. Usually something starring Tony Leung, Chow Yun Fat or Raymond's favorite, Jackie Chan. Those tests then somehow managed to skip the line with A1 priority. He was diligent, honest and fast, the key characteristics of a great forensic technician. For Raymond, knowing Bloch made life easier. There was a certain cachet of cool that came with being her friend. Doors opened. And more importantly for Raymond no one bullied him any more. Bad-tempered bosses and even jacked-up, gym-rat PIs stopped giving Raymond shit. In that respect, being Bloch's pal was like having a nuclear weapon in the backyard. Nobody would ever risk pissing you off in case you aimed it at their house.

In Molly Green's apartment, months ago, Bloch had ignored Raymond as he swept the apartment with the same equipment he was using now. In Molly's apartment, Bloch had a particular point of focus.

She remembered staring at the Monet print that hung on the wall – the water lilies.

She remembered sniffing the air.

Whatever chemical smell she had detected on her first visit to the apartment was now gone.

She had approached the picture, examined it. It sat flush to the wall. Bloch put her hands on the frame, tried to tilt it upwards to take it off the picture hook, but it didn't move.

It must've been stuck on with picture tape.

Instead, she pulled gently, and then lifted. The picture came off the wall with a slight cracking, sucking sound. Her first thought was that she had been right, the picture had been stuck to the wall. But when she checked the frame, she didn't find any stickers. None on the wall either. There was a single picture hook.

She had looked closer, saw that some flecks of white paint had come away from the wall, and were now stuck to the frame.

She had called for Raymond then.

That moment of discovery. Of finding something that had been hidden, it gave most investigators a thrill. A surge of adrenaline and dopamine that was the juice of the job. Not for Bloch. She felt different. She felt as if something wasn't quite right. An itch. An annoyance. And revealing the truth fixed the problem.

It was soothing, but, in a strange way, not completely satisfying.

Raymond was up on all the latest forensic techniques, including retrieving blood and DNA in all kinds of situations.

Bloch had helped him that afternoon in Molly's apartment, carefully sanding and removing layers of paint to reveal – bloodstains on the wall, behind the paint. Raymond explained that once paint dries, it forms a discreet layer. In a way, it's just like wallpaper. If the layer of paint is carefully peeled from the wall with a sharp blade, then whatever was beneath it can be properly examined.

Raymond had processed the bloodstains that he could find, and a DNA analysis had revealed that it was Molly Green's blood.

Now Bloch knew why she and Lake had smelled that solvent aroma when they'd first visited Molly's apartment. It was fresh paint. Someone had painted over Molly's bloodstains on the wall.

Why they had done so was not clear to Bloch, Lake, or even Eddie.

Why paint a wall to hide a victim's bloodstains when there was a pool of her blood on the floor? That was a question that continued to plague Bloch, but it established a method of operation. Painting over blood to hide it.

Now, as Raymond swept the light over floors of Patrick Vanderpool's Hamptons beach house, Bloch got the same curious feeling. She left Raymond in the grand hallway of the Hamptons house, and moved into the kitchen. It was a vast space with a long wooden dining table with a dozen wicker seats on either side. At the end of the kitchen was a glass-paneled bi-folding door that led straight out onto the beach. It was an overcast day, with dark gray clouds that sat over a chalk-green ocean. The sand was still wet with recent rain and looked more like clay in this light.

White foam brushed the beach, waves breaking far away and rolling in toward the house. It should have been a beautiful sight, the whole room was designed to frame that view, but Bloch felt only loss. She had always been slightly fearful of the ocean, recognizing its power and how often people underestimated it. Watching the tides, Bloch could easily see how a young Teresa Chase could have been swept away in those waves.

Taken and never returned by an unforgiving sea.

It would be easy to sell such a story.

But the more time she spent in that room, the more she thought that this house was just as dangerous as the sea outside.

Something wasn't right in this house. Something had been hidden.

She and Raymond had to find—

'Bloch,' called Raymond.

She turned and followed his voice. The way he had said her name just now. The tone – she knew before she even saw him that Raymond had found something.

40
The Journal

Patrick's beach house was beautiful.

And at the same time, terrifying.

He parked his Ferrari and leapt out, came around and opened my door for me. I'd never been in a car this expensive. The smell of leather and the noise from the engine, which sat behind us, and now the house, it was all just too much for me.

He opened the door, then turned off the alarm and gave me the tour.

It had seven bedrooms, although he said most of them had barely been used. He said I could put my bag in the main guest bedroom, but his smile told me that I wouldn't be sleeping here.

There was a lounge, a games room, a huge kitchen that was made for partying with a glass wall that folded away to open the space up to a veranda and then the beach and the blue ocean beyond. We walked out onto the outside dining area, and Patrick kicked off his deck shoes and made his way down a small flight of steps to the beach. I slipped off my pumps and followed.

It was one of those beautiful autumn days that still clung on to the last breath of summer, but later in the day would remind you of the winter to come. The sun had been warming the sand all morning, and it was pleasant beneath my feet and creeping in between my toes as I joined Patrick. He leaned on a fat wooden pillar jutting out from the sand. There were two rows of them, like the teeth of an alligator, that made their way from the house down to the water, as if they'd once supported a pier that stretched into the sea.

'We don't have a pool,' he said. 'No point, when you have this. I opted for the tennis court instead. Would you like to swim?'

The thought of it made me feel sick.

'Maybe. Will you be joining me?' I asked.

He didn't give an answer. He didn't need to. He stripped off his shirt and his shorts as he walked to the shoreline. I looked around, and couldn't see another house for miles. Nothing that led directly onto the beach anyway. Right before his feet touched the wet sand, he lost his underwear and tossed them over his shoulder, then bounded into the water and dove quickly beneath a wave. When his head surfaced, he tossed his wet hair back and laughed.

'Come on in. The water's great,' he said.

That whole weekend could be summed up by how I felt on that beach in that moment.

I had desperately wanted to get to this house. I'd longed to walk around it. To comb every inch of it. To let my soul inhabit it in the hope that it would touch on another who had stayed here. I don't know what I had expected to find. Something, some hint of her spirit, or some article of hers left behind. A trace of her.

Some remnant of Teresa.

But there was nothing here. I knew that much just from walking around the house with Patrick. This had been the last place she had been alive.

Standing on that beach, seeing Patrick run out to those waves.

I wondered how he could do that. Knowing that she had been lost out there.

Which made me think that maybe she hadn't been lost in those waves after all.

Could he have dived in without so much as a care in the world knowing that someone he'd been with had died out there? Swept away? Could he be so callous, or was this all in my head?

I stripped off to my underwear as I made my way to the water's edge. As the dying wave licked my toes, I felt its icy touch, like death.

I shivered, but not from the cold. I waded out, my body trembling, covered in gooseflesh. My teeth were rattling by the time I got to him.

'Is it safe to swim here?' I asked.

His smile faded, briefly, then he said, 'It is at this time of day. This time of year. The tide isn't so strong. It's okay. I've got you. I would never let anything happen to you . . .'

I felt his arms around my waist.

Then his lips, wet and salty, on mine.

I pulled back gently.

'What about your wife?' I asked.

'She'll never know,' he said.

'Won't she suspect something?'

'Don't worry. She will never find out. Things haven't been so good between us for a while now. Soon as I saw you, I knew I'd married the wrong person. I think I'm falling in love.'

'You don't know me,' I said.

'I want to know you. I want to know every inch of you.'

A wave hit me, and I almost lost my footing, but he grabbed me and held me, and kissed me.

And right then everything I thought I knew fell away. I was lost in that sea, and I cried. At least I think I did. It was hard to tell. All I knew was that he was strong, and full of life, and powerful and rich and he held me tight against those waves.

There was very little chance someone could drown when this man was beside them.

'I'm scared,' I said.

'Don't be afraid. I've got you. Nothing will happen to you when you're with me.'

'I'm not a great swimmer. Didn't someone, a girl, drown on this beach?'

He stared at me, cold, dead eyes boring into mine.

'I never heard anything about that. You're fine.'

He kissed me, and we held each other in the waves.

He'd lied.

And I knew then, for sure and beyond any doubt in my mind.

This man had murdered my half-sister.

41
Eddie

'The People call Dr. Morrow,' said Riley.

Medical examiners all have that same kind of look.

Dr. Morrow was a young man in a somber suit with a somber expression on his face. He made his way to the witness stand and took the Bible, repeated the oath. He had superbly clean hands and thick white fingers, like sticks of chalk. That same pallor spread over his face. It was always the same with those who work with the dead. Perhaps it was because they spent hours in basement morgues with no sunlight, or maybe they took on the color of the bodies who were the subject of their work. I don't know which, but I'd never met a coroner or a medical examiner with a tan.

'Dr. Morrow, you examined the body of Molly Green. Correct?'

Riley's assistant DA had a laptop open in front of him, about to cycle through a series of photographs of the victim's body, and the horrific way that she had been mutilated. Part of this was to generate the evidence that was required, through Morrow's testimony, to prove how the victim died, but there were parts of that chain that were missing. Maybe Riley would ask Morrow to stretch the truth, to get a win. I would have to wait and see. The other reason to call him to testify was to shock the jury. To show them the visceral effects of murder. This wasn't Hollywood. This wasn't a TV show or a movie. This was real life, and murder was nasty and disturbing and violently real.

Part of it would lean toward tapping into the jury's emotions. Breaking their hearts. Scarring their minds.

As my mind ruminated on all of this, that last thought stuck there for a second, like a spinning wheel.

Emotion.

Riley's weak point with a jury.

The easiest way for a prosecutor to access the raw emotional anger of a jury toward the perpetrator of a crime was to make the victim a real person, and not just a photograph.

I opened my trial bundle, found the DA's list of potential witnesses. Not all of them would be called, and the list ran to seventy-four names. Way more than would ever be used in this case. That's an old prosecutor's trick. Flood the defense with a huge witness list. Let them waste time chasing down irrelevant people, interviewing them, investigating them, burning through the defendant's cash reserves on billable hours and distracting from the real work, the relevant witnesses, the prime issues in the case.

Very few of the witnesses would fulfill an essential element in the DA's case of making an emotional connection between the jury and the deceased victim. The prosecution's motive was that the only way to make a jury grieve for a victim is to show them someone else's grief. There were some of her work colleagues on the list, people from Patrick's campaign team, but none of her friends and, more importantly, none of her family. No one who would really grieve her loss.

Riley began settling Dr. Morrow as a witness, running through a series of questions on his qualifications and experience to establish him as an expert and to impress upon the jury that whatever this man said was fact. I turned to Harry, whispered so our client wouldn't hear.

'It's just hit me – there's no one from the victim's family on the DA's witness list. Just work colleagues.'

'Riley doesn't have the same years of experience as we do, probably just an oversight,' said Harry in a hushed whisper.

'I think he's good enough to know his weaknesses. Something is wrong here.'

Harry frowned, leaned back in his chair, then began to rub the top of his head, letting his fingers comb through his gray hair. He often did this when he was thinking.

Suddenly, he leaned forward, grabbed his trial bundle and began flicking through the pages. I kept an ear on Riley and Dr. Morrow, still on his work history with the city. They hadn't gotten to the meat of his testimony yet. Vanessa was listening to the witness, but I saw her glance at Harry and I, just to see what we were up to. She soon turned back to listening to the testimony.

Ripping a page from his trial bundle, Harry handed it to me, said, 'You're right. Something's wrong with this picture.'

The document was only a paragraph long. A statement from a uniformed cop, one of the officers who had attended at the crime scene – Officer Garcia. In the statement he said that he had attended the morgue and accompanied Alison Karim who identified the remains as that of Molly Green, from her body shape, approximate height and a small tattoo on her left wrist of a dolphin.

'There's nothing about Garcia making an effort to get her driver's license, birth records or any kind of search for a family member,' I said, keeping my voice low.

'Maybe he did, but he couldn't find anything,' said Harry. 'We know nothing about this young woman, and Riley hasn't done the leg work on her life either.'

This was all too strange. It wasn't a coincidence.

I texted Lake, told him to see what he could find in public records for Molly Green including any family history. Surely, the NYPD would have made an effort to contact her family. It's protocol. It had to have been done, but Garcia didn't make any note of it in either his statement about attending the scene, nor this statement about body identification.

Lake texted back, said he was on it.

'What do you think?' asked Harry.

'Could be three things. Either the NYPD didn't do their job, Riley didn't do his due diligence or they couldn't find anything.'

'What does that even mean? They would've found something,' said Harry.

'Not if Molly Green wasn't who she said she was. What if she was working for Patrick Vanderpool under a false identity? What if she had an alternative agenda? This murder could be about a lot more than a scandalous affair.'

'Dr. Morrow, did you examine the body of the victim in this case, Molly Green?'

'I did. I carried out a full postmortem examination . . .'

We were now getting into real territory with Dr. Morrow. I gave him my full attention, and tried to push thoughts of Molly Green to the back of my mind. Nothing about this case was straightforward.

An image flashed on the large screen for the jury.

The headless body of a young woman.

A few members of the jury gasped. Some looked away, then forced their gaze back at the screen.

The image came up without warning to the jury. No words of comfort from Riley, no apologies for showing them the result of an evil, murderous act of violence. He knew most, if not all, of those jurors would take that picture to their grave. That they would close their eyes at night, for a long time after this trial was over, and they would see this young woman lying on a steel table.

It was what he wanted. What he counted on.

Riley wanted to shock.

He got it.

I heard Vanessa sniff, softly. It was then I noticed she was crying.

Her face wet with tears, the grief and loss writ large on her features. Normally, I tell my clients not to react to anything in the courtroom. Just look neutral, let me do the reacting.

But there was no hiding this.

This was what the prosecution case lacked – genuine grief, empathy.

I caught some of the jurors staring at Vanessa.

They were trying to figure out if she was crying because someone she had known had been murdered and mutilated in this way, or if she was staring back at her own handiwork with shame and disgust.

Was she crying for Molly? Or crying for herself?

Harry gave her a handkerchief, and she dabbed at her eyes, reddening now from crying.

'Dr. Morrow, what in your expert opinion was the cause of death?'

I leaned in, listening carefully.

There was only one possible answer from his point of view. The same conclusion that was in his preliminary report. He had to say that cause of death was likely unnatural, but he could not say exactly what caused her death. That was the only reasonable, professional opinion he could stipulate.

Dr. Morrow shifted his attention from Riley to the jury, and spoke directly to them when he said, 'Probable cause of death was blunt-force trauma to the skull.'

Riley couldn't resist shooting a smug grin in my direction.

Now we had a ball game.

42
Lake

Multitasking wasn't Gabriel Lake's thing.

He stared at the screen of his laptop, balanced on the wheel of his Pontiac Aztek.

Then he looked ahead, down the street, at Julian Vanderpool's building.

No movement from the building. Father and son had been inside for a couple of days now, along with his security team, hunkered down, running interference in the media. Judging by the sheer volume of articles coming out of his newspapers, the coverage on the news programs on his network and the thousands of bots and trolls constantly running hate and conspiracy theories on social media, Vanessa Vanderpool was the most vilified woman in New York, a cold-blooded killer.

The headhunter, the trolls called her.

None of the principals he was watching had left that property in days.

He turned back to the laptop.

Now that he was ex-FBI, Lake didn't have access to the same kind of databases as Bloch, so his online searches would be more generic.

So far, he was coming up short.

Too short.

No voter registration details for Molly Green.

No driver's license issued by New York or any of the surrounding states.

No online presence on social media.

He was about to look up birth records when something caught his eye.

Movement from the Vanderpool home.

A huge man in a black leather jacket, gray jeans and black military boots. He looked both ways, checking for cars before he crossed the street and that's when Lake clocked it was Dekker. Two of his goons with him. Smaller, but sharp-looking men. The last two survivors from his unit. They hustled across the street, got into a blacked-out Mercedes SUV and Lake saw the taillights firing up.

He closed his laptop, placed it on the passenger seat and used the voice control on his phone to text Eddie and Bloch.

Dekker on the move. Two men with him. I'm following.

Turning the ignition key in the Aztek, the engine coughed, then coughed again and nothing happened. The starter motor turned over and over.

Lake swore, turned off the ignition, waited a moment.

The black Mercedes ahead of him pulled away.

He tried it again. This time determined.

'Come on, baby. You know I love you,' he said.

The Aztek sputtered into life, but it wasn't sounding good. He selected drive, hit the gas and the engine backfired.

By now, the Mercedes had already made it through the lights and was speeding along the next block.

Lake swore and put his foot down, to little or no effect. Neither the swearing nor the depression of the gas pedal seemed to make any appreciable difference. Pressing the pedal all the way to the floor, the pitch of the engine increased and the Aztek seemed to find the next gear, and backfired again.

Still, he was moving. And the Mercedes was still in sight.

Lake bit his nails and drove, pushing the car as hard as he dared.

He told himself the car problems were probably a blessing. When he was in the FBI, he had a habit of tailing cars way too close. It was the anxiety in him. He didn't want to lose his target. No amount of coaching from the precision driving instructor helped. Eventually, he was advised to take meds for the condition.

Lake ignored the advice. It was his anxiety that kept him sharp, made his brain tick along at high speed and made sure he never got into a situation he hadn't already planned for in his catastrophic way of thinking.

The Mercedes pulled into what looked like a mechanics' garage, stopping at the roller shutter doors. One of Dekker's men got out, used a key to open the lock on the doors then rolled up the shutter. Dekker rolled the Merc inside and the goon followed, closing the doors behind him.

Lake pulled up twenty feet away, checked his location on the maps app on his phone. No way to follow them inside.

He would wait for them coming out.

It was a redbrick building in the Bronx, with steel shutters for windows and a faded hand-painted sign above the door advertising the old car-repair business. Too bad they were no longer in business. The Aztek probably needed a shit ton of work. It had been running fine yesterday, but that was the way of old cars. No telling when they might decide to stop functioning. Lake thought this gave the car character. And it was true – the Aztek had plenty of character – too bad it was a comedic character.

He bit his lip, kept the engine running. No way he was going to risk turning it off. It may never start again.

Lake watched the building, chewed his nails and let his heel bounce on the floor. It shook the car slightly, but not enough that anyone outside would see. No way he could go back to the laptop, not just yet. This needed his full attention.

As an agent, and now as a private investigator, of sorts, he was used to spending hours simply observing. Sitting and watching. Staying alert wasn't a problem. Sleeping, that was a problem.

He checked his watch with difficulty. Hard to see it. The clock on the Aztek read two thirty in the morning, so that was no help. How long had he been waiting now? Fifteen, maybe twenty minutes. Maybe longer.

Give it more time.

He told himself he would wait another twenty.

He only managed five minutes before he reluctantly switched off the engine and got out of the car. Leaving the engine running in a normal car and abandoning it in any major US city was tantamount to giving the car away. He had thought hard about turning off the Aztek's engine. No one was likely to steal this car. And even if they did they probably wouldn't get very far.

Still, it was his, and he needed it. So he took the keys with him and opened the trunk. Slipped off his jacket, put on a ballistic vest, then his jacket back over the top. He moved his Glock from his shoulder holster to a quick release on his belt, shut the trunk, locked the car to make sure the laptop was secure because it cost more than the vehicle, and crossed the street.

No way to see inside from this face of the building, so he ran around the corner and found a steel emergency exit door. Locked. He moved quicker now. On the opposite side of the building from where he'd parked, he found another roller shutter door that led directly onto the street. This one was up.

He went inside, cautiously. A single-story garage. Apart from the emergency exit, which he'd seen already, there was no staircase and no other way out of the building other than the roller shutter doors and a single door exit on this side.

The roller shutters were up. There was nothing else here apart from – the Mercedes.

He called Bloch.

'I lost Dekker and his boys. I'm pretty sure they switched vehicles in a garage. The roller shutters on the opposite side of the building were up. Wherever they're going, they didn't have time to stop and close the doors. Are you still in the Hamptons?'

'Yeah,' said Bloch.

'Any trouble there?'

'No.'

'I'm sorry. I shouldn't have lost them. My car—'

He could almost hear Bloch's eyes rolling in her head at the mention of the Aztek.

'It happens. Don't worry,' said Bloch. 'Eddie, Harry and Vanessa are safe in the courthouse. I've got a lawyer here from Vanderpool's firm. He's pissed, but I have it under control.'

'Did he make a call to anyone since you've been there?'

Silence.

Then, 'I'll check,' said Bloch.

'Call me back,' said Lake.

43
Bloch

'Can you hand me that fine sandpaper?' said Raymond.

Bloch hung up on Lake, reached down, fetched a fresh sheet of fine sandpaper from Raymond's bag and handed it to him. He was now in white coveralls, head to toe, and a breathing mask with a mesh dust filter. A white sheet spread out from the base of the wall, and Raymond stood on it, lights flooding the surface of the wall as Raymond sanded it down.

'This is criminal damage to property, you know?' said Corbett.

He was on a kitchen stool, watching Raymond work. When he had begun to sand the wall, Corbett had begun to make threats and take pictures of Raymond.

'Like we told you, he's testing for dry rot,' said Bloch.

'I don't care. He's damaging the property and he's not authorized—'

'Eddie Flynn has a court order for an expert to undertake an examination and valuation of this property,' said Bloch. 'He's examining and evaluating.'

Corbett smirked, then went back to his phone.

'Did you call anyone and tell them what we're doing here?' asked Bloch.

'You're damn right. I called my boss, Mr. Duff, and he called the judge. Your client, or your firm, is going to pay for the damage and then some, mark my words. Do you even know whose house this is?'

Bloch told Raymond she'd be back in a second. She was just getting some equipment from the car. Stepping down onto the gravel driveway, she texted Lake.

The associate spoke to his boss at the firm.

Lake texted back straight away.

Vanderpool's firm?

Yes.

Three dots jumped on her phone screen as Lake was typing out a message.

She popped the trunk, lifted the floor covering and removed her tactical vest and a long item wrapped in a leather cloth. She propped it up on the side of the lip of the trunk.

Lake's text came through.

It's probably nothing to worry about. Could be me being paranoid. Just watch your back.

Bloch looked at the vest in her hand, and the long mysterious item that sat by the trunk. If she brought these things inside, it would only inflame the situation with Corbett. He was almost at the point of calling the police.

Lake worried a lot. Too much, sometimes. It was part of his gift, thought Bloch. He could always see the worst in people, and therefore put himself in their shoes, figure out their moves, motives and how they committed the terrible acts that were so alien to others. That's how he caught them.

Well, most of them.

She put the vest and the leather cloth item back in the Jeep and closed the trunk, made her way back to the house.

She texted him again.

Where are you now?

His reply came fast.

Waiting on Triple A. Car won't start.

Bloch texted, Are you worried?

Yeah, but what else is new?

In the hallway, Corbett was pacing back and forth. He was pissed and panicking. After all, the damage had happened while he was supposed to be supervising the visit. But what was he supposed to do? Bloch knew the cops wouldn't do anything, because the property itself legally belonged to the couple, and Raymond was engaged on behalf of Vanessa. Even if he wasn't a realtor, he was there on official business for a client. The cops would say this was a civil matter, and leave it at that.

Still, Corbett was on edge. He could expect to eat a shit sandwich when he got back to the firm because this had happened on his watch.

Through the hallway, past the staircase, past the lounge and into the kitchen, Bloch saw Raymond scraping at the wall opposite the dining table with a knife.

'You nearly done?' she asked.

'I need more samples, another two hours maybe.'

Bloch nodded, walked through the kitchen to the glass doors that looked out on the beach. The wind had picked up. Dark clouds had gathered over the steel-gray ocean, its surface becoming choppier.

'A storm is coming,' said Bloch.

44
Eddie

'Dr. Morrow, what makes you believe the victim died of head trauma?' asked Riley.

'It's a simple logical conclusion based on my medical examination of the body. Even though the victim's head had been severed between C5 and C6, this was not the cause of the death. In my opinion, the removal of the head was carried out postmortem. Meaning, after her death.'

'How do you know the decapitation occurred after she'd already died?' asked Riley.

'The marks left on the skin, and the marks left on C5, indicate a blade with a serrated edge was used to saw through the skin, tendon, muscle and bone. This was done in a single cut, level and quite square. If the victim had been alive, I would have expected to find several different cuts with the same blade as the victim struggled.'

'Is it possible the victim was merely unconscious when this mutilation occurred?'

'I suppose it is possible, but unlikely in my opinion. The vast majority of major limb amputations that I have seen have all evidently been carried out postmortem. After death, I mean.'

Riley paused to let the jury take in this point before expanding it.

'Dr. Morrow, why then do you conclude that the cause of death was trauma to the head?'

'Really it was a logical course of eliminating other potential fatal injuries. Having examined every inch of the victim's body, there was no evidence of any natural cause of death. Heart, liver, kidneys, all major organs were in excellent health, there were no signs of disease and more importantly no signs of any other kind of trauma to any other part of the body which could possibly have been fatal. There was a cut on the sole of the foot, but that would not have been a potentially mortal wound. That led me to conclude that any fatal injury must have occurred to the skull and brain, which were of course missing.'

'Dr. Morrow, you have had cause to examine a jewelry box, is that right?'

'Yes.'

'Does this box have the necessary weight and—'

'Objection, Your Honor,' I said. 'The witness is now speculating.'

Tanner gave me a side eye, then smiled at Riley and made sure I saw it.

'Your Honor,' he began, 'this witness has cause to examine what we believe to be the murder weapon and posit his expert opinion on whether or not it could have been used to cause the type of injuries which in his opinion caused the victim's death.'

Very few judges would have let Riley proceed. This was way beyond the medical examiner's expertise, considering there was no evidence of any head trauma that the DA had to offer.

'I'll allow the question,' said Tanner.

Before Riley could restate and finish his question, Dr. Morrow shot out his answer.

'The box weighs almost three pounds, it's solid and has sharp corners. There is no question in my mind that this could have caused a skull fracture and fatal brain injury if it had been used as a weapon.'

'Thank you, Dr. Morrow,' said Riley, who sat down like he'd gotten away with murder. He was getting an easy ride from the judge, and I was getting fines.

I stood up and moved around the defense table, closing the distance between me and the witness stand. I felt Riley tense, almost up on his toes already. I could sense it. The judge too was watching me with hawk eyes. Dr. Morrow sensed it also. I could see his eyeline flicking between the judge and Riley. His protectors. At any moment, either one of them was ready to jump on me and rip me apart.

I didn't want to keep them waiting.

'Dr. Morrow, you're altering your testimony to suit the prosecution's case against my client. Isn't that right?'

'Obje—'

Helpfully, Riley didn't even have to finish this word.

Judge Tanner said, 'Mr. Flynn, you have been warned about this line of questioning repeatedly. That question will cost you another thousand dollars.'

'I'll rephrase, Your Honor,' I said. 'Dr. Morrow, you filed two autopsy reports on this victim. Correct?'

This question was short, sharp, to the point. Factually accurate and no way for Riley or Tanner to argue about it.

'That is correct.'

'The jury have only seen your second report, correct?'

'I believe so, but—'

'They only saw your second report – yes or no, Doctor?' I had to risk cutting him off. I didn't want to give him time to explain himself.

'Yes,' he said.

The next question had to be carefully worded. If I straight up asked him why the jury had only seen his second report, you can be sure he would give a perfectly convincing explanation. The risky thing about asking questions in a murder trial is that sometimes witnesses answer you. I didn't want an answer. I wanted to carefully control every word out of his mouth so I could build a narrative for the jury.

'Your first report, which has been hidden from this jury, has a different conclusion on the victim's cause of death – yes or no?'

'The reason there's a difference—'

'I didn't ask you for a reason. I didn't ask you to give this jury poor excuses. I asked you a simple question with a simple yes or no answer.'

Riley was on his feet again – rookie mistake. 'Your Honor, Dr. Morrow can answer Mr. Flynn's question in any manner he chooses, as long as he answers it.'

Before Tanner could speak, I shot back at Riley, not for the judge, but for the jury to hear.

'Your Honor, I'm exploring why Dr. Morrow and the district attorney's office decided to hide relevant evidence from this jury. Obviously, Mr. Riley doesn't want the jury to know the truth, but I'm determined that they hear it.'

I saw Riley's expression change, a wince, like he'd just walked into a wall accidentally. He had only one option now. If he was smart, he would take it.

'Your Honor, actually, having considered it, I withdraw my objection. Let Mr. Flynn waste his time. I don't mind.'

I could take the barb on the end of that statement. I'd shut him up, and he would think twice about interrupting me again now that he knew I wasn't giving him any free rides.

Before Tanner decided she would fine me again, I moved things on quickly.

'Dr. Morrow, your original report stated that the cause of Molly Green's death was inconclusive, but may have been caused by decapitation. Again, that's a *yes* or *no* answer.'

He hesitated, looked to Riley for assistance. Given how the last exchange went, Riley was warming the bench for a while and the judge didn't have any wiggle room to hit me, not yet.

'Yes,' said Dr. Morrow, finally.

'Let's be clear for the jury, when you wrote your second report, your final report, you had not re-examined Molly Green's body, correct?'

'Correct.'

'I just wanted to rule out any possibility that there was some other injury you might have found on a second examination, maybe something that you neglected or missed the first time?'

You can always tell when a professional witness feels insulted. They sit up straighter, or lean forward, or their expression hardens and their gaze focuses on you instead of the jury, who they're trained to look at when they deliver their answers. Dr. Morrow chewed his lip, then leaned forward and looked at me when he said, 'I don't miss important details when carrying out postmortem examinations. I never have, and I never . . . I mean . . .'

He paused while giving his answer, but he wasn't stumbling over his words – he was reading me. I'd raised an eyebrow, like I didn't believe he could possibly carry out a competent examination. His neck flushed red, stark against the white collar of his shirt and the rest of his alabaster complexion. He was really pissed now.

'I mean . . . I don't make mistakes, Mr. Flynn.'

'Really? Not once?' I asked.

'Not. Once,' spat Dr. Morrow.

'Your opinion on the victim's cause of death changed. That's because the district attorney gave you a jewelry box to examine, which supposedly had the victim's blood on it, and told you it was the murder weapon. Isn't that right?'

'I am entitled to alter a preliminary opinion when I have taken all the relevant facts into consideration,' he said, rather too grandly.

'It is not a fact that the jewelry box is the murder weapon, though, is it?'

'I was informed by the district attorney's office that this was the murder weapon.'

I had a comeback for this, a real doozy, but it would take me off point and likely cost me a thousand dollars. I decided I would try and work this answer back into my last question.

'Dr. Morrow, there is no point of fatal impact on the body you examined which would be consistent with a blow from this jewelry box, is there?'

He hesitated, said, 'It's obvious the victim's head was removed to hide any such point of impact.'

'So you're a detective now as well? Are you psychic too?'

'Objection,' said Riley.

'Sustained. Be careful, Mr. Flynn,' said Judge Tanner.

'You did not examine the victim's skull, Dr. Morrow, did you?'

'No, for obvious reasons.'

'So you don't know if the victim sustained thirty blows to the head with a long, pointed object, do you?'

The medical examiner opened his mouth, paused, then said, 'No, but I can take other evidence into account.'

'There was bruising on the victim's neck. You don't know if the victim was strangled, do you?'

'That bruising is likely to have been caused during the amputation at the throat.'

'But you don't know that for sure, do you?'

'No.'

'The victim could have been shot in the head, stabbed in the head, or possibly even smothered to death. Isn't that right?'

'It's possible, but like I said I am entitled to take into account extraneous evidence when forming my opinion.'

'You're referring to the jewelry box, so you think, in your professional opinion, that if the district attorney tells you they found the murder weapon you are entitled to change your entire opinion on cause of death?'

'I am entitled to take that into account, yes.'

I was finishing up, just one more question to set up the final blow.

'It is the district attorney's case that Molly Green was murdered with that jewelry box, correct?'

'Correct.'

'The first question I asked you was if you've changed your opinion to suit the prosecution's case, and you've just proven that this is exactly what you've done.'

Riley tensed, put his hands on the prosecution table, bent his elbows, ready to spring to his feet to object. The judge watched him. Waiting for him to give her a chance to knock me down again.

His lips tightened, his jaw flexed, and then he relaxed back into his chair, leaned back and covered his mouth with his hand. He didn't know if I'd set him a trap, and the question was legit. Too risky.

Dr. Morrow looked at the judge, who stared back at him. No help there.

I didn't mind the awkward pause. In fact, I stayed quiet. I didn't push him. It was good to let the jury see him squirm.

'Yes,' he said, with some difficulty, 'I changed my opinion.'

I looked at him for a few seconds, enjoying this moment. The jury met my eyes, and they were fully switched on now. This wasn't an open-and-shut case.

'Your Honor,' I said, 'I have no further questions at this time, but the defense may need to recall Dr. Morrow.'

She nodded curtly, and I muttered in her direction, under my breath, 'And you owe me a grand.'

'What was that, Mr. Flynn?' she asked with a lot of heat in her tone. She'd probably heard me just fine.

'Apologies, Your Honor, I was just muttering to myself. I said the prosecution's case isn't going to plan.'

Riley rubbed his forehead, sighed and Judge Tanner looked so embarrassed she actually hung her head, looking for the ground to swallow her up. She'd asked the question, after all, and I'd just answered it. Someone on the jury chuckled.

As I made my way back to the defense table, I had a feeling that I was making up some ground. But I knew all that work could fall apart at any moment. A successful defense is a long tightrope walk. A sudden gust of wind could be catastrophic.

That's trial law.

Riley was about to hit back.

The wind was going to start blowing.

I just didn't know how hard.

45
Bloch

Bloch waited.

Bloch watched.

The wind gathered speed.

The tree branches swayed. The foliage rustled.

And . . .

The black tires of a gray panel van rumbled over the gravel outside the East Hampton house. Slow, unhurried. The driver was a tall young man with blond hair so light that it was almost white. The man in the front passenger seat was older, smaller too, judging by how low he was in the seat, with dark hair.

The van came to a stop. The passenger door opened. The small man with black hair got out and his boots crunched their way up to the front porch. He wore gray coveralls, way too big for him. At least, they were once gray, and maybe he'd lost weight. The overalls were covered in different colors of paint, mostly pale but some yellows, greens and reds too, and the same smattering of paint was on his boots.

He had a hard face, weathered and full of experience. His sleeves were rolled up to reveal thick forearms. For a small man, he was well put together. Not stocky, but thick. Years of working paint brushes and rollers will build a certain physique. The sticker on the side of the van said *Perfect Finish, We Paint Houses.*

The small man walked up the porch steps as Corbett opened the front door to greet him.

'You took your time,' said Corbett. 'I think he's finishing up in the kitchen, but he's made a goddamn mess of the wall. Look, our client is super important to us, so we need you to match the paint and make sure it looks like nothing happened in there. You got it?'

'Got it,' said the small man as he took blue gloves from his hip pocket and put them on. 'So the guy's finished?'

'Almost,' said Corbett. 'I saw him packing up about ten minutes ago.'

'Is the owner here?'

'No, just those two. The realtor and the investigator from the wife's law firm. They're getting the house valued and their valuer was checking for dry rot or some shit. It looks terrible. We can't risk pissing off this client.'

The tall, blond driver got out of the panel van.

Bloch had been wrong when she'd assumed he was tall.

When he stood on the gravel, his head was above the roof of the van. He was gigantic. Thin and wildly pale, like a corpse that had been stretched on a rack. His overalls and boots were similarly stained with paint and were comically too small. The bottom of the pants swayed around his ankles, three inches from the top of his boots. He walked around the van and opened the sliding side doors to reveal tarpaulin wrapped in rope, buckets and brushes, aluminum poles and lots of large paint cans inside.

Another man climbed over the cans in the back and leapt out onto the gravel. Average height, shaven head. Tattoos from his neck snaking up behind his ears. Tanned and muscular.

The giant picked up the tarpaulin, tossed it aside and lifted a roll of thick blue rubber sheeting out and dumped it onto the gravel. He then took a five-gallon bucket of paint by the metal handle and together they walked over to the porch.

Following him, the bald man hauled the rubber sheet over, then dumped it on the porch and rolled it out.

Corbett stood by the open door, the small dark-haired man beside him. The tall blond put the bucket on the porch and opened it. From inside he took out a length of rope, which he placed in his teeth, and then he took a roll of plastic garbage bags from his pocket. He tore off a bag, opened it and then whipped it through the air, fanning it out, and walked around the porch, coming up behind Corbett.

'How long is this going to take?' asked Corbett.

The small man said, 'Not long at all.'

The giant flung the bag over Corbett's head, cinching it tight at the neck. Corbett's arms flailed uselessly, his cries muffled. The giant then took the rope from his teeth, and wrapped it round Corbett's neck, holding the bag in place.

The small man casually drew a silenced pistol from his overalls and shot Corbett once in the head.

But his body didn't drop. The tall man, his fists holding the rope around Corbett's neck, ducked low and turned and then leaned forward, hauling Corbett's body up so that it rested on him, back to back, so he was carrying Corbett. The giant's fists clenched over his left shoulder, holding the rope.

Suspended on the back of the giant, Corbett's feet dangled in mid-air.

The small man with the pistol watched the front door, listening to any movement inside.

'Hurry up,' he said.

On command, the bald man bent down and undid Corbett's right shoe and then took off his sock. He brought the five-gallon bucket over and rested Corbett's bare foot inside it. Then he produced a knife and sliced the sole of his foot.

Blood hissed into the bucket.

'Keep him steady,' said the bald man.

Makes sense, thought Bloch.

A recently deceased human still has a high-pressure blood system inside them. The heart would still beat for a few seconds, even after brain death, and there are no major arterial sprays from the bullet wound in the skull to alleviate that pressure. They were using gravity to drain the system. After ten seconds, the bald man took the still-bleeding foot out of the bucket, but the blood flow had drastically reduced. The giant arched his back, dumped Corbett's body on the tarpaulin.

The bald man took something from his pocket and gave it to the giant: a fine wire, maybe four feet long, with what appeared to be corkscrew handles on each end, like a garrote.

But this wasn't a garrote.

The bald man drew a gun from his coveralls, and stood beside the small dark-haired man. Each of them fell into a firing and moving stance, pistol grip supported by both hands as they entered the house.

The giant looped the wire completely around Corbett's neck, then stood over him, both handles in his hands, maybe twelve inches in front of Corbett's face. The giant put a huge boot on Corbett's chest, then pulled on his right hand, which lowered his left. Then pulled on his left, which lowered his right. It was a pump-action motion, which drew the wire back and forth across the entire surface of Corbett's neck in a sawing motion.

The giant pumped his fists, faster and faster, the loop of razor wire tightening.

Within five seconds, Bloch heard a whine from the steel sawing through bone.

Less than ten seconds. The giant reached down, picked up the bag containing Corbett's severed head and placed it in the bucket.

He had some blood spotting on his hands, but not much. Draining the arterial flow of blood first had cut down on the spray. The giant then put the lid on the bucket, knelt down beside Corbett's headless corpse and rolled him into the rubber mat. He squatted and heaved the body onto his shoulder, then picked up the bucket with his other hand and walked to the van.

Total time since they'd arrived, less than three minutes.

It was efficient. Practiced. Smooth and unhurried. A quiet, clinical execution and dismemberment, as if these men were not dealing with a human being. They were body disposal operatives. Like men who had worked in a meat processing plant all of their lives.

This was human processing.

'Jesus Christ, what have you got me into?' whispered Raymond.

'You got this on video?' she whispered back.

Raymond, holding up his phone, nodded.

'When you see a chance, get out of here on foot. Call Lake.'

Bloch put her index finger to her lips. Raymond had finished twenty minutes ago, but she'd told him to leave his equipment and follow her out the back doors of the kitchen, across the sand through the trees enclosing the property until she could get a good look at the entrance unobserved.

Just because Lake was paranoid didn't mean they weren't coming to get her.

She grabbed the long item lying beside her on the bed of rotten leaves. Unwrapped it. Slowly, she made her way through the foliage of the evergreen trees surrounding the house. As long as she kept the soft earth beneath her boots, the giant wouldn't hear her coming. The noise from the wind buffeting the trees would help.

The storm was coming in fast now.

His two friends, the short one and the bald one, would take two, maybe three minutes to clear the house. Maybe half that time had gone already.

Ninety seconds until they came around the side of the property, following her and Raymond's footprints in the sand.

She had never seen these men before. Between Lake and Bloch, they had photographed and researched every single man on Patrick and Julian's security team.

These three men were not part of that detail.

It was important to keep as many of them alive as possible.

One of them would talk. One of them would confess to who had hired them.

The giant put down the bucket at the back of the van, opened the rear doors with his free hand and then, as he dumped Corbett's body in the back, Bloch stepped onto the gravel.

He spun round, his eyes locked on what she held in her hands.

Bloch pointed the working end of a Beretta 1301 tactical shotgun at the giant.

Center mass.

Stock tucked tight to her shoulder. The Beretta fired with lower recoil than most models and its gas system fed the next round into the chamber automatically. It was loaded with six twelve-gauge shells in Bloch's preferred load out. Two slugs, two buckshot, and then two slugs. The slugs were for penetration, and the buckshot for stopping power.

At this range, Bloch could put a hole in the giant that would never be filled.

'Hands in the air,' she said.

In thirty seconds, the small man and his bald friend would emerge from the left side of the house, pistols drawn, looking for targets, pissed and high on adrenaline. When that happened, she needed to be somewhere else, under cover and silent so she could pick them off without being seen.

The giant was unarmed. She had to take him down quickly and quietly. And make sure he could talk.

But he wasn't following her instruction.

His arms hung by his sides like legs of beef on a meat hook.

'Hands up. On your knees. Now,' said Bloch.

The giant didn't move.

He just stared at her, almost as if he was wondering if he could break the shotgun in half before he got to her.

Five feet between them.

Twenty seconds until Bloch had company.

Her eyes flitted, half a second, no more, to the house and then back to the giant.

He was big, but not stupid. He knew he had back-up on the way.

All he had to do was delay.

Should she risk stepping closer to him, to take him out quietly? And maybe having to wrestle him for control of the shotgun.

Or pull the trigger and give away her position to two armed men hunting her and Raymond?

There was no safe option here. Two choices. Both high risk.

What was the right choice?

She now had eighteen seconds to decide.

46
Eddie

Most lawyers say the key to winning a trial is in preparation.

I'd done mine.

A text on my phone confirmed that my prep was about to pay off.

I stood outside the courtroom in the dingy hallway, lined with reporters, witnesses, cops and the prosecution team, and I stared at the beige walls and dark, stained tiles on the floor. I thought about the kind of preparation ordinary lawyers do: assembling briefs, reading reports and statements, workshopping their cross-examinations, writing and rewriting their speeches. Hundreds, sometimes thousands of hours of prep and planning.

Me? I'd ordered donuts.

The delivery guy exited the elevators wearing an all-weather motorcycle suit and carrying a large plain white box containing a dozen glazed. I'd already slipped a twenty to the courthouse security guard manning the scanner that morning, told them to send my donut guy straight up and to text me when they let him through.

I wouldn't want to miss this.

He looked around the hallway. There were maybe thirty people standing around and a few occupying the benches outside the double doors that led to the courtroom. He pulled a delivery docket from a chest pouch. Checked it.

I'd given a detailed description of the intended recipient.

The delivery guy checked the crowd again. Spotted his target.

He wasn't easy to miss.

I couldn't hear what was said, but I watched him hand over the box of donuts to a bemused, but somewhat delighted, Detective Ben Larkin. There were two assistant DAs around him, and they smiled and laughed. As did Larkin, when he opened the box.

The delivery guy handed Larkin an envelope, then left.

Larkin shared out the donuts and both of the ADAs took one. No sign of Larkin's partner, Detective Carey, but I guessed she wasn't far away. Maybe in the bathroom. He took one of the donuts and disappeared half of it in one bite.

The big smile on the big man's face turned into a big surprise when he opened the envelope. I don't know what he was expecting. Maybe a note from a loved one, a family member or perhaps a kind word of encouragement from his fellow police officers in the precinct. His face said it all. Warm curiosity became confusion and then swiftly, fear.

He closed the box.

Stood.

Looked around.

I turned my attention back to the dirty floor tiles, just keeping Larkin in my peripheral vision. He put the note back into the envelope and quickly stuffed it into his inside jacket pocket.

The donuts he tossed into the trash.

It looked like the envelope had had the desired effect.

Harry strode up and said, 'The judge is about to come back out.'

'How's Vanessa?'

'She's okay, I think. She keeps staring at the judge. Have you noticed?'

'I haven't been keeping an eye on her. Maybe she's pissed that we have a partisan judge. Most people expect a fair trial. It can take a while for the reality to sink in. We need to prepare her for what comes next. Only way out of this is to put the blame on the husband.'

'Things are about to get rough.'

'The security footage looks bad. I've been thinking, maybe there's a way to spin it?'

'Is there a way to spin a wife leaving her husband's mistress's, apartment with what looks like the mistress's head in a bag?'

'Yeah,' I said. 'I think there might be.'

47
Bloch

Split-second decisions seemed to take a long time in Bloch's mind.

Time is relative.

With a giant killer in front of her and two armed hitmen coming for her, time was real slow.

Fire the shotgun and give away her position to the hit team.

Or . . .

Take her chances dropping the giant quickly and quietly, keeping him alive as a living witness. Someone who could testify about who hired them and why.

Only one option led to the truth.

She dropped the barrel of the shotgun as she stepped forward and then reversed her grip. The blonde giant grinned and spread his arms wide as Bloch advanced, ready to grab her. He looked strong enough to take her head off bare-handed. She held the shotgun like a club, close to her body, but instead of swinging it she ducked and lunged and then drove the stock straight up under the giant's exposed throat.

But she wasn't aiming for his windpipe – she wanted bone. The stock found it. This wasn't unexpected, considering the man's chin was the size of a porcelain sink.

He dropped to his knees, his head rocked back, but Bloch was already moving past him at speed, the stock now at her shoulder and the barrel pointed at the right-hand side of the house, the iron sights trained on the corner of the building. Her focus stayed there as her boots found the porch steps, and she ascended them stepping sideways, the shotgun levelled at the corner at all times.

A head poked round the corner.

Bloch pulled the trigger.

A cloud of brick dust blew off the edge of the building. The dust cloud cleared to reveal a bloodied, bald head. The body followed it to the floor. She had missed him, but the brick shrapnel dislodged from the shot had done the job for her.

The pistol fell from his dead hands.

Bloch's right shoulder hit the wall of the house and she scraped along it toward the end, keeping tight, narrowing the angle for the short man with the black hair wearing the baggy overalls. He was the leader, Bloch had guessed, and he had yet to put his head round the corner. Considering what had happened to his bald friend, he might just think twice about poking any body part round it.

She shut her mouth, tried to slow down her breathing.

Listened.

All she could hear was the beating of her own heart.

Shit.

The short guy now had the advantage.

Right now, he could be doubling back, coming through the house and be out the front door in twenty seconds. If he did that, he would be behind her, with Bloch's back against a wall and no cover. Or, he could play the double bluff and come around the corner of the house shooting at tight angles.

Shit.

Only way to play this was to beat the odds.

She should widen her killing field. Run back to her truck and get behind it, giving her a broad field of fire covering the corner of the house and the front door.

She lowered the shotgun, looked at her Jeep.

Thirty feet away.

Her boots would be hammering on that gravel.

There were three poor options here.

Go through the house, but maybe he was heading that way and had already taken cover in the kitchen with a kill shot lined up for Bloch soon as she stepped onto those tiles.

Try for the Jeep. Play the odds. But thirty feet of open ground lay between Bloch and the perfect firing position.

Or stay put.

Which was the biggest risk?

House. Jeep and cover. Or stay on the corner.

Three different ways to survive or three different ways to get herself killed.

This last armed man already knew Bloch must've dealt with the giant quietly. And his bald partner was down.

This wasn't the short guy's first rodeo. He was trained and experienced.

The only question was how smart this man would be in this situation and how clearly he would think his problem through. Given his professionalism, he'd probably been killing people for a long time.

That meant he was either really smart, or really lucky.

In moments like this, death comes fast and easy. But it's not making the wrong decision that takes a life, it's freezing up and not making any kind of decision at all.

She didn't like any of the three options.

She decided to make a fourth.

Bloch angled the shotgun toward the sky, pulled the trigger twice.

Double tap.

Blowing through the second slug in the chamber and the buckshot.

She immediately dropped to the gravel. Belly on the ground, stock at her shoulder.

The short man would've heard the shots.

He knew the last thing Bloch wanted to do was give away her position.

He would think that she was shooting at the only other possible target.

The giant.

Which meant she would be at the front of the house, probably behind the Jeep. Facing the giant at the van. The short man would know distraction was the biggest weapon he had in his arsenal. If he was a pro, he would come tearing round that corner, running at full speed, trying to get to the van and shooting while he moved.

He wouldn't anticipate Bloch had stayed put. That she would be low, and waiting, and that she had fired into the air to lure him out. Because he knew she was smart enough not to take that chance.

The short man burst from the side of the building, firing at the Jeep.

The stock kicked into Bloch's shoulder as she fired the remaining slugs.

The short man's feet left the gravel, and he would never stand up on them again.

She lowered the empty shotgun, put one hand on the wall to steady herself as she rose to her feet. Adrenaline always made her feel a little light-headed.

Footsteps on the gravel.

Big, heavy ones.

Moving fast.

Bloch turned, saw the elbow slam into her face, heard the dull echo of her skull bouncing off the wall and her vision blurred. The shotgun fell from her grip. Massive hands took hold of her jacket and slammed her body against the wall. This time, she tucked her chin into her chest so only her shoulders hit the bricks but it was still enough to knock all the air out of her.

She stared up at the face of the giant. His lips drawn back, teeth bared, his jaw already swollen on the left side from when Bloch put the stock of the shotgun through it.

The pain from the blow to the face and her skull being smashed against the wall was beginning to bite, hard. She welcomed it. The pain blew away the drowsiness and Bloch started to think.

If the giant stayed on his feet there was only one way this was going to go, and that wouldn't work out well for Bloch. Her magnum was on her hip, but he was too close and there was no way to draw and fire without him grabbing it from her. He was way too strong for that kind of move.

Instead, Bloch leaned in close, tucked her feet behind her and used the weight of her body falling as momentum. She grabbed the giant's left thigh, wrapping her left arm around it, and sank the heel of her right palm into the side of his left knee.

Pulling his thigh with her left.

Pushing on the side of his knee with her right.

His stance widened and he tried to get his left foot off the ground to straighten it and alleviate the pressure, but Bloch already had all of her weight on that leg.

A clubbing blow landed on the side of her head.

She pulled.

She pushed.

The giant screamed as his knee separated, then he landed on his back like an oak tree that had been felled.

Bloch was on her knees, panting, shaking her head, trying to clear it. She had to put him out, now. Or pull the magnum and put a bullet in him.

One thought permeated the haze of adrenaline.

Keep him alive for Eddie. They needed to know who had sent him.

She had a better idea. No point in wrestling him into a sleeper hold. Another blow on the head with the butt of her magnum would put him out like a light.

She reached for her gun, nicknamed Maggie.

'Freeze! Police!'

The voice came from her left.

Captain Landry had his police weapon drawn, and aimed at her.

'Nice and slow, finger and thumb on the butt of that magnum. Draw it and toss it.'

Bloch did as she was asked as Landry approached her in a shooting stance. She was fast, but she couldn't get the gun up and pointed at Landry before he could pull the trigger.

No point.

She had no other choice.

Bloch tossed the weapon at Landry's feet.

Something distracted her attention as she raised her hands in surrender.

Blue and red flashing lights through the foliage. Landry must've parked his patrol car at the property gate and walked in quietly.

'Don't you move. Hands behind your head. And don't try for that shotgun. You're not that fast,' said Landry.

Bloch locked her fingers together behind her head.

Ten feet from her now, Landry knelt down and picked up her magnum with his left hand, keeping his own pointed at Bloch in his right hand.

The giant was still on his back, gasping, clutching his knee.

'Is he shot?' asked Landry, as he drew level with the incapacitated giant.

'No,' said Bloch.

Landry stood up to full height. Casually pointed Bloch's magnum at the giant.

And blew his head off.

He dropped Bloch's magnum, aimed his own weapon at her head.

'Where's the guy who called this in?'

Raymond.

Damn, she should have told him not to call the local cops.

'He ran,' said Bloch.

'I'll find him. By then it will be too late. He will have caught a bullet. Maybe from that shotgun of yours. The fewer survivors, the easier this will be to clean up. Looks to me like you killed four men in cold blood. But one of them managed to get a good shot on you before he died. Chest shot, I think.'

Bloch thought about her tactical vest. It was a Mil-Tec tactical combat vest. With two polyethylene plates in the carriers. One in front. One in back. Each plate gave level-three ballistic protection, but weighed only three and a half pounds. She hadn't skimped on the plates. They would stop a standard NATO round, and were five pounds lighter than a steel plate.

If Landry shot and hit the chest plate . . .

Bloch would be sore. But just fine.

The vest would save her.

Too bad it was still safely locked in the trunk of her Jeep.

Bloch closed her eyes.

And waited for the shot.

48
Bloch

Bang!

She flinched.

Eyes shut.

Waited for the pain. The fear crushing her chest like an anvil was pressing on it.

Nothing.

No pain.

Bang!

That sound again, but hearing it for the second time, it didn't sound like the crack from a .45 or a .22 caliber pistol.

It was different.

The second time she heard it, she sensed that it was closer.

Landry still had the gun on her. He hadn't fired, but it was pointed square at her chest.

And he was looking over his left shoulder.

Staring at the driveway.

Then Bloch heard a different sound.

An engine.

Not a healthy one.

It was the sound of a six-cylinder V6 running on maybe three, maybe two cylinders.

Revving high.

A shit-colored Pontiac Aztec came tearing up the gravel driveway at speed.

Landry checked Bloch hadn't moved. She was still on her knees.

He turned back to the car, completely taken by surprise. Bloch imagined he had no clue who the hell was in this shit heap. But he was a police officer, a captain no less, in uniform, with his gun pointed at a suspect. He could send whoever it was away just as fast as they arrived.

The Aztec's brakes slammed on with a high-pitched whine and it backfired again, sending a huge cloud of black smoke from the exhaust.

That was the sound Bloch had heard.

She didn't move.

Not an inch.

The wind blew the cloud of black smoke back over the car, masking the identity of the driver as they opened their door.

The smoke cleared in just a few seconds, and Landry stared at Gabriel Lake, who was pointing his Glock straight at the police captain. Landry turned away from Lake and focused all his attention on Bloch.

'Put the gun down, Lake, and get on the ground.'

'You can't take two targets. If you shoot her, you'll be dead before her body hits the ground. You know that. I'm guessing you want to keep this quiet, so you don't have back-up on the way. It's just you and me now. Bloch is unarmed. Put your gun down and we can figure this out.'

Landry said nothing, but Bloch saw the pistol in his hand begin to shake as he weighed up his options. They were limited.

'Okay,' said Landry. 'Let's do this together. Why don't we both put our pieces away and then we can talk.'

Lake's arms were spread through the open windowsill of the Aztec, using the body of the door for cover. He was perfectly still. Aim zeroed.

Ready to rock.

It was then that she noticed Raymond, hands over his head, ducking down in the passenger seat of the Aztec.

'Okay, let's put our guns down and figure things out together,' said Lake.

Landry didn't move at first. He kept his eye on the iron sights of his pistol, trying to aim for Bloch and keep his aim straight.

'Okay,' said Landry.

His neck began to turn to the left, to check Lake's position, so he could mimic his movements, and together they would put down their guns.

Soon as Lake appeared in his field of vision, his aim moved off Bloch, just a fraction, but enough.

Crack.

The top of Landry's head came off, and he dropped like a stone.

'I guess I figured it out on my own,' said Lake.

49
Eddie

Detective Lorraine Carey wore a brand-new gray pant suit and a cream blouse. Her hair was tied back and she'd had her nails done. This was her big day in her career case. The make-up didn't fully mask the dark rings beneath her eyes, which suggested she hadn't slept much. It was only to be expected that she would be nervous. As she sat down in the witness box, I saw her cross her legs, then uncross them and put her feet down flat on the floor, then place her hands on her knees. Her knuckles were white, and her neck flushed red.

Riley established her credentials as the lead detective on the case, but didn't ask her about her experience, since she had none. Instead, he went straight into the interview with Vanessa in his questions, and at various points asked for the recording to be played in court.

The jury heard Vanessa denying she knew Molly Green, and denying that she had ever been to Molly's apartment.

'Was there anything in your subsequent investigations which may have cast doubt on the version of events given by the defendant?' asked Riley.

'Yes, two key pieces of evidence directly contradict the defendant's version of events,' said Carey, delivering her answer in a deliberate monotonous tone. It sounded rehearsed to me.

'What were those pieces of evidence?'

'The first was a jewelry box, which my partner, Detective Benjamin Larkin, had examined in our forensic laboratory. He can speak to that piece of evidence in more detail. The second was security camera footage which I obtained.'

'The People shall be calling Detective Larkin to deal with that evidence tomorrow, but for now can you tell us more about the footage from the security camera?'

'Yes, I'd noticed a security camera at the rear entrance to the property. The building behind had been demolished and there were plans for construction. The owner of that site wanted to make sure it was secure for parking while construction plans were approved so he installed a camera overlooking the temporary lot. I obtained the footage from the camera for the night of the murder and viewed it.'

'The People enter exhibit one-one-three into evidence, with Her Honor's permission. Let's just play the relevant parts of that footage for the jury and you can talk us through it, Detective.'

Having heard Vanessa deny she'd visited Molly's apartment, the video evidence stirred some double takes from the jury.

'What is the time stamp on the video?' asked Riley.

'That's twenty-two, thirty-two,' said Detective Carey.

'And can you describe the female shown entering the victim's building?'

'She has blonde hair, tied in a ponytail, white pants, light-colored fawn coat and white shirt. We can't see a face in this video, but this person resembles the defendant, Vanessa Vanderpool.'

The second portion of video footage then played. Riley paused the video at the exact moment Vanessa seemed to stare up at the camera as she left the building.

'What is the time stamp on the video?'

'Twenty-three, fifty-eight.'

'Who is the person shown in this still image?'

'That is clearly the defendant, Vanessa Vanderpool. This shows the defendant exiting the victim's building.'

'Please describe the woman in this video.'

'It's Vanessa Vanderpool, her hair is the same and she's wearing the same outfit of white pants, white blouse and light brown overcoat. Only this time she's carrying a black Nike gym bag with a white tick logo in her left hand.'

'Detective Carey, was the victim's head ever found?'

'No.'

'Would this bag be large enough to conceal the victim's severed head?'

'Yes.'

'From your examination of the security camera footage for this building, did you see anyone else enter or leave the building prior to the arrival of the officers who discovered the defendant's body?'

'No.'

A middle-aged female juror shook her head, stared wide-eyed at the image of Vanessa on screen with that bag. Another juror, a young man in his twenties in a white button-down shirt silently mouthed 'wow' and turned to the jurors on either side of him. The older man beside him just nodded, while the elderly lady made the sign of the cross, blessing herself and quietly muttering, before they all turned again to stare at the screen.

'No further questions,' said Riley.

Before I could get to my feet, Judge Tanner said, 'Court is adjourned for the day. We will begin tomorrow with the cross-examination of Detective Carey.'

If there was a way for a judge to pour salt into a wound, this one was about the closest. You adjourn the case for the day after the jury has heard the most damaging piece of evidence in the whole case, so they have the whole rest of the night and the next morning to allow themselves to make up their minds that the defendant has to be guilty.

It was as good as the judge telling the jury that there was no coming back from that, and that they could take it easy for the rest of the trial, safe in the knowledge the verdict had to be guilty.

Harry leaned over to me, whispered so as to make sure Vanessa didn't hear him, 'Do you want to know my expert legal opinion?'

I nodded.

Harry said, 'We're fucked.'

50
Eddie

Harry was right.

Those two words didn't leave my mind for a second.

I sat on a stool in the Taco Bell restaurant in Times Square. I chewed the paper straw that sat in my soda cup.

I wasn't thirsty, and I don't eat here. I just wanted something to chew on.

It was about the last place on earth you'd find anybody who actually lives in New York. This place was tourist central. Thousands of people passed through these doors. None of them would be remotely connected with the Molly Green trial or the investigation. In the unlikely event a local did come in, they would order takeout. Having a secret meeting in one of the busiest restaurants in the world didn't sound like a smart plan, but it worked. Hiding in plain sight didn't get much better.

Larkin was five minutes late when he walked through the doors. He clocked me, stopped dead in his tracks and swore. He went up to the counter and ordered, then came to the table and set down a soda and a side of nachos in front of him.

'Come here, Eddie,' he said, and held his hands out to embrace me in a hug.

He wasn't being friendly. I embraced him, let his hands pat my back, my sides, then my pants pocket, and finally the inside pockets of my overcoat. I patted his back, and his sides, to make it look like we were glad to see each other when in fact he was patting me down, looking for a wire.

'You got a phone in your jacket pocket,' he said, as he let me go.

I took my phone out of my pocket, placed it beside my soda cup.

'Turn it off, please,' he said as he sat down opposite me.

I switched off my phone. He was paranoid about being taped. I'd guessed as much.

'You have the photo I sent you?' I asked.

'I should've known it was you,' he said.

'Who were you expecting?'

'I don't know,' he said as he took out the photo I'd included in the box of donuts I'd sent him earlier that day with instructions on the back to meet here, at this time.

'If you know that many people who might want to blackmail you, I would seriously consider making some lifestyle adjustments.'

He put the photo on the counter, the one of him receiving a package from Dekker. The picture that Bloch took many weeks ago when she was trailing the cops and trying to figure out their angle on the investigation.

'Fuck you, Eddie,' he said.

'I'm here to help you, Larkin. You've had Internal Affairs crawling over your skin before. I thought you might want to take all available steps to stop that from happening again.'

He put several nacho chips into his mouth at once and began to crunch them. The dust from the chips coated his lips and fell onto his blue tie.

'I have two options for you,' I said, taking a cigarette lighter from my pocket and placing it on the table. 'I can burn this photo. Pretend like it never happened. I didn't see it. Bloch didn't see it. It never existed. Or, I can burn you. That's your choice.'

'Not much of a decision, is it?' said Larkin, and as he spoke small fragments of nachos erupted from his mouth like the waste pipe on a woodchipper.

'Not really. But this is all your fault. You used to be a good cop, before you fucked up an investigation by cutting corners. If you hadn't been so good, they would have canned your ass and saved the money on your pension. This could be another chance for you. But you've gotta do exactly as I say.'

He washed the chips down with a slurp from his soda, and asked, 'How much?'

'I don't want money. I want something else.'

'What do you want?'

'I want you to do the right thing. For a start, your employment with Julian Vanderpool is unofficially at an end. Now you work for me.'

'What if I arrested you now for trying to blackmail an investigating officer during a murder trial in which your client is the sole defendant? You'd be disbarred, you'd serve ten, maybe fifteen years for perverting the course of justice. How about that?'

He had lowered his voice, looked me in the eye as he spoke.

I said nothing for a moment. Then smiled.

'You almost had me going there, Larkin. How about this? If I don't make a phone call to Harry Ford in the next thirty minutes, he serves that photograph on the court, and the DA, and I ask you on the witness stand why you were accepting a suspicious package from the employee of the father of the only other viable suspect in a murder you were investigating?'

Larkin stared at me for a second, took another sip from his soda.

'Good,' I said, 'I'm glad we've cleared that up. First thing I want to know is, what was in the package you got from Dekker?'

'You don't know?'

I had no idea what the hell was in that package.

'Of course I know,' I said, 'I just need to hear it from you. You need to trust me, and I need to trust you. Or one of us might be going to jail and it's not going to be me.'

Larkin's head fell forward, he grunted, then sat up again and put more chips in his mouth.

As he chewed, he said something that I didn't really catch, and then, '. . . and fifty Gs.'

'Fifty grand, was that a down payment or the full amount?'

'Half. I got another fifty when we indicted the wife.'

'And what was the first thing you'd told me was in the package? I couldn't make out what you'd said.'

He took another slurp from his soda, smacked his lips then said, 'Molly Green's journal.'

'What's in the journal?' I asked.

'She was playing a part. Molly Green was a false identity. This woman was lying to everyone to get close to Patrick Vanderpool.'

'Why'd Dekker give you the journal? Surely that's motive for Patrick. Why the hell would they give that to the police?'

He leaned back, took a long drink from the straw until he was slurping at nothing but air. Then put it down and said, 'Dekker chose me. He knew I was a good cop, at heart. Yeah, I might have lost my way, lost some evidence here and there when it suited me, but I wasn't going to cover up the murder of an innocent girl even if it was for a hundred K. He wanted me to know Molly wasn't innocent. He told me to read the journal, that I'd see she was deranged, cunning and dangerous too. She was gearing up to kill somebody, so I figured it did no harm to make sure I was protecting the right people. The real victims.'

'Patrick Vanderpool is a victim?'

'He could've been, if this crazy chick had gotten her way. He told me to focus on the wife, Vanessa. That she'd taken matters into her own hands with Molly. That she was the real killer. And that in the investigation we should keep quiet about who Molly really was, that exposing her would only make things complicated for Patrick and his run for governor. He told me to read the journal, and then burn it after.'

'And did you?' I asked.

'It's in the glovebox of my car. I figured it was an insurance policy. That if I ever needed a favor from the new governor I could use it.'

'The journal is in your pocket,' I said.

He stared at me.

'I patted you down too. Give it to me.'

'Why should I?'

'I want to make sure you're not lying to me. I can hurt you with that photo, remember?'

He reached into his coat pocket, hesitated. His eyes roamed the room while his mind wandered. I didn't know what he was thinking, but, whatever it was, he was struggling with it. Either he was wondering how much damage I could cause him with that photo, or maybe something else. The photo alone would just be the starting point for Internal Affairs. It wouldn't take them long to look into his investigation and his finances. Cops are shit at hiding dirty money. But right then I wasn't a hundred per cent sure that self-preservation was the only thing on his mind.

Cops don't start out dirty. Some join up because it's in their blood – long family lines of blue-blood cops. Some join up for the pay and the pension and the job security. It's rare for cops to get laid off in this city. For a few, a section of recruits, they join for one of two reasons. Either they just want the power from the uniform, or they want to do some good – they want to help people and put away bad guys.

I wondered, just for a second, why Larkin joined the force. His early career was stellar, and he could have been one of those golden cops. He took out the journal and placed it on the table in front of me beside my soda.

As he put it down, he breathed out. A long sigh. Like he was laying down a burden, and lightening the load he carried around on his shoulders. No matter how far a person falls, there's always a part of them that wants to climb back up.

I put the journal in my coat.

'What else did you do for Dekker?'

'I handled some cash payments. Dekker wanted to make sure witnesses would play ball.'

'The neighbor, Alison Karim. Who else?'

'That's all I'm saying for now.'

'The judge?' I asked.

'You're a real piece of work, Eddie. Yeah, her too. But, look, that's it. That's all I got. I'll never testify to any of this. I'm not going to jail for doing the right thing.'

'The right thing?'

'Yeah, look, I made sure that the right person went down for this. That's all. It don't matter one heap of shit what I've done. I believe your client killed that girl. I didn't fuck around with forensics, Eddie. It's her DNA on that jewelry box, and the vic's blood too. She beat that girl to death with that box then took her head. She killed Molly and tried to frame her husband. And I made sure she didn't get away with it. You ask me about any of this shit on the stand, I'll deny it all. I'll say Dekker gave me the journal and I gave it to you. That we didn't use it because it painted the victim in a bad light for the jury. That the NYPD is not in the business of trashing murder victims. You can't prove any of the other shit I told you, so we're done here.'

'You mean, *you're* done. You're finished. Do the right thing and I can get you FBI protection. You're being manipulated. Patrick and Dekker, they're trying to frame the wife and you're helping them.'

'Listen to yourself. You believe your client? She's a liar. She said she'd never been to Molly's building. She didn't know about the security camera in the back of the building, though. Like I said, we're done here.'

He got up, left his soda and nachos, took the photo, and then left.

That hadn't gone the way I'd expected.

I picked up my soda, pulled the straw out, then opened the lid and tipped the cup. The mini microphone fell into my hand.

Reaching under the table, I pulled the duct tape loose and retrieved a phone. Swiped the screen to open it and then stopped the recording.

It was an illegal clandestine recording. It may not even be admissible in court. If I let Judge Tanner hear this, my best guess was she would be worried about Larkin exposing her. And she wouldn't want Larkin to be in any kind of trouble in case he made a deal with law enforcement. Taking out a corrupt judge is a way bigger prize than a corrupt cop. Tanner would bury this recording, and then try to bury me and Vanessa.

Still, the recording was ammunition.

I just needed to figure out the best way to use it.

As I got up from my seat, I thought about Larkin. He was corrupt and he deserved to go down for this. I could understand his reasoning. Most cops who go bad do it for what they believe to be the right reasons – stretching the evidence, hiding inconsistencies in their case, all with the aim of putting bad people away. They manipulated the system for their cause.

In some ways, Larkin wasn't so different from me.

I just hoped I was on the right side of this case.

Weaving my way through the crowds at Times Square, I reached the subway station, got on a downtown train and found a seat in the carriage.

I took out Molly Green's journal, and read.

51
Vanessa

Eddie was late.

She was pacing the floor, clenching and unclenching her fists. The skin on her hands was raw, and she'd moisturized them a few times, but it didn't help. She was washing them way too often. It was almost seven when Vanessa heard the knock on the door of her hotel suite.

'They're here,' she said.

Voss sat on the edge of Vanessa's bed, and placed her index finger over her lips to confirm they should be quiet. Vanessa closed the bedroom door, then made her way through the living area and opened her hotel room door.

Eddie looked tired.

Harry looked as though he'd had a few stiff drinks. As he entered the suite, and passed close by, she could just about smell the whiskey on his breath. Not overpowering. Just there.

'There's a lot to catch up on. I think you should sit down,' said Eddie.

Vanessa nodded, settled into the couch, Eddie and Harry on the couch opposite.

Eddie said, 'My investigators are currently talking to the FBI. A friendly agent I know is handling. Basically, three men killed one of your husband's lawyers, then tried to kill my investigators and our DNA expert after they found blood on the walls of your Hamptons home.'

Vanessa pressed her nails so deep into her palms she thought she might have pierced the skin. She looked at her palms, the marks there, and was thankful she wasn't bleeding.

'Why did they kill the lawyer?'

'They were a clean-up crew. They don't leave witnesses.'

'What blood did they find? Is Patrick alright? Is he hurt?' she asked.

'He wasn't there. It was old blood. The wall had been painted over to cover it up, but we have a damn good forensics guy called Raymond who is up on all the latest pioneering methods of detection. As long as the paint can be scraped away carefully enough, the old bloodstain can be analyzed. It's not perfect, but it should help us. One wall of Molly Green's apartment had been freshly painted, and he found Molly's blood there too. Although, why someone would paint over blood on that wall when there's a pool of the victim's blood on the floor is still a mystery. But the fact that they painted over the stain established a pattern of concealment. That's what took us to the Hamptons house.'

'Why would that take you there?'

'Because we believe a young woman named Teresa Chase was murdered in that house six years ago. A body was found in the woods, but the body didn't have a head and no formal identification could be made. Patrick was seeing Teresa, and he reported that she'd been ripped out to sea while swimming at the beach. We think he killed her and had help covering it up. We'll have a DNA sample from the Hamptons house to compare with the DNA from the unidentified body found in the woods. We think it will confirm that this Jane Doe was murdered in that house.'

Her hands flew to her mouth. Tears welled in her eyes, her fingers trembling.

'And you . . . you think he killed Molly, and . . . and . . . had it covered up the same way?' she asked.

'We think so, but there are differences. This clean-up team cut the bottom of the lawyer's foot to drain his blood. Molly had that same cut on the sole of her foot. The body found in the woods didn't have a cut on the foot, so it's not a complete match. The team that my investigators took out were professional killers, experts in body disposal. We think they were sent there by Patrick. You are now in a lot of danger, Vanessa. You have to stay indoors, and don't move out of this room unless we're beside you.'

'But why?'

Harry said, 'We think Patrick, maybe his father too, are now in damage limitation mode. They might think it's cleaner to have you killed.'

'Oh my God? Wait, wait, this doesn't make sense. Why would Patrick kill this woman, and why would he kill Molly?'

'You told us yourself,' said Eddie, staring at Vanessa's arms, always covered by long sleeves. 'He's violent. He loses it sometimes. I saw it. And you showed us those burn marks on your arms. We don't know why he killed Teresa Chase. Maybe he just lost it and things went too far, but we think we have a motive for why he killed Molly.'

'Why?'

'Because Molly wasn't who she said she was. We think Molly Green was an assumed identity. She had no relatives, and very few of the usual identification documents you might expect to find. We can't find birth records, tax records only go back about eight months and the social security number looks to be fake. We can't prove this, but we think Patrick found Molly's journal in her apartment, and read it. A friendly police officer gave me the journal. We think Patrick figured out that Molly was Teresa Chase's half-sister, a woman called Willow Chase. We think Molly was really Willow, out for revenge. That's why he killed her, before she could do something to hurt him or kill him. And then Patrick had these men come to the apartment and cover up his crime.'

'Jesus Christ, I can't believe it . . .'

'You said you went to Molly's apartment on the night of the murder to warn her about Patrick and his temper. To tell her that she was making a mistake, that he could be violent. What did Molly tell you?' asked Eddie.

'She said she didn't believe me, that I was just a jealous wife.'

Vanessa dabbed at the tears beneath her eyes now, trying not to smear her make-up. Her chest felt like it was going to explode and her head felt hot, as if it was boiling.

'You can't testify about Patrick's confession to you that he killed Molly. But we need you to testify that you believe he killed her. We need you to tell the jury about his violence, about how he has physically abused you, burned you with spoons, everything. You need to tell them Patrick was having an affair with Molly and he killed her. It's the only way out of this for you, Vanessa – you've got to tell the jury your husband went back and killed Molly after you left the apartment that night. Now, there's a problem about what you can and can't say on the stand, because of marital privilege. But Harry is working on a way around that.'

Vanessa nodded. 'I'll do it. I'll tell the truth.'

She tried hard to listen to Eddie and Harry, but her mind was racing and her pulse was beating so hard she felt it throbbing in her throat, like a constant drum that echoed inside her head and through her whole body.

Eddie took a pen, made a note on a legal pad, tore off the page and gave it to her.

'What's this?' she asked.

'That's what I want you to wear tomorrow,' he said.

'Okay, I can do that. Any reason?'

'Best if you don't know,' said Eddie.

They talked for another ten minutes, making sure she was okay, that she could hold it together for the rest of the trial, then Eddie and Harry left.

As she closed the door to the hotel room, and listened for their footfalls as they walked away down the hall, she turned and caught a glimpse of her reflection in the full-length mirror on the wall. She had lost weight, her cheekbones sharper than they had been since she was in her teens. So much for trying to keep her make-up intact. Her face was a mess with tears.

She stood in front of the mirror.

Shaking.

She wiped her face, smearing the make-up further, and then returned to the bedroom.

Voss was standing there, waiting for her.

'I heard everything,' said Voss. 'Do I have to remind you what will happen if you accuse your husband of this murder?'

Vanessa shook her head.

'I think I do,' said Voss. 'If you tell that jury Patrick was having an affair, if you tell them he's a violent man, if you tell them you think he killed Molly . . .'

'I know how dangerous my husband can be. Trust me,' said Vanessa.

Voss collected her coat, buttoned it and marched out of Vanessa's room, letting the door slam closed behind her.

Vanessa lay down on the bed, breathed in and out. The pressure in her head had been building for hours and now it felt like it would explode.

How long could she keep lying to Flynn?

More importantly, how long could she keep lying to Voss?

If you lie to everyone, sooner or later, you will be found out. She told herself she had to hang on for just a little while longer. Flynn was smarter than Voss, and he was going to find out all about Molly Green.

Her only hope was to pray that Flynn didn't figure everything out. She wanted to trust him. If it came right down to it, she would have to tell him the truth.

But not yet.

Flynn was a lawyer, but he wasn't like other lawyers. He had a good heart and a moral code. His ethics were clear, he knew right from wrong and he couldn't be bought, but his judgement was twisted somehow. He did what he thought was right and the law be damned. She knew he would lie and manipulate witnesses, and do whatever he had to in order to protect her.

How would he react if she had to tell him she was a killer?

52
Patrick

'Home' is a strange word, thought Patrick.

For some it is a comfort. It's a warm blanket they wrap around themselves.

For others, it is a needle of ice being scraped across their skin. It is fear, it is danger, it is the creeping dread that lives in the pit of their stomach.

For Patrick, *home* was something else. Something more complicated. Unlike most people, as a result of his father's insane wealth, home wasn't rooted in a specific house or apartment. There were many properties that his parents lived in depending on his father's career priorities and the time of year. Later, he would learn that their locations were also influenced by whichever woman his father was enjoying an affair with at any particular moment.

Whatever genetic advantages Patrick had, in terms of looks especially, came from his mother, June. She had been a model, of course, because his father wouldn't really have been interested in her otherwise. For Julian, it wasn't enough that a woman was beautiful, she had to be known for her beauty and desired by others. His choice of partners was then driven just as much by status as everything else. He was a self-made billionaire, but Patrick wondered how much of that skinny kid whose first job was hauling paper in a printing works remained in his father. Perhaps a lot. He had a chip on his shoulder the size of Nebraska.

Julian had already ditched his first wife when he met June, who would go on to be married to Julian for seven years and then secure her place as the reigning champion among the sorority of ex-Mrs. Vanderpools that littered the planet. Or at least she would have, if she had survived. Divorce was on the cards at the time. Even at six years old, he had seen the signs. The fights got more brutal. His mother would unsuccessfully hide bruises on her arms, neck and shoulders. He liked to watch her put on her make-up in the morning, standing at the door to the bedroom. She would sit at her dressing table and pat concealer and foundation onto her bruises. One time, he tripped over his own feet in their garden at the house in Los Angeles, and the next day a purple bruise appeared over his kneecap and shin.

'That looks sore, honey,' said his mom.

'It's okay. We can just put some of your magic make-up on it, and it will go away,' Patrick had said.

He never forgot her face in that moment.

When he thought of her, that was the face and the expression he saw. Thinking of it now, in the bathtub in his father's massive townhouse in Manhattan, he wondered if the face he saw in his mind's eye was really his mother. After she died, his father had all of her pictures taken down from the houses. Perhaps the face he saw was one he had invented.

Maybe he had forgotten his mother a long time ago, and all he had now was the image he had created.

That water in the tub had long gone cold.

Patrick examined his fingers only to find the pads had shriveled and swirled because he had submerged them for far too long. His hands were slender and fine. He'd never worked a day in his life. The calluses he had built up rowing in college were long since gone, smoothed by a daily moisturizer that cost six hundred dollars a tub.

He stared at his hands, at the wrinkles around his knuckles and the fine lines of approaching middle age. They were not nearly as mottled and aged as his father's, but they did look similar. These hands had hurt and loved. And sometimes, when he was very angry, they were not his own. They become someone else's hands.

His father's perhaps.

He got out of the tub, dried himself with a soft white towel and dressed.

Standing at the top of the stairs, he listened for sounds of his father. It was always possible to tell where he was in any house by the sound of his voice. It was deep and rough and carried everywhere. He thought he heard him downstairs, but couldn't be sure. The one place he wouldn't find his old man would be the kitchen. He didn't think his father had ever set foot in there.

As he reached the bottom of the stairs and turned toward the kitchen, he heard that voice.

'What have you been up to?'

The voice came from the lounge. Patrick checked his watch. It was almost nine. He had spent the entire day upstairs, on his laptop, checking for news of the trial, scrolling social media and feeling like a prisoner. His father had insisted he hunker down until the trial was over. It didn't matter what press he got now, every question, every single piece online or on the news or in print would mention Molly Green and his wife's trial. Patrick had to avoid all of it, at least until the verdict. And even then he could speak to the press again only if the jury came back with the right verdict.

His father was spread out on the white leather couch, a remote control in one hand, his ubiquitous cigar in the other, and several cell phones spread out on the coffee table beside him, like he was a goddamn drug dealer. The large-screen TV above the fireplace was playing his news channel. He looked at him, cocked an eyebrow, waiting for an answer to his question about what Patrick had been doing.

'I've been checking for news on Vanessa's trial. Staying out of the way.'

'Any word from the DA on when you'll be called as a witness?' he asked.

'I'm on their list of witnesses, but I haven't heard anything yet.'

Julian nodded, said, 'Good. And don't worry about the campaign. You can pick it back up in a month or so, when all this is a distant memory.'

'A month? I'm not going to be able to run now. I've been thinking of pulling out, Dad, maybe running again next cycle. Maybe . . .'

He wanted to say, *maybe he could do something else*. That maybe politics wasn't his bag. That maybe he was going to move out of the city, to get as far away from his piece-of-shit father as possible. That his father was a monster, and he wanted Patrick to be just like him, and he wasn't going to have any part of it. Not any more.

But of course he didn't say any of that.

'You always were a pussy,' said Julian, turning his attention back to the TV. 'Look at this,' he said. The news anchor was talking about US miliary action in South America. The banner of rolling news on the bottom of the screen detailed updates on war in the Middle East, the government's threats to invade a NATO ally's country on the basis of establishing US security, five teenagers dead in a high-school shooting in Texas, fresh allegations that members of the government were involved in child sex trafficking, a Russian bomb killed thirty-civilians in . . . and on and on and on . . .

'The news cycle has never moved this fast. The world is spinning out of control. There's a high-pressure hose made up of death, corruption, war, rape and murder that's aimed at everyone in the world through their phone screens twenty-four hours a day. With thousands of gallons of shit being thrown at them, they're going to miss a few smaller turds. Little shits, like you. Despite the media coverage of this trial, most of your voters don't even know Vanessa has been arrested, never mind someone in your campaign got murdered. Give it a month after the verdict, and then you'll be back.'

'I know what you mean, but it's just—'

'This isn't your decision. I can make you governor, son. But you're going to do it on my terms. Or you won't do it at all. Now, go start making plans to relaunch your campaign.'

Patrick stood there, dumb. Like that little boy who lost his mother, and grew up terrified of his father. Patrick was old enough now to realize that being scared of this man was the smart thing to do. He should be scared.

Everyone should.

He heard boots on the tiled hallway, coming closer.

He turned, saw Dekker coming toward him. The man had a black leather coat on, and his face was flushed either from the cold or the rage that came with way too much anabolic steroids and nobody to tear apart. The South African didn't even acknowledge Patrick. He walked past him like he was part of the furniture.

His father sat up when Dekker came in, said, 'Get out of here, Patrick.'

He did as his father asked, turned and left, but he remembered that Dekker hadn't closed the door. Patrick made it look as if he was heading for the stairs, but he stopped, held his breath, and put his back to the wall, just a few feet from the door, listening to the two men in the room beside him.

Dekker spoke first. It was hard to hear all of it. He at least kept his voice low.

Something, something, something, '. . . dead bodies . . . Hamptons . . . FBI on scene.'

'Fuck me,' said his father.

He had no trouble hearing that.

'Did anyone see you?'

'No, we changed vehicles before we left the city.'

'Do we know the special agent in charge?' asked his father.

'Bill Kennedy. He's an old friend of Flynn's.'

'Fuck me.'

'What do you want me—'

'Take out Flynn. Soon as possible.'

Silence.

Patrick had been in the room for those silences before. His father had a way of taking every ounce of oxygen out of the atmosphere, and your only choice was to take a moment. Think. And make sure your response was what he wanted to hear.

'That could be difficult, and may not suit us in the long run,' said Dekker.

'Why not?'

'If Flynn disappears, the defendant can get the trial adjourned. I thought you wanted this over.'

'No, it doesn't work that way. Vanessa has co-counsel, Harry Ford. He'll take over. Just make sure Tanner doesn't grant an adjournment or a mistrial. Have Larkin tell her there's an extra hundred thousand in it if she can give me my verdict in the next three days. That should sweeten her.'

'Larkin has been quiet. I'll have to talk to him in person.'

'I hope our dirty cop isn't developing a conscience. Tell him we need him to see this through.'

'What about Bloch and Lake?'

'They're too hot right now. We'll get them after. A month or two, maybe. Flynn is the priority. I don't care how you do it. I don't care how you make it look. I want him dead in the next forty-eight hours.'

53
Eddie

'This office is a lot better than that last shithole you had in West Forty-sixth Street,' said a voice. A man's voice.

A voice I hadn't heard in person for a long time.

Harry had gone home to walk Clarence, and I needed to call in to the office and catch up with work. Bloch and Lake were standing around their desks sipping hot drinks from their mugs. Coffee for Bloch. Some kind of herbal tea that once passed through the digestive system of a Guatemalan cat for Lake. Behind them, I clocked the man who sat sprawled out in Bloch's chair, with both feet on her desk. He wore a pale raincoat over a navy suit. White shirt. Tie pin. Gold. Silver ballpoint pen in his jacket pocket. He was thin, barely fitting his shirt, and the circles beneath his eyes looked deeper and darker than the last time I'd seen him, which was some years ago now.

'You remember the last time you broke into my office in West Forty-sixth Street?' I asked him.

'As I recall, you put both of my agents on medical leave for a week. One guy had a bruise on his arm the size of Lake Tahoe, and the other had a couple of broken fingers. You still carry a set of brass knuckles?' he asked.

'I prefer ceramic these days. They don't set off metal detectors. How are you doing, Kennedy?'

He swung his long legs off the desk, got up and we hugged.

I'm not a fan of the feds. Law enforcement and I don't see eye to eye very often. But I made an exception for Kennedy. I'd saved his life once, and in turn he had saved mine. While we'd spoken on the phone a few times, we hadn't seen each other in years.

'You've lost weight, Eddie,' he said.

'You were always too skinny,' I said.

'You okay?'

'I've been worse, and I've been better. How's the family?'

'Growing up fast, and you?'

'I haven't seen Amy in a while. Christine is mad at me. Maybe it's for the best until this case is over. Thanks for looking after these two.'

'My pleasure. Your forensics guy got the paint crew on video taking out a lawyer. That helped clarify the situation for the locals and my field agents. The dead police captain is a little more difficult. We're looking into Landry's finances which should help corroborate their story. It might be best if Bloch and Lake aren't found surrounded by any more dead bodies for a while.'

'Can't make any promises,' said Bloch.

Kennedy and I exchanged a look.

I said, 'See what I have to deal with?'

'Makes a change from you creating the corpses,' said Kennedy.

'When is Raymond going to come back with some DNA results on the paint in the Hamptons house?' I asked.

'Thirty-six hours,' said Bloch. 'But maybe we don't need to wait that long. The video Raymond took of the lawyer getting his head cut off, the paint job at Molly's apartment and at the Hamptons house, we now know who killed Molly Green. We can show that to the jury, right?'

'We don't know who those men were working for,' I said. 'Not for sure. So far there's nothing solid to link them to Patrick.'

'But the lawyer, Corbett, he called his firm. They would've called

Patrick straight away and he called the disposal crew. He was the only person with motive who knew we were there.'

I hung my head.

'Patrick, maybe his father too, were the only people who knew Raymond and I were investigating the Hamptons property, right?' asked Bloch.

I looked at her, shook my head, said, 'I told Vanessa. I had to.'

'When?'

'Right before you arrived at the house.'

'Did she call anyone and tell them we were there?'

'Not to my knowledge.'

'You were with her in court the whole time, though, right?'

'No, she used the bathroom.'

'When?'

'Right after I told her.'

'So she could have tipped off the disposal team?'

'I don't see why, though? She said she knew nothing about Teresa Chase.'

'But she could have called someone?'

'It's possible.'

I had a thought that I didn't want to speak out loud. Not yet.

'What about the crew's phones?' I asked.

'Burners,' said Bloch. 'But the evidence. Two women beheaded? Both of them in relationships with Patrick, and Patrick reports one of them missing at sea when actually she'd been murdered?'

'Let's not get ahead of ourselves. We need Raymond to process the DNA from the Hamptons house. If that DNA matches the headless Jane Doe then we're a little way forward, but remember there's no DNA profile for Teresa Chase. If the DNA from the Hamptons house and the missing girl line up, that doesn't prove it's Teresa, it just proves this woman was murdered there.'

'Still,' said Lake, 'that's two decapitated women. And we have the crew who probably did it on film.'

'It throws suspicion on Patrick, but it's not enough. But there is something that might change things.'

'What?' asked Lake.

'Molly's journal. It's an account of her creating a persona, an identity, so she could get close to Patrick Vanderpool. In the journal, reading between the lines, she wanted to go to the Hamptons house to check it out. To look for evidence. If I'm reading the journal correctly, she was seeking revenge for her sister. She wanted to get close to Patrick so she could take him down. Molly was Teresa Chase's half-sister, Willow, who has been missing for years. I didn't make the connection until we worked out Molly wasn't who she said she was. Now, reading that journal, it fits together. Tell Raymond to do a DNA comparison on Molly Green and our Hamptons Jane Doe. I'm betting we get a familial match. That's a much stronger point in Vanessa's defense.'

'Wait, we searched for a deceased Willow Chase and found nothing in the records. Let's say you're right. Molly is Willow Chase. If Willow's DNA was logged under the false name, Molly Green, wouldn't that DNA profile have thrown up a match with the Jane Doe already?' asked Lake.

'No,' said Bloch. 'DNA profiles are stored on seven separate databases in the US, all with different categorizations and they don't cross-reference each other unless you separately search each database. To protect fourth amendment rights to privacy, you can't search a database without probable cause. The Jane Doe case wasn't listed as a murder. It was processed under *unidentified persons* and listed on that database. If Molly's DNA was fed into the *victim* database, then it wouldn't show up as a match, because the Jane Doe profile wasn't listed there. I'll get Raymond on it, now we have cause to cross-reference those DNA profiles.'

'One thing still bothers me,' I said. 'Why did the killer paint over the bloodstains on the wall of Molly's apartment? It's not like they moved the body – they just took the head. And there was blood on the floor. I don't get it.'

'This wasn't like the Hamptons house. This a building full of people in Manhattan. We know they didn't use the back entrance because they weren't caught on camera, and there's no cameras out front. They could hide the head in the paint bucket, and no one would know, but even if they wrapped a body in tarpaulin, or one of their rubber sheets, it's still going to look like a body in a rubber sheet. And they have to bring that right out onto the public street. It could be that there were people outside the building that night. It was probably too risky to move, so they just took the head,' said Bloch.

'Maybe, but I don't know for sure. Just ask Raymond to be quick with the DNA processing from the Hamptons and the profile searches. If everything comes through as we hoped, we have reasonable . . .'

I couldn't finish the sentence.

For the first time in this case, there was a realistic hope and a narrow path to getting Vanessa an acquittal. I had a bad feeling in my stomach that had only grown as this case got closer to trial. Now, the mere thought of it made me feel sick. But I couldn't hold that poisonous thought inside any longer.

'Harry always thought Vanessa was innocent,' I said. 'He and I had the same thought: women, even deranged killers, don't decapitate their victims.'

'So?' asked Lake. 'You're doubting your client now? After we saw on video exactly how those men murdered and mutilated their victims?'

'That's the thing. We still don't know. We're assuming a chain of events that may not make perfect sense. I think we can say Patrick found the journal in Molly's apartment, realized who she really was and either he killed her and called his father for the clean-up crew, or he left her alive and had his old man send the crew out to kill Molly, and they got there after Vanessa had left the apartment. That's all possible. But something else is equally possible. What if

Vanessa killed Molly and then *she* called the clean-up crew? No matter what way you think about this case, it still comes down to two suspects. Patrick, or Vanessa.'

'Are you really doubting her?' asked Bloch.

'I'm doubting myself,' I said. 'You don't know this, but I once represented a guy on kidnapping charges and got him off, even though right before the verdict came in I realized he was guilty. That man walked free because of me, and he almost killed a young girl named Hanna Tublowski. That young woman's life was torn apart, and that was all my fault. I just don't want to make the same mistake.'

Kennedy put a hand on my shoulder, said nothing. He didn't need to.

'I thought you'd moved on from that, Eddie,' he said, and then put his hands in his pockets and looked at the ground. Men have a hard time talking to each other.

'I don't know if I ever will. Hanna is doing a lot better these days. Look, we all have theories about this case, yet none of us know the truth. We know a young woman was murdered. We know Patrick lied to the police, and continues to deny the affair. We know our client lied to the police, and lied to us about the affair and being at Molly's apartment. And she still hasn't told us how her fingerprints got on that jewelry box.'

'What do you want to do?' asked Bloch.

'We're in the middle of this now. We have to see it through to the end, one way or another. We have to keep going, but I want to know what really happened in that apartment. There's justice, and then there's the law. Sometimes those are two different things. Let's keep fighting, for now. Let's see what Raymond finds out. In the meantime, I have another favor to ask of the FBI.'

'Of course,' said Kennedy. 'It's not like we have anything else to do. What do you need?'

I said, 'I need you to arrest somebody.'

'Anyone in particular?'

'Sure, but you're not going to like it,' I said, then played him the recording from my conversation with Larkin, and told him who I wanted arrested.

'The recording is inadmissible. That means I can't show it to a judge as probable cause for a warrant. You want me to make an arrest, then I need probable cause.'

'I think I have some,' I said.

'What?'

'Well, you're gonna have to pretend that I'm working for you, but, really, that's only a little white lie. I'm always happy to assist the FBI.'

54
Eddie

'I've been thinking,' said Harry as we walked along Center Street toward the court building at eight fifteen on a fresh morning.

'Was any alcohol involved in this thinking process?' I asked.

'Of course,' said Harry. 'I do some of my best thinking when I've had a glass or six.'

'Anything helpful come out of this drinking session?'

'You mean thinking session. Anyway, I've been researching spousal privilege like you'd asked. It's interesting. That particular door swings both ways, Eddie. I found a few pieces of case law that might help. The privilege is a shield that is supposed to protect both spouses as a marital unit. There's a similarity to the fifth amendment right against self-incrimination. These are the head notes,' he said, and drew out a page from his old leather satchel.

I read it as we walked. 'You got copies of these cases for the judge and Riley?'

'This isn't my first time in a courtroom.'

'You got any more bright ideas?'

'I don't know. I'll get drunk again tonight and let you know what happens.'

Vanessa sat in court, dressed exactly how I wanted.

She still didn't know why, but that was okay.

Better she didn't know.

Detective Lorraine Carey resumed her seat on the witness stand and Judge Tanner glared at me like I was something unpleasant that she'd found on the sole of her shoe.

The jury had had all night to take in Carey's testimony and the security video footage. Leaving court yesterday with that footage in their minds was one hell of a disadvantage for me. DA Riley and Judge Tanner had seen to it that the jury had time to think on all of that damning evidence without a word of response from the defense. The jury all looked a little more relaxed today, as if they didn't have to pay much more attention to what happened in this trial. The jury, it seemed to me, had already decided that Vanessa was guilty.

Sometimes, luck plays a little part in a trial. It shouldn't, really. There is only the testimony and the evidence and the words from the lawyers, but very occasionally lady luck lends a hand. Can that tip the scales of justice one way or the other? Not really.

Can it help?

Sure.

Detective Carey held her chin up high, her legs crossed and her hands in her lap. My little slice of luck came in her outfit choice.

She was dressed all in black today. Black business suit. Black blouse. Black shoes.

Confident and assured today after her strong performance yesterday. The video footage proved that Vanessa had lied to the police when she said she had never been to Molly Green's apartment. And the jury had seen her being the last person leaving that building before the victim's body was found, together with the contents of a Nike gym bag that looked, for all to see, as if she was carrying the victim's head in that bag.

As I stood up to cross-examine Carey, she gave me a smug grin.

Just to piss me off.

Then quickly returned to a neutral expression before the jury saw it.

She had done well yesterday.

Today would be different.

I stared at her for a moment, letting the anticipation build. Came around the defense table and stood in front of the jury.

I opened my mouth, hesitated, then returned to the defense table and picked up the three empty glasses that sat there. A fresh jug of water was provided by the court staff every morning. With my back to the witness, I poured two glasses of water. One for Vanessa, one for Harry. I placed Harry's glass in front of him, and Vanessa's in front of her. She mouthed a thank you.

I poured a glass for me, took a sip.

I could almost hear Tanner's blood pressure surging.

'Ask you quite ready, Mr. Flynn?' she asked.

I put down the water, turned and faced the witness.

'Yes, Your Honor. Detective Carey, how can you be sure the woman in the video footage the jury saw yesterday is my client, Vanessa Vanderpool?'

This was about the worst question any defense attorney could have asked. And I put it in the worst way possible. A pure, open question. The equivalent of an underarm pitch in professional baseball that a half-blind batter could send into the fourth row of the bleachers. Carey now had an opportunity to lay out her case against the defendant, and repeat all of the worst parts in great detail.

Two of Riley's assistant DAs whispered something, tried to suppress their laughter.

Riley wasn't laughing. He was smart enough to know if I was going to show my ass in court there had to be a good reason.

'Can I refer to the footage of the security camera again, please,' said Detective Carey, and Riley's assistants put it on the big screen for the whole court to see. Then she doubled down on the damage she'd caused yesterday.

'This woman shown entering the building is wearing white pants, white blouse and light brown overcoat. She has long blonde hair, and although we can't see her face in this clip we do get a better look when she exits the building. Can we see that clip?'

The prosecution loaded up the second clip.

'As you can see,' continued Carey, 'this is the defendant. We can get a very clear view of her face. It's a much closer angle, and we can see she has the same hair and she's wearing the exact same outfit – white pants, white blouse and light brown overcoat. Only difference this time is she's carrying a Nike bag with what we believe to be the victim's head inside.'

Carey smiled at me when she finished her answer.

This was a lot easier than she'd expected. I had to start pushing back. Just a little.

'You don't know for sure what is in that bag, do you, Detective?'

'No, I don't.'

'And you are sure that both women seen in those clips are in fact the same person, the defendant, Mrs. Vanderpool?'

'I am certain. The images, especially the second image, are crystal clear. It's high resolution so I can almost read the brand label on the top button of her pants. The image could not be clearer.'

'Let's be sure. Mrs. Vanderpool, would you just stand up for a second, please?' I asked.

As Vanessa stood, I saw a creeping realization spread over her face.

Now she knew why I'd asked her to dress like this today.

In court, she wore white pants. A white blouse, and a light colored, fawn jacket. Not the same overcoat, but the same color of jacket.

I approached the defense table, stood in front of it and turned back to Detective Carey.

'Do you mean an outfit very similar to this?'

As I asked this, staring at the witness, I drew my right hand up, by my side, to point at the defendant.

My hand hit the full glass of water at speed, sending it tumbling over the defense table and Vanessa.

'Oh, I'm so sorry,' I said, as Harry reached into his pocket for his handkerchief.

Vanessa brushed the water off her shirt, jacket, but mostly her white pants which were now dark with cold water.

'Yes,' said Carey, smiling at my incompetence. 'That's an almost exact match for her clothing. Apart from the sta—'

She stopped herself. Shut her mouth tight.

The other shoe had dropped.

'Go on, Detective. Finish your answer.'

'I've finished,' she said.

'I think you were going to say it's a match apart from that staining that's on her clothes now. Correct?'

She didn't answer.

Didn't have to.

'This is one of the photographs taken by your forensic photographer of Molly Green's apartment.'

Harry brought up an image on screen. A picture of a large wet bloodstain on the carpet.

'That's a thick pool of blood, correct?'

'Yes,' said Carey as she uncrossed her legs and put both feet firmly on the floor. She wasn't so relaxed now.

'So it's your case that the defendant entered the victim's building, crushed her skull with a jewelry box, leaving traces of the victim's blood on the box, used some kind of tool, which you have never recovered, to then saw off the victim's head, and then take it with her in that bag when she left. Is that right?'

She swallowed, then said, 'Correct.'

'And she did this without getting one single drop of blood on her clothes?'

'I don't know,' said Carey.

'You do know. You testified that this is a high-resolution picture of the defendant leaving that apartment, and because of what she's wearing we would be able to see any bloodstaining very clearly, wouldn't we?'

I turned to Vanessa. She hadn't known what I was going to do, but she followed along and at least had the good sense to remain standing.

'I'm not sure,' said Carey.

'Just a simple water stain is clear enough now. Blood would stand out even more, wouldn't it?'

'I suppose it would,' said Carey.

'There's another entrance to this building. Isn't that right?'

'Yes.'

'The front entrance, otherwise called the main entrance.'

'Yes.'

'And there's no security camera covering that entrance?'

'No.'

'So anybody could have come to that building after my client left and visited Molly Green's apartment and you wouldn't know anything about it, would you?'

'There's no security camera covering that entrance.'

That wasn't the question I'd asked. I was about to double down when Riley came to his senses.

'Objection, Your Honor. Mr. Flynn has staged an inadmissible reconstruction in court by pretending to spill water on his client's clothes, which I'm sure she was instructed to wear today. I move that the entirety of this cross-examination be struck from the record and the jury instructed to ignore it.'

'The water was an accident, Your Honor. You can't—'

She wasn't interested in my excuses.

'Sustained. The jury will disregard everything they have heard today. Mr. Flynn, that's another thousand-dollar fine for contempt. Next time, I'm not going to fine you. I'm going to have you thrown in a cell, do you understand?'

'I have an objection, Your Honor,' I said. 'I think your actions are confusing the jury, my client and everyone else in this courtroom.'

'What on earth do you mean?' asked Tanner.

'I just think it would be a hell of a lot clearer to everyone in this courtroom if you came down off the bench and just took your seat beside Mr. Riley at the prosecution table. That way my client and the jury won't confuse you with an unbiased judge.'

I heard a few intakes of breath from the jury.

I'd made my point.

I didn't have to look at Harry. I could feel him staring at the back of my head.

'This case is adjourned for one hour,' said Judge Tanner. 'Bailiff, arrest Mr. Flynn.'

55
Eddie

In a strange way, I like jail cells.

It's quiet. There are no distractions.

I have time to think.

I was pretty sure I had most of this case figured out.

It seemed clear to me that the paint team Bloch took out at the Hamptons house was involved in the murder of the woman known as Molly Green. Maybe they were planning on moving her body, to make it look like a disappearance, and that was why they painted over the bloodstains on her wall.

That was a rational explanation, but this case defied logic on so many levels.

There was more to it. Much more.

As I lay on a concrete bench in the cell, I looked up at the wall beside me. It was covered in graffiti. Gang tags, names of former occupants of this cell, trial dates, band names and slogans, some of it in ballpoint pen, but mostly it was scratched into the surface.

I put my hand on the wall, closed my eyes and let my mind wander.

Something was bubbling to the surface of my consciousness. Something that had been working there for a while. I turned my head away from the wall to the chipped cream paint on the cell bars and door. Beyond them, in the hallway, I saw a notice to prisoners pinned up on the wall. Jailhouse rules.

I sat up.

I had an idea.

Footsteps were coming down that hallway.

Harry Ford leaned over and peered through the bars at me.

'You're spending more time in a jail cell than a courtroom these days,' he said.

'I wish I did have more time in here. I think better.'

A Department of Corrections officer joined Harry outside my cell. He took a thick bunch of keys from his belt and unlocked the door.

'Judge says you'll have cooled off by now,' said the CO.

I got up, grabbed my jacket and left the confines of the cell. As we walked down the hallway, I slipped my jacket on, asked Harry for his cell phone.

'You'll get yours back in a second,' he said.

'Can't wait that long,' I said.

He handed me his phone. I dialed Bloch's number from his contacts.

'It's me,' I said. 'The van that the paint crew arrived in. You said there was all kinds of kit in the back, paint buckets, tarpaulin, rubber sheets. Do you remember seeing any pictures in there?'

'Pictures?'

'Framed pictures. Ask Bill Kennedy to get his agents to send you photos of the contents of the back of the van. The Monet picture you saw in Molly's apartment looked to you like it didn't belong. Do you remember?'

'I remember. They must've put it there to help hide the paint job.'

'They weren't trying to hide the bloodstains, Bloch. How's Raymond doing with the DNA samples from the Hamptons?'

'I talked to him an hour ago. He just got the dried scrapings processed and they're in the rapid DNA testing machine now. He should get results in an hour or two and then it'll take another few hours at least to upload and search on the DNA databases.'

'Tell him to put a hold on it for now. There's something more important. Get him over to Molly's apartment again and sweep that wall.'

'We swept the wall with the black light – there was nothing more to see.'

'I don't need you to sweep with the UV light. I need you to use a metal detector.'

I hung up, giving Harry back his phone as we got to the end of the hallway and the CO's station. They gave me back my personal items with my phone, money and my father's Saint Christopher medal, which I wore every day. The only time I took it off was when I was in a jail cell, which was increasingly too often.

'The judge is going to ask you to apologize to her in front of the jury,' said Harry. 'If you don't, it might be easier just to give me your stuff and I'll hold on to it while you spend the night here.'

'Who is Riley calling next?'

'We've got Geoff Gilbert, Patrick's campaign manager. I think he's just going to call him as a representative witness to establish bad blood between Vanessa and the victim. Then it's the forensics officer, then Ben Larkin, and last should be Patrick Vanderpool.'

'Then let's get through this as fast as possible. I have no choice now but to blow up Larkin. I'll ask him if he's been paid to target Vanessa and when he denies it, I'll try to use the audio recording from Taco Bell.'

'You think the judge will allow that?'

'Clandestine recordings can be tricky at the best of times. With this judge, I doubt it. But we have to try.'

'Your Honor, I apologize for my remarks,' I said.

Riley was practically rubbing his hands. The jury watched somewhat impassively. But I noticed that three jurors in the front row were leaning forward, listening intently to this exchange. I didn't want to get my hopes up. I only needed one juror to have reasonable doubt, but it certainly gave me the impression they were at least interested in the dynamic between me and the judge.

Harry had his head in his hands, but he was peeking at me between his fingers. Our client was stony-faced, as we'd asked her to be.

'Is that *all*?' asked Judge Tanner with a little hot sauce poured onto her tone. She was clearly still pissed at me.

There's a long line of judges that I've pissed off. They're at the back of a longer line of police officers and district attorneys. To me, that was a source of pride.

'I apologize if my remarks offended you,' I said.

This wasn't exactly a good apology. Not my best, but definitely not my worst, as my ex-wife could attest.

She slowly tapped her pen on her desk and stared at me. The three jurors watched closely.

I stared back.

I smiled.

This didn't go down well.

She shook her head, turned to Riley and said, 'Call your next witness.'

The political consultant, Geoff Gilbert, wasn't the type of guy you wanted in your corner. He wore an expensive, tailored suit, a bespoke blue shirt, navy tie, handmade shoes and a Rolex hung off his hairy wrist. His beard was neat and trimmed, as were his eyebrows and his coiffured hair. He gave the appearance of a guy pretending to be rich, even though I was quite sure he was a rich man. The money didn't suit him. It looked like he'd stolen what he was wearing.

Taking his time, Riley led Gilbert through establishing testimony for the jury, questions designed to elicit who Gilbert was, what he did for Patrick Vanderpool and who else worked on the campaign, including Molly Green.

'It was clear from the way she spoke to Molly that Vanessa hated her,' said Gilbert. 'She was jealous of a young beautiful woman being around her husband so much. Not that anything ever happened between Molly and Patrick, of course not. But that didn't stop Vanessa's insane jealousy. I overheard her once, Vanessa, that is, threatening Molly. She told her to stay away from her husband.'

'Did you form the impression that this was a threat?'

'You're damn right it was,' said Geoff.

'No further questions.'

'You want to do this one?' I asked Harry.

'Sure. I was thinking short and sweet. A one-two combination punch?' he said. Harry often thought of cross-examination like a boxing match.

'Go for it.'

That's what all the greats do. Young inexperienced lawyers have legal pads filled with questions for every witness in a trial. They're trained to do it. The fact that they charge by the hour is only partly responsible. Often, they ask witnesses lots of questions out of fear of missing out some important detail.

They forget that sometimes it doesn't matter what the answer is to the question. Sometimes the question is way more important than any answer.

Harry rose to his feet.

Threw a left.

'How much do you earn working on Patrick Vanderpool's campaign?' asked Harry.

Gilbert looked toward Riley, then the judge. He was waiting for an objection. His earnings weren't relevant in his mind. No objection came from Riley, who was still wary of wading into unknown waters with an objection he wasn't sure about. Just in case it came back to bite him.

'Do I have to answer that?' asked Gilbert.

The judge nodded.

'Four point three million dollars a year,' he said, and cast his eyes down toward his knees and brushed some imaginary fluff from his pants. Like he wanted to brush away the question.

Two of the jurors visibly reacted to that by making O shapes with their lips. That's a lot of money.

Harry threw his right.

'Who pays you that salary?' asked Harry.

This time, Gilbert had nowhere to hide so he just answered fast.

'Patrick Vanderpool.'

He was waiting for another question.

Harry announced, 'That's all I need to hear. Thank you, Mr. Gilbert.'

TKO.

Gilbert looked around, puzzled and a little alarmed. That was it. He was expecting to be in the witness box for hours, to be contradicted, to be called a liar, a real battle.

He got none of it.

The jury heard this guy was paid millions of dollars and nobody is going to sabotage that kind of meal ticket. And Harry's final dismissal of the witness, 'That's all I need to hear,' had painted a clear and precise picture for the jury.

Damn, he was good. He should've done this whole trial.

'Members of the jury,' said the judge, 'whether a witness is in the employment of someone else who is involved in this case is neither here nor there, and does not affect the truthfulness of their answers. You understand?'

Of the three jurors in the front row who had watched my apology to the judge, one of them, a lady in a blue sweater, raised her hand.

'Yes?' asked the judge. 'Do you have a question? Just whisper it to the jury keeper if you wouldn't mind.'

The jury keeper came forward and the lady in the sweater whispered something. The jury keeper, a woman of about the same age, smiled and nodded.

'Well?' asked the judge.

The jury keeper said, 'The juror asked if she and her fellow jurors get to decide the verdict, or if it's your decision, Your Honor?'

Judge Tanner looked directly at the juror, said, 'The jury gives the verdict, as I explained to you at the beginning of the trial.'

The juror in the blue sweater raised her hand again. The jury keeper approached, the juror whispered, the jury keeper's eyebrows shot up and then she turned to the judge and said, 'This juror says if the decision has to be made by the jury, then respectfully, Your Honor, stop telling the jury what to think.'

Several jurors in the front row nodded, two in the back as well. I could've kissed them all.

That's the special thing about juries. They're ordinary decent citizens who have two eyes, two ears and the best of them have an open mind and an open heart. You can only lie to people for so long before they call bullshit. Sometimes, for all of its faults, the legal system is beautiful.

'Call your next witness, Mr. Riley,' said the judge, doing her best to ignore the statement from the jury. The jury keeper, who had to deliver that reply from the juror, looked just a little smug. You don't always know what goes on behind closed doors with judges. Those who were cruel or didn't treat their court staff well sometimes got a little pushback. And it was always good to see.

'The People call Derek Reading,' said Riley.

This was the forensics officer who took the victim's blood and the defendant's DNA off of the jewelry box.

'If it helps the court,' I said, 'we will stipulate that the victim's blood and the defendant's DNA are both on the jewelry box, as long as we can make submissions to the jury about the manner in which our client's DNA got onto that box.'

The judge looked to Riley. He was handcuffed now. He'd been planning a long, boring but devastating exchange with the forensics officer about blood and DNA, all of which would be damning for

Vanessa. There was nothing we could do to challenge it. Her DNA was there and so far Vanessa had no explanation. No point in dragging out the inevitable.

'You have no problem with that, Mr. Riley?' asked the judge.

'I can't really object, Your Honor. The defense is admitting the defendant's DNA and the victim's blood are on the murder weapon.'

'No,' I said. 'Your Honor and the jury know very well, we are stipulating as a fact that the defendant's DNA and the victim's blood are on the jewelry box that was in the victim's apartment – that's all. There is no evidence to show when, or how, the DNA or the blood got onto that box. And it's a matter for the jury to decide if this is the murder weapon, or not.'

'The jury will have understood that, Mr. Flynn,' said Judge Tanner, and looked at the jury sympathetically. She was trying to win back their favor, and appear as if she was on their side. I can't say it worked for all of them.

'Mr. Riley, those facts are admitted. Call your next witness,' said the judge.

Riley looked around at the back of the courtroom, then leaned over and whispered to his assistant. Then looked up at the judge as he spoke.

'Your Honor, may we have a short recess? Detective Larkin would be our next witness, but he is not in court, presently.'

'Go and find him,' said the judge, and rose from the bench.

We all stood and watched her leave, followed by the jury. As soon as the last juror cleared out of the room, Riley got on his cell phone.

Harry and I looked at each other.

We both had the same thought.

'Well, I mean, Larkin was probably told he wouldn't be needed today. I'm sure he was instructed to come to court tomorrow,' said Harry.

'He was here for the opening of the case. He hasn't shown up to court since we talked in Taco Bell,' I said.

Harry whispered, 'How much did he get from Dekker?'

'A hundred grand, all in. That's not enough for a cop to disappear.'

'Maybe he asked for more. Or maybe he told them about your little talk.'

'He wouldn't have said a word. He gave me that journal, but he didn't have to. I didn't push that hard. He could've lied about it. I wonder if some part of him wanted to do the right thing. Either he's somehow gotten more money from them, enough to disappear, or they figured he'd been turned and took him out.'

'If they took out a cop, that means they're getting desperate,' said Harry.

'I don't know,' I said. 'Sometimes I wonder about the way the world has turned. Laws and rules don't apply when you've got all the power. Fewer people are willing to stand up for what's right any more. They can shoot people on Fifth Avenue and walk away now. Just like they said they could.'

Harry said, 'The world may have changed, but people are still the same. There will always be people who fight back, who call out the injustices.'

'We're a dying breed,' I said.

'Speak for yourself. I've got a lot of drinking to do when this case is over. I'm not planning on dying for a long time.'

'You're a real badass, Harry.'

'That's what my ex-wives say. Well, something like that.'

Hanging up his phone call, Riley came over to me with a dark look on his face.

'We can't find Detective Larkin,' said Riley.

'You mean you've lost him,' I said.

'No, he's just not answering his phone.'

'Has anyone seen him since yesterday?'

'No.'

'Then you've lost him,' I said. 'That's quite an achievement. He's six foot three and four hundred pounds. He's unlikely to have slipped down the back of your couch.'

'We'll get him. In the meantime, I have one more witness. It'll take an hour to get him here, but I'm going to call Patrick Vanderpool.'

56
Eddie

In the lawyer consultation room, Vanessa was still mopping at her pants and blouse with napkins.

'I'm sorry about the glass of water. I could have warned you, but it would have looked fake if I had.'

'I understand,' she said. 'The jury seemed to get the point.'

'I'm glad you saw that. If we keep on this path, there's a chance we can get an acquittal. But only if you do what we discussed. After Patrick testifies, the prosecution have one more witness. If they can't find them, I think the judge will push the case on and give the DA permission to call Detective Larkin later. That's okay – we won't object. Larkin was a hand grenade. He could go off in anyone's face. There's no way of knowing how that would've played out. He might have admitted to outside interference in the case, or he might not. It would have been messy and risky for all sides. You just remember what we talked about. Remember exactly the answer we gave you and repeat that precisely.'

She nodded. 'I'll do it. I won't let you down.'

Harry came into the room and said, 'Patrick Vanderpool is here. We're due back in court.'

'Remember, Vanessa, you can't reveal anything about personal conversations you've had with your husband. No matter how much they push you. Just give them the answer we discussed.'

'I've got it. Don't worry. I've . . .' she said, then paused, as if thinking about something, or weighing up a decision. 'Wait, there's something else. I can't remember if I've told you about it or not. I guess in the beginning I was protecting him. I was afraid of him. But this time away from him, it's made me think more clearly. I think Patrick gave Molly a really expensive gift, not long before she was killed.'

'What kind of gift?' I asked.

'A diamond bracelet, in white gold. I found it hidden in his medicine cabinet one morning, not long before our anniversary. I thought he'd bought it for me, you know? So I didn't say anything to him about it. But he never gave it to me. I got a purse for our anniversary, and dinner and a show. He was trying to make up for cancelling our anniversary party at the Hamptons house. There's been so much happening I forgot all about it. I don't know if it's even relevant, but I remembered last night Patrick asked me if the police had mentioned the bracelet when they were questioning me. Again, I don't know if it means anything. I just thought I should mention it while I remembered.'

Harry and I stared at each other for a moment.

'There was no bracelet listed in Molly Green's possessions, and there's—'

'I know, my DNA on her jewelry box, but I swear I've never seen or touched that box before.'

'And you didn't mention this before, because . . . ?' I asked.

'I don't know. I'm sorry. I probably should have, but, like I said, I didn't know if it was relevant. I've been so scared. You don't know what it's like living with . . .'

As she trailed off, she scratched at her right forearm, where she'd shown us the burn scars.

'Okay, I'm sorry,' I said. 'I can ask about it. We don't have this bracelet to show him, and it could come back to bite us, Vanessa. Do you want me to ask about it?'

She nodded, said, 'I think it could rattle him.'

'Okay,' said Harry. 'Well, let's go nail your husband.'

57
Patrick

Falling.

That's what it felt like to Patrick, as he sat in the witness box, concentrating on Riley's questions, focusing as hard as he could on answering him and keeping his statements short and to the point. He could have no fat on his words at all. His heels were pressing down hard on the wooden floor to help keep his posture upright, so he could look assured and confident.

But inside his feet were dangling as he fell through the air. His body was screaming *danger, danger, danger* . . .

His mind began to wander, the adrenaline soaking his back with sweat. His collar was too tight, and his jacket too. Dear God, he hoped he wasn't sweating through his jacket. This suit was professional, but perhaps a shade too light. Christ, he had to focus.

Listening hard to Riley's questions, clinging to them, he felt as if his body was tumbling through open space.

This is how the old family friend, and his father's former number two in the business, Boris Cherry, must have felt as he jumped off the top of his building. Maybe this was how Boris felt as his father fired him. Patrick could never forget that man's face, his world crumbling around him.

'Mr. Vanderpool, could you describe your relationship with your wife, the defendant?' asked Riley.

Patrick put his hands on his knees and pressed down, rooting himself to the present, as he said, 'We had no problems until this case. Vanessa was a very loving and supportive spouse. Since I learned of the evidence in this case, I could no longer be part of the marriage, so I instructed my lawyers to file for divorce.'

'And are you legally divorced now?'

'Not yet. It has to work its way through the courts, but the relationship is over. I couldn't be with someone who could do something like this to anyone, never mind one of my campaign staffers.'

'You believe your wife murdered Molly Green?'

'Objection, Your Honor, pure speculation,' said Vanessa's lawyer.

Flynn had been quiet up to now. So much so that Patrick had almost forgotten he was there.

'Move on, Mr. Riley,' said the judge, with a sigh. Patrick formed the view that the judge had reluctantly taken Flynn's point, but it was clear there was no love lost there.

'The victim was a smart, attractive young woman, Mr. Vanderpool. Given your knowledge of your wife, is it possible that she was jealous of such a woman working in close proximity to you every day?'

'She was insanely jealous, and she hated Molly.'

'What makes you say that?'

'We fought about it. She said—'

'Objection, Your Honor . . .'

Flynn again. This time, Patrick wrinkled his nose at the defense lawyer. He wasn't used to being interrupted by anyone, except his father.

'The witness and the defendant had many conversations when they were married, and all such conversations are privileged, and neither spouse can divulge the content of those discussions. Mr. Ford has precedents he will hand up.'

Flynn's partner, or lackey, the old man in the tweed jacket, Ford, got up from his chair and gave a pile of documents to the judge and Riley. They scanned the pages.

The courtroom was quiet, like a funeral parlor. Patrick hated funerals. They always reminded him of his mother's. He saw her face in the coffin again, eyes closed unnaturally, like she wanted to open them, but they were glued shut. Her skin had so much make-up on it, layers upon layers, like she was hiding her bruises, even in death. He remembered the little boy that he had been back then, wondering if his mother's face had been horribly beaten, and if all that product on her face was there to hide the horrors beneath.

'Mr. Riley, what do you say to this?' asked the judge.

'Your Honor, this isn't matrimonial court. This is a murder trial. A young, innocent woman is dead and we have to be able to get to the truth, for the jury.'

'Did you read this? Is there any reason why I shouldn't be bound by these decisions?'

'Your Honor . . .' began Riley, then tailed off. He had nothing.

'I have no choice, I'm afraid. Objection sustained. Move on . . .'

'Mr. Vanderpool, were you at the victim's apartment on the night she was killed?'

This was it. The tricky part. The uncomfortable admission. Patrick remembered his media training, and put on a somber look, deepened his tone to a respectful depth and said, 'We were working on my political campaign. It wasn't unusual to have long days. Sometimes I needed to go over notes for meetings the next day and I would occasionally do that in Molly's apartment. It saved her the expense of travelling to my home, or the office. I left around ten fifteen.'

'Right before your wife is shown in the security camera footage entering the victim's building?'

'Correct.'

'Did you know she was there that night?'

'No, not until I heard about the charges in this case.'

'Mr. Vanderpool, I have to ask this, because Mr. Flynn will likely ask you. Did you kill Molly Green?'

Patrick lowered his head.

He had prepared himself for this question. He knew it was coming. He had rehearsed his answer in the mirror many times. When he raised his head, there were tears in his eyes. He looked at the jury . . .

And lied.

'No, I did not kill Molly Green.'

58
Eddie

Damn, he was a convincing, slimy son of a bitch.

I know a tell. A lie leaves the lips, but the eyes hold on to the truth.

His emotion wasn't fake, though. That looked real. That felt real. Whether he was channeling some dark, tragic incident from his past, or maybe he was allowing his true emotions for Molly to come to the forefront, I couldn't quite decide.

His testimony had not done as much damage as I'd thought, which was largely down to Harry's research and Riley not being prepared. The DA had been caught off guard and hadn't recovered. If he'd been smarter, or better prepared, Patrick could have won this case for him. Instead, he let uncertainty cloud his judgement. The number-one thing you want to avoid while running a trial is making a mistake. It's almost better to do too little, than too much. The more you're talking, the greater the chance you will slip up.

I decided to take my own advice.

There was only one question I had to ask – did he kill Molly Green?

But the prosecution had already asked it.

I decided to keep this short. Dangerously short.

And leave a little mystery for the jury.

'Mr. Vanderpool, did you have a sexual relationship with Molly Green?'

'Absolutely not,' he said.

'Did you ever buy her an expensive piece of jewelry?'

I saw his eyes widening, but only for half a second, a brief flash as the question hit him, like the shutter on a camera, before he could again contain his reactions and keep himself calm and relaxed.

'No, I never bought her any jewelry,' he said.

I stood there and stared at him for a moment.

Until I was sure the entire jury had their attention on me, waiting for my next question.

I put on a broad satisfied smile. The kind of smile that somebody wears when they know they've won.

'No further questions,' I said.

Patrick's head swiveled quickly to the DA. Then the judge, then the jury. Perplexed. Worried. *What the hell has just happened?* written over his face.

I sat down.

The jury would think I'd nailed Patrick. That I had caught him in a lie.

It was Vanessa's suggestion. But we didn't have the final card to play. There was no Perry Mason moment of me being able to produce a receipt or a picture or anything else to contradict him.

I had nothing. No bracelet. No evidence.

All I had was Vanessa's testimony where she would deny killing the victim.

I had the advice and the prepared answer I had given to her, which would set a trap for Riley. But I really needed Bloch to come through with something from Molly's apartment.

That would be the third weapon in my arsenal. If she found what I hoped she would, that weapon could prove to be nuclear.

I checked my phone.

Text from Bloch.

Something is beeping in the wall. We're digging.

'Your Honor, subject to the right to call Detective Larkin at a later stage, with the agreement of the defense, the prosecution rests.'

'Call your first witness, Mr. Flynn,' said Tanner.

I stood, said, 'The defense calls Vanessa Vanderpool.'

As she took the oath, and promised to tell the truth, the whole truth and nothing but the truth, I thought about the one rule I lived by in trying criminal cases – it's nearly always a mistake to allow the defendant to testify.

This time, I had no choice.

The next few minutes would decide Vanessa's fate.

59
Vanessa

Vanessa was good at hiding her feelings.

She'd had plenty of practice now.

Her heart was beating fast, and her mouth was so dry, yet she knew if she took even one sip of water she would be sick, right here, in front of the whole courtroom.

She crossed her legs, and locked her fingers together over her knee, and pulled, as if she was anchoring her body to that seat, bracing her body, and her mind, for the storm to come.

'Mrs. Vanderpool, what is the current state of your relationship with Patrick Vanderpool?'

'He has filed for divorce. We haven't seen each other in some time.'

'But you're still married?'

'Yes, we're still legally married.'

'Do you understand that, because of your marriage, certain legal protections apply to what you can and can't testify about in this courtroom?'

'That has been explained to me, and I understand marital privilege.'

'The security footage shows that your husband left Molly Green's building at twenty-two eighteen, on the night of the murder, and you entered the building at twenty-two thirty-two. What did you see when you entered Molly Green's apartment?'

Vanessa let go of her knee, uncrossed her legs.

Leaned forward and spoke directly into the microphone in front of her.

'On legal advice, I assert my right to silence on the basis that my answer might incriminate my husband.'

She leaned back, away from the microphone, as if it was a fire she had just lit.

The DA leaned over his desk, shaking his head, and began to sift through the pages of case law that Harry Ford had given to him. He wasn't expecting this.

Flynn was a clever son of a bitch. He had found a way for her to say *nothing*, but in a way that said *everything*.

'Mrs. Vanderpool, was your husband having an affair with the victim, Molly Green?'

Vanessa slowly closed her eyes, and opened them again, leaned into the mic.

'I refuse to answer on the basis that my answer may incriminate my husband.'

Thump, the sound of Riley's fist hitting the desk.

She craned her neck to the side, saw the judge making notes, and giving Flynn a look of utter contempt.

'Mrs. Vanderpool, is your husband a violent man?'

'I refuse to answer, as the answer may incriminate my husband.'

'Would you please roll up your shirtsleeves and show the jury your arms?'

'Object—' began Riley, shooting up from his seat, but with a look of confusion on his face. He didn't want this to happen. He had objected on pure instinct, but before he could get the full sentence out of his mouth, his brain told him that this was an area he didn't want to venture into. He didn't know what was coming next, and he didn't want to get into an argument about relevance.

'Apologies, withdrawn,' he said.

Flynn nodded, and Vanessa rolled up her sleeves and showed her scars to the jury, and the courtroom.

'What caused those scars?'

'A red-hot spoon, sometimes a flame, being held on my skin,' she said.

'Who did this to you, Mrs. Vanderpool?' asked Flynn, keeping his voice soft, as if the question was a balloon, floating over the whole courtroom.

'I refuse to answer, on the grounds that it may incriminate my husband.'

A sound broke the silence that fell over the room. The sound of a woman's heels marching across a floor.

She saw Voss, walking quickly toward the door of the courtroom, looking over her shoulder at Vanessa, a hard expression on her face.

Vanessa knew then, while she may be saving herself from a life sentence, that life may not last very long.

Not if her plan didn't work.

'One last question, Mrs. Vanderpool,' said Flynn, 'for the sake of total clarity, did you kill Molly Green?'

Vanessa gave all her focus to the jury, watched their faces, as she spoke.

'No, I did not.'

She held the jury with her eyes, looking at each one in turn.

Wondering if they realized she had just lied.

60

Eddie

'No further questions,' I said.

Vanessa had done well. She had said nothing.

Yet the jury had gotten the picture. Juries are smart. They understand the subtext, the nuance. They were putting together a picture of what they thought had happened in Molly Green's apartment.

And it didn't involve Vanessa.

Riley stood tall, in the center of the court, Vanessa straight in front of him, the jury to his right. He had rehearsed this moment in his mind. This interaction. Each question he was going to ask had been carefully weighed and considered.

Until I'd come along and thrown a hand grenade at him.

I knew by his first question he was way off his game.

'Mrs. Vanderpool, why did you lie to the police when you told them you had never been to the victim's apartment?'

To most, this might seem like a good question. It's completely valid, but utterly ruined by one single word – *why*.

Cross-examination should be tight, leading questions that demanded a single one-word answer.

He should have said, *You lied to the police, didn't you?*

No way out of that for Vanessa. The simple answer is *yes*. And then right away he's nailed her as a liar.

By asking her *why* she lied to the police, he gave her way too much room.

Now she was going to tell him why, and he wasn't going to like it.

Not one bit.

'I refuse to answer on the grounds that it may incriminate my husband,' said Vanessa.

Riley stepped up a gear, raised his voice and spat his next set of questions at Vanessa.

'You lied to the police because you murdered Molly Green in a fit of jealously because you suspected she was sleeping with your husband, didn't you?'

'No.'

'You picked up the nearest thing to hand, a jewelry box, and you swung it at her so hard that you bashed her head in – that's what really happened?'

'No.'

'Then, realizing your horrible mistake, you took steps to hide your crime. You cut off her head and took it with you, disposing of the evidence linking you to the murder?'

'No.'

He caught his breath, thought for a moment. What else could he ask that wouldn't give her an opportunity to implicate her husband? He wasn't happy. This had been much harder than he had been expecting.

Better to cut his losses. Use the testimony he had gathered already.

'Nothing further, Your Honor.'

'Court will reconvene at nine tomorrow morning,' said Judge Tanner. 'Mr. Flynn, have your next witness ready.'

The courtroom cleared, the jury silent and unreadable as they left.

We had a chance. It would all come down to Bloch's work with Raymond tonight. She would be in his lab all night, knowing I would call her to testify tomorrow morning.

*

We met Lake outside the court building, sitting in the driver's seat of his shitmobile. The Pontiac Aztek looked even worse than usual. It backfired and sent a plume of black smoke from its exhaust as Harry and Vanessa got in the back. I knocked on Harry's window and he wound it down.

'You're not coming back to the hotel?' he asked.

'I need to be ready for tomorrow. I have to think. A walk will do me good. Best if you all stay in the hotel tonight, with Lake keeping watch. The cat is out of the bag now. The way Voss stormed out of court, I'd say whatever threats she's been secretly making to you, Vanessa, they are going to try to fulfill.'

'You knew?' she asked.

'I got the impression she had been talking to you on the sly. Making all kinds of threats against you if you decided to accuse Patrick on the witness stand. I'm not stupid. There was no other reason for her to be around.'

'I took your advice. I did what you told me,' said Vanessa.

'I know. You did well, but now is a dangerous moment. Be safe, all of you. And listen to Lake. That goes double for you, Harry.'

The Aztek backfired, startling Vanessa, and me, and a few passers-by. Neither Harry nor Lake flinched. Harry was a war veteran, and Lake . . . well, he was Lake.

'Apologies about the transport,' I said. 'If you do make it to the hotel, call me so I know you're safe.'

'I'll look after them,' said Lake.

'I know you will,' I said.

I watched them pull away, pulled up the collar on my coat and started walking.

Movement always helped me think. There's something about walking, the rhythm of my feet on the sidewalk, the sound of tires rolling on blacktop, horns, engines, snatches of conversations from people passing by, street vendors hawking pretzels, music and laughter and arguments drifting out of bars, the smell of garbage and exhaust fumes and hotdogs and beer, the chiaroscuro of neon lights burning over dark doorways, the burnished glass skyscrapers catching the last of the day's sun like a tilted lake of fire, the mottled stone towers of old wealth and power, the sad and happy and terrified and determined faces of people who survive in this city and love it for all its contrasts and contradictions, all of its joy and its heartbreak.

Damn, I love New York.

I don't know how long I walked, but I found myself in West 46th Street, and my gaze drifted to the window, where I had my old office and apartment.

I stopped and stared, and wondered about all the shit that had happened since I hung out my shingle from this place and started practicing law. I wondered about all the mistakes I'd made, and the people I had helped, and the people that I'd lost.

Something hard bit into the back of my skull.

My vision blurred and dulled.

I was aware I was falling, but I was out before I hit the ground.

61

Eddie

The last walk

The best time of your life lasts less than a second.

When you hold your newborn in your arms for the very first time; when you meet the one you know that you will love with your whole heart until the moment you die; when you look around you and realize that everyone you love is happy and well and safe.

It's a fleeting moment of joy.

The worst times of your life seem to last an age.

Right now, I was having one of those moments.

I'd just woken up in the trunk of a moving car.

My head felt like there was a rusty nail rattling around inside my skull. The cut on the back of my scalp was still bleeding, and I could taste the fumes from the exhaust pipe and hear the rumble of tires on the road and the drone of the engine. I couldn't see anything, too dark. The only thing in my vision were occasional white stars that penetrated the black, probably the result of the head injury.

My hands weren't tied. I felt around in my jacket and coat pockets.

No phone. No wallet. No cash. No keys. I put my right hand down, tried to move.

It was too cramped. My feet and legs were tucked up into the corners.

The bed of the trunk felt strange. It wasn't hard plastic. It wasn't that rough fiber that lines most trunk beds.

It was thick plastic.

I felt all round the edges of it.

This plastic had been taped to the inside of the trunk, so that I wouldn't leave any blood, hair, saliva or fibers behind. There would be nothing for forensics to find.

Nothing to prove that this was the car that drove me to my final destination.

Every second in this trunk felt like a hundred years.

This was the moment.

It had been in the mail for a long time.

Some day.

Sometime.

This was always going to happen.

In my life, I've hurt a lot of people. Some of those people I loved. Some I hated. It didn't matter – I always tried to do the right thing, even if it meant killing somebody.

I felt the car slow and lean left.

We were turning.

No idea how long we'd been on the road.

One thing was for certain, we were no longer on the highway. The suspension now had to work hard, and in the trunk every bump sent a fresh shot of pain through my head. We were on a dirt road, somewhere.

The end was close now.

I'd been in tight spots before.

But not like this.

Not with so many unanswered questions. I had a pretty good idea who had grabbed me off the street, though. I'd pissed off a very dangerous family. My ability to get myself into trouble was kind of a gift. Not that Christine saw it that way.

I thought of her, and my daughter, Amy. How would they react when they were told I was missing? Judging by the professional approach of the two guys up front in this car, and it was always two guys in a street grab like this, my body would probably never be found.

It was strange, but right then, that was the thing that pissed me off the most.

My family and my friends not being able to grieve properly. Not knowing where I was, but pretty sure that I was dead. I had known loss and pain, and I'd seen the damage it could do to others – their lives torn to pieces. I didn't want that. I definitely didn't want that for my daughter.

I didn't care about myself. Everybody has to go sometime.

And one grave is as cold as the next.

It was the people I would leave behind.

That's what hurt.

I should have seen this coming sooner.

Sometimes, we are so blinded by what's right in front of us that we don't see the real danger.

The car slowed.

My weight shifted as it turned.

I felt the vehicle roll over rougher ground. A series of bumps in the earth, rocks maybe, threw me around in the trunk.

I knew then the two men up front were professionals.

This gave me a chance.

Amateurs don't think things through. They can try, but killing somebody and hiding their body is one of those few tasks where you can only really learn on the job. There's no manual, and the guys who do it and get caught can't really learn from their mistakes.

After a few minutes of getting thrown around, the car stopped.

The engine died.

Two doors opened.

I felt the weight shifting in the front suspension as two men got out.

Two doors closed.

No footsteps.

We were on dirt or grassland.

Not hard asphalt.

I closed my eyes, lay perfectly still.

The trunk opened.

Even with my eyes closed, I could still sense a flashlight, maybe two, pointed right at my face.

'Get out,' said a voice. Male, older. Not a New York accent. A hint of something familiar, though. South African?

Dekker. And he was undoubtedly a pro.

I didn't move. Waited for a few seconds.

No shots were fired.

That meant the guy with him was also an experienced killer.

Amateurs take no chances. They'd be worried that I might make a play and lunge for a gun, or make a run for it. Amateurs shoot you in the trunk. Safer. No chance for escape. But then they've made themselves a bigger problem. Now they've got to put their hands on me again, and manhandle my body out of the trunk, onto the dirt, and carry my bleeding ass to a place where I can be buried.

Amateurs carry bodies.

Pros make the bodies walk to their own graves.

'Get out or I'll put one in your knee,' said the voice again, unmistakably Dekker.

I blinked, raised a hand in front of my face to shield the light.

It did no good. I couldn't see a goddamn thing.

With great effort, I sat up. The nausea returned. I'd been hit on the head harder than I'd first thought. Probably I had a mild concussion. That didn't help when I had to think my way out of eating a bullet in the next few minutes. I got up on my knees, threw my left leg over the lip of the trunk, found the earth with my foot then shifted and turned and got my other leg out, like climbing off a bike.

They'd left the headlights on in the car. I was in woodland. Thick trees reached for the sky. A dirt track on the right cut through the forest. I could barely make it out, but it was there. I couldn't see the men holding the flashlights. One flashlight was lower than the other, so I guessed that guy was shorter. The other, much bigger man had to be Dekker.

'Turn around. Start walking, straight past the car. Don't run. You'll regret that,' said Dekker.

I wanted to vomit. I couldn't stand up straight. I had to lean on the car. My head felt like it was on fire. I looked around, hoping to see distant lights from a landmark somewhere. But there was nothing. Just black forest. Not even a sound. No birds, no bats, no animals. Not even wind.

The forest seemed like it was a dead zone. And it could be anywhere. I had no idea how long I had been in the trunk. We could be in Jersey, or upstate, Rhode Island or Virginia for all I knew.

I stared down at the car.

It was a dark blue Honda. Something disposable.

'It doesn't have to end like this,' I said. 'There's got to be a way of working this out.'

'You're done. The only options you have left are whether it will be slow and painful or quick and easy. Do what I tell you and it will be quick and easy. Keep running your mouth, you're gonna wish you were dead.'

I turned and walked along the side of the car, using it for balance. I couldn't see far ahead. The flashlights blazing at my back threw my own shadow in front of me, long and dark, into the trees beyond the hood of the car. I glanced through the rear passenger window, saw a pick and a shovel lying across the back seat. They needed these tools, and obviously didn't want to hand me either of them in the trunk. Same reason that they would take them out of the back and carry them to wherever we were going.

It was so dark they needed flashlights to see where they were going.

Dekker was the senior man. He would have a flashlight in one hand, his handgun in the other. He's not the guy to haul the heavy digging tools. Or share the load.

But his friend? He would need a flashlight, and he would need to carry the tools.

So he had to put his gun away.

I knew when we eventually reached the spot they wouldn't toss the tools to me and tell me to start digging either. Amateur mistake. Even if you have a gun, you don't give the target a weapon, because they know the writing is on the wall and if you hand them a shovel, they're going to use it to fight for their lives.

No, when we got to the gravesite, I'd be shot. And then I would lie quiet while they dug the hole for me.

Everything I knew about these two guys told me this wasn't their first rodeo. They'd done this before. And that at least gave me some knowledge that I could exploit.

I stumbled, lost my footing and went down on one knee right beside the driver's door.

No one was coming to rescue me. Nobody could track me. No one had seen the grab on the street.

I was on my own. Two gunmen behind me. Nowhere to run. No weapon.

I only had one move.

One chance.

And it was probably going to get me killed.

If I messed up, they would adjust their plans accordingly. A quick bullet to my temple, and then they would drag my ass to the grave. Not ideal, but safer, and professional.

I stood up, inched along the car, put my hand on the passenger-side wing mirror to steady myself.

'I'm going to be sick,' I said.

I leaned over, my knees bent, hunched my back.

The side mirror was in my hands, concealed from the two men behind me.

I leaned all my weight on it, both hands around it, held it tight to my stomach.

And started to work the hinge, twisting it as I pretended to vomit.

'Jeez,' said the other man. This guy had an American accent. I heard him move toward me as he spoke, then I heard the rear passenger door opening. He was right behind me.

I waited for one second while he opened the door fully.

Another second for him to lean into the back seat.

I heard the clink of the shovel head hitting the pick as he grabbed them.

One chance.

Still bent over, I planted my left foot in the ground.

Raised my right knee to my stomach.

Then kicked back with my right heel, swinging it as hard and as fast as I could, straight into the open door behind me.

I heard the man behind me cry out, and glass breaking, and I swung around.

The American had collapsed on the passenger seat, holding his head, broken glass from the passenger window all over him.

Now Dekker would shoot me. Just put me down right now. No point in taking chances. There was only one problem for him.

He couldn't see me.

In fact, he couldn't see shit.

When I kicked the door into his pal's head, I'd wrenched the side mirror off the bracket, and it was in my hands now, reflecting the wide beam of light from Dekker's flashlight right back into his face.

He reacted instantly, his face turned away, his eyes closed and he tugged the flashlight to the sky. I saw the gun shining in his other hand.

I had seconds.

I leaned through the broken passenger window, grabbed the shovel from the back seat and started to move.

Dekker was seven, maybe eight feet from the car. That meant I had to be seven or eight feet from the car, right now. The shortest distance between two points is a straight line, but that was a bad idea. I stepped to my left, my shoes making hardly any sound in the soft dirt road, and I came at him in an arc because I knew exactly what he would do.

He squinted, returning his focus to point to the last position he'd seen me, but he still couldn't see – his retinas were still burned from that blinding reflection of his flashlight, which, if anything, had only increased its brightness. He let off three shots, fast, pumping the trigger on the pistol, and I heard more glass breaking, and a metallic thud from a slug hitting the steel body of the car.

Blinking, he turned toward me. Maybe he'd sensed my movement, or heard me, and the flashlight fell over me as I closed my eyes and whipped my torso, shoulders and arms in a wide sweep like I was trying to swing a baseball bat through a fastball with every ounce of strength and speed I could muster. My hands shook with impact, my wrists and forearms instantly numbing with the shock and I let the shovel go, stumbled and fell, such was the force of the swing. I got onto my hands and knees instantly, scrambling toward Dekker, when my fingers touched his gun lying on the cold earth. I got to my feet, pointed the gun at him. He lay flat on his back, his legs twitching violently.

The flashlight lay on its side, pointing at the car. I brought the gun up, following the flashlight beam. The other guy was the stocky blonde that had taken me to see Julian Vanderpool, and who I'd hit on the knee with a tire iron later. He was wide-eyed, his shirt soaked in blood, and his dead hand still clutching his throat. One of Dekker's shots at me must have taken him out. To make sure, I felt for a pulse on his wrist. Nothing. I closed his eyes, grabbed the flashlight off the floor, pointed it at Dekker's face.

Then turned away.

I didn't want to see that.

The gun felt cold and heavy in my hand. I watched Dekker's legs twitch and thought about putting a bullet in his head. It was a fleeting thought, but his legs became still suddenly. I felt for a pulse.

Nothing.

I felt his pockets and found a phone in his jacket. There was no signal.

As the fear and adrenaline subsided, the pounding in my head came back with a vengeance. I swept the flashlight around.

We were on a dirt road in a forest, more of a track really, that wound higher and deeper into the trees. Either going back down or going higher might help with the phone signal.

As the beam hit the road, I saw tire tracks heading up. They weren't fresh, but they didn't look that old either. I looked back down the hill, examined the tracks we'd made coming up.

Same tire tread.

I followed the older tracks up the hill, and they stopped dead just twenty feet from where we'd parked.

Footprints in the dirt. Boots. Two different treads. And shoes too. The shoes were much bigger than the boots. Three people. Heading into the trees, I trained the flashlight into the foliage.

Shit.

I checked the phone.

One bar.

My hands were shaking so hard it took me a good thirty seconds to punch the number into the phone. I hit dial.

'Harry, it's me, I—'

'Where the hell are you? I've been calling. Bloch found your phone on the street in West Forty-sixth Street.'

'I don't know where I am. Dekker and another guy hit me from behind, stuffed me in the trunk of a car and drove me God knows where . . .'

'Are you alright?'

'I took a hard hit, but I've got a hard head.'

Silence.

Then, 'Are they . . . ?'

'They're dead, Harry.'

I took a moment to catch my breath – last thing I wanted was to pass out now.

'I need you to call Bill Kennedy, give him this number and tell him to call me and trace my location. I need him and his team up here, fast. I need someone I trust at this scene. I can't spend another night in a jail cell. Also, tell him I'm looking at a big fresh mound of soil in the woods.'

'Are you alright?' he repeated, slower this time.

'No, but I'm a lot better than I've any right to be. I was lucky. Jesus, I was so lucky.'

'What's the mound of soil?'

'Judging by the size of it, I think I've found Detective Ben Larkin.'

62
Eddie

'We're here,' said Kennedy.

I must have dozed off on the highway in the back of the SUV. Looking around, I saw we were outside the Center Street Courthouse and the sun was up. Staring at my watch, I couldn't make out the time. Either my brain or my eyes hadn't fully adjusted to consciousness.

'What time is it?' I asked.

'Eight thirty-five,' he said. 'You're not seriously going into court?'

'No choice. Don't worry. I called ahead for fresh clothes,' I said as I saw Harry with a suit bag in his hand coming toward the car. I looked down, saw the mud on my pants and the blood on my shirt.

'It's not your outfit I'm worried about. You should have gone to hospital for a CT scan and some real stitches in that head wound.'

'The paramedic put some paper stitches on it. It's fine.'

'It's still bleeding.'

'I'm okay,' I said, and as I undid my seat belt another shot of pain went through my skull. 'Thank you, Bill. I mean it.'

'You don't have to thank me. Just get checked out when this is all over, okay?'

'I will,' I said, with no intention of getting checked out. I'd taken enough blows to the head in the ring, and in life, to know when I needed to be worried. I probably had a mild concussion, but feeling around my head I was pretty sure I didn't have a skull fracture. I was alive, and for now that felt like a win.

I thanked Bill again, got out of the car and stood facing Harry Ford.

'You look like shit,' he said.

'I feel a lot worse.'

He dropped the suit bag on the sidewalk and hugged me. 'After this we should take a long vacation. Go somewhere warm, with a beach and a bar. Forget about this city. Maybe forever.'

'That sounds good to me,' I said.

'If you want, we could get drunk in that beach bar. Maybe even get arrested, just for old times' sake.'

'Is everyone here safely?' I asked as he let me go.

'Lake got Vanessa and me here in an Uber. The exhaust and the rear axle fell off the Aztek this morning. Bloch is inside already. She says she's got something you'll like.'

When I lifted my head out of the sink in the men's bathroom on the eighth floor of the courthouse, the water was a dirty, reddish brown. I used my shirt from the night before to dry my face and chest, then dabbed my hair dry, carefully. The cut was really stinging now.

I wore a fresh pair of pants and shoes, and I was already feeling a little better.

Bloch handed me a clean shirt. I slipped it over my shoulders.

'Raymond's DNA analysis report has been handed in to the DA and the court, along with his video of the painters at the Hamptons house,' she said.

Harry was already in court with Vanessa and Lake. The case was due to start in ten minutes. He was going to hold the fort while I got ready.

'There's something else I found – thought you would like it. I already gave it to the DA and the court,' she said as she handed me a one-page report from the New York City Department of Finance.

I let the shirt hang open, read the report carefully.

Then read it again.

'You're shitting me,' I said.

Bloch gazed at my chest and said, 'You have a lot of scars.'

She was that kind of person. She said what was on her mind. I looked down at my chest.

'Maybe Harry's right,' I said. 'Somewhere in the world there's a dirty, run-down beach bar with a couple of empty stools for Harry and me. I've been lucky, Bloch. Sooner or later, luck runs out.'

'Not today,' she said, staring at the document in my hands. 'Not today.'

The judge and jury were already seated when I entered the courtroom.

The stares from Tanner were hard enough to cut glass.

I ignored her, went straight to my client.

Before anything else happened in this case, I needed something from her.

I leaned over the defense table, whispered to Vanessa.

'We're going to make a new deal, between lawyer and client. I know two things. I know you didn't kill Molly Green. I know you've been lying to me since the day we first met. I'm going to win this case for you now, but not in the way you think. When this is all over, you and I are going to have a sit down. And you're going to tell me the truth. Either you agree to this now, or I walk out that door with my team and you can find yourself another lawyer.'

What she said next was unexpected, but really I should have seen it coming.

'The judge won't let you walk away.'

I let that sit for a moment, then said, 'She can put me in jail for a while, but you don't want a lawyer that doesn't want you for a client. I can throw you under a bus with this jury just as fast as I can save you. Think quickly, Vanessa.'

She breathed in, thought for a moment and said, 'Okay.'

'Good, because when we talk, I'll know if you're lying to me.'

I moved to the prosecution's table. Riley got up as I approached.

'Mr. Flynn, we are waiting . . .' said the Judge.

'I'm sure you're getting well paid for it,' I said.

'What did you just say?' she asked.

'My apologies, I said, *I'm sure it will be worth it*, Your Honor. I just need a quick word with Mr. Riley. We have some new evidence in this case.'

I lowered my voice, so no one but Riley would hear.

'I'm using this new evidence today. You should listen carefully to it. You've got a decision to make.'

'What the fuck does all this new evidence even mean, Eddie? I don't get it.'

'You will, but don't worry about that for a second. I'm not trying to mess with you – I'm not playing a con here – I'm trying to help you. You heard the FBI pulled Ben Larkin's body out of a shallow grave this morning?' I asked.

'I heard.'

'I was the one who found him. This whole case stinks and you're smart enough to know it. You have some talents. You have a perfect record of convictions. In another year, you can walk into a good job in a decent firm on a great salary. Don't let this case put the same smell of corruption on you. Because if that happens there's no future for you in this city. The only way out of this is for you to drop the charges.'

'I can't do that. The DA will fire me. The evidence all points . . .'

'The cops and the judge have been paid to look in one direction only. That's why the evidence points to the wife. Trust me, for your sake. I'm going to call a witness, and then you're going to stand up and ask for the indictment to be withdrawn, on a without prejudice basis, in light of this new evidence. Nobody in the DA's office will criticize you for that, and some of the more liberal-leaning law firms in this town will look at your résumé a lot more favorably for it. They'll think you're a straight shooter, a man who follows the law – maybe the last powerful person in this city who thinks the law means anything.'

I could see from the look on his face that this was landing, but he wasn't sure.

'How do I know you're not conning me?'

'Two reasons. Listen to the testimony and, if you're not convinced, don't do it. Second, I didn't have to say shit to you. I could have let this go to a verdict and just kicked your ass.'

'Why do you want me to withdraw the charges without prejudice? That means we could charge her again in the future. Surely you mean *with* prejudice.'

'I know what I mean. *Without* prejudice. Don't ask me why. I know every lawyer in your office thinks I'm a criminal and a conman, and I'm not going to defend the things I've done, but I will say this – I always did what I thought was right. This feels right. And that's all I have to say. Now you've gotta do what *you* think is right.'

I swung away from Riley, said, 'The defense calls Melissa Bloch.'

63
Eddie

It took almost ten minutes to go through Bloch's testimony about her experience working as a cop in various jurisdictions, and her record as a special advisor and training specialist in the areas of control and restraint and advanced driving. By the time we were done with that, the jury couldn't take their eyes off her.

'. . . I currently work for you, Mr. Flynn, as a fully licensed private detective.'

'Thank you, Miss Bloch. Would you please talk the jury through this video we are about to show. And I just want to warn the jury that this is shocking to watch.'

We played the video which Raymond had recorded on his phone, of the paint crew arriving at the house in the Hamptons, shooting the lawyer in the head, then holding his body in mid-air and slicing the bottom of his foot to drain his blood into a bucket.

'In your opinion as an experienced homicide investigator, why did the killers cut this victim's foot?'

'It's simple physics and biology. Even though the victim was dead, and his heart had stopped pumping, his circulatory system was still under high pressure. The laws of gravity dictate that liquid flows in one direction. They sliced the bottom of his foot, which contains major veins, to relieve the pressure in his circulatory system. This does not drain all the blood from the body, far from it. But what it does do is significantly minimize blood spatter when the subsequent dismemberment is carried out.'

The rest of the video played out in silence. Most of the jury watched the whole thing, but some men and women turned away when the lawyer's head was placed in the bucket. I couldn't blame them. So often, murder is a messy, rage-filled mistake. But sometimes it's purely clinical, methodical and even casually evil.

'Miss Bloch, could I refer you to both of the reports prepared by the medical examiner in this case? We have already discussed the differences in relation to his findings on cause of death, but both reports refer to an injury to the victim's foot. Would you read this section I have highlighted, please?'

I handed her both reports. Bloch read the identical entries from each.

'The victim had a deep cut on the sole of her left foot.'

'Did you visit the crime scene in this case, the victim's apartment?'

'A number of times, yes.'

'Did you find any bloody footprints in that apartment?'

'No.'

'To your knowledge, did the NYPD forensics team find any bloody footprints?'

'No.'

'It is the prosecution's case that the victim was murdered by the defendant striking her on the skull with a heavy jewelry box? Is that consistent with your findings at the crime scene?'

'No. The victim did not die from being struck on the head by a jewelry box.'

Riley leaned forward. The jury were mesmerized by Bloch's matter-of-fact delivery.

'Please explain your answer in more depth for the jury.'

'When I first attended the crime scene, I noticed an odor. I thought it might have been a chemical or solvent used by forensics, but I now believe I was smelling relatively fresh paint. There was a framed print in the victim's apartment, which didn't match the decoration. When I attended on a subsequent occasion with the defense's forensic expert, I noticed this picture was stuck to the wall not only with a hook, but it was stuck to the paint work. This meant the picture had been placed there before the paint dried. I witnessed our forensics expert use a chemical and a black light to scan the wall for traces of blood beneath the paint. We found blood-spatter traces, scraped away the paintwork and those traces of blood were analyzed for DNA.'

'What were the findings?'

'The blood DNA was a scientific match for the victim, Molly Green.'

'Miss Bloch, why, in your experience as an expert homicide investigator, would the murderer paint over blood spatter on the wall and then hang up a picture? The jury have already seen a pool of the victim's blood on the floor of her apartment.'

Bloch nodded, took a breath and said, 'This was the question which bothered me. I returned with the defense's forensic expert yesterday and we again scanned the wall with the luminol and black light to look for further blood traces beneath the paint. We found none. However, having witnessed the method of operation of the execution team at the Hamptons property, and seeing that their van also contained numerous cans and buckets of paint and painting materials, we scanned the wall with a metal detector.'

I paused for a second, watched the jury, made sure they were following. Then continued.

'And what did you find?'

'The metal detector sounded an alarm for metal in two locations on the wall. We then began to dig at those locations. One we found was to do with internal wiring, the second exploratory hole revealed a .22 caliber slug buried in the wall.'

Bloch took an evidence bag from her jacket, held it up. Inside was a small, misshapen item that looked to be about the same size as a large cashew nut.

'This is what we found. This slug had been covered up with fresh plaster, and then hastily dried and painted over. To make sure it was covered up, they hung a picture too in case the plaster and paint left the wall uneven.'

'What was the caliber of the weapon used to kill the man shown in the video?'

'The exact same as this one, .22 caliber.'

'Was this slug further analyzed?'

'Yes, the report has been served on the prosecution and the court this morning. The forensic analysis shows traces of blood, and of organic matter, most likely skin or brain matter, on the slug. The DNA analysis confirms, to a recognized scientific standard, that the blood and organic material is from the victim, Molly Green.'

'For the benefit of the jury, what does this mean to you as an expert investigator?'

'It means the victim was shot in the head, and the round exited the victim's skull and became buried in the wall. The killers then removed the victim's head, methodically, and identically to the method shown in the video, and took steps to hide the method of murder by repairing the wall. This murder was carried out by the team shown in the video. While they could move freely in and out of the building with painting and decorating materials, it would have been too risky to move the victim's body, even wrapped in cloth or rubber. I discovered there was a road crew carrying out overnight repairs just outside the front entrance to the building. The killers would have been seen taking the body away. It is likely they removed the victim's head from the building in a large paint bucket, as you've seen in the video.'

'But, Miss Bloch, isn't this just a theory? The prosecution could argue that the victim was shot by the defendant. What evidence is there that this team of executioners were anywhere near the victim's apartment on the night of the murder?' I asked.

Bloch leaned into the mic, said, 'The New York Department of Finance proves that this execution team were there on the night of the murder.'

'How is that possible?' I asked.

'The New York state license plate on the killers' vehicle is clearly shown on the video. I carried out a search on the vehicle plate, and there is a record of a parking fine being issued to that vehicle on the night of the murder by the PVB, the Parking Violations Bureau, who are part of the Department of Finance. The vehicle was illegally parked on the street outside the victim's apartment on the night of the murder. The times of the parking fine confirm the vehicle was present after the defendant was shown on security camera exiting the rear of the building. There are no security cameras covering the front of the building, but the fine was never disputed. And it was never paid.'

'Thank you, Miss Bloch.'

I turned away from her, checked the crowd in the gallery, looking for one face. SAC Bill Kennedy sat in the back, ready to choose his moment.

Riley stood up slowly.

He looked at the jury. They were done. It didn't matter what he said, or what questions he asked. There was no coming back from this.

'Your Honor, in light of this new evidence, the People request that all charges in the indictment against the defendant are withdrawn, without prejudice to further prosecution.'

'This is highly irregular, Mr. Riley,' said Judge Tanner. 'Surely you have an objection to some of this new evidence?'

'No, Your Honor. And if this evidence was put before the grand jury at the outset of this case they never would have indicted the defendant.'

Tanner tapped her pen on the judge's bench, gave Riley a look that I'd become accustomed to and said, 'This is unacceptable, Mr. Riley. As you've asked for this in open court, I have no choice but to report both counsel to the New York Bar and I will be recommending disciplinary charges. The indictment has been withdrawn. The jury is discharged.'

She stood, and was about to turn away when she saw the man in the dark suit striding down the center aisle of the court. He took a badge from his jacket and showed it to the bailiff as he walked past the defense tables and then made his way around the judge's bench and up the stairs.

'SAC, William Kennedy, FBI. Elizabeth Tanner you are under arrest on federal charges of perverting the course of justice and corruption in public office.'

I'd asked him if he would arrest somebody, but I'd told Kennedy to wait until the case was over.

'What is the meaning of this?'

'We obtained a federal warrant to look into your financial history, ma'am. It seems there are sums of money that have been lodged in your accounts, which tend to show you have been paid to influence cases.'

'That's preposterous! Any warrant would be illegal. You have no probable cause to look into my affairs.'

'But we do. Mr. Flynn has been assisting us with our investigation. On our instruction, he gave you five thousand dollars, cash, in person. He bribed you on our behalf.'

The change of color in her face was something I'd never seen before. A bright red angry hue at her cheeks turned white as the shock hit her.

'That was payment for fines, which will be accounted for in court funds at the end of this trial. He said he was paying this money on account, the arrogant prick.'

'That's your story, ma'am. Mr. Flynn tells it differently. But it gave us probable cause to investigate your checking accounts. You have to come with me now.'

I turned around, looked for Vanessa.

'She said thank you,' said Harry, 'before she left. She said she needed to get away before the press could get to her. She said she would call you to arrange a meeting.'

I sat down at the defense table as the turmoil and chaos enveloped the courtroom and the arrest of the judge gathered noise around me. I leaned my head back and looked at the ceiling.

Then closed my eyes and tried to stop the pain pumping through my skull.

'Eddie . . .' said a familiar voice. I opened my eyes. Bloch was standing in front of me, her phone in her hand. She handed it to me.

'Raymond got the results back on the DNA comparison between Teresa Chase and Molly Green, checking for any familial connection.'

On Bloch's phone was Raymond's email with the results.

I read it, said, 'Tell Raymond I need him to do one more thing.'

64
Vanessa

'Penn Station, as fast as possible, please,' said Vanessa to the cab driver.

She closed the passenger door and caught her breath in the back of the cab as it pulled away from the courthouse. A crowd of reporters had followed her out of the courtroom, but she had managed to get the elevator before they could jump in beside her. They gathered outside the court building, and didn't see her get into the cab.

She exhaled, tried to bring down her heart rate.

Flynn was brilliant. But way too smart for his own good.

She would meet him. Like she had agreed. She didn't want this man for an enemy, and maybe the truth would make him an ally. But not yet. She couldn't agree to see him for a while.

She had work to do.

Vanessa took the burner phone from her coat and typed out an SMS message to her husband.

The police will come for you. But they don't have enough to charge you.

I can change that.

I have the bracelet. That's why my DNA was on the jewelry box.

I'll text you details of where we can meet. I need other people around. I'll give you the bracelet, you give me what I want in the divorce. You'll need time to prepare the papers.

I'll send you details. If you come after me, I'll make sure the police get the bracelet.

She hit send.

She'd set a chain of events in motion.

Nothing could stop this now.

Patrick would show that message to his father. That's what he always did when he was in trouble, run to his daddy.

And Daddy would try to save him.

She had been so focused on texting Patrick that she had become unaware of her surroundings, and was surprised when the driver pulled up at the station.

She paid him, in cash, got out and made her way to the main hall of the station.

There was a small line of people waiting at the Amtrak Baggage service, but it moved fast. In a matter of minutes, Vanessa was at the front of the line. The storage bill could have paid for rent for a month, but she didn't care about the charges. Amtrak had manned bag services, for extra security.

She displayed the QR code on her phone, and the baggage handler scanned it, disappeared behind a service door, then came out of the back storage area with a black Nike gym bag with a white swoosh.

Vanessa thanked him, and took the bag to a corner of the main hall, away from the crowds pounding their feet over the tile. She knelt, opened the bag and checked its contents.

Everything was there, securely wrapped.

One item was the bracelet she had taken from Molly's jewelry box, now sealed in a transparent ziplock bag. She placed it back inside, checked the rest of the bag.

She took one item from the bag, and held it close to her chest.

A red leather Valentino purse. Holding it close to her chin, she opened it, peered inside . . .

A small silver revolver lay cosseted in rich, dark, padded leather.

A .22 caliber revolver.

She snapped the purse closed, put it in her coat pocket, zipped closed the Nike bag and made for a train headed west.

In two weeks, it would all be over.

65
Vanessa

There is one law for the poor, and another for the rich.

Vanessa had come to understand this. But what she had never fully appreciated, not until these past two weeks, was that there was a third strand to that saying.

One law for the poor.

Another for the rich.

And no laws for the ultra-rich.

This was America. Maybe the rest of the world too.

While she had spent most of the two weeks following the trial moving around the mid-west, never staying in the same place twice, paying cash, just to be safe, she had also followed the news and fallout from the trial with forensic interest.

The prosecutor, Riley, had resigned from the district attorney's office the day after the case had finished. Some reporters mentioned that he was being headhunted by several law firms. The judge was on bail facing federal charges. The FBI said in a press statement that, while their investigations continued, there was no evidence to tie any of the money received by the judge to a single individual.

But there was a link to Detective Larkin's murder. The NYPD stated that he had been killed by a rogue former special forces operative, acting on his own, and probably suffering from PTSD.

One law for the poor.

Another for the rich.

No law for Patrick and Julian Vanderpool.

But that didn't matter tonight.

She sat in the driver's seat of her Mercedes and checked her black Gucci purse.

Cell phone.

Keys.

A perfume bottle.

The bracelet wasn't in her purse. She had it in a clear plastic baggie, taped to her stomach. This was a dangerous situation, and she didn't want to have to hand it over right away. Not until she had made sure she could go through with her plan.

The little silver revolver was still in her red Valentino purse, safely secured in the glovebox of the car. She couldn't risk bringing it inside.

She swung the Gucci purse over her shoulder with the silver chain strap.

She reached for her shoes which were in the passenger side footwell. Black open-toed high heels. Too difficult to wear while driving. She slipped them on, got out of the car and felt those heels sink into the gravel of the driveway. Vanessa would need to be careful in these heels. They suited the little black cocktail dress, though they were uncomfortable and ugly in their own way.

But entirely necessary for tonight.

Just like the perfume bottle.

The cocktail dress was sleeveless. Ordinarily, she would never have worn a piece like this to one of Patrick's functions. Both he and Vanessa were conscious of her scars.

Now, having revealed them at the trial, Vanessa felt no shame about displaying her bare arms in public. If anything, she was proud.

Most of the guests had their own drivers, and they weren't

taking up space in the drive of what was, at that time, still her house in the Hamptons. Or at least half of it was hers, but only for the moment.

As she looked at the house, her memory flashed on the murder of the lawyer from Buchanan and Duff, and she shivered.

Two burly men in tuxedos stood outside the entrance.

Security for Julian and the guests.

There was no discreet way of doing this in public, and making the exchange in Julian and Patrick's lawyer's office would only raise more questions, or so Vanessa had maintained. She would only agree to this, an exchange at the house in the Hamptons, during the relaunch party for Patrick's campaign for governor.

His second time running for the office.

Inside were thirty-four high rollers – all of them friends of Julian. Or at least they pretended to be his friend. Like Patrick, his father didn't really have any friends in the traditional sense. These were powerful, vastly wealthy individuals who would pledge money as long as they knew they would get something in return when they needed it. Preferably something that would increase the stock value of their companies. That was the thing Vanessa had learned about the rich – they were lonely. Every relationship, even with those of their own wealth class, was purely transactional.

They liked it that way.

As arranged with Patrick, Vanessa would enter via the back staircase, which would mean she could meet Julian and Patrick in the second-floor lounge area, away from the guests. No one would see her enter. No one would see her leave. Yet she had the security of knowing there were sixty or seventy people downstairs, moving around freely, and she could scream and draw their attention if she felt threatened.

Vanessa picked her way through the gravel to the front door.

One of the security men in a penguin suit held out a hand with thick fingers.

'We just need to search your purse, ma'am.'

She opened the Gucci purse, and he looked inside. Then nodded to his colleague.

Were they checking her for weapons, or making sure she had the bracelet on her?

It didn't matter.

'I'll take you to the rear staircase,' said the security guard. Before she went round the side of the house, Vanessa looked past the security, through the glass doors.

The hallway was lit with tasteful lamps and candles, just as she had planned. Melissa, the property manager, had decorated the house just as Vanessa had instructed. Rattan chairs, the oars on the wall, and the ship's wheel, the barometers, and most important of all, the ship's lamps.

This was exactly how she had envisaged it. Melissa had carried out her instructions to the letter.

This was how the house was supposed to be decorated for her anniversary party that Patrick had cancelled. Two years married.

She also saw fleeting glances of the assembled guests in their black ties and chic designer dresses. Mostly old men and young wives.

She followed the security guard round the side of the house, through a door and up a flight of stairs. This was essentially a well-decorated fire escape.

Patrick stood at the top of the staircase. Hands in his pockets. He moved aside as she came to the wide, spacious second-floor landing.

The guard left via the main staircase, and stood at the bottom to make sure none of the guests ventured upstairs while business was being conducted. Sitting on a couch behind the large sea-view window, Julian Vanderpool waited in a sharp black tuxedo. This area was her favorite part of the house. The landing spread from this generous upstairs lounge area, round to the right where there was a bathroom. Beside it stood a hall table arranged with smooth white sea stones and distressed wood, and a ship's lamp burning with warm light. Beyond that were the bedrooms.

No one else on this floor.

This was private, family business.

On the table in front of Julian were three glasses of champagne.

'I need a drink,' said Patrick. 'Thought we could all use one.' He took a glass for himself and handed one to Vanessa.

She couldn't help but notice Patrick's hands shaking, ever so slightly, as he gave her the glass. She took a sip.

So did Patrick.

'What the fuck is this? A reunion?' asked Julian. 'Give me an account number, Vanessa, and I'll wire you one hundred million dollars now, and you'll sign a no-fault divorce and you get ten per cent of Patrick's net worth. I'll arrange the transfer of the money right now. But I want to see the bracelet first.'

Taking another sip of the champagne, Vanessa never took her focus from this old, dangerous man. He was hard to look at. The blood-drenched eyes betrayed the liver problems that had plagued him from a long history of alcohol abuse. Not that he cared. If anything, Julian enjoyed causing those in his company some level of discomfort however he could.

'I said I wanted half of Patrick's worth. That's what we agreed. I want to see that divorce agreement,' said Vanessa.

'You want three billion dollars? Because that's what this amounts to, half of his worth. You weren't with Patrick for his good looks and charm. You're a player. You may have fooled my idiot kid, but you never fooled me. Where's the bracelet?'

'I want this over tonight. I need the heads of agreement signed by me and Patrick. The lawyers can work out the legalese, but I need something binding.'

'You're a real piece of work,' said Julian. 'Show me the bracelet.'

'Show me the agreement. You know, Patrick shouldn't have

bought that bracelet at Seinfeld's. They have meticulous records of their client's purchases. I know – I have one of their rings,' she said, and glanced at her engagement ring. 'The bracelet will have Molly's DNA all over it. And Seinfeld's will confirm Patrick bought it. A gift like that? What, eighty grand's worth of diamonds? That's a gift for a lover, not a PA. That's the evidence the DA will need to prove the affair. It won't take long for them to figure out it was you who sent the painters to Molly's apartment after Patrick panicked and called you that night. You want me to give the bracelet to you, or the police? If you want it, I need to see the agreement.'

Patrick shifted his weight on his heels nervously, rocking side to side.

'Dad, just show her the agreement,' said Patrick.

'Fuck the both of you,' said Julian, and took a document from his tuxedo jacket.

He threw it on the floor. Patrick knelt down, picked it up and gave it to Vanessa.

A single page, agreeing to divorce and equal split of Patrick's total net worth, an estimated payout for Vanessa of three billion dollars.

'Do you have a pen?' asked Vanessa.

'Before you sign this, I need to see what we're buying. It's not in your purse, I know that,' said Julian.

'I have it on me. I just need some privacy to retrieve it. Couldn't really just pop something so valuable in my purse, now, could I?'

Patrick drew a pen from his pocket, and signed and dated beside his name.

Then waited.

'I'll just be a moment,' said Vanessa.

It was ten feet to the bathroom, in the corner of the landing. She entered, closed and used the key to lock the door. She placed her glass of champagne by the sink and stared into the mirror.

Her jaw trembled.

If she didn't get a hold of herself now, Julian would realize something was wrong. Yes, he would expect her to be nervous, but not shaking with fear. He had a better sense of her true self than her husband ever had.

Another hit from the champagne.

That would help.

She had a plan. One that had been adjusted recently, but everything was in its place. There were things that had to be done, right now.

There was no going back.

She opened her purse, took out her perfume bottle, carefully pulled off the atomizer from the top and tipped enough liquid into her champagne glass that it would appear level to when she had come into the bathroom. It would be enough. The liquid was powerful. She replaced the atomizer on the top of the perfume bottle.

She put her perfume back in her purse, then knelt on the floor in front of the toilet.

Reaching around behind the cistern, her right hand searched, feeling along the cold, dusty porcelain until . . .

Her fingers touched the handle of the flathead screwdriver. She pulled, twisted, and yanked it free from the duct tape that had held it in place. Still on the floor, she placed the head of the screwdriver into the shut-off valve for the water supply.

Turned it off.

There was now no water coming to the toilet or the little sink.

She put the screwdriver in her Gucci purse, stood and flushed the toilet.

She listened.

No sound of the cistern filling. The water at the bottom of the bowl sank until it all but disappeared.

Vanessa lifted her dress, peeled the baggy containing the bracelet from her belly, and adjusted the hem back down, smoothing out the fabric.

She chanced one last gaze in the mirror.

This was it.

She unlocked the bathroom door, took the key, put it in her purse and shut it. Then bracelet in one hand, champagne flute in the other, purse over her shoulder, she left the bathroom.

Julian had got up from his seat and stood now a few feet from Patrick. Waiting for her. Patrick's eyes met hers, and she read the alarm in his expression.

At first, she couldn't figure out what was wrong. Then, she saw it.

Julian held one of his expensive cigars in one hand, and a mother-of-pearl-handled cigar cutter in the other. He clipped the cap off the cigar as he watched her come closer. He put the cutter in his pants pocket, then patted his jacket for a lighter.

'Do you want this?' she asked, and tossed him the bracelet.

He caught it with his free hand, then placed the cigar between his teeth while he held the bracelet and baggy in both hands, turning it over, then holding it up to the light. Once he was satisfied, he took the cigar from his lips and held it, unlit in his right hand.

'Seinfeld's have some lovely pieces. This one is a little more expensive. I can give you fifty for it,' said Julian.

'I thought we had an agreement,' said Vanessa sternly. She would have liked to work up to this moment, to argue and allow the situation to become increasingly intense, but now Julian had the cigar in his hand she had no time.

'We had a deal,' she said.

'You didn't really think you were going to get three billion dollars, did you?' he said, smiling.

Now was the moment.

She flung the glass at him, holding on to the stem, making sure that the liquid hit his stomach and chest and didn't go anywhere near his skin or eyes. Then let the flute fall to the carpeted floor.

'You're a real bitch,' he said. 'You'll do well to walk out of here alive. Patrick, get this fucker out of here. She gets nothing from us.'

He pushed her out of his way, then gripped his wet shirt and tuxedo, pinching it so that the soaked fabric stayed off his skin. He strode into the bathroom and closed the door.

Vanessa took the bathroom key from her purse, ran to the door.

Carefully, silently, she inserted the key.

And locked the door.

She heard him inside, swearing, and then, the sound of the cold-water faucet running. It wouldn't take long for whatever residual water there was in the system to drain away.

She took the key from the lock.

Held it in her hand.

And stared at her husband, maybe for the first time.

He was trembling. Tears streaked his face.

Vanessa listened to the pipes groan as air was forced through them, the water almost gone.

'I'm sorry,' said Patrick.

'I know. I'm sorry too.'

She walked forward, gave him the key and said, 'I can't do it. It has to be you.'

He stared at the black key in her palm.

His shaking hands reached for it.

Vanessa was transported back, months before, to the last night she had spent in the house in Manhattan.

She was headed up the staircase, away from Patrick, away from his questions about the bracelet, when he said to her,

'There's something I need to tell you . . .'

She had later told Flynn that Patrick had confessed to her that he had killed Molly. Another lie. But a necessary one, just like all the others.

What Patrick had told her that night was very different. And Vanessa had no doubt that it was the truth.

'There's something I need to tell you . . . I didn't kill Molly. And you might not believe me, but for the first time in my life I'm going to

tell you the truth. The whole truth. Yes, I was sleeping with her, and I'm sorry, but I swear I didn't kill her. I found her journal and I panicked. She wasn't who she'd said she was. Her real name was Willow Chase. She was out for revenge. She got close to me so that she could ruin me, ruin my political career. Maybe even worse. Maybe kill me. I thought . . . I thought I loved her. I told her I'd found her journal, that I knew she had been lying to me, and that I now knew who she really was, and I stormed out of that apartment without another word and called my dad. I told him what had happened, and he said he'd take care of it. Like he did with Teresa, only, I swear, Teresa was an accident.

'We were young and we were partying, I was still taking coke and too much booze, and Teresa, she was pretty wild too. She fell, Vanessa. She was dancing on the kitchen counter in the Hamptons house and she slipped, and she fell on her head. There was so much blood. I was out of my mind on drugs, and Teresa, she . . . she was dead. She'd broken her neck. She was gone. There was nothing I could do. I called my dad, and he told me not to call the paramedics or the police, that I should just change my clothes and get out of the house. He said he would take care of it, that this could ruin us.

'Molly, she . . . she was Teresa's half-sister. The one they could never find, Willow Chase. She had come after me. I only read the first few pages of her journal, but it was clear what she had in mind. My dad said that he would have to take care of Willow, that we were in too far now. That I shouldn't worry, that he would do it. I swear I didn't know he was going to kill her. I thought he was just going to pay her off. I can't live with this any more. I swear to you, Vanessa, I'm telling you the truth. He's a very dangerous man, and he could kill me too, if I tried to tell anyone. He'd kill you too if he found out that I'd told you any of this. I don't know what to do. I'm so scared, and I'm so sorry.'

Vanessa said, 'Patrick, I believe you, but we have to stop him now. He's framed me for Molly's murder. He covered up that poor girl's death in the Hamptons and you've been carrying that guilt ever since. Together, we have to make sure he can never harm anyone else ever again. He's tortured you for your whole life. He wants you to be like him. But you're not, Patrick. You're not your father. There's still time to stop him. To put an end to this once and for all before it's too late for you and me . . .'

Now, standing in the second-floor living area, the pipes wailed as the water in the system ran out.

Vanessa handed Patrick the bathroom door key.

He took it, gave her the divorce agreement and his pen.

'Leave,' he said.

'No, I have to make sure you go through with it. Do it. Do it for yourself.'

He nodded, and together they walked to the locked bathroom door.

'What the fuck happened to the water?' said Julian, his voice muffled behind the thick mahogany door.

Vanessa slipped off both of her open-toed high-heel shoes. She tossed one, the other she placed on the floor, with the open toe pointed at the tiny gap between the door and the carpet. Vanessa took her perfume bottle, sprayed the door, then took off the atomizer and poured the contents of the rest of the bottle onto the insole of the shoe.

The liquid slipped down the leather, cascading at a rapid pace through the open-toe gap, and underneath the bathroom door.

It wasn't perfume – it was ether, taken from a can of engine-starting fluid, and it would burn like nothing else on this earth.

'What is this? What the hell is wrong with this plumbing? It's all over my shoes.'

The door handle suddenly turned so fast that it frightened Vanessa, and she stood up and backed away from the door, now barefoot.

'What the . . . Get me out of here . . .'

'Do it,' said Vanessa. 'Do it for yourself. Do it for your mother. He made her suffer just like you suffered.'

Patrick picked up the ship's lamp from the table, the wick red hot. She could smell the kerosene from a few feet away.

'Dad, I'm not weak. Not any more. This is for Mom, and Molly,' said Patrick, and he threw the lamp at the door.

The flames burst into life instantly, the floor and the oak door roaring into flame.

The screams came next, his father burning like that wick.

Burning like the devil he was.

Patrick and Vanessa moved fast. He leaned over the balcony, shouted down to the security guards on the stairs below.

'Fire! Get everyone out now!'

'Where's your father?' called the security guard, as he turned and started to run up the staircase.

'He must be outside already. I think he took the back stairs. Get everyone out, now!'

The guard hesitated, uncertain what to do.

The fire alarm on the second floor blared, deafening everyone. People in the crowd below started shouting, women screaming.

'Get them out!' cried Patrick.

The guard turned on his heel, leapt the last two stairs to the hallway and began to holler at everyone to get out of the house.

Vanessa grabbed Patrick's arm, and they made for the back staircase, but she couldn't resist a glance back toward the bathroom.

The door was ablaze, and the ceiling now too. The fire was spreading rapidly, fueled by the oil from the lamp.

Together, they ran down the staircase, and out into the cool night air.

Vanessa reached for Patrick's hand and took the key from him.

He let her, there was no resistance. She locked her fingers in his, and then they ran to the back of the house, across the grass and Vanessa's toes soon bit into cold, gray sand.

She let go of Patrick and ran to the water's edge, the vast horizon dark and ominous.

She hurled the key into the churning water.

Then turned to look back at the Hamptons house.

A red blaze of fire had eaten through the roof and was sending black smoke into the night.

66
Eddie

I hadn't been to Fort Washington Park in a long time.

I used to come here as a kid. To this exact spot.

The spot where I now saw Vanessa waiting for me.

The sun was going down over the Hudson River. All the impressive might of the George Washington Bridge hung above me, and just ahead, standing on a hook of land that anchored one of the great pillars of the bridge, was a little red lighthouse.

Vanessa leaned on the black railings that surrounded the lighthouse. I first came here as a kid because I'd read a picture book called *The Little Red Lighthouse and the Great Gray Bridge* that my mom had borrowed from the public library for me. I couldn't believe there was a real lighthouse, so small, and yet so brave, and I had to see it for myself.

I never got tired of looking at the thing. It was made up of steel, painted bright red, with a conical top and a railing around the light. I'd heard you could get a tour of the lighthouse, but I'd never had the time. It was only forty feet high, and had been rendered redundant when the George Washington Bridge had been built, and its lights lit the river for all passing barges and boats.

Still, the lighthouse stayed.

It was a plucky underdog. If any building in this city exemplified New York and its people, it was that little red lighthouse.

'Why did you want to meet me here?' asked Vanessa.

The weather was mild, but she still wore a long coat, with black boots, black gloves.

And held a small red leather purse in her left hand.

It was a Valentino purse – I recognized the branding – and it was the same red as the lighthouse, almost as if she'd chosen it to match.

'It's quiet,' I said. 'And I like it here. I thought we could have that talk.'

'Sure,' she said. 'What do you want to talk about?'

'Your late father-in-law, for one. I thought you might tell me the truth. I think you owe me that.'

'I paid you, and I can't thank you enough for helping me, but what else can I say? You're a lawyer. Don't you have rules? How do I know whatever I say will be confidential?'

'You answered your own question. I'm still your lawyer. Client confidentiality. Anything you tell me, I will take to my grave. Unless you tell me you're going to harm someone, then I have an obligation to help prevent that. But as far as anything that happened in your past goes – my lips are sealed.'

'Alright, I'll play along for now. I do owe you that much.'

'That was a serious fire at the Hamptons house. How did it start?'

'Who knows? You'd met Julian, he never had a cigar out of his mouth. The fire department think it had something to do with that.'

We were about five feet from one another, and there was nobody else around at this time of the early evening. The river was calm, and the birds were circling over the bridge.

'Is that what the arson investigator found?' I asked.

'Cause is unknown, but probably the cigar they said. Patrick was very grateful to the East Hampton Fire Department for all their efforts to save his father. I believe he made a large donation to their fund.'

I nodded, and then noticed there was something on the ground, behind Vanessa's boots. The light was fading, but I had a good idea what it was.

'And your divorce?'

'Granted, last week. I took three billion in the settlement. I didn't want it, not really. I never really wanted any of it, but I had to take it.'

'I know,' I said, and she angled her head at that statement, gave me a strange look.

'I know a lot more than you think, Vanessa. Let me see if I got this right. Patrick found the journal in Molly's apartment. He believed Molly was coming after him for revenge, because Patrick killed a young woman named Teresa Chase . . .'

'He didn't kill her,' said Vanessa.

'He talked to you about it?'

'They had both been drinking and doing drugs. Teresa was dancing on the counter and she slipped and hit her head, and broke her neck. Patrick panicked and called his father. Julian made sure to cover it all up, because he had big ambitions for his son.'

'And you believe Patrick?'

'I know a liar, Eddie. I know what they sound like. I know how they think. I know how they lie. What Patrick told me about Teresa is the truth.'

'Okay, so he leaves with the journal, calls his father. Then you go into the apartment. And you do almost exactly what you told me. You warned Molly about Patrick.'

She hung her head, said, 'I did. She didn't . . . She . . . I told her to run like I had before. This time she believed me. She said she would get out of town, but she was too late. They got to her before she left. Julian's crew of house painters.'

I took another step toward Vanessa. We were close now. Eye to eye.

'That's not the whole truth, is it?' I asked.

She gripped that little red purse tighter.

'Patrick didn't kill Molly. And you didn't kill Molly. But, in a way, you're both responsible.'

Her left eye shone with a tear forming.

'I did my best. I told her . . .'

'You told her the truth. About you . . . about who you really are . . .'

The wind blew across us. That tear was caught in the gust, and was carried right off her cheek.

'We had DNA analysis carried out. To confirm that Molly and the Jane Doe were related. Turns out, they weren't. So I asked Raymond to do another DNA comparison. This one was just right. Molly wasn't Willow Chase. *You are . . .*'

She took a deep breath, let it sit in her chest for a few moments, then it staggered out as panic and fear took hold.

'That wasn't Molly's diary. It was yours. You clocked Molly. You knew she was playing a game, pretending to be someone she was not. That's the game you had been playing for two and a half years, so it was easy to spot. The night before she was killed, you confronted her, told her back off. Told her that Patrick and his father were dangerous. Maybe she didn't believe you. Maybe she thought you were just a jealous wife. And then you let her read your journal. When Patrick found the journal in the apartment, he thought, naturally, it was Molly's. We all did. If you hadn't tried to warn her, if you hadn't let her read that journal, she might still be alive.'

'She was way out of her league. She had no idea of the lengths that Julian would go to in order to protect his son. A son he hated, by the way. Julian never wanted Patrick to succeed for any other reason than his own selfish ends. Julian wanted more power. He wanted to control the country, not just the media. But yes, as much as it hurts, I feel as if I killed Molly. I gave her that journal. I knew she should've been more careful and yet I gave it to her. And ultimately that's what got her killed. Just as Patrick is responsible. He read the first two pages of the journal. He said he couldn't read any more, and he believed Molly was Willow Chase coming after him for revenge. He called his father, and that got Molly killed. We both killed her, Eddie.'

'And were you planning on killing Julian all this time? Seems a long time to wait to kill one old man.'

'Until he told me the truth, on that last night in the Manhattan house, I thought Patrick had killed Teresa, and covered it up. Teresa and I were close when were kids, and we fell in with the wrong people after we lost our parents. I got hooked on heroin, and drifted away from her. When I came out of that nightmare, I discovered she was missing. That she had drowned. My sister could have swum across that river behind us. I knew straight away something awful had happened. I tracked down an old cop, called Paul Winchester, but I couldn't tell him who I was, or why I was asking questions. I didn't know if I could trust him. But I got the impression he had fought to find out what had really happened, and someone had made sure that he suffered for it. That's when I decided I wasn't going to let this stand. I wasn't there for Teresa when she needed me. She was the only good thing I ever had in my life. We had let ourselves get hurt by men way too often. I was going to make sure that the man who killed my sister paid the price. I wanted my revenge. I wanted Patrick dead.'

'Then why didn't you do it before? Why marry him? Why not kill him the first chance you got?'

'The one useful thing about being a junkie is you get to meet a lot of criminals. I got close to one guy, dated him for drugs. He had money and he knew how to hide, how to pay off the cops. That's what he taught me. How to build a façade that no one could penetrate. How to become someone else. But he was only able to do that because he had money. You know how this works. You've seen it. The law doesn't apply to those with power. You only get power in America through money. If I was going to get away with killing the man I thought had murdered my sister, it wasn't enough to kill him. I had to take everything he had. I had to take his power.'

'You mean you had to take his money.'

'I didn't want it for myself. I wanted the power that came with it. The power that came from that kind of money. The power to stand above the law. There was only one way I could do that.'

'The sunset clause in your divorce,' I said. 'If you split up with him, or if something happened to him the first two years of your marriage, you would get virtually nothing. You had to be married for two years before you got any spousal entitlement.'

'I was going to do it at our anniversary party. Our two-year anniversary party, in the same house where I thought he'd killed Teresa. But the party was cancelled, and Molly got killed and then Patrick and I had a heart to heart. He told me the truth about my half-sister. If you spend a long time walking around in the mud of a lie, the truth shines brightly, like a diamond. We made a deal. We had to make it look like we were against each other in the trial, so no one would suspect we were working together. There was one man who was ruining our lives, and we had to stop him. Julian butchered my sister's corpse. He hid her death away from me. Dumped her body like it was trash. That one act started me down this path. And the lies and the killing were just getting worse. He killed Molly. He had tortured Patrick for years and possibly even beat his mother to death. We had to stop him.'

I tensed before I asked my next question. The answer would dictate what happened next.

'I almost died. Bloch and Lake too. Other people weren't as fortunate. So I have to ask this, and I need you to be honest. Remember, I will know if you're lying. Did you tell Patrick that Bloch was searching the Hamptons house with Raymond?'

'I did, but he never told his father. It was the lawyers, Buchanan and Duff. They told Julian as soon as their associate called it in. And Julian got Dekker to call the painters, like he did before with Teresa and Molly.'

'Why did you tell him?'

'Because I needed him to trust me. If he found out that you were investigating the house and Teresa's death, he would assume that I knew you were doing that. It would look like I was trying to double-cross him. His father always said he was weak. I needed to be there, by his side, to make sure that he went through with the plan. I never wanted to put your team at risk, I swear.'

'I take it Patrick doesn't know who you really are?'

She shook her head. 'And he never will. He thought Molly was Willow. I never told him otherwise.'

I looked down at Vanessa's boots, tilted my neck, saw exactly what was there on the ground.

'You want to tell me who Molly really was? Better still,' I said, gesturing to the ground, 'show me.'

She stepped to the side, picked up a black Nike gym bag with a white swoosh on the side.

She handed it to me. In her other hand, she held that red purse tight.

I took the gym bag, put it on the ground and opened it.

Inside was a phone, a laptop, a notebook and a small, framed photograph. The photo was of a man in his fifties or sixties, with white hair, in a sharp suit, holding a baby girl in his arms.

'There's no blood in that bag. There never was a head in there. Molly gave me her stuff in case Patrick came back and started tearing her apartment apart. I should have taken her with me.'

'I think she knew the risks,' I said.

'That's Molly and her father. Molly was her real name. But her surname wasn't Green. She was Molly Cherry. That's the only photo of her and her father, Boris, who worked for Julian for years. A week after that photo was taken, Julian fired Boris. Patrick was there when it happened. I've heard him talk about it, talk about how nasty his father was to this man. Patrick believed his father fired Boris to teach Patrick a lesson in cruelty and ruthlessness in business. Six months after he was fired, Boris Cherry threw himself off the roof of his building, and his family disintegrated. Molly's mother lost herself in alcohol, and died three years later. Molly spent her childhood being ferried around different foster homes, with foster parents who were much more interested in Molly's trust fund than making her a decent meal, or looking after her at all. When she grew up, she had nothing. No money, no prospects, a juvie record and one family to blame for it all. She knew the most important thing in Julian's life was his son. He wanted Patrick to have political power. Molly wanted to get close to him so she could find some dirt on him, something to ruin him. And if she couldn't find it she was going to do a tell-all exposé to the press about the affair. So I don't blame her for what she tried to do. I was doing the same thing.'

The rumble of a large truck on the bridge above filled the silence between us.

'So you and Patrick are on decent terms now?'

'Yeah, you could say that. We've agreed to part. The police investigation against him for Molly's murder won't go anywhere, because there's no link between Patrick and the paint crew, not enough evidence to charge him and no new evidence to find.'

'So they never found the bracelet?'

She shook her head, said, 'I took it the night Molly was killed, thought I might be able to use it against Patrick. Like an insurance policy. Proof of his infidelity. When Patrick told me the truth, I used it to get the meeting with Julian, pretending to blackmail Patrick.

'And those burn marks on your arms – I take it you did that to yourself?'

'I had no choice. I met Patrick on his first election campaign. I was a staffer, just like Molly, and Patrick was married then too, although that relationship was already going off the rails before I came along. Geoff Gilbert is a great political campaigner, but a lousy judge of staff. He often says he doesn't have the best campaign staff, but he does have the hottest. A low-cut top and a smile go a long way in certain branches of politics. So I was able to get close to Patrick, just like Molly. But I'd been a junkie for too long. I'd gotten clean, but there's only one way to hide scars from those kind of needles.'

'You're a formidable person, Willow. I've got a good sense of when people are lying too. It's kind of my thing. I think you've told me the truth tonight. Thank you for that.'

I turned away, but I felt her gaze on me.

I stopped.

I let her see my back. I didn't turn around.

'You don't need the pistol in that purse,' I said. 'I'm glad you never had cause to use it. From the sounds of it, Molly knew the risks, and she was playing a very dangerous game. If I were you, I'd go start that new life. Lots of people died, and that's something you have to live with. Julian Vanderpool came after my daughter and he tried to have me killed, so I only have one question – was he conscious when he started to burn?'

A bird called overhead. The river lapped gently at the shore.

'Yes.'

I nodded. 'Good luck. Go make a good life. I'm going to forget about you, Willow. I suggest you forget about me.'

I started walking away, back along the riverbank to my car. After a minute, I turned around.

Willow was gone.

'Pack your bags, Eddie. We're going to Rio in the morning,' said Harry.

The office was quiet, for once. Bloch and Lake were kicking back in the reception area with Denise. Harry was on his laptop.

'You've booked the tickets?' I asked.

'Not only that, I got us a great hotel, right on the beach, with a little dive bar not far away. There are pool halls, casinos and all kinds of trouble we can get into.'

The main door to the office opened.

A young girl stood there with a large backpack which she let fall to the ground.

'Dad, can I stay with you?' said Amy.

I hadn't seen her since she was in the hospital. Christine wouldn't allow it. I had texted her to make sure she was okay. The pictures of her drugged and lying outside that hotel had vanished from the internet quickly, and whatever gossip had gone on at her school had died down.

I held out my arms, and she rushed into them.

'Harry, maybe you should cancel my reservation, and book another three tickets. Take Lake, Bloch and Denise with you. Hell, see if Raymond wants to come along. Put it on the firm's dime. You all deserve a vacation. I'm staying right here.'

She buried her head in my chest and said, 'I missed you.'

'I missed you too. Does your mom know you're here?'

'No, I can't take it there any more. They won't let me see you.'

'I'll call her and let her know. She's not going to be happy.'

'Tell her it's just for a few days. Let's see what she says.'

I hugged her close.

I told her not to worry. Told her everything would work out just fine.

I wanted to believe that, so badly.

Things can get rough. Life can be hard. Sometimes it feels like there's no way to catch a break.

Then I remember there are a lot of good people in the world.

I heard someone say this once, I don't know who, but it stuck with me.

In the end, everything will be okay.

And if it's not okay, then it's not the end.

Acknowledgements

I would very much like to thank my wife and first reader, Tracy, who continually makes these books, and my life, so much better – I love you.

Thanks to Jon Wood, Safae, Sam, Tristan, Katharina, Stephen and all at RCW literary agency who continue to sell my work all around the world. Thanks to Toby, Joe, Alexia, Becca and everyone at Headline Publishing in the UK. Thanks to Sean, Ali, Maudee, Jessica, David, Diana and all at Atria Books in the USA. I am delighted to be working with you all, and thank you for what you do for me and the books every single day.

Thanks to my family, friends, my faithful dogs Lolly and Muffin.

And, of course, my biggest thanks goes to *you*, dear reader.

You keep all of us employed by buying and reading these books (dog treats don't come cheap and Muffin, in particular, is very grateful) I can't thank you enough for your time and your support. I write these books for my readers, so it's really important to me that you enjoy the time you have spent with the characters. This is the tenth Eddie Flynn novel, and I can't believe I'm writing that sentence. I never thought I would write ten books in a series, but I have, and it's all down to you. It's because I love writing about these characters, and I get to do that because you seem to enjoy reading about them.

Long may that continue.

In the meantime, thank you again sincerely, for reading my books. I hope they give you some enjoyment and pleasure, and in the time you spend in these pages I hope you forget your troubles, whatever they may be.

Until next time, I give you and your family all my best wishes and hopes for our futures.

Steve Cavanagh
April 2026.

RAISING READERS

Books Build Bright Futures

Dear Reader,

We'd love your attention for one more page to tell you about the crisis in children's reading, and what we can all do.

Studies have shown that reading for fun is the **single biggest predictor of a child's future life chances** – more than family circumstance, parents' educational background or income. It improves academic results, mental health, wealth, communication skills, ambition and happiness.[1]

The number of children reading for fun is in rapid decline. Young people have a lot of competition for their time. In 2024, 1 in 10 children and young people in the UK aged 5 to 18 did not own a single book at home.[2]

Hachette works extensively with schools, libraries and literacy charities, but here are some ways we can all raise more readers:

- Reading to children for just 10 minutes a day makes a difference
- Don't give up if children aren't regular readers – there will be books for them!
- Visit bookshops and libraries to get recommendations
- Encourage them to listen to audiobooks
- Support school libraries
- Give books as gifts

There's a lot more information about how to encourage children to read on our website: **www.RaisingReaders.co.uk**

Thank you for reading.

hachette UK

[1] OECD, '21st-Century Readers: Developing Literacy Skills in a Digital World', 2021, https://www.oecd.org/en/publications/21st-century-readers_a83d84cb-en.html

[2] National Literacy Trust, 'Book Ownership in 2024', November 2024, https://literacytrust.org.uk/research-services/research-reports/book-ownership-in-2024